I0670276

MONK

FALCON'S REST MC
BOOK FOUR

TAMSEN SCHULTZ

DEVIL'S GATE PRESS, LLC

MEET THE MEN OF
FALCON'S REST MC

Book 9, Mystery Lake
Noah **"Mantis"** Streak – with Charlotte "Charley" Warwick

1) Simon **"Stone"** McLean – with Juliana Morganstern
2) Jackson **"Viper"** Bond – with Lina Kato
3) Gabriel **"Philly"** Walker – with Calypso "Callie" Parks
4) Collin **"Monk"** Wilde
5) James **"Lovell"** Church
6) Spencer **"Juan"** Watson
7) Mateo **"Dulcie"** Flores
8) Isacc **"Einstein"** West
9) Lonan **"North"** Cardinal
10) Jonah **"Scipio"** Arias
11) Cruz **"Marley"** Murray
12) Marcus **"Superman"** Garza
13) Luke **"Wesson"** Riggs
14) Nicholas **"Hawkeye"** Cline

CHAPTER ONE

Monk stood in front of the familiar custom-made wrought iron gates and stared down the long driveway. Dormant vines and rosebushes lined the road, their twisting, gnarled branches and thorns urging him to turn back. Instead, he lifted his gaze to the towers of his father's home, the four structures peaking over the horizon. The castle, shipped stone by stone from Italy to the Napa Valley decades ago, a testament to Roger Wilde's ego.

Monk tipped his head as a red-tailed hawk soared overhead, hunting the tiny prey that called the two hundred acres of vineyard home.

He winced. What the hell was he going to do with two hundred acres of prime vines? Not to mention an actual fucking castle? Or the four hundred acres his father owned in two of California's other prestigious wine regions?

Had owned, he corrected himself.

Satan had finally sent the reaper to bring Roger Wilde home. Monk hoped he had a long, hot, and bumpy ride.

A car drove by heading north on the iconic Silverado Trail. He glanced over his shoulder as a black livery vehicle rounded a bend in the road. He never understood why so many people traveled to the valley to wine taste. As wine regions went, it wasn't a huge one, not like the sprawling hills and estates of France or Italy. And the traffic, tourists, and expensive lodgings overshadowed any enjoyment. Or he imagined they would if he ever did any real tastings. He'd left home at eighteen and hadn't once come back.

Until now.

The crunch of tires on the berm had him turning once again. Despite the chilly December temperatures, the top was down on the vintage hunter-green MG.

"Is it open today?" the driver asked. The older white man looked as if he'd be better served keeping the top of the convertible sealed. Even from thirty feet away the red of his scalp shone through his thinning gray hair.

"We heard the owner died," his companion, a woman with large sunglasses and a sun hat, said. "But you'd think the business would stay open, wouldn't you?"

Monk hadn't spoken to his father for seventeen years. He had no idea how Roger ran his empire, and the woman raised a good question. Surely Bacco employed enough people to keep the tasting room open.

"Still closed," he said, gesturing to the locked gates.

"We were so looking forward to visiting," she said. "It's been on our list forever. We even had a reservation." She paused, then shrugged. "But life throws us curveballs..."

The couple gave a jaunty wave before pulling back onto the road. His gaze lingered until they disappeared around the bend. In the silence that followed, his thoughts turned to his truck. He'd left it several miles away on the edge of town and, hoping it would burn off his restless anxiety, walked to Bacco. It wouldn't be hard to turn around and walk right back, to climb in and drive home to his family, to the safety of Mystery Lake.

His body swayed, and he lifted a foot. Only the step led him toward the side gate. Not toward his escape. Another step took him closer and before he could stop himself, he typed in the security code his father hadn't changed in decades and walked through.

His feet fell nearly silent on the well-tended drive as he traveled the half mile to the castle. The vines appeared sturdier and the rosebushes larger, but not much else had changed.

As he drew closer to the castle, memories of what went on inside when the doors closed at night dripped through his mind like acid. The violence and depravity of the dark, taunting thoughts rendering the serene beauty of his surroundings absurd.

That had been his life, though. On the surface—glamorous, wealthy, *perfect*. In reality—ugly, sick, and twisted.

Until he left.

Until he joined the army and met his family—his real family. Fourteen men he served with. Fourteen men who'd grown up similarly enough to understand one another in a way that both anchored and freed them all.

Thinking of his brothers brought a swift punch of confidence, and he straightened his back and lengthened his stride. He'd chosen to make this trip alone. But he wasn't truly alone. He'd never be alone again.

The castle came into sight as he followed the gentle curve of the drive. Two towers anchored the north and south ends of the building and two more flanked an arched entrance to a charming inner courtyard. For years, people had sat and laughed and enjoyed one of the valley's most prestigious wine labels in that courtyard. He wondered what they'd think if they knew what went on in the rooms buried deep below their feet.

A pair of crows cawed to each other as they swooped over the south tower, drawing his attention away from the clean-cut lawn and potted roses. The top two floors of the south tower had been his room. As far away from Roger and the "parties" he threw as Monk could get. Not that it always helped.

For the hundredth time, he wondered why the hell he'd come. He knew the details of his inheritance—millions he wouldn't keep, land he didn't want, and a castle he'd raze to the ground if given the chance. He wanted nothing from the house, and the lawyer could handle any paperwork required by the estate.

So why had he come back?

He paused as the question percolated, only one answer bubbling to the surface. Ego. Only this time, it was his, not Roger's.

Everything his vile, hateful father had owned was now *his*. His to do with what he wanted. And while he didn't have any fixed plans, the options he'd contemplated on his three-hour drive to the valley would leave Roger rolling in his grave if he hadn't been cremated.

His lips twitched with a smile he wasn't proud of as he continued toward the employee entrance. Considering all the ways the castle, grounds, and money could be used that would piss Roger off wasn't healthy. But Monk was also practical enough to know it would get him through the next thirty minutes, so he let the ideas flow.

Maybe a retirement home. Or an art gallery. A private library, open to the public, was an option, too. As incongruous as it was, Roger had been an avid reader and collector of books. Monk didn't know if any of the rare books he'd managed to get his hands on were still in the castle library, but it was a thought.

Rounding the corner of the building, his gaze swept over the wine caves his Moldovan great-great-grandfather had carved out over a hundred years ago. The floor of the Napa Valley was relatively flat, except in a few spots. His long-dead ancestor had chosen land with a rise specifically to build the underground labyrinths—tunnels with natural temperature moderation essential to storing wine before cooling systems were even a glint in anyone's eye.

But like everything else on the property, they appeared empty and silent, their gates closed and locked. Almost ominous.

A cold breeze rolled up the valley, the chill snaking down his collar and wrapping around his neck, yanking him from his thoughts.

And his avoidance.

He'd come to walk through the castle, to face his past with the eyes and experience of an adult. The sooner he did that, the sooner he could think logically about what to do with both his inheritance and his memories.

Taking the last few strides to the employee entrance, he climbed three steps to the wide threshold and eyed the security pad tucked into a nook between several large stones. He knew the code; the lawyer had given it to him. Yet an almost physical pull on his body held him still.

He lifted a hand, his finger outstretched. The tip brushed the ridges of a number engraved in the tiny metal buttons. As he pressed down, a ripple of awareness ran up his spine.

He stilled.

Opening his senses, his world grew both narrow and open. A mockingbird trilled up on the hill. A woodpecker banged away on a tree to his left. Another breeze shifted the dormant vines, carrying a hint of...lavender?

He frowned. Napa Valley had its share of lavender, but in December?

He inhaled again. The scent of dirt, recently dried from rain a few days earlier, mingled with the ever-present undertones of fermentation and decaying agriculture. And there it was again, lavender.

Dropping his hand, he scanned the parking area before shifting his gaze to the vines forty feet away. His eyes swept from left to right, covering two-thirds of the view before swinging back like a magnet to a spot directly in front of him.

There, flanked by rosebushes, a single white blossom incongruously in bloom, leaning toward her, almost brushing her arm, stood Helia Shaw.

His body seized, imploding like an icy avalanche before rolling back outward in a wave of heat.

Their eyes locked, and even from a distance he could see hers widen in recognition, her lips part on a small gasp.

A blur of jeans and puffer vest and flannel and wild honey-gold hair flew toward him before she leaped, her body slamming into his. He staggered back as her legs wrapped around his waist and her arms squeezed his neck, her chin digging into the flesh of his shoulder. His arms closed around her and a heartbeat later, the reality of her body pressed against his hit him.

Helia Shaw was once again in his arms.

He loosened his hold, hoping she'd do the same and he could set her down.

She squeezed him tighter. "You're here," she said, her voice muffled against his leather jacket. "I didn't know if you were alive or dead or unreachable and now I don't know whether to be grateful you're okay or furious that you never wrote me."

Furious would be easier. "You feel kind of grateful to me," he said instead.

She drew back enough to look him in the eye but didn't let go. "You should have written."

The brown in her hazel eyes expanded, almost covering the emerald green. He'd thought about her ever-changing eyes more than he should while in the army. They'd eased him into sleep, following him into his dreams, more than once.

"Collin?"

He blinked at the sound of his name. No one called him Collin anymore. He'd left that name behind years ago when his teammates dubbed him Monk.

"I should have written," he said. He didn't mean it. There'd been a reason he hadn't. One he lived with nearly every day but never let himself formulate, let alone voice—not even in his own head.

Her eyes narrowed, then a beat later, her grip loosened and she slid away. He couldn't help it; he glanced down at her left hand. No ring. Ten years ago, he'd run into her brother at the airport in Berlin. Monk had been sitting at a bar, nursing a beer, debating whether to re-up for another few years. Kaden and his husband walked in, on their way to California to attend Helia's wedding. Monk had reenlisted the next day.

"I'd say I'm sorry about your dad..." she said, her eyes searching his.

"But we don't have to pretend," he finished.

Sympathy flashed across her face. "You going in?" she asked, gesturing to the door with her chin. He nodded. "Want company?"

He glanced at the heavy oak door. He'd done enough therapy over the years to know his reaction to being back at the castle could be unpredictable. He didn't feel the beginnings of anything—no panic attack skulking around the periphery of his mind—but he hadn't set foot inside yet.

He shook his head. "I need to do this on my own."

Her head tipped a fraction and again, sympathy flashed in her eyes, only this time concern vied for space, too. Her jaw tightened and her lips thinned, but she nodded. "Will you come by after?"

Her family's property bordered the Bacco vineyards. They'd run back and forth between the two estates dozens of times a week as teenagers.

"It might be a while."

She reached out and squeezed his hand. "Just come. Or call if you can't." She pulled out her phone and without thought, he did the same. A few seconds later, she'd AirDropped her contact information to his device.

She hesitated, as if unsure whether to leave. Despite what he'd told her, he felt the same uncertainty. He didn't want her to witness whatever might happen to him once he set foot inside, but he didn't want to watch her leave either.

She squeezed his hand again, then went on her toes and brushed a kiss across his cheek. "I'm glad you're here, Collin. If you don't show up in two hours, I'm coming back for you," she said. "I'm not going to let another almost-two-decades pass before I see you again."

And with that she turned, skipped down the steps, and walked away.

She slipped down a row of vines, the bright red of her flannel shirt a shot of color in the muted browns of winter. She'd always been a beacon of color, of brightness, in his life. Even when she hadn't been a part of it.

When he could no longer see any hint of her, he noted the time on his phone, then slid the device into his pocket.

Two hours. She hadn't intended to—or maybe she had—

but Helia had given him something he needed. A time frame. He didn't need to face all his demons today. He didn't need to immerse himself fully in the hell of his past. He could give it a cursory inspection, dip his toe in. Two hours only. Really, only ninety minutes, as it would take a little more than twenty minutes to walk to her family's place. He could survive most things for ninety minutes.

CHAPTER TWO

He had a beard. A trim one. One that looked soft and yet still...beardy.

"I'm focusing on the irrelevant because..." Helia muttered to herself as she traipsed across the Bacco property—Collin's property now—back to her family's land. "Because he's back," she finished on a near silent huff. "He's back," she repeated.

Her first best friend, her first lover, her first a lot of things. Her *everything*. Until he'd left. She hadn't known—still didn't—everything that had gone on between him and Roger in the castle. She'd known it hadn't been good, though. A fourteen-year-old boy, already built like a man, didn't hide in her family's storage barn for no reason when he had a thirty-thousand-square-foot literal *castle* to sleep in.

Seventeen years later, the vivid memory of finding him, curled up with a pillow and a thin blanket in the bucket attachment of their tractor, still haunted her dreams. As did the wary way he let his guard down as she stayed in the barn talking with him for four hours. In the years since he'd left, she'd been tempted to be angry with him for never reaching out, never letting her know he was okay. But how could she stay mad at someone running from something she couldn't even imagine?

She'd missed him, though. His quiet smile, the way his eyes creased when his lips curled up. The dubious yet tender look he gave her every time she proposed one of her crazy ideas. He would have done anything for her—both a gift and a responsibility. The feeling had been mutual, though, and one of the reasons she'd let him go seventeen years ago without a fight.

"Did you check the wine?" her mother asked, walking toward her with a bouquet of white roses sprinkled throughout with red winter berries, startling Helia out of her trip down memory lane.

So lost in her thoughts, she'd arrived at Sundaram—her family's property and business—without even noticing. Or doing what she'd set out to do in the first place.

She winced. "Sorry. I, uh...Collin is back."

Her mother paused. The afternoon sun caught her face as she tipped her head. With her sharp bone structure, deep indigo eyes, and smooth, even skin, she'd always been a beautiful woman. That hadn't changed at sixty-five.

"For his father's memorial?"

Her parents had taken Collin in when she'd befriended him that long-ago winter. She hadn't thought anything of it at the time—her family had always been a loving, welcoming one. As an adult, though, she recognized that they'd known things weren't right in the Wilde household and they'd wanted to give Collin a safe space to be, to come.

"I doubt it," she replied. "But I don't know." It would be scandalous if he didn't attend, and gossip flew up and down the Napa Valley faster than the tourists' cars. Collin wouldn't care, though.

A sympathetic look crossed her mother's face. "Will he stop by? I'd like to see him."

She nodded. "He said he would. I gave him two hours before I went looking for him again."

Her mom smiled. "An ultimatum, Helia? Really?"

She wrinkled her nose. "Maybe not the best idea given that I—we—haven't seen him in years." She paused. "But it worked. I think." Then, not wanting to delve into the reality of Collin being back any longer, she nodded to the bouquet. "How's everything coming together?" They had a sunrise wedding the next day followed by brunch for a hundred people, then, five hours later, a dinner reception for four hundred. The whole event a mix of Indian and American traditions.

"The florist just left. Everything is sitting in the cooler, but I wanted to see a centerpiece vase on one of the tables," she replied, holding up the one in her hands. With its wide rounded base and narrow neck, it looked like a filigree-covered wine decanter. Beautiful, but unusual.

"Are you going back to check on the wine?" her mom asked.

Helia inclined her head. "I'll have to. I'm sure Alessio left it where he said." Alessio Venzago was the fourth generation of Venzagos to make wine for the Wilde family. Collin's three generations of grandfathers had held the role of head wine-maker, with the Venzagos being their right-hand men. When Roger inherited, he'd had no interest in making wine, so had handed the reins fully over to Alessio.

Her mother nodded. "While you're waiting for Collin to stop by, can you check in with Akin and make sure he has everything he needs?"

She nodded and headed toward the building that housed their industrial kitchen to talk with the chef. A visit that would likely take less than five minutes. Akin was a man on top of things, as connected to the success of their business as the family itself. Prone to culinary curiosity, he thrived at Sundaram, where they'd made a name for themselves as *the* place for mixed-cultural weddings in the Napa Valley. It wasn't all they did, but if a couple coming from two different cultures wanted a wedding that seamlessly, and beautifully, blended both, Sundaram was the name that everyone spoke. From food to decorations to officiants to transportation to music, she and her family made it happen. And Akin adored the challenge. Indian and Chinese? Done. Azeri and French? Not a problem. Argentinian and Senegalese? He had it covered.

"Hi, luv," he said, spotting her at the door. "Everything okay?" he asked, returning his gaze to the sauce boiling in a pot.

She smiled. "I'm here to ask you that."

He flashed a smile, his teeth a slash of white against his dark skin. Like so many of the people who worked at Sundaram, he embodied a blend of cultures. His smooth dark skin and high cheekbones coming from his Nigerian mother and his startling gray eyes from his white British father.

He nodded. "The crew was in earlier. I sent them home to get a few hours of sleep before they have to be back at three."

"At least it's December," Helia said. A sunrise wedding in the summer, when the sun came up at five thirty rather than seven thirty, meant the crew arrived shortly after midnight.

He wiggled one eyebrow, then dropped his gaze back to his sauce.

"What's that?" she asked, walking closer.

"The rosewater syrup for the gulab jamuns," he answered, referring to one of the desserts they'd serve with dinner. This couple had decided on a sit-down meal but wanted a dessert station with an assortment of their favorite sweets from their respective childhoods—everything from homemade Ho Hos and Oreos to kheer, kulfi, and of course, the gulab jamuns. The latter, deep-fried milk curd balls, needed to start soaking in the syrup by midnight to ensure the right flavor and consistency.

"I'll bring the wine over first thing in the morning. The champagne is already chilling. Need me to make any calls? Rattle some cages?" she asked.

Akin grinned again. "No, luv, we're good. Everything else is ready to go." She hadn't expected anything less. Akin disliked drama and chaos more than he disliked a messy kitchen. A trait that bred loyal kitchen employees *and* kept everyone's blood pressures low.

She nodded. "Holler if you need anything. You know where to find me," she said, leaving him to his work and heading to the office.

"Hey, sweetie," her dad said, holding the door open as she approached.

"Where are you off to?" she asked.

"Your mom had a question about the placement of the agni she wanted my input on," he replied, referring to the small firepit that played a significant role in most Hindu weddings, including the one taking place tomorrow.

"Can you tell her Akin has everything under control?"

Her dad chuckled, his dark eyes glistening with an easy humor. "When doesn't he?"

Helia inclined her head and smiled back. "I saw Collin."

A tiny frown twitched on his lips. "Wilde? He's back? Did he come for the memorial?"

"Yes, yes, and I don't know."

Her dad studied her before turning his head and looking toward Bacco—not that they could see the castle from Sundaram. "Is he doing okay?"

She hesitated. "I don't know." He raised an eyebrow. "I mean, he's okay, as in, he's alive. I don't know if he's still in the military or not or how he feels about..." She waved in the general direction of the castle. "Although he seemed a bit lost when I saw him."

Again, her father turned his head. He gave it a subtle bobble—a trait he'd picked up from his Indian mother—and shoved his hands into the pockets of his quilted jacket. "I imagine he is. Will we see him?"

"He said he'd come by." Now that she'd left him alone with all his memories, she wasn't so sure he *would* stop by, but he had her number. Too bad she hadn't gotten his.

"Then he'll stop by," her father said. "Make sure to find your mother and me when he does. We'd like to see him, too."

"Of course," she said. Her father's gaze swept over her face, then he nodded and walked toward the event space.

She watched him go, wondering how her parents seemed to make love—relationships—look so easy. Sure, they fought occasionally, and sure, they got on each other's nerves. But when the chips were down, they turned to each other. For more than forty years.

Whereas her marriage lasted a whopping four. She consoled herself that it ended with a whimper, not a bang—just two people realizing they wanted different things out of life. Adam was currently somewhere in Mongolia shooting a documentary on a nomadic tribe, doing what he loved. The same as her. Event planning might not be the sexiest job, but she loved it, especially weddings. And she was damn good at it.

Her dad disappeared into the south side of the stone building where they hosted events when the weather wasn't agreeable to an outdoor venue. Her maternal grandparents had built the facility when they first bought the property sixty-five years ago. It had hints of French influence from her grandfather with an Argentinian flair from her grandmother. They made wine and used the space as their tasting room. When her parents took over, they leased the vineyards to a local wine-maker and focused on hosting events. A few years into it, they added a new-but-built-to-look-old stone barn to host larger receptions like the one tomorrow.

A familiar truck pulled up the drive before she had a chance to slip up to her office. With a sigh, she mentally rearranged her schedule, fitting the final review of tomorrow's timetables into a slot between dinner and the final setup check.

An hour later, she waved goodbye to Juan Mendoza, the delivery driver for the linen service they used. When his truck passed through the portico, she started toward her office, but again, the sound of another car slowed her steps.

A bright yellow Maserati cruised into the courtyard. Her stomach somersaulted at the sight, and she debated making a run for it.

Unfortunately, that wouldn't solve the problem.

Taking a deep breath, she reminded herself that her history with the driver went back far longer than the events of the past four months. They'd been, if not friends, then friendly acquaintances. Not the exes he thought they were now since they never really dated. Yes, they'd been on two dates, but both had gone south so fast she hadn't bothered to figure out how or why.

Derek stopped his car, leaving it running as he leaped out. "We need to talk, Helia," he said, stalking so close she took a step back.

"We don't, Derek. There's nothing to talk about." Something she'd told him three times since she declined a third date. "And we have an event we're getting ready for." Unwilling to show any weakness, she held his gaze. His generic brown eyes were average and uninteresting in every way. Except for a frantic glint in them that gave her pause. A glint that made every internal danger radar she had go off. A new, and disturbing, development.

"Helia, we're good together. You know it, I know it. Why are you playing hard to get?" he insisted, taking another step forward. She hated herself for taking a step back, but her reflexes kicked in before she could consider holding her ground. If ever there was a time to do that, it was now. He wouldn't press her too far—not here, not with people moving around the property preparing for the event. But her logic didn't work as fast as her instinct.

"Derek, you know that's not true," she said, still confused how he could think any of those things. They were as compatible as oil and water, and not once in her life had she played hard to get.

"You're lying, Helia. I don't know why, but you are," he said, his hand closing around her upper arm before she could move away. "We're good together, Helia."

Her heart rate took flight like a swarm of hummingbirds when his grip tightened. She'd have her thick flannel to thank if she walked away without bruises.

"Let go of me, Derek," she said, jerking away. When he didn't give an inch, true fear rolled through her body like an earthquake, leaving her legs shaky. She desperately wanted to be one of those strong kick-ass women she saw on TV or read about in books. But deep down, she wasn't prepared for this to happen *to her*.

"Come now, Helia. Talk to me. At least talk to me." He pulled her close, his face inches from hers.

A thousand thoughts raced through her mind—should she stomp on his foot, or scream? Maybe knee him in the nuts, or slap him with her free hand? Like a deer in the fucking headlights, though, her body refused to cooperate with any of those options.

Fighting to breathe, her chest rose and fell in jerky, uneven spurts. Distantly, she knew she needed to do something soon, to protect her body as well as her pride. Rocking back on her heel, she shifted her weight to lift her knee.

A sharp squeal ricocheted through her ears, but her knee connected with nothing but air. A heartbeat later, Collin stood between her and Derek, his stance wide as he faced her not-ex. "She asked you to let her go," he growled.

CHAPTER THREE

Monk wrestled with the beast inside him, the one that wanted to remove whoever this dude was from Helia's orbit. Possibly permanently. He'd seen the fear in her eyes. And the heartbreaking confusion. As if doubting her own experience. Helia wasn't the first woman he'd met so stunned by physical aggression that she froze in disbelief. He hated seeing that look on anyone, but on Helia? Nope, not acceptable.

"Who the hell are you?" Hunched to his left and holding the shoulder where Monk had strategically pinched a nerve, the dude's question came out more a squeak than a demand. It took less than a second to dismiss the pretty boy as any sort of real threat—at least to him.

"A friend," he replied. Helia inched up behind him, her shoulder brushing against his leather jacket in a swirl of lavender.

"This is a private conversation." Beady brown eyes narrowed as he spoke. Monk supposed he was a relatively good-looking guy, in the way every other rich, entitled bro he'd ever come across was.

"This isn't a conversation at all," Monk replied. "Climb back into your compensation car and drive away. If Helia ever wants to see or talk to you again, it will be on her terms. And you will not touch her," he added. He thought about qualifying that with "unless that's what she wants," but the words wouldn't come out.

The dude shifted, as if he could sway Helia with his gaze like that python in *The Jungle Book*. Monk shifted with him, keeping her from his view. His eyes narrowed again, making his nose and chin look out of proportion to the rest of his face. Monk took a small step toward him. Predictably, he stepped back.

Monk flashed him a menacing smile and leaned forward. The guy's eyes widened, foretelling his imminent capitulation.

Three...two...one.

"We're not through discussing this, Helia," he said, before spinning away and lowering himself into his ridiculous car. Not that Monk disliked the Maserati; they were sweet rides. But if this guy knew how to properly handle one, Monk would eat his leather jacket.

The yellow car turned and raced down the drive. Monk snorted at the cloud of dust. Yeah, predictable.

"Thank you."

Turning, he met Helia's gaze. The surprise in her eyes when the guy grabbed her told him it was likely the first time anything like that had happened to her. Still, the shame he saw there now had his stomach twisting in on itself.

"I'm glad I could help. He an ex?"

Her gaze darted to the empty drive before traveling back to him. She shook her head. "I've known Derek for five or six years. We went on a few dates this fall. It never went further than dinner. We had zero chemistry. Rather than let it drag on, I told him we were better off as friends, nothing more." Again, her eyes traveled to the road, and she caught her lower lip between her teeth. "I'm not even sure that's a good idea anymore."

It wasn't, but he wouldn't tell her that. She'd just had one man try to bully her; she didn't need another.

Wanting to erase the confusion and fear of the past few minutes, he slowly turned in a circle, taking in his surroundings. "The place looks great. It's changed since we were kids." The big house had always been there, as had the large outbuilding. But the squat square building to his left, the stone barnlike structure, and a second cottage were new. As were the extensive gardens. "It looks like a movie set. Even in the winter."

She smiled when his eyes met hers again. "It's been in a few movies, actually."

"No shit? Uh, sorry. I mean, really?"

She laughed, the sound easing the tightness in his chest. "Really. Six of them. Some only for standard background shots, but one, a mystery, filmed almost the entire movie in the hall," she said, nodding to the original outbuilding.

Once again, he took in the setting. Sundaram had always been special—especially to him—but now it was stunning. Almost fairy tale–like.

"Is that you, Collin?"

He turned toward the newer barn structure to see Vanessa and Harry Shaw walking out. He had no idea how long they'd been married—maybe forty years—and yet they came toward him holding hands.

"Mrs. Shaw, Mr. Shaw, it's good to see you," he said, a smile touching his lips for the first time since he'd heard of his father's death. In the four years between first meeting Helia and leaving to enlist, the Shaws had welcomed him into their home and their family. They'd never asked about what they most certainly knew, or guessed, about his home life. Instead, they'd offered him love and laughter and acceptance, teaching him more about family, real family, in those four years than he'd learned in the prior fourteen.

"Now that we're all adults, Vanessa and Harry is fine," Vanessa said, letting go of her husband's hand and opening her arms to him. He didn't accept physical affection from many people, but the Shaws were one of the few, and with zero hesitation, he stepped into her embrace, familiar even after all these years. Her hands lingered on his shoulders after she released him, and he thought she might be blinking back tears, but Harry moved up and nudged her out of the way. Always an affectionate father, he didn't bother with a handshake and embraced Monk as well.

"Why don't we head into the house, and I can make us all a cup of tea or coffee?" Vanessa offered. "We have wine, too, of course, but we have a very early morning tomorrow and I'm not sure if you're staying?" She let the question hang, her obvious preference for him to stay written on her face.

"I'm heading home tonight. But I'll be back," he said. Three sets of eyes flashed with disappointment. "I'll stay longer next time," he added. Relief replaced the disappointment. "Coffee would be great."

Vanessa smiled and hooked her arm around his. "Excellent, and you can tell us all about what you've been up to these past years. You're certainly taking care of yourself," she said, patting his biceps.

"Mom!" Helia protested on a laugh as they started toward the main house.

"Just stating a fact," Vanessa called over her shoulder.

He might have been gone for nearly two decades, but the

table Vanessa gestured to as they entered the living quarters remained the same. No surprise since it had lasted two hundred years before being shipped to California by Vanessa's French father from some old farmhouse the family owned in the south of France.

"Now," Harry said, taking two mugs from his wife and sliding one to Monk, "tell us everything you've been up to since we last saw you."

All three members of the Shaw family looked at him wearing almost identical expressions of curiosity. He saw no judgment, no censure, for essentially leaving them behind. More than anything, that made him regret he'd done precisely that. At the time, it had felt like what he'd needed to do—leave everything about his life in Napa Valley behind. But now...now he wondered.

"You're here now," Helia said, as if reading his mind.

"And we're glad," Vanessa added. "I mean, we're *really* glad —not just that you're here with us, but that you're here at all. You know we supported you going into the army, but don't think we haven't worried."

"I should have let you know," he blurted out. Hindsight was twenty-twenty and all that, but these people had been his family. Then again, he hadn't fully appreciated what that meant until he'd met his brothers.

"You can let us know now," Harry said. "Let's start with the obvious, are you still in the service?"

Monk shook his head. "I live in Mystery Lake. Have been there for almost seven years."

"Only three hours from here," Harry said.

"They have some nice wineries north of there," Vanessa added.

"Why Mystery Lake?" Helia asked.

They seemed genuinely curious, so he told them. Told

them about how a motorcycle ride with five of his brothers turned into forever when Dulcie got a flat tire, forcing them to stop. He told them about the men who made up the club and the businesses they ran in town—all seven of them. And he told them about his new "sisters" as four of his brothers had recently found women they intended to spend the rest of their lives with.

They were finishing their second cup of coffee when someone knocked on the door. "Come in," Vanessa called.

A blond head popped around the corner of the door as it opened, her gaze sweeping over them before landing on Helia. Her expression set the Shaws on alert, and they straightened in their seats.

"Everything okay, Beatrice?" Helia asked.

Beatrice grimaced. "I heard from Alice at the market, who heard from Joe in the dispatch center, that Justin Flannery was found dead in his house this morning."

Judging by the sharp inhales of his hosts, Monk figured whoever this Justin was, the family knew him.

"No," Helia said. "Do they know what happened?"

Beatrice shook her head. "Not yet. Or not that Alice knew." She paused. "I wanted to tell you..."

"Thank you. I appreciate that," Helia said with a concerned frown. "I'll stop by his mother's house tomorrow."

Beatrice lingered, then nodded. "I dropped the invoices from the market on your desk," she said to Harry. "They'll come electronically as well, but you know how Alice is loath to rely on technology."

Harry chuckled. "Thanks, I'll get to them once we're through with the wedding tomorrow."

Beatrice nodded, then gave a tiny wave and left, closing the door behind her.

"Wow, I was not expecting that," Helia said, her hands wrapped around her mug, her gaze resting on the table.

"A friend?" Monk asked.

Vanessa nodded. "We've known the family since we moved here. Justin grew up with his dad on the East Coast but moved out here for college and stayed. We met him when he began helping Gina—his mom—with her wine accessories business."

"We dated for a couple of years," Helia said. She'd married, divorced, and dated more than one guy—obviously she hadn't pined for him. He hadn't wanted that for her, but he felt the sharp sting nonetheless.

"I'm sorry for your loss." He wanted to ask why she ended it, but it wasn't his place. It also wasn't appropriate given the Shaws had lost someone they obviously cared for.

Harry's knowing eyes landed on him. "And how are you doing?"

He lifted a shoulder. "It's been...interesting. Roger's death came as a surprise, mostly because I haven't thought about him in years. But in some ways, I'm surprised it didn't happen earlier." His father was no stranger to illicit drugs or a reckless lifestyle.

"Will you be here for the memorial?" Vanessa asked.

He shook his head. "I don't want to stand there and pretend I feel anything about his death." He hadn't told the Shaws much about his home life, but he hadn't needed to. "Let the valley bury one of their own with their illusions of him intact." Aside from his uncanny business acumen, fooling people was Roger Wilde's other gift. Assuming things hadn't changed, the valley would mourn the loss of a philanthropist, a fourth-generation winemaker, and an active member of the food and wine community.

Monk didn't feel the need to correct them. He had no interest in dredging up the past, but also didn't want to risk harming the reputation of the Bacco label when he didn't know what he'd ultimately end up doing with the property.

He frowned. "That reminds me, do you know why the tasting room is closed? My father was never involved in running it, and I assume that hasn't changed, so I was surprised to see it all but abandoned."

Vanessa barely refrained from rolling her eyes. "All of Bacco's employment contracts stipulated that the winery would close for a month after his death and the employees would mourn him. Some sort of weird fascination with Victorian death rituals, and his lawyer went along with it."

Yeah, that sounded like his dad...the world according to Roger Wilde, with him at the center. "Please tell me he at least arranged for them to be paid?"

Helia nodded. "He did, thankfully." A month of no work could be a death sentence for some in the valley, many of whom lived paycheck to paycheck. "Alessio said he even included bonuses to make up for the tips the tasting room staff would miss out on."

"Generous guy," Monk muttered. He didn't doubt his father's generosity had more to do with preserving his reputation than out of respect for the people who worked for him. But at least he could rest easy knowing his father hadn't fucked over the staff with his bizarre demand.

"I should get going," he said, pushing back from the table. "You all have a big day tomorrow, and I have a three-hour drive home."

"I didn't see your car when I was at Bacco earlier," Helia said, rising with him. Vanessa and Harry followed.

"I needed to burn a little energy, so I parked in town and walked up," he said, gathering their mugs.

"Why don't I give you a ride back?" Helia offered. "I'll

swing by Bacco on my way home and grab the cases of wine Alessio left out for me."

"For the wedding tomorrow?" he asked.

"I'll take those," Harry said, holding his hands out for the mugs.

Monk hesitated, then handed them over with a "Thank you."

Helia nodded in response to his question. "That's why I was over earlier. I wanted to check where Alessio left them. I planned to head over later and pick them up. I can do it now instead."

Another knock at the door stopped him from responding, and they turned as Vanessa called out for whoever it was to enter. Monk didn't like how lackadaisically they took security, but since the Shaws' living quarters were on the third floor of the main house, he supposed not many people who weren't known to the family popped by.

The door swung open and a man wearing jeans and a long-sleeved Henley stepped through, followed by a woman dressed nearly the same. Both wore badges on their hips.

"Jess, Carter, what a surprise," Vanessa said.

The arrival of two detectives not long after receiving news of Justin Flannery's death had Monk's instincts coming to attention in a swirl of unease.

"Mrs. Shaw," the male detective said with a nod before his gaze landed on Helia. "Earlier today, Justin Flannery was found dead in his home. If you wouldn't mind, we have some questions for you, Helia."

CHAPTER FOUR

Helia's parents cocked their heads at the detectives.
Collin's dark, watchful eyes remained on her.

"Of course," she responded, a rote answer more than anything else. She hadn't spent any time with Justin in several years, but she wouldn't say no to speaking with the police.

"We'll stay, if you don't mind," her mom said.

"I appreciate that, Mom, but there's no need," she said. "You wanted to check the reception room before dinner. I'll be fine."

Her parents eyed her, then, interestingly, both turned to Collin. "I'll stay with her," he said.

She hid a grimace and hoped Carter and Jess didn't ask anything too personal about her relationship with Justin. She didn't have anything to hide, but talking about her love life in front of Collin made her feel a little squirmy.

"Do you mind if we head to my place?" she asked the detectives. Both shook their heads and stepped to the side, clearing the way to the door.

Collin's fingers settled on her lower back as he followed her out, staying so close that the side of his body brushed against hers.

"You don't live here anymore?" he asked, his breath warm against her ear, sending a chill down her spine.

She shook her head as Jess and Carter fell into step behind them. "I'm way too old to be living with my parents. I love them, but it was better for all of us to have my own space." They pushed through the door that closed off the private third floor from the floors below and headed toward the grand central staircase. "Did you see that stone water tower when you walked over?" He nodded. "We built that six years ago. I live there." The space wasn't huge, but she'd designed every inch and loved it to bits. The ground floor held a sitting area, a small kitchen with a breakfast nook, and a powder room. It also had a fireplace as well as gorgeous French doors that opened out to a flagstone patio. Her bed and bathroom were on the second floor. The third was a covered rooftop deck where she often sat with her morning coffee or evening glass of wine, watching the sun rise or set over the valley.

"Collin? Collin Wilde, right?" Carter asked. "I was two years ahead of you in school."

Collin drew away from her as he turned to talk with the detective.

"Sorry about your dad," Carter said, shaking Collin's hand.

It didn't surprise Helia that Carter recognized Collin. He'd grown a couple inches upward and *several* more in muscle, but his eyes and facial features hadn't changed much. He'd also been the sole heir to the Wilde legacy and fortune. As one of the earliest European families to settle in the area, the Wilde family was Napa Valley royalty. People knew them even if they —Collin—didn't know them back.

"I understand the memorial is the day after tomorrow.

How are you holding up?" Carter asked. Helia frowned at the question. It seemed awfully personal. Maybe even a bit nosy.

"I have a supportive family," Collin replied. Carter might be hoping for more from the Wilde heir, but he wasn't going to get it. Helia smiled. She'd always been protective of Collin. Maybe she didn't have a right to be anymore, but their estrangement changed nothing.

"You're married? Nice, any kids?" Carter asked.

"We're here," Helia announced, cutting off the need for Collin to reply. Family came in all shapes and sizes. And as a thirty-five-year-old woman, she was mightily tired of correcting people when they assumed every time she mentioned family she meant a husband and kids. She didn't want to hear Collin have to do the same.

Crowding around her small kitchen table, Collin took the seat beside hers. She considered offering drinks, then opted not to. She still had a lot to do today and the sooner she got through this conversation, the faster she could get to it.

"How can I help you?" she asked.

"You heard about Justin?" Jess started. Relatively new to the valley, Jess had moved twelve years ago to be closer to her aging parents. Helia had always liked the practical, no-frills woman.

She nodded. "You know the valley vine. Beatrice told us a few minutes before you arrived."

"How well did you know him?" Jess asked.

Her gaze slid to the view through the French doors. "I knew him well, once. Or thought I did. But it's been a couple of years since we spent any time together."

"You dated?" Carter said. She nodded. "For how long?"

"Two years."

"And how long ago did you two break things off?" Jess asked.

"Three years ago."

"Why?"

She tensed at the question. She had nothing to hide, but she didn't like talking about it.

"You don't have to answer." Collin's quiet voice drew her attention. Jess and Carter shifted. Probably in annoyance. "You're under no obligation to talk to them and can choose what or how much to say," he added. The confidence in his voice piqued her curiosity. He hadn't mentioned anything about working with law enforcement as part of the *seven* companies his MC owned and ran, but she didn't doubt his certainty.

"I have nothing to hide," she replied, her eyes still locked on his.

He gave a tiny shake of his head. "It's not about having anything to hide. This is a courtesy conversation. You aren't obligated to say anything. Talk only if you're comfortable talking."

She gave a shaky nod. "It's embarrassing more than anything," she said, then wrinkled her nose. "Which really shouldn't stop me, since I'm not known for my restraint."

Collin didn't smile but humor glinted in his eyes.

"We broke up because we had different definitions of what it means to be monogamous," she answered, darting a look at Collin. Had he just growled?

"There's only one definition of monogamous," he said.

She snorted a laugh. "Yeah, I thought so, too."

"He cheated on you?" Jess asked.

She nodded. "Three times. That I know of. I ended things the day I found out about one of them. The others I learned about *after* we broke up."

"Fucker," Collin muttered. Carter's gaze flickered to him.

"While you were together, were you aware of any health issues he might have had?" Carter asked.

She tipped her head. "You know, I never asked how he died. I assumed he had a heart attack or something. He's young for that, but my brother-in-law's father dropped dead at forty-two from a heart attack, so I know it happens."

An anticipatory silence filled the room. Collin shifted beside her. Jess tapped the table with her forefinger. Carter drummed a pen on his notebook. She stilled, puzzle pieces she hadn't even considered sliding into place. She gasped and sat back. "It wasn't a natural death, was it?"

Collin slid his hand beneath the curtain of her hair and started gently rubbing the tension from her neck. Between the heat of his palm and the touch of his fingers against her skin, the urge to close her eyes and rest her head against his shoulder beckoned.

"It's an ongoing investigation," Carter replied. Resisting the temptation of Collin's comfort, she narrowed her eyes. "But there are unusual circumstances," he conceded.

Unusual circumstances—such a quaint phrase for what she assumed meant murder. Her stomach lurched at the possibility. Justin hadn't been good to her, but he didn't deserve to be *murdered*.

"No heart or blood pressure issues or things like that," she answered.

"What about other things?" Carter asked.

She hesitated, for Gina's sake. "I know you can't promise to keep things confidential, but if it turns out to be irrelevant...?"

"We'll do our best," Jess said.

Helia huffed. "He had...issues. You know..." She gestured to her crotch area.

Jess tipped her head. "He had erectile dysfunction issues?"

Heat crawled up her neck. "He did with me. Maybe I was the problem, though?"

"You are not the problem," Collin muttered.

Carter darted a glance at him before clearing his throat and turning back to her. "While you two were together, the only drugs you saw him take were to address ED?"

She nodded.

"And have you seen him lately?" Carter asked.

She shrugged. "Here and there."

"Meaning?" Jess pushed.

"I saw him at a fundraiser at the Hayeses' two months ago. Then again at the grocery store a few days after that. He's also been delivering orders here the past several months." She paused. "Actually, now that you ask, it's kind of weird. After we broke up, I could go ages without seeing him. But in the last, maybe four or five months, he popped up, not exactly like a whack-a-mole, but more frequently than usual."

"What kind of deliveries did he make?" Jess asked.

"Stuff from the business. Wine pourers, glasses, that sort of thing. Some of our higher-end weddings like to put together adult-style goody bags for their guests. Gina's company often supplies products for those."

"And the Hayeses' gala?" Carter asked.

"That was...weird," Helia said, pulling up the memories from that night. The event hadn't happened that long ago, but charity blowouts in Napa Valley blended into each other. Even ones with fireworks. Although how they'd managed a license and permission for that, Helia wasn't going to guess.

"Weird?" Carter pressed.

The inflection in his voice hinted that he already knew why. "He approached me and wanted a second chance. I turned him down," she answered flatly.

"Fucker," Collin muttered again, making her lips twitch. A

man was dead. She shouldn't be laughing. But Collin's running commentary was keeping her grounded. It wasn't every day the police questioned her about a murder.

"Did the conversation get heated?" Jess asked.

"Sugar Raymond told you it did, didn't she?" she asked, not hiding her irritation. Turning to Collin, she explained, "Sugar moved here six years ago. Divorced, widowed, and divorced again, she's been after Justin for *years*.

"The conversation was intense on Justin's part," she continued, returning her attention to the detectives. "He tried cornering me a few times throughout the night, but I managed to slip away. When he finally got to me, I figured I'd let him have his say, decline, then move on."

"And what did he say?" Carter asked.

Helia wrinkled her nose. "I know this sounds weird, but I don't actually remember. I kind of tuned him out while he was talking. Sundaram had a huge wedding two days later, and rather than listen, I took the time to work out some kinks in the timing I needed to sort through."

A deep chuckle sounded from beside her, sending a little frisson through her body. Carter and Jess, on the other hand, stared at her, their expressions cautiously blank.

"You remember nothing of what he said?" Carter clarified.

"I remember him asking me for a second chance," she replied. "After that, I knew my answer would be 'no way in hell,' so I didn't feel the need to listen to the rest." She paused, then added, "The wedding went off beautifully. Those ten minutes he had me cornered were very productive."

Another chuckle from Collin. Another head tilt from the detectives.

A beat later, they shared a look. Silent communication passed between them before they rose in tandem. She and Collin did the same.

"Thank you for your time, Helia," Carter said, holding his hand out. She shook it, then Jess's.

"I'm sorry I couldn't help more. I know very little about his life since we ended things," she said.

"If you remember anything unusual, you know where to find us," Carter said, moving across the room.

She nodded and opened the door. A few seconds later, she closed and leaned against it. "Was that weird?" she asked as the detectives' footsteps faded.

Collin crossed his arms, his gaze on the picture window, but not really looking through it. "It was a fishing expedition."

"Meaning?"

"Justin Flannery didn't die of natural causes, and they're trying to figure out if it was an accident or murder."

She blinked. She hadn't considered an accident; that made more sense than murder. "An accident. It had to have been an accident. I don't remember the last time we had a murder. We have violent crime. Usually related to tourists who come up here, drink too much, and do dumb things. But murder?"

His gaze refocused on her, and damn if those deep brown eyes didn't pull her back to all the feels she had for him in their teenage years. "I could be wrong. Maybe he had a weird health issue."

"I'm guessing you're not," she said.

He smiled. "I've worked with a few police departments. Their tactics aren't unfamiliar to me."

She cocked her head. "None of the businesses you mentioned would involve regular communication with the police."

He grinned. "A story for another time."

She studied him, letting her gaze drift over his face—so familiar, yet so unknown. She considered pressing him for answers but decided to use his promise as an excuse to see him again.

"Another time, then," she said. "Ready to head to your car?"

He nodded and a few minutes later, they climbed into one of the Sundaram vans.

"How many cases of wine?" Collin asked as they pulled out of her driveway.

"Thirty," she answered, her arms already aching at the thought of loading it all herself. At least she'd have help unloading it when she returned.

"After you drop me at my car, I'll follow you back to help," he said.

His offer to return to Bacco so soon after his initial visit surprised—and concerned—her. She didn't want him making himself uncomfortable for her.

"That's okay, I got it," she replied.

"Helia."

"No, really, it's not a problem."

Silence.

She managed to drive a full mile before she caved. "I don't want you to be there any more than you have to, so I got this," she said. "Really. It's not as if I've never loaded cases of wine."

"Helia."

She kept her eyes fixed in front of her knowing if she looked at him, she'd cave even more. Because the truth was, she didn't want him to leave. She wanted to hear more about his family and his life in Mystery Lake. She wanted to know what his days were like and where he lived. What she *didn't* want was to make his coming back to Napa even harder than it already was by making him visit the one place that drove him away.

"I'll follow you back. You know the code, right?" he said, nodding to the gates as they passed the entrance to Bacco.

The stubborn mule wasn't going to let her do it on her own. Whether she wanted him to or not, he'd follow her. She huffed a "Fine," then added, "Alessio stored the cases in the caves. You don't have to go into the house."

"I appreciate your concern, but I'm going into the house." She whipped her head around to find him staring at the side mirror through the window. "I'm going to stay until they figure out what happened to Justin Flannery."

CHAPTER FIVE

M onk stood in the parking area watching Helia drive away. He should have gone with her and helped unload. Eyeing his truck, he contemplated that course of action. And whether it would seem too eager given they'd just spent several hours together. Or whether, possibly, it was a way to avoid the consequences of the decision he'd made.

A curtain fluttered in one of the third-floor windows of the castle, drawing his attention. His gaze lingered, a place to rest his eyes while he processed what he'd chosen to do—stay in a place he'd vowed long ago to never set foot in again.

Well, he'd already broken that vow earlier. Not that he'd set foot too far inside. He hadn't made it to the second or third floor. Or the towers. Or the basement Roger referred to as the dungeon. He knew himself well enough not to tackle that subterranean space on his own. He'd call his brothers in to help with that.

His brothers. He needed to let them know his change of plans. They'd worry if he didn't make it home. Also, being on the phone with one when he reentered the castle seemed like a good idea. Pulling out his device, he brought it to life, then hesitated. He didn't want to call Mantis. As their president, he'd be expecting Monk's call. But Mantis's ability to read him —to read anyone—was more than Monk wanted to deal with.

There were thirteen others to choose from, but it didn't take more than a few seconds to settle on Lovell. Understated and sparse with his words, Monk would get the connection he needed without a lot of questions.

Scrolling through the numbers, he tapped Lovell's name and a second later, the phone started ringing as he walked to the employee entrance.

"You good?" Lovell asked when the call connected.

"Been better, but okay." Monk paused to type in the code. "I'm going to stay a few days, though," he said, pushing through the door. It snicked shut and the familiar smells of oak, leather, and wine wrapped around him.

"You're gonna stay." A question, but also a statement.

He reset the alarm before walking down a hall lined with offices, private tasting rooms, and a small kitchen, before stopping at the entrance to the large public tasting room. His gaze scanned the area: five high tops, three groupings of chairs, two long couches, a synthetic Christmas tree decorated in the corner, and a fireplace, its mantel cheerily bedecked with holiday greens and ornaments. Continuing toward a group of leather chairs, he sank into one closest to the unlit hearth.

"Yeah. I...need to be here."

"Why?" Lovell didn't say a lot, but he also didn't beat around the bush.

"Helia."

"Helia Shaw?" All his brothers knew about the Shaws. "What about her?"

He hesitated. His gut told him the situation was off, but

what did he know? He hadn't seen Helia in years. He knew nothing of her life or the people in it. Still...

"Her family's property abuts the winery's. I went over to say hi to her and her parents. When I got there, a guy she'd dated a couple of times was insisting she give him another chance." The scene played out in his mind. The fear on Helia's face solidifying a quiet rage inside him, like a core of cold steel.

"He had his hand on her," he added. Lovell remained silent, but Monk felt his brother's anger through their connection. All the Falcons had grown up in violent homes, and none of them took that shit lightly.

"You gonna look into him?"

He'd been too distracted by Justin Flannery's death to consider that, but it was a good idea. Both men needed looking into.

"Yeah, but that's not the end of it. Less than two hours later, two detectives knock on her door wanting to talk with her. Turns out one of her exes—a real one this time, she dated the guy for two years—turned up dead this morning. After he, too, tried getting back together with her."

"No commentary on Helia, but I don't like it."

"I don't either," Monk replied.

"What'd the guy die of?"

"The detectives didn't say, but it sure as shit wasn't natural. Whether it was murder or an accident, like an over-dose, I don't know." He kicked his feet out and considered starting a fire when he ended the call. The tasting room didn't hold the same memories that the rest of the castle did. Maybe he'd sleep on the sofa down here.

"Call Leo," Lovell said, referring to a friend of the club who had mad cyber skills. And one who'd likely become family sometime in the next six months if Monk had to guess. His girl-friend Josephine, aka Joey, was Charlotte's twin sister, and everyone expected Mantis to propose to Charley over the holidays. Monk had his money on New Year's Day and figured Leo and Joey would follow soon after.

"Yeah, I might do that." He'd dig around on his own first.

"When's the memorial?"

"Day after tomorrow."

Lovell made a noise somewhere between a grunt and a "hmm." "Call if you need anything."

"I will. Let the others know? I'm on shift at Rita's in a few days. Hopefully, I'll be back by then." This close to the holidays, Rita's, the bar the club owned, was a busy place seven days a week.

"We got it if you're not."

"Roger that. I'll keep you posted." They ended the call, and he sat in the silence that followed—there was nothing like the quiet that filled a space typically bustling with people. It held a weight that other kinds of quiet didn't.

A creak sounded above him, and he lifted his eyes. When several seconds passed and he heard nothing more, he blew out a breath and rose. All buildings settled, especially at night. Even a monstrous castle.

Checking the woodbin, he found enough to get him through the night, especially since the fireplace was gas-assisted. With the hearth only slightly smaller than the one anchoring the main gathering room at the club, the gentle flame would bring a welcome familiarity.

A few minutes later, he'd collected his go bag from his truck and was kneeling at the hearth adjusting the gas level as the small, tentative flames caught. When they licked and curled around the logs, he rose. Only to be met with a growl of protest from his stomach. Other than the scone he'd had at Sundaram, he hadn't eaten since morning. His gaze traveled through the windows, across the courtyard, to the back corner of the castle. Where the industrial kitchen sat.

The fire danced and crackled soothingly at his back. Delivery it was.

Another creak had him flickering a look at the south hall as he opened the delivery app. He paused. A small kitchen that serviced the tasting room lay two doors down. He hadn't searched the cabinets earlier, but maybe he could scavenge enough charcuterie and cheese to get him through the night.

A chuckle rumbled through him at that thought. He'd survived on a lot worse than prosciutto, gourmet salamis, and high-end Napa Valley cheeses before. Yeah, he'd get by. Assuming the cleaners left the kitchen stocked. Those items didn't tend to go bad quickly so should have been left.

Fifteen minutes later, he sat in front of a roaring fire, a plate stacked high with seven types of cured meats, four cheeses, a bowl of olives, a pile of dried apricots, a mound of marcona almonds, and a stack of crackers. He'd even poured himself a glass of wine, his first-ever taste of the Bacco brand. He'd give credit where credit was due, Alessio made a damn fine zinfandel.

Pulling out his phone as he ate, he typed Justin Flannery's name into the browser. Several links popped up about his death, although none speculated about the cause. Toward the bottom of the page, he found a few articles about the business he ran with his mom.

As he read one, then another, he admitted the wine accessory business was bigger than he imagined—or bigger than he would have imagined if he'd ever given it any thought. Justin and his mom sold wine pourers, decanters, openers, glasses, chillers, and more. The designs ranged from classic simplicity to whimsical and charming to art deco.

The article included pictures of Flannery, who reminded

him of the douche he'd seen at Sundaram that afternoon. What had Helia called him? Derek, that was his name. Yeah, Derek and Justin had a similar look. Lean, well-dressed and - groomed. Tall, but not too tall. Brown hair, brown eyes. Good-looking, he supposed, if not memorable.

A log toppled from the stack, and he rested his gaze on the flames. Was he being paranoid about the reemergence of both men in Helia's life followed by Justin's death? Was he using it as an excuse to stay? An excuse to spend time with Helia? He'd left her and the whole valley behind years ago. He didn't have any right to claim space in her life. Was this his way of doing that without pulling on his big-boy boxers and *admitting* he wanted to spend time with her?

He snorted, then took a sip of his wine. It could be both; he could be using the suspicious timing of the events as an excuse to stay *and* they could be a legit concern.

One of those things was easier to deal with than the other, though. Without pausing to overthink it, he sent a quick text to Leo. Thanks to the license plate he'd memorized when the douche fled Sundaram and Leo's access to certain databases, less than five minutes later, he had the man's full name and basic deets.

Derek Jason Weber. Thirty-nine years old, resident of Napa. Manager at one of the Michelin-star restaurants—a one-star, though, not a three-star.

He drove a flash car for being the manager of a restaurant, even a high-end one. A lot of people who lived in the valley had family money, though. Derek could be one.

Opening another browser, he started digging. Twenty minutes later, he'd finished his food and wine and knew more about Derek Weber than he had this afternoon, but not enough.

He'd moved to the valley six years earlier when the restaurant hired him, with gigs in San Francisco and Cabo San Lucas before that. He supported several charities and popped up in a range of photos from fundraising runs to galas to feeding the firefighters after the deadly Napa fire.

He appeared to be an all-around decent guy, but the dirt on either Derek or Justin wouldn't be found in news articles and write-ups of charity events. Logging on to the club's fake social media account—one they used to dig into people's lives without giving themselves away—he started scouring personal pages.

The further he delved into his search, the more posts he found that included both men: pictures of them raising wine-glasses at a charity tasting event, sharing a beer after a fun run, laughing with two women at what looked like a black-tie New Year's party. It could all mean nothing, though. Both appeared popular on the charity scene, and the valley wasn't that big.

Clicking on yet another charity event page, his breath caught at the first picture. Derek and Justin, dressed in tuxes, flanked his father. All three held glasses of sparkling wine. All three smiling for the camera.

Forcing a slow inhale, he turned away from the image. The twisting beauty of the flames soothing him as he absorbed what he'd just seen. For the first time in seventeen years, he'd laid eyes on Roger Wilde. With two men linked to Helia.

Drumming his fingers on the arm of the chair, he contemplated that last thought. He had no wish to see any more photos of Roger, but his memories of the man were just that, memories. Justin and Derek posed a more pressing, timely, problem. If the three men were connected in any way, he needed to know.

Bracing himself, he returned his attention to his phone and typed Roger's name into one of the social media apps. Twenty minutes later, he set it back down, what he *hadn't* found more interesting than what he had. Roger, Derek, and Justin had a lot of pictures with the same people at the same events, but very few together.

Taking the last sip of his wine, the soft glow of the fire easing the tension in his body, he considered continuing his research. But finding out about his father's death, driving to Napa, seeing Helia again, then learning about Derek and Justin made for a long day.

He had time to dig more tomorrow. For now, he deserved another glass of wine and a quiet session in front of the fire with his e-book.

CHAPTER SIX

Helia rolled her head against her silk pillowcase and looked at the clock. Fifteen minutes before her alarm was set to go off at five thirty. She'd never *not* woken up before her alarm and often wondered if that was a blessing or a curse. She liked having a few minutes to enjoy the coziness of her bed, but some mornings, a little extra sleep wouldn't go amiss.

Not worried about falling back asleep, she turned the alarm off. In the early-morning quiet, she picked out the familiar hum of Sundaram preparing for a morning wedding. The shuffling of feet across the courtyard as the team carried over the last of the flowers to the ceremony location. A burst of laughter, muffled in the morning darkness. The beep of a truck backing up near the kitchen; the last of the food supplies for Akin.

As the sounds faded in and out, her mind drifted to Collin. And to him sleeping in that massive house all alone. She could have invited him to stay with her, but she only had one bed. And while he'd grown into a man she'd look at more than twice if she saw him in a bar or restaurant, their history stretched between them. It didn't make her uncomfortable—or him, it appeared—but he had enough on his plate that she didn't need to dredge *that* past up.

Still, she didn't like the idea of him in that huge place all alone. It was creepy and hollow and a little cold. But the memories were probably worse than any physical discomfort.

Grabbing her phone, she opened her texting app, grateful she'd remembered to get his number the night before. It was early, but he likely kept his device on silent while he slept.

Helia: *How'd you sleep?*

To her surprise, the dots immediately started glowing.

Collin: *Fine, what are you doing up? Your mom said she and your dad are covering the ceremony and lunch and you're not taking over until the reception*

Helia: *When did you talk to my mom?*

Collin: *When I got here ten minutes ago*

She bolted up.

Helia: *You're here?*

Why would he be at Sundaram at just after five in the morning?

Collin: *Yeah, helping your mom and dad with a few last-minute things. I don't know shoot about weddings, but I can carry things*

Collin: **shit* about weddings...giving autocorrect*

Collin: **fucking* autocorrect*

She laughed.

Collin: *Or maybe it's my fat thumbs*

Her mind flashed to his hands. There was absolutely nothing wrong with his hands.

Helia: *I'll be out in ten*

Hopping out of bed, she pulled her hair into a bun as she

darted to the shower. Ten minutes later, she emerged from her water tower, showered, dressed, and ready for the day.

It didn't take her long to spot Collin crossing the courtyard carrying six chairs. He slowed when he saw her, lifted his head, then continued toward the ceremony location.

"The bride emailed last night. Some extended family from Vancouver decided to surprise her. They flew down yesterday, and now we have twenty additional guests," her mom said, joining her. "Collin appeared about twenty minutes ago and offered to help. It's nice to have the muscle. And it's nice muscle, too."

"Mom!" Helia said over a laugh, hip-bumping her mother.

"You going to tell me it's not? He was a good-looking boy. He's grown into his looks even more as a man." She paused as he exited the ceremony location on his way back for more chairs. He glanced their way but kept walking. "And thoughtful, too. Hard to believe he's lived so close all these years."

And never came to visit was left unsaid. Helia recognized the pang lancing through her at her mom's words. Hurt. It hurt that he'd been so close and hadn't ever dropped by or called or even sent an email. Her email address hadn't changed since he left; he could have found her.

But she didn't want to go there. Maybe someday, he'd tell her why he'd stayed away. Or maybe not. For now, though, he was here. And he didn't seem like a man who needed to run anymore. Nor was she a woman who'd let him. She'd missed him too much to do that again. Now that she had his phone number, she had no intention of letting him slide into the shadows of her life a second time.

"What needs to get done?" she asked, turning to her mom. "I know you and Dad have this covered, but I'm up."

Her mom rolled her eyes. "You're always up."

"What can I say, I'm a spry chicken, mama hen. Now put me to work."

And to work she went. For the next hour, they touched up flowers, finalized the seating, made sure Akin was set, prepped the lunch buffet table, and checked waste bins and bathrooms.

When the families began arriving, she dragged Collin to her home to feed them both. They were halfway through their egg-and-sausage sandwiches, and well into their second cups of coffee, when someone knocked at her door.

"You expecting someone at"—Collin looked at his watch—"seven forty-five in the morning?"

She shook her head but pushed back from the table. Crossing the room, she opened the door to find Jess and Carter on the other side.

"Detectives," she said. "This is a..."

"Surprise," Collin said, from over her shoulder. She hadn't heard him move, let alone approach her.

"Morning," Carter said. "Mind if we come in?"

She stepped back, bumping into Collin. He set a hand at her waist, but seemed reluctant to move and let the pair in.

"Sorry to bother you so early," Jess said. "Especially when you have an event going on."

"But we have a couple of follow-up questions," Carter finished.

Helia frowned. "I don't know what more I can tell you, but I'm happy to help. Can I get you both coffee?"

"This isn't a social call, Helia," Collin grumbled. She looked up at him, but his eyes were fixed warily on the two detectives.

She frowned at the expression on his face. "I know it's not social. But since I had nothing to do with Justin's death, if I have answers to any questions they have, I'll help. His mom deserves that."

Collin's gaze dropped to hers. They stood inches apart, his hand still resting on her hip, the heat of his body curling around her. His eyes held steady, but she didn't fool herself. His mind was working a mile a minute. On what, she didn't know, but after an uncomfortable stretch of silence, he nodded. A slight tightening of his lips the only evidence of his unease.

She dragged her gaze from his, then cleared her throat. "So, coffee? Tea?"

Jess and Carter shook their heads.

"Okay," she said, leading everyone into her small sitting room. She and Collin sat on the sofa, his thigh flush against hers. Carter sank into the one chair, while Jess leaned against the wall, setting the backpack she carried on the ground.

"What can I help you with?" she asked.

Carter pulled out his phone, tapped the screen, then handed it over. "Do you recognize that knife?"

She took the device and studied the image. Collin's weight shifted as he leaned closer to look as well.

"It's part of a set," she said, handing the phone back. Both the blade and the handle were covered in suspicious stains, and her skin crawled at the idea that it might be Justin's blood.

"So you recognize it?" Jess asked.

She nodded. "It's in the kitchen, or the rest of the set is. Akin had a sous-chef, Marcel Laurant, who worked here two summers ago. It was his," she said. After a moment's hesitation, she added, "It always seemed weird to me that he left it. Knives are a critical part of a chef's trade. They tend to have their favorites and guard them almost religiously. But it's a beautiful set. Unique. We assumed it was meant as a thank-you for Akin."

"Can you get us Marcel's information?" Carter asked.

She nodded. "It's in the computer in the main building. I can get it for you when we're done here. Was that knife used…"

Jess ignored her lingering question. "Who would have access to the set?"

Helia shrugged. "Pretty much everyone who works here. The last time I remember seeing them was about a month ago, and they were in the drawer that holds extra knives."

"You've touched them?" Carter asked.

Collin shifted beside her, bringing his entire side flush against her body.

She frowned. "I guess, maybe once or twice. They're beautiful pieces. The scrollwork is delicate yet solid. But if, or when, I did, it hasn't been for a while."

"Why?" Collin asked. Carter's and Jess's gazes shifted to him.

Rather than answer, Carter tapped his device again and handed it over.

She wasn't sure she wanted to take it this time, but Collin had no qualms. He plucked the phone from Carter's hand and studied the screen. She watched his face rather than read over his shoulder. The corners of his eyes tightened before they narrowed. His nostrils flared a hint. And even through his beard, she saw his jaw clench.

"Collin?"

His lips disappeared into a thin line as he tipped the phone in her direction. She hesitated, then leaned over. On the screen was an image of a page torn from a notebook. Scrawled diagonally across the paper in large letters were thirteen words.

Why, Helia, why don't you listen? Why are you doing this to me?

She read it, then reread it before looking at Collin in confusion.

"I don't understand," she said. "What does this mean?"

Carter shifted, and she turned back to the detective. His gaze flickered to Jess, then came back to her.

"Where were you on Wednesday night, Helia?"

CHAPTER SEVEN

Rage rolled through Monk's body at the insinuation that Helia was involved in *anyone's* death, let alone that of a man she clearly hadn't wanted anything to do with.

Helia opened her mouth to answer, but he slid a hand over her knee, gave it a gentle squeeze, then spoke over her. "Between what hours?" he asked, his voice clipped.

Carter and Jess might think themselves clever in shocking her, but he'd been around the block a time or two. He knew their tactics.

The two detectives shared another look before Carter answered, conveying his displeasure at Monk's interference with his narrowed eyes. "Between four and ten p.m."

Monk brushed his thumb over Helia's knee. "Between four and ten on Wednesday, what were you doing?" he asked, hoping she'd understand that she was not obligated to—and shouldn't—answer any more than the specific question.

Her hazel eyes, now more brown than green, held his. A beat passed before she nodded and turned to Carter.

"We had a phone meeting with the bride," she started, nodding in the general direction of the hall where said bride was currently becoming a wife. "It started at four thirty. I was in my office before that, and my parents joined me at four fifteen. We took the call from there. It was scheduled for an hour, but it went over, wrapping up around five forty-five. My parents stayed for another fifteen minutes or so while we worked out the final plans, then I took another fifteen minutes to print the schedules for everyone on staff, then dropped them into the staff mailboxes."

Carter scribbled in his notebook, and Jess nodded. Helia set her hand on his. Without pausing to think, Monk flipped his palm and intertwined their fingers.

"After that, I popped out to the Roadhouse to grab some takeaway. I arrived there at six twenty-nine. Those were the first three digits of one of our phone numbers when I was a kid, and it was a little thing I remember noting." She paused and took a breath. "Marielle was working. She took my order, and I sat at the bar with a Pellegrino while it was being prepped. I don't know how long that took, maybe twenty minutes?" Her brow furrowed. "I also saw Miles as I was leaving, Officer Hooper. He and my brother were in the same high school class, so I know him. We waved to each other as I pulled out of the parking lot and he pulled in. From there, I drove home and, well, ate and went to sleep."

Her words trailed off as she finished, as if realizing she had no alibi from about seven fifteen when she left the Roadhouse to ten. He squeezed her hand.

"You keep the gate closed at night, don't you?" he asked.

She nodded. "Unless there's an event, it closes at five and doesn't open until eight the next morning. Not without the code."

He nodded, then turned to Carter. "There are CCTV

cameras all over the facility," he said. They were discreet, but he'd noticed them while helping earlier. "You'll be able to check the gate logs for when Helia returned from the Roadhouse and the cameras will show that she didn't leave again." He didn't know that for certain; he and Helia hadn't talked about it. But he knew her. Knew her in a way he didn't really understand other than to be certain that if she'd gone out again, she would have said.

Carter studied them, then glanced at Jess, who nodded. "Thank you, Helia. Can you show us the rest of the knives?"

She grimaced but nodded. "I can, but the kitchen is getting ready for a hundred-person brunch/lunch buffet. They work like a well-oiled machine, and if we set foot in there and disrupt the mechanism, it throws things off." Carter opened his mouth to speak, but she talked over him, making Monk smile. "I'm not saying we can't go in, but would it be possible if I took only one of you with me?"

Surprisingly, the detectives didn't pause to share another look. Jess pushed off the wall and grabbed her backpack. "Yeah, that's fine."

Helia rose, dropping his hand. "The ceremony is underway, but we'll take the back paths in case one of the photographers is taking pictures of the grounds," she said, leading them through her door and onto the walkway.

"One of the photographers?" Carter asked, falling into step beside Helia ahead of him. Jess came up alongside him in yet another predictable move—as if separating him from Helia would stop him from protecting her.

"There are seven for this wedding. And three videographers," Helia answered. As Jess asked him, "You grew up here?"

He nodded.

"What was that like?"

Internally, he sighed. As a general rule, he didn't talk about his life with people he didn't know. Unfortunately, if he dodged too much, he'd give them more of a reason to focus on Helia.

"I left at eighteen, if that tells you anything."

"You're back now."

"Carter mentioned my father dying yesterday, so I know you know why I'm back."

"When'd you get here?"

"Yesterday."

"He died over a week ago."

"We weren't close."

"Where do you live now?"

She knew the answers to these questions. If she thought he'd give her some great insight, she was in for a disappointing chat. "Mystery Lake."

"Not far, but you never came back."

"Nope."

"You and Helia seem close."

His jaw clenched. He didn't want anyone prying into his and Helia's past. "Our properties abut. We grew up together."

"But you hadn't seen each other in years before yesterday," Jess said. An assumption on her part. She might have found out he hadn't been back since he left, but the world was a big place. He and Helia could have met up anywhere. They hadn't, but that wasn't the point.

"Some friendships stand the test of time," he responded as they approached the back entrance to the kitchen.

"Who's going with me?" Helia asked.

"I will," Jess answered. Which would give her time with Helia and Carter a chance to talk with him. Monk nearly rolled his eyes at the orchestration. Again, he didn't begrudge them their job. He hoped they found whoever killed Justin Flannery. But they were wasting their time with Helia.

The two women slipped through the door, the sound of pans clattering, raised voices, and ovens running filtering out before the door shut, sending him and Carter back into silence.

"You going to stick around and run Bacco?" Carter asked, leaning against the dark wood of the building.

Monk crossed his arms and let his gaze rest on the vast vineyard stretching north. "Haven't decided."

"You don't seem especially cut up about your father's death."

He sliced the detective a look. "As I told your colleague, we weren't close."

"Justin did some work with your dad."

Monk shrugged. "Bacco has a tasting room. I understand Flannery and his mother ran a wine accessories business. It doesn't surprise me they did business together."

"But you never met him?"

Monk shook his head.

"Helia never talked about him to you?"

"Not until yesterday."

"They were together two years, and she never mentioned him?"

Monk shrugged. "Like I said, never heard the name until yesterday."

Carter's gaze stayed fixed on him; he could feel it. He didn't mind. The detective could look all he wanted. Monk wasn't easy to intimidate.

"What'd you do when you left the valley?"

"Joined the army."

"You out now?" He nodded. "How long?"

At least the tedious conversation passed the time while they waited. "Seven years."

"And you live up in the mountains?"

He nodded. "Run a few businesses with a couple of guys I served with. Was the knife the murder weapon?"

With his eyes still on the vineyard, he felt more than saw Carter's focus. "Who says he was murdered?"

"I'd prefer not to play this game, Detective. If you don't want to tell me whether the knife was the murder weapon, then say so. But no need to pretend this isn't a homicide investigation."

Carter grumbled a short string of words Monk didn't catch before answering. "The knife was found at the scene. The ME is still deciding if the wounds were self-inflicted."

He locked eyes with Carter. Monk had once sat on a rock on the side of a mountain looking through the scope of his rifle for fourteen hours without moving. The detective wasn't about to win this staring contest.

Three minutes passed before Carter shifted his gaze on a huff. "That's a fucked-up skill to have," he muttered.

Monk fought a grin. "Jealous?"

Carter wagged his head, then crossed his arms. "Maybe a little. You learn that in the army?"

"It's not a course they teach, but yeah. I don't use it that often, though."

Carter chuckled. "But for Helia, you will?"

"She's not involved in this at all. You know it. Jess knows it. I know it," he said. "I get that you have a job to do. And it's cliché for me to point out that time you spend focused on her is time you're wasting not focused on the killer. So what do you need to clear her and move on?"

"The letter is an issue. It implies they had a conflict."

"Or," Monk said, "it's the ramblings of a desperate man unwilling to accept a woman doesn't want him. Of the two scenarios, mine seems more plausible."

"Justin Flannery showed no evidence of desperation in any other part of his life."

"And Helia shows homicidal tendencies?" Monk countered. Helia's voice filtered through the din as she and Jess headed their way. "Get the CCTV, clear her, and move on."

"You the detective now?"

"I get it, I irritate you. But it's obvious the Shaw family respects you, which means you have integrity and intelligence. I want you to clear her because the hairs on my neck are standing on end, and I think there's more going on here than just Flannery's death."

Carter straightened. "The hell? What do you know?"

Jess called out a hello to someone, her voice close.

"I don't know anything. But I don't like that two men Helia dated have both been sniffing around her again and now one is dead."

"Two?" Carter asked, but Monk didn't have a chance to answer before Helia and Jess exited the kitchen.

"The rest of the set," Jess said, holding up a sealed box she must have unfolded from her backpack. "There are six total, five here."

"You sure the set isn't larger?" Carter asked.

"They're stored in a leather carrier that has six individual pouches. One is empty, the other five are in here," Jess replied. Monk gave her credit for keeping her tone even as Carter questioned her skill.

"Can we download the CCTV footage?" Carter asked Helia with a nod to the main building.

Helia didn't look thrilled but nodded. "If it would be helpful."

"I know it seems intrusive, but yes," Carter replied.

Rather than allow the detectives to separate him from Helia, he stepped to her side, set a hand on her lower back, and nudged her forward. He remained by her side, walking in a silence occasionally punctuated by sounds of chanting coming from the wedding ceremony. If anyone else noted the odd juxtaposition of two people happily starting a life together on one end of the property and four people focused on the brutal end of life on the other, no one said.

Again, they entered through the door farthest from the ceremony, following Helia to the second floor and into an office. She took a seat while he stood to the side, arms crossed, feet apart.

"You were Delta Force," Carter said, finally acknowledging, as subtle as it was, that they'd investigated him.

He nodded. Helia's eyes flickered up but she said nothing, returning to her task.

"How many tours?"

"Delta doesn't have tours," he responded. "We deployed."

"You traveled a lot?"

Monk studied the man. He didn't want to assume the questions had nothing to do with the investigation, and he doubted Carter was making casual conversation. He couldn't figure out how they were related, though.

He inclined his head in response.

Carter grinned. "Is it anything like the movies?"

"Is police work?" he countered.

"No," he replied without hesitation. "But I don't mind. I like investigating. What did you like about Delta?"

"I emailed you the footage from the night you requested," Helia said, the sharpness of her voice punctuated by the scrape of her chair across the floor as she rose. "Six hours total."

Carter's gaze lingered on him, then slid to Helia. "Thanks, we appreciate it."

Helia nodded. "Is there anything else? I need to get back to work."

Carter and Jess shook their heads. "Thanks, but this should do it for now. We can show ourselves out," Jess said.

Helia smiled, not a friendly one. "Sorry, it's against our policy to have unescorted guests on the property unless they are part of an event. We'll walk you down."

Monk fought the twitch of his lips. He had no idea if that was true, but he liked the steely sweetness of her response. No one could say she was being rude, but no one would be dumb enough to argue with her either.

Sensing the shift, the detectives nodded and moved into the hall. Once Helia shut and locked the door, he took his place beside her again. A few minutes later, they watched the white SUV cruise down the driveway.

He turned to his childhood friend. His childhood...everything. A breeze caught her hair, lifting the ends, displaying the delicate line of her jaw and her elegant neck.

"Well, that was interesting," Helia said, her hazel eyes meeting his. "I've never been accused of murder before."

"Not accused, investigated. Big difference."

One dark eyebrow went up. "Didn't feel different."

"Says the woman who has never been accused of murder."

As he'd hoped, her expression lightened, and her eyes took on a sparkle that was distinctly Helia. "Come on, He-man," she said, looping an arm through his. "Let's see if the staff needs help getting food from the kitchen to the dining room." She squeezed his biceps. "If you're going to keep these guns in top shape, lugging chairs isn't going to cut it."

CHAPTER EIGHT

Monk sat in front of the unlit fire, debating whether to light it. He'd spent the day yesterday helping the Shaws and hadn't returned to the castle until well after midnight. He'd fallen into a restless sleep on the couch, his dreams filled with darkness. Helia made an appearance a time or two. But on waking, the images he remembered most were vague and ominous, leaving him uneasy in the muted late-morning light of the tasting room.

It didn't help that his father's memorial started in four hours.

He had no intention of going and had almost convinced himself that he felt nothing about the situation. But he couldn't stop the coil of anger twisting through him at the thought of so many people gathering to pay their respects to a man who couldn't deserve it less. The community would mourn and reflect on the wonderful man they thought Roger Wilde was—the same man who fed people drugs before luring them into orgies that frequently crossed the line into outright violence. Men, women, even his own son; Roger hadn't cared who attended so long as he found it entertaining.

Nausea curled in his stomach as the memories peeked through the thick wall he'd constructed to keep them at bay. He'd been thirteen the first time his father drugged him and brought him to a party. Monk didn't remember everything from that night, but he remembered enough. He remembered his father encouraging a woman three times Monk's age to play with him. He remembered his father watching, laughing, as she coaxed him into a state that allowed her to do things that should never be done to a child or anyone unable to consent. And he remembered the shame. The shame of waking up and knowing his body had betrayed him. He hadn't wanted what had happened to him. And yet, young and drugged, his body had succumbed.

That had been the first time.

Beside him, his phone rang, jarring him from his dark journey down memory lane. Glancing at the number, he connected the call.

"Leo," he said.

"Monk. I did some digging. I don't have answers yet, but I have a few interesting bits of information."

Between taking down the lunch buffet and preparing for the dinner reception, he'd called the cyber expert and asked him to look into both Flannery and Weber.

"On?"

"Flannery's death. It appears to be from self-inflicted knife wounds."

"I'm assuming since you used the word 'appears' and two detectives were here yesterday, there's some question."

"You would be right. The cleaner had been in that day. She left at two, stating that Flannery was usually home by three and he preferred she be out of the house by then. According to the file, he left work at the usual time, stopped by the grocery store where he purchased two steaks and a quart of premade broccoli salad—"

"Weird thing to buy if you're planning to kill yourself."

"Agreed. Based on the timelines, the police believe he arrived home around fifteen minutes before four. The time of death isn't between four and ten, but between four and seven, although I'd say closer to four than seven."

"Why?"

"Nothing in the house was disturbed other than the room where they found him. He parked in the garage as usual, took his shoes off in the mudroom, and put the steaks and salad in the fridge."

"Then?"

"Then comes my hypothesis."

"Which is likely to be closer to the truth than the police's."

"I appreciate that," Leo said. "What I think happened is that someone came to the front door. His work bag was left on the floor in the kitchen, and his footprints—in socks, not shoes —were found on the newly vacuumed carpet in the living room, the room he'd show a guest into."

"He was found in the living room?"

"He was. The shutters were closed, so no witnesses from outside, but that's where it happened. The pictures aren't pretty. Arterial spray is nothing to scoff at."

Monk knew that all too well.

"They found him, in his work clothes, with his throat cut, and the police are still considering a suicide?"

"To be fair, I think it's the chief, more than the detectives. Napa isn't an area with a high murder rate, and I'm guessing she'd like to keep it that way."

"But the detectives are still investigating."

"Aside from the anomalies you summarized, there's one more." Leo paused.

"You're being dramatic. Sabina is rubbing off on you." Sabina was Leo's boss, and she had a thing for the dramatic pause. Monk was sure she read too much Agatha Christie and Sherlock Holmes.

A chuckle rumbled over the line. "Sorry. In addition to the anomalies you noted, they found another footprint."

"On the newly vacuumed rug?"

"Exactly. A shoe. Men's size eleven dress shoe."

"What size is Flannery?"

"Nine."

"I didn't know grown men had such tiny feet."

"Because you and your brothers are all giants. But you're right, it's not common. Not in a man of Flannery's height."

"Okay, so murder. Not a big shocker. I wonder how the knife got there," he said, having filled Leo in on the detectives' visit and their interest in the custom knife set. "Did the killer bring it, or did Flannery pick it up during one of his deliveries?"

"That I don't have insight into. There are fingerprints on it, but while they could be Flannery's, they are too smudged to be conclusive."

"Smudged? As if someone wiped them?"

"Or maybe Flannery stole the knife at some point, leaving his prints, and then the person who used it wore gloves, smudging them."

"What about Weber? Did you find anything on him?" he asked.

Leo chuckled. "Now he's a walking cliché if I ever met one."

"His hundred-dollar haircut and compensation car gave that away. What else did you find?"

"Car's leased. He doesn't own it."

"Figures."

"Still, it's not cheap. And not an expense your average restaurant manager would be able to afford. Not on top of the six grand he pays per month for rent."

"What's his story?"

"Nothing obvious popped up on him except he does have a conviction for assault back in Florida, where he's originally from. It was twelve years ago, and he hit his girlfriend."

A growl rumbled up from his chest.

"From the arrest picture, it looks like she got a few good ones in herself," Leo added.

"Too bad she didn't finish the job."

"His mama might miss him, but I doubt many others would," Leo agreed.

Monk stared at the darkened fireplace. He was willing to concede he might be overreacting to the situation, but the letter found at Flannery's didn't fit. Was it possible he'd become obsessed with Helia? Was Weber? And if either of those were true, did it tie into Flannery's murder?

"Am I reading too much into this?" he asked. He didn't like not trusting himself, but with Helia in the mix, his thoughts felt jumbled.

Leo hesitated. "I don't know. As weird as it is, it's Weber that muddies the water, not the murder. A single murder would be easy to write off. But the fact that both men wanted Helia back at the same time *and* Weber is... Well, I don't know what's going on yet, but my Spidey senses are telling me to look deeper at him. I focused on Flannery for obvious reasons, but..."

"Do you have the time? Do you make that noise in front of Joey?" he added when Leo snorted.

"She loves me and of course I have time. I'm curious now, and I don't do well with loose ends. *That* annoys Joey. Despite the fact that she loves me," he added.

"Smug bastard," Monk muttered, meaning it despite being happy for the couple.

Leo chuckled again, then promised to check in the next day before disconnecting. Less than a minute passed before Monk's phone dinged with a text. He smiled when he saw the name.

Helia: *You sleep in?*

Monk: *A bit, you?*

Helia: *Not as much as I wish I could. I never do, seems like I should give up that ghost at some point, but no, I still hold out hope that someday, I'll sleep in until ten. What are you up to today?*

He lifted his gaze and scanned the tasting room, a reminder of his father. And the pending memorial.

Monk: *Not going to the memorial*

Helia: (eyeroll emoji) *I didn't ask you what you're not doing. I know what you're not doing. Or at least one thing you're not doing. But what are you doing?*

A creak sounded over his head, and he glanced up. He needed a shower, which was on the second floor. He'd skated past without one yesterday, but after all the lifting and carrying, he smelled a little ripe. Felt grungy, too.

Monk: *I need to shower, which means I need to go upstairs. Since I'll be up there, I should probably start going through Roger's stuff*

A pause followed before the dots appeared.

Helia: *If you haven't gone upstairs yet, where have you been sleeping?*

He grimaced. He should have thought through his response better.

Helia: *And don't lie to me*

Monk: *You're bossy*

Helia: *I have leadership qualities*

He chuckled.

Monk: *The couch in the tasting room. It's not so bad*

Helia: *You could have stayed at my parents'. Your room is still there*

The room might be there, but the boy he'd been—the boy who'd needed it—was gone. He was eternally grateful for everything the Shaws had done for him. But he was an adult now. He was stronger, he had family, he had responsibilities. The memories were brutal, but that's all they were, memories. They couldn't hurt him anymore—his father couldn't hurt him anymore.

Or so he told himself as his gaze lingered on the ceiling. If that was true, why hadn't he managed to climb the stairs to the private part of the castle?

A low growl of frustration rumbled in his throat.

Monk: *I appreciate that, but I need to be here*

Helia: *Do you need me to be there with you?*

His heart hitched in a funny little beat. He hadn't seen or spoken to Helia in years and yet here she was, sliding right back into his life as if she'd never been gone.

Monk: *Why aren't you mad at me?*

A pause again before the bubbles.

Helia: *I'm not going to pretend not to know what you're talking about. I missed you when you left. A lot. But it made me sad, not angry. Now that you're back, I can either be happy about it or mad that you were gone for so long. I choose to be happy*

Monk: *You're a better person than I am*

Helia: *This is getting deep for an early morning text*

Monk: *This fucking castle inspires maudlinism*

Helia: *Not a word, but it should be (laughing emoji). So do you want company?*

He considered it. It would be nice to have her with him, to have the light she carried inside her as he stepped back into the darkness of his past. But he had no idea what he'd find, and he wouldn't risk subjecting her to any of Roger's depravities.

Not that she'd talk—he knew her better than that—but she didn't need any more insight into his childhood.

Monk: *Not today, but maybe dinner tonight?*

The offer both surprised him and didn't. He hadn't asked a woman out in ages. Well, truthfully, ever. Not that he hadn't gone out with women or dated them, but on the rare occasions he did, the woman initiated it.

But this wasn't a date. It was two friends grabbing a meal together.

Helia: *Only if you take me to Guichos. They have the best al pastor tacos. It's a food truck, but they set up a tent with a heater, and you can bring your own beer*

He chuckled. Leave it to Helia to ask to be taken to a food truck for tacos and beer.

Monk: *Deal. I'll pick you up at five*

Helia: *I'll walk over. I have a ton of paperwork to do, I'll want to stretch my legs*

Monk: *Fine, but call or text if you change your mind and I'll come get you*

Helia: *Be kind to yourself today*

Five simple words that pulled the breath from his lungs. A reminder he needed to hear.

Monk: *I will...and thank you*

She ended the conversation with a heart emoji, and he shoved his phone into his jeans pocket as he rose. Another creak sounded from the second floor, and he cocked his head. When nothing else shifted, he let it go and grabbed his bag. He'd once known every little squeak and scrape of the castle, but seventeen years aged a building.

Heading to the south side of the castle, he paused at the bottom of the stairs leading to the second floor. Gripping his bag tighter than its weight called for, he took the first step. Without giving himself time to think, he climbed steadily to the third floor and walked to his old room, hoping Roger hadn't renovated it to some other use.

He set his hand on the closed door, the thick wood plank with an aged bronze fixture cold beneath his touch. Nudging it open, he kept moving, as if it might keep the memories at bay. He didn't harbor any illusions he'd outrun them, but maybe he could stay far enough ahead that only wisps and pieces filtered into his mind until he felt strong enough to face them head-on.

Striding into the room, he noted it hadn't changed much since he'd left. The pictures on the curved plaster walls were now Italian landscapes rather than posters, and a tapestry graced the space behind the headboard. Roger had left the custom armoire but traded the bed out for a dark, gothic four-poster king one, and a thick Persian carpet with deep red and brown tones covered much of the wood floor.

Turning to his right, he entered the bathroom. Again, mostly untouched, though updated. Vaguely, he noted the marble floors and shower, the intricate tile work on the walls, the expensive fixtures. A far cry from the subway tiles and simple shower he'd had, but in a way, he was glad it wasn't the same. Glad it wasn't one more memory pulling him back to that time.

As the water slid down his body, some of his anxiety washed away with it. By the time he stepped out fifteen minutes later, he decided that the room was different enough that he could try sleeping there. And after shaving and dressing, the rest of the castle didn't seem so daunting.

Leaving his bath kit on the counter and his bag on the bed, he made his way to the corridor that ran along the front section of the castle with views down into the courtyard. Worried that his bravado might fail him, he didn't stop at any of the rooms. When he reached the north side of the castle, he jogged down to the second floor, passed through another hallway, then stepped into his father's room.

Pausing in the doorway, he scanned the space. The cleaners had obviously been in since his father's death, and the bed was freshly made. Through an open door, he glimpsed the bathroom counter and his father's personal effects—his shaving cream, toothbrush, and a few other items—laid out in a neat row.

Crossing the room, he entered the enormous walk-in closet. The original castle had twenty-four bedrooms. By the time Monk left, Roger had converted seven of those into either bathrooms or closets. Now, unless he'd done more renovation, which wouldn't surprise Monk as his father was a perennially dissatisfied sort of person, it hosted seventeen bedrooms, each with an en suite bath. And many with closets the size of an average living room.

Standing in one such closet, he took in the tailor-made suits lining one wall, the rack of Italian shoes, and the polished wood cabinets that held who-knew-what.

Turning in a slow circle, his skin vibrated with an awareness that meant only one thing. "Okay, Roger," he said on an exhale. "What the hell will I find here?"

CHAPTER NINE

D rugs. In addition to a wardrobe worth the cost of an average house, Roger had a stash of drugs. Monk stared at the box filled with tiny plastic bags, each of those filled with a crystal-like substance. He'd found the container in a hidden compartment behind the shoe rack. Along with a gun, a pair of gold handcuffs—an impractical material if there ever was one—and a whip. He could understand why Roger hadn't left the handcuffs down in the dungeon where all his "parties" took place, but the whip was an odd one. It didn't appear to be valuable, and Roger wasn't a sentimental man. Monk didn't feel the need to pick it up and examine it, though.

Grabbing the gun, he slid the shoe rack back into place, an audible click securing the items back in their hidey-hole. Then pulling out his phone, he tapped a contact.

"Monk." Mantis's familiar voice soothed some of his anxiety.

"Yeah."

"You need company?"

"I found a bunch of drugs in Roger's room. I don't know what it is so don't want to dump it."

"You made it into his room?"

Monk walked out. "And my old one." And then, because he didn't feel the need to hide anything, he added, "I've been sleeping in the tasting room, though."

His brothers knew enough about the castle that Mantis would understand how much he *hadn't* explored.

"Dulcie's there already. I'll send Lovell, too. One can stay with you, and the other can bring the drugs back. HICC can test it, then we'll know how to dispose of it."

He'd spied Dulcie following him from Mystery Lake but hadn't seen him since arriving, although it didn't surprise Monk he'd stuck around. Now that he'd broken the metaphorical seal and made his first foray into parts of the castle littered with memories, it would be good to have a brother with him for the rest.

"I'd appreciate that."

"Lovell told me about Helia. Any news there?"

Monk didn't blink at the question. There were very few secrets among the Falcon's Rest men.

"Leo's looking into it. Flannery was murdered, although they aren't public with that yet. Two detectives questioned Helia yesterday, but her alibi is airtight. Still, it rattled her."

"I'm sure it did. How's she doing otherwise?"

He'd been one of the lucky ones to have someone looking out for him. Someone who cared about him and gave him a safe place when his father started doing, well, what Roger did. Knowing his relationship with Helia and her family made them important to his brothers, too.

"Good. Running an amazing business with her parents. They had a massive wedding yesterday and no one even broke a sweat. I'm talking a four-hundred person sit-down-five-course meal preceded *and* followed by dancing."

"Damn, even Dottie would be impressed," Mantis murmured, referring to their own house manager/house mom. Dottie kept the club running and fed with an efficiency that seemed almost mystical at times.

Monk chuckled as he made his way down to the tasting room. He'd venture upstairs again when Dulcie and Lovell arrived, but he'd had enough for now.

"She'd definitely be impressed."

Mantis hesitated. Monk knew the next question his club president wanted to ask but wasn't certain if he should. Taking the choice away from him, Monk spoke. "She's divorced."

To his credit, Mantis didn't take the next logical step in the conversation. "She okay? Was it messy?"

"It was a while ago," he said. They'd touched on the topic over breakfast the day before, but she hadn't gone into detail. "I didn't get the sense it was messy. Sounded more like they drifted apart, then realized they wanted different things. No kids, so fewer complications."

"Probably still hard, but I'm glad she seems okay."

Yeah, Monk felt a tad guilty for how good it felt not seeing her cut up about another man. He had no rights to her in that way, but he didn't make a habit of lying to himself.

"Me, too."

"The memorial is today."

"Yep."

"I assume you're not going. Do you need anything other than Dulcie and Lovell?"

"Definitely not going and no. I'm going to research where I can donate Roger's clothes. I'll get his room cleaned out, then move on to the rest of the house."

"Dulcie will stick around in case you need him."

Before going down to the dungeon, was left unsaid. Monk hated even thinking the words. Aside from the memories, it was such a cliché. Not that he'd prefer his father to be a less-cliché criminal asshole, but referring to the basement as the dungeon made it sound like a set in a two-bit porno. Admittedly, it hadn't been far off. But unlike a professional film, the drugs Roger pushed on people, sometimes without their knowledge, made it impossible for anyone to consent to the activities that took place down there. Himself being a case in point.

"Thanks," he muttered, shifting a pillow out of place and taking a seat in one of the leather chairs.

"When are you seeing Helia again?"

"You better not start fucking betting on anything," Monk muttered. Charley came from a large family that bet on *everything*. It hadn't taken much to drag the Falcons into it.

"Between Charley, Joey, and Leo, that's like asking the tide to stop," Mantis said on a laugh.

Monk grumbled. He didn't really mind, but the idea of them betting on him and Helia in any way made him think of Helia *in that way*. A topic that had no business occupying his brain. He'd only walked back into her life after years apart.

"We're going out for tacos tonight. Some food truck she likes," he replied.

"I want credit for changing the subject and not responding like a teenager right now."

"Depends on what you're going to change it to. I might prefer prurient comments about my lack of relationship with Helia."

Mantis chuckled. "I was going to make a taco comment, actually. All joking aside, how is seeing her again? She and her family were good to you. They were a big part of your life before you left. But the good mixes with the bad sometimes."

Monk considered his answer. In truth, he hadn't really let himself think too deeply about slipping back into her life. Or what, if anything, it might mean to reconnect with the Shaw family. Maybe he should, or maybe it wasn't worth over-thinking.

"It's not hard," he replied truthfully. "I'm not reading anything into that, though. Only that it's easy and they aren't bringing back any of the bad memories. They're still the good people I knew; we just look older now."

"And have more years—more experience—under our belts."

"That, too."

Mantis paused. "Okay, Lovell is on his way. He'll pick Dulcie up and be there in three hours or so. Call if you need anything more."

He promised he would, then rattled off the gate code and ended the call. Glancing at the fireplace, he considered making a fire, then ixnayed the idea. It wasn't all that cold, and he'd have to let it die out before heading to the taco truck with Helia. Maybe he'd light it before bed.

Setting his phone on the side table, his gaze lingered on the gun from his father's closet. Pistol, if he cared to be precise. A pocket Ruger—powerful enough to pack a punch but easy to conceal and carry. He'd never seen Roger carry a weapon or even shoot one.

Picking it up, he turned it over in his hand, his gaze lingering on the serial number. On a whim, he grabbed his phone and texted the string of digits to Leo, asking him to run it through their system. When the message was delivered, he set the device down and held the weapon in his palm, testing its weight. With a frown, he checked the magazine. Why the hell did Roger have a fully loaded weapon in the house?

There could be dozens of answers to that question. He

hadn't seen his father in years. And Roger wasn't exactly a bastion of good behavior. Who the hell knew what he'd been up to.

His phone dinged, a message from Leo confirming he'd look into it. Not knowing what more he could do or learn about it, Monk set the pistol on the side table and focused on more productive things—finding the right place to donate his father's clothing and shoes.

Two hours later, he'd made arrangements with a second-chance program that helped formerly incarcerated men find employment, including providing them with interview-appropriate clothing. He'd have to drive to San Francisco to drop it off, but the city wasn't that far.

Leaning back in the chair, he closed his eyes and contemplated a nap. He had an hour or so before Lovell and Dulcie arrived and another hour after that before meeting Helia.

The heavy weight of sleep danced on the fringes of his mind when a scraping sound yanked him from Morpheus's embrace. Keeping his eyes closed, he dialed his hearing in.

Another scrape, a shuffle, then the low mumble of a voice, more a vibration than a distinct sound.

In silence, he palmed the pistol. Maybe Helia had come early. If so, she didn't need to see it.

That thought—as tenuous as it was—fled when he heard the security code being entered.

Living behind a gate and down a half-mile drive had lulled him into forgetting a very basic security practice. As the door swung open, he added changing the code, and locks as well, to his to-do list. And while he was at it, he'd install security cameras, too. Having footage of his visitor's arrival—and pending retreat—could have come in handy.

"It's his fucking memorial today," a voice rumbled. It didn't sound familiar, but Monk hadn't expected it to. Napa had changed a lot in the years he'd been gone, and there were too many newcomers to assume he'd recognize someone.

A quiet response followed. He didn't catch the words, but the intense vibe of the reply had him hooking his finger around the trigger.

"I don't know who's truck that is, but no one will be here, not even Alessio," the first voice said, looking over his shoulder as he stepped into Monk's line of sight.

"You got that wrong," Monk said.

The first man leaped three feet, bounced off the wall, and spun. Dressed in a black windbreaker, black ball cap, and a scarf wrapped around his face, all Monk could catalog were the basics: a hair shy of six feet, lanky build, bordering on thin, dark eyes, and a nervous energy. Monk considered asking why he concealed his appearance if he didn't think anyone was there, but maybe he thought the tasting room had cameras. Most did these days, so not an unreasonable assumption.

"What the fuck?" the burglar shouted.

The second man stepped into view, dressed in the same type of hat and scarf but with a black hoodie. Monk couldn't see his face, but his build seemed familiar.

"You're not supposed to be here," Man One said, his voice rising in what Monk assumed was supposed to be a threatening manner.

"And yet here I am. I could say the same for you."

"We have the code. That means we have permission to enter."

Questioning the man's grasp of the law didn't seem like a good use of Monk's time. "Permission denied. Get the fuck out."

"Who the hell are you?" the same man demanded. Man Two stepped farther into sight. A prick of familiarity hit Monk at the way his hand swung at his side, but nothing clicked.

"Someone who *is* supposed to be here. Now again, get out."

Both men puffed up at the challenge. Monk bit back a sigh.

Man One looked at his accomplice. They may as well have shouted their silent communication.

"I wouldn't go the path you're considering," Monk said.

"Two on one isn't such bad odds," Man Two hissed, taking another step forward.

"Maybe if you tell me what you came here for, I'll let you grab it and go." He wouldn't, but he was curious.

"Or maybe we'll have a different kind of conversation," Man One said as Man Two pulled a bowie knife from the pocket of his hoodie.

"Is that a threat?" Monk asked. Sure, he was baiting them. But they were thirty feet away, and he seriously doubted either had the skill to hit him at that distance.

"The mountains called, and they want you back. We'll take you there in pieces."

Being called a mountain man struck him as funny, and Monk laughed. But when Man Two's shoulders stiffened and he started forward, Monk lifted the pistol and with zero hesitation, fired. The shot hit six inches in front of his toe, sending shards from where it struck the stone flying into the air as the bullet ricocheted and embedded in the wall above the man's knee.

"Jesus fucking christ," Man Two shrieked, leaping back. Man One plastered himself against the opposite wall.

Monk grinned and waved the gun. "I have a few more bullets if you want to try me."

"You're fucking insane," Man One shouted. More like squealed, but Monk didn't need to kick a man while he was down.

He shrugged, his shoulders sliding over the leather at his

back. "You're the one with a knife at a gunfight. Are you sure I'm the insane one?"

The two men shared a look. Monk casually pointed the pistol in their direction. "You're breaking and entering into *my* home." Words he never thought he'd say. He didn't mean them, though, so figured he hadn't damned his own soul by calling the castle his home. "I have no obligation to retreat and every right to defend myself—your threat and that knife made sure of that. But I won't shoot you in the back, if that's any consolation." He wouldn't shoot them at all, but they didn't need to know that. "Make good choices, gentlemen."

Man One grumbled a curse before bolting down the hallway without a backward glance at his crime buddy. Man Two stared at him. The feeling of knowing washed over Monk again. Before he could place him, though, the erstwhile thief spun and disappeared down the hall, too. Less than two seconds later, the door slammed shut.

Monk remained where he was until he heard footsteps on the gravel outside. Rising from his comfortable seat, he followed their path down the hallway and stepped outside. He didn't feel the need to pursue the intruders, but he did want to know in what direction they fled.

Pausing on the porch, he tuned in to the sounds around him. Two birds calling to each other, a third interrupting every few seconds. The breeze rustling the winter vines. The clink of the gate at one of the wine caves, shifting in the wind.

Then he heard it. Gravel dislodging and rolling down the hill. He zeroed in on it and a few seconds later, he heard a branch crack. Making a mental note to place a few cameras with views of the mountain, he returned to the alarm keypad.

A quick internet search gave him the information he needed and a few minutes later, he had a new code. With his nap no longer an option, he ventured to the parking lot and eyed the castle. He had enough time before Lovell and Dulcie arrived to make a plan for the CCTV.

An hour later, his phone dinged as he added the last item to the list of equipment he'd pick up the next day. He smiled at the image. Lovell's souped-up electric Mercedes waiting for the gate to open at the entrance of Bacco.

Rounding the front of the castle, he waited as Dulcie and Lovell pulled up the drive. The sleek black car with tinted windows slid to a stop in front of him, and a beat later, his brothers climbed out.

Both paused, their gazes sweeping over the monstrosity he'd called home. Neither said a word, though, opting instead for a hug and a back slap.

"Murder, drugs, and creepy exes, you've had a busy few days," Dulcie said as they walked inside.

"Considering I've barely left this room other than to go to the Shaws', yeah, it's been interesting," he replied, ushering them into the tasting room.

Lovell paused where the hall met the room, and Monk turned to see him studying the floor. He remained silent as Lovell noted the dings in the wall from the stone shrapnel before he lifted an eyebrow at the bullet still lodged in the plaster.

With a chuckle, he turned to Monk. "Looks like it's been even more interesting than we were led to believe."

CHAPTER TEN

Helia tugged her down vest around her body, grateful she'd had the foresight to throw it on before walking to Collin's. She'd been either moving all day, taking care of the wedding cleanup, or in her office and hadn't realized how far the temperatures had dropped. At least by Northern California standards.

She crossed over to his property and paused to send him a text.

Helia: *ten minutes out*

Collin: *Door's unlocked, come in when you get here*

She stared at the text for longer than the few words required. In the past three days, the reality that he was back hit her at odd times. The reality that he was once again within walking distance. That she talked and laughed with him several times a day. Not quite like no time had passed, but damn close.

Smiling, she tucked her phone back in her pocket and continued down the row. Seeing Collin daily was definitely no hardship. Although she probably shouldn't think about that too much. She had no idea if he was dating someone or other-wise spoken for. He didn't wear a ring, but many people didn't these days. Although the way he'd touched her, held her hand...no, he wouldn't have done any of those things if there was someone in his life.

A hawk swooped overhead, then dived between two rows of vines, no doubt leaving the vineyard with one less mouse. The bird made her think of Collin's found family, the Falcons. He'd told her about each of them, how they'd met, how they'd ended up in Mystery Lake, what they did now. As the castle came into view, she wondered if she'd ever meet them. She didn't plan on letting Collin slip out of her life again, so maybe one day she would.

Coming to the end of the row, she stepped onto the packed-gravel parking area, a second car parked next to Collin's truck drawing her notice. He hadn't mentioned anyone visiting, but maybe Alessio had borrowed a friend's car.

After wiping the mud from her Blundstones, she pushed through the door and headed down the hall.

Mustering her best Desi Arnaz impression, she called out, "Honey, I'm—"

She cut her greeting off and drew to a halt when three men rose from one of the tables. Collin held two cards in his hand, the rest of the deck scattered across the tabletop in what looked like a messy game of blackjack. It wasn't the cards that drew her attention, though. The two men standing with Collin managed that.

When faced with probably five hundred pounds of muscle packed into two fit bodies, she did what most red-blooded women would do: She stared. One of those bodies, a stunning Black man with eyes so green she could see the emerald color from where she stood, stared back. The other, a vaguely Latino-looking man an inch taller than Collin but a good two inches shorter than the green-eyed man, studied her with a hint of amused curiosity.

"If I ever get into a fight, I want you on my team," she said, pointing to the Black man. His lips twitched, although it didn't turn into an actual smile.

"You're crushing my soul, woman," said the other man.

She dragged her gaze to him, swept him with a once-over, then smiled. "Somehow, I doubt that."

"Helia." Her eyes bounced between the two one more time before meeting Collin's. "Two of my brothers, Dulcie"—he gestured to the shorter of the two—"and Lovell. Or Mateo and James, if you prefer."

"Oh no," she said, walking into the room. "It's not about what I prefer." Lovell held out his hand, but she ignored him. "I come from a family that hugs. You're Collin's brothers and he's like family to me, which makes you family to me. Unless it makes you uncomfortable, I'm coming in for a hug."

Lovell blinked, then held his arms out. She stepped into them, her head only coming to his pecs as his massive guns wrapped around her. Dulcie was ready for her when she dropped her arms from Lovell. Collin's brothers were good huggers. She approved.

"Which do you prefer, Lovell and Dulcie or James and Mateo?" she asked. Both men shrugged. She crossed her arms. "It doesn't work that way. Now that I know Collin only lives three hours away, I plan to be a part of your life for a good long while. If you have a slight preference for one and I pick the other, in twenty years it's going to annoy the shit out of you, so *you* have to decide. Besides, it's your name. I'm a big advocate of people being able to decide how they want to be referred to."

Collin chuckled when both Dulcie and Lovell looked at him.

"You'll get used to me," she added.

Lovell's lips twitched again. "Call me James. Named after my grandfather. Would be nice to be reminded of him every now and then."

She gave a sharp nod, then turned to Dulcie. "Dulcie's good. Every time I hear someone call me Mateo, I look around for my mother."

"There, settled," she said. "Now, I'm starving but want to know why there's a bullet embedded in the wall. One of you can tell me while we drive to tacos."

"We'll need to stop for beer," Collin said, ignoring the other half of her comment. She'd caught sight of the bullet a split second before James and Dulcie distracted her. There'd been no time for panic to kick in before her attention diverted.

"No, we don't," she said, crossing the room and slipping behind the tasting bar. "Marisa, who runs the tasting room, keeps a few beers in stock just in case."

"In case of what?" James asked. "This is a winery."

She inclined her head before dropping down behind the bar to the mini fridge. "Yes, but we get all sorts here. Ninety-nine percent of visitors are great, but every now and then, you get a real dick, usually a guy." She popped up holding two four-packs of IPA from Twisted River, a local brewery located on the south side of the city of Napa. "A guy who's brought a date up to the valley and wants to swing his imaginary big dick around so he orders beer to show he can get what he wants when he wants." She set the two four-packs on the counter. "It's really satisfying when you can smile and hand him a glass like he's not special at all."

All three men blinked.

"Swing his dick around?" James repeated.

"Metaphorically, of course. Most of the time," she added, remembering a particularly raucous wedding Sundaram hosted a few years back.

"How do you know it's not actually big?" Dulcie asked.

"Dude," Collin said.

"She said it's imaginary, maybe it's not," Dulcie pointed out. "Not that it would give him an excuse to *be* a dick, but you know, just curious how she knows."

"Some people have a good gay-dar. I have a really good big-dick-dar," she replied. James's lips twitched again; Dulcie snorted. One of Collin's eyebrows went up. "It's not a super-power or anything. But it's like the whole alpha-male thing, which I know is scientific bullshit, but in pop culture, it's a thing. A true alpha will never talk about it. They just *are*. It's the same with big dicks. Men who have them *know* they have them and don't feel the need to swing them around. Metaphorically or otherwise."

"Right," Collin said, walking over and grabbing the four-packs. "Let's go get those tacos." He tossed a four-pack to Dulcie and the other to James. "I'll drive so you can charge your car before leaving tonight, Lovell."

"Perfect," she said, rounding the bar and slipping her arm around Collin's. "And you can tell me all about that bullet."

By the time they arrived at the taco truck, Collin had relayed the events of the afternoon. The ones relating to the bullet, anyway. The experience would have left her shaking like a leaf in a storm, but after ten years in the military, spec ops no less, Collin wouldn't have called his brothers down because of a break-in. They'd come to town for another reason. A reason they weren't telling her. Probably something she had no right to ask. That wouldn't stop her, of course. But she'd wait to catch Collin off guard. In her experience, surprising people had a better chance of leading to the truth than easing into a conversation.

They ordered their food, then grabbed one of the three picnic tables. The spot was popular with field workers, but they'd arrived between shifts, so while a few folks lingered, waiting for to-go orders, they were the only people sitting.

James handed a beer to everyone, and as she popped the top, the sun setting over the western mountains, she inhaled a breath of appreciation. Napa Valley wasn't an easy place to live for a lot of people—housing was expensive, jobs were limited, the general cost of living high—but she had a job she loved, on land that had been in her family for decades, and now Collin was back. Plus, she was eating tacos. Life was pretty damn good.

"What's it like being an event coordinator at such a big place?" Dulcie asked. "My younger sister works at a restaurant in Sacramento doing the same thing, but smaller scale. She's always mega stressed when there's an event going on."

"I get that. I love my job, but it's stressful. Even with the great team we have. Sometimes I think it would be nice to be a little smaller scale, a little more intimate. But it's hard to complain about being the victim of your own success. Events your sister works, at restaurants, are different than the events we hold, though. Ours are usually part of a bigger celebration —a wedding or holiday party or birthday, that sort of thing. At a restaurant, the focus is almost entirely on the food and the dining experience. There's no distractions if it isn't perfect."

James nodded, Collin studied her, and Dulcie smiled. "So you're saying I shouldn't tell her to chill?"

She snorted. "Has that ever worked for you?"

Saved from answering by Jose, the food truck owner, calling Collin's name, Dulcie chuckled as he rose to retrieve their food.

They settled into comfortable conversation, occasionally punctuated by moans of satisfaction, when she spotted a familiar figure lingering in a group of field workers. Snagging

Collin's attention, she nodded to the man. "That's Miguel," she said. "Your vineyard manager."

"My what?"

"He manages the care of the vineyard. Him and his team. Do you want to meet him? You'll want to at some point, but it doesn't have to be tonight."

"I assume he's good if Alessio keeps him on?" he asked.

She nodded. "He's solid. The family had a little bit of a setback recently when his daughter got involved with the wrong kind of guy. Shook them up a bit, but they managed to get her out. She and her son live with her parents now."

A little boy zoomed around the corner of the truck and launched himself at Miguel. "And there's the grandson now." Miguel set his hand on the boy's head and smiled down at him.

"Let them be. I'll meet him later," Collin said.

"Helia?" All five turned at the voice calling from the far side of the food truck. "Oh my gosh, it is you."

"Trish?" Helia said.

"It's been years," Trish said, hurrying toward her.

"What are you doing back in town?" Helia replied, hugging her old friend. She and Trish had met the first week she'd moved to Napa. They'd gone to different schools but played soccer together in the local premier league and stayed close growing up. They'd drifted apart during college, but still occasionally kept in touch via social media.

"I'm moving back," she answered, smiling as she stepped away. Her gaze flickered to the three men before landing back on her with an exaggerated you-go-girl look in her eye.

Feeling like a teenager again, Helia laughed. Trish had always been boy crazy. "Join us?" she asked. Her three companions shared a look Helia didn't understand and didn't have the time to contemplate because Trish squeezed her hand and wiggled her eyebrows.

"Don't mind if I do. Let me place my order and I'll be right back," she said before darting off. Helia watched her, noting how little she'd changed since high school. Still all long, lean muscles and gorgeous wavy black hair, Trish had definitely aged better than the average bear.

"Hope you all don't mind? I figured we're going to be here for a while, what with your second dinners and all," she said, turning to the men.

"Not a problem," Dulcie replied. "Old friend?"

Helia nodded and sat again, Collin beside her. "We were close for several years. Then I went to UC San Diego for college, and she went to Tulane in New Orleans, and we drifted."

"And now she's back," Collin said.

"Apparently," she replied, her gaze darting between her companions. She narrowed her eyes. "What's going on?" she demanded. She'd bet her house they were holding a different conversation among them than the one happening out loud.

Three sets of eyes studied her.

"Good thing I happened to stop at the store on my way here," Trish said, setting a six-pack on the table and sliding onto the bench. A pang of annoyance rippled through Helia at the interruption. Only it wasn't really an interruption because that implied Collin, Dulcie, or James would have answered.

And for whatever reason, she was certain that hadn't been the case.

CHAPTER ELEVEN

Helia wasn't happy with him. Or Dulcie or Lovell. But what would he say to her? Having three people from her past suddenly show up and want to reconnect wasn't *that* weird, even if one was recently murdered. And yet the odds felt off to him. How, or if, they were tied together, he'd find out. But until he was satisfied they *weren't* intertwined, he'd stick around.

"Where are you moving from?" Lovell asked.

Trish flashed him a smile as she popped the top on one of the drinks. "Miami. Great city, but I'll admit, I'm not going to miss it. Not much."

"You were there a long time, weren't you?" Helia asked.

"Over ten years. I left some good friends behind, but it didn't feel right to stay once Mark and I separated. Besides, my dad needs the help as he gets older."

"Sorry about Mark, but glad you have a place to land," Helia said.

Trish nodded. "You and me both. Hopefully I'll find a job soon, though."

"What kind of job?" Helia asked. "I can keep my ears open."

Trish smiled as both her and Lovell's orders were called. "I'll get it," Lovell murmured, waving Trish to stay seated.

"Mark, my soon-to-be ex, ran a lighting company. I managed all the import and export logistics. I figure I can find a similar gig here, but likely smaller scale. With all the wine shipping out of the region and equipment being shipped in..."

"With each state having their own liquor import laws, I assume that means more work possibilities?" Helia replied.

Trish nodded. "Hopefully. I can work the food angle, too. A lot of restaurants here are locally focused, but several import specialties from abroad."

Helia nodded, then adjusted her deep green beanie down over her ears. The color made her eyes look like smoky emeralds. Monk wondered if smoky emeralds really existed. He'd heard of smoky diamonds, but not emeralds. If they did, though, they'd look like her eyes.

Dulcie nudged him. "Helia asked if Bacco needs any help? Since Trish is looking for a job."

The look in Dulcie's eyes reflected Monk's opinion—no way in hell would he hire Trish without a thorough background check. Even if he needed help, which he wasn't sure he did.

"I don't think so, but I'll keep you in mind if that changes," Monk replied. He assumed Bacco had some sort of business manager since Roger certainly hadn't taken on that role, but he didn't know who. One more thing to find out.

Both Trish and Helia beamed at him, Helia's smile wider and more authentic than Trish's. Like the difference between a ray of sun and a table lamp.

"Sorry for the delay, they forgot to add the extra three al pastor tacos I ordered," Lovell said, sliding a container in front of Trish and taking a seat across the table from her on the other side of Dulcie.

"Enough about my boring life, what about you three?" Trish asked. "What brings you to our lovely area?" So the rest of the evening went. Trish metaphorically batting her eyes at the three of them and peppering them with questions, while they deftly avoided anything of substance. They'd each learned the art of misdirection from the cradle, then honed the skill while in the military. Nobody would learn a thing about them unless they chose to share it.

Using the cold weather as an excuse not to stay and finish the six-pack Trish brought, Monk herded Helia and his brothers to his truck. When they arrived at Sundaram, Helia extracted promises from Dulcie and Lovell that she'd see them again as they escorted her safely inside. Her sincerity caused funny feelings in his chest he wouldn't explore too deeply. And while both brothers glanced at him before answering, they readily agreed.

"I already texted Leo about Trish," Dulcie said when they left Sundaram. "I didn't catch a last name, but it's probably not hard to find a Trish who was married to a guy named Mark who owns a lighting company in Miami."

"Leo will have that info in less than ten minutes," Monk agreed. "You want to stay or drive home tonight?" he asked Lovell as they turned into the drive to Bacco.

"Tonight," Lovell said as Monk punched in the code and the gates started their slow inward swing. "I don't want a box of drugs sitting in my car any longer than necessary."

Monk chuckled. Yeah, he wouldn't either. "What about you, Dulcie? Want to move out of whatever hotel you've been staying at and crash here?" he asked as the castle came into view.

"Not tonight. Maybe if I stick around," he responded. "I

have my stuff there and already paid for the night. Doesn't make sense to leave now. The beds are comfortable." He paused. "The walls are thin, but the beds are comfortable."

"Amorous neighbors?" Lovell asked, grinning.

"A couple with three kids under four," Dulcie countered. "Cute as hell and not bad kids, just the typical chaos."

Having helped raise his sisters, Dulcie was the most outspoken about loving kids. Despite her husband's flying fist, his mom had managed to keep both her relationship with her kids and their relationship to one another tight ones.

"Well, you won't have that problem here. The walls are ten inches of stone in most places," Monk said. Although the wide-plank floors on the upper floors creaked more than he remembered.

No one mentioned the fact that he still had a bed set up on the tasting room couch. He'd left his things in his old room but hadn't fully committed to crashing there yet.

A few minutes later, he let himself into the castle, toeing off his boots at the entrance. Halfway down the hall, he detoured into the small kitchen to grab some water, drawing up short when he spied a glass, half full, sitting on the counter.

Silently, he shifted, putting his back to a wall rather than the open doorway, and listened. No one could have entered the castle while they were out, not without the new code, which nobody knew but him. He was equally certain, though, that none of them had left the glass there when they'd gone for dinner.

Which meant someone had been in the house when they left.

The military had taught him the benefit of patience, and he settled in. The long hand of the clock hanging on the opposite wall ticked by. Ten minutes passed, then another six. Then he heard it. A creak coming from the second floor.

Staying light on his feet, he exited the kitchen and headed for the side stairwell, bypassing the three squeaky steps as he made his way up.

When he reached the landing of the second floor, he stilled once again.

There, the sound of footsteps above him, hurried, but muted and sure. Without overthinking it, he continued up the last flight.

Moving swiftly, he cursed Roger, again, for being the person he was. Had he put cameras in the tasting room, like every other major winery in the area, Monk would have some idea what he was hunting. As it was, all he knew was someone was in the castle with him. Someone who might have been there a while, maybe all along. And if that wasn't creepy as fuck, he didn't know what was.

With his own weapon locked away and Roger's pistol on its way to HICC with Lovell, he quickly went through his options as he hit the landing of the third floor. Unless his father had changed things up, there should be several sets of armor along the western hallway. The swords they held would be dull as shit, but they'd be heavy.

Turning left, he darted toward the back of the castle. Rounding the corner, eight suits of armor came into view. As did a flash of white. A flash of white that disappeared around the far corner, heading away from him along the north hallway.

Stalking down the hall, he grabbed a sword along the way and considered what he'd seen. Not a man; it was too small, and the glimpse of the garment he'd spotted seemed too fluttery to be men's clothing.

Was it a woman?

Roger Wilde liked nothing more than to surround himself with willing women, so it wouldn't surprise him to find one loitering around. But he had the security app on his phone and except for his arrivals and departures, no one had come and gone.

Christ, how long had she been in the house?

That question brought him up short. Slowing his steps, he pulled out his phone and brought up the app, clicking through to find the history. On the day Roger died, someone, presumably the cleaning crew who found him, entered at seven in the morning, resetting the alarm behind them. Twenty-one minutes later, it disengaged again, likely for the first responders. At four twenty-two that afternoon, the system reengaged. None of the doors had been opened again until his arrival a few days ago.

The situation wasn't adding up. He hadn't been to the castle in nearly two decades, but nothing looked missing, messed up, or tossed. If someone wanted to get away with hundreds of thousands of dollars of art and antiquities, they could have easily done it.

So who the hell was in the castle?

The quiet snick of a door being carefully shut echoed through the silent building. He knew the sound of that tumbler. Whoever it was had entered the hall closet two doors down from his old room. He smiled; if his intruder had explored the house at all in her time there, Monk knew exactly where he'd catch her.

Doubling back the way he came, he approached his room from the opposite direction, ensuring he wouldn't pass the closet. Slipping inside, he waited in the shadows.

Two minutes passed before he heard another familiar click. Slowly, the door to the enormous armoire opened. Very few people knew the castle hosted a labyrinth of secret passageways. Centuries ago, they'd been designed to hide people— servants, those being persecuted for whatever happened to be a popular topic at the time. Roger used them to sneak in on people. Usually women he'd drugged with enough coke and ecstasy that when he showed up, they had no idea what they were consenting to, only that they wanted sex.

A toe peeked out from the armoire, pulling him back to the moment. Barefoot with a small chain clasped around the ankle, the thin leg that followed wasn't a woman's.

Monk's stomach felt as if someone had launched it from a trebuchet. A girl. A girl was living in this house. As vile as Roger was, to the best of Monk's knowledge, he'd never been interested in children. The thought that his tastes might have changed nearly had Monk running to the bathroom to throw up.

Her torso emerged as she stepped backward from the armoire. A long white cotton skirt swirled around her legs, at odds with the tight black crop top she wore. Her dark hair fell straight, ending an inch below her earlobes, and he caught sight of two earrings dangling from her left ear.

With both feet firmly on the ground, she closed the door so gently it made no sound, then turned.

"Fuck!" she cried, jumping back against the armoire. The word, and the strength of it, catching Monk by surprise. She sounded much older than she appeared and less scared than angry at being caught.

He crossed his arms and leaned against the wall.

The imp mimicked him, a belligerent glint in her eye.

"Who are you?" he asked.

"Who are you?" she shot back.

He searched her face, the defiance there almost hiding the fear. And worry.

"Collin Wilde," he replied. He meant the girl no harm, so the least he could do was be the first to offer information.

Her eyes narrowed. "You related to Roger?"

"To my ever-loving chagrin, yes. I'm his son."

"You don't like your dad?"

"My father was a predator and parasite," he said, wanting her to know exactly where he stood on Roger Wilde's existence. She didn't look the sort who'd believe him right away, but he'd at least lay the groundwork.

Some of the tension eased around her eyes. "Kendall," she replied.

"You know my father?"

She shook her head, both her hair and her earrings swaying with the motion. "But my mom does."

"I'm sorry." He didn't know her mom's story, but if she partied with the likes of his father, then Kendall's life couldn't have been easy.

"She's a good mom," Kendall said, lifting her chin.

Monk refrained from pointing out that she obviously wasn't that good since she'd left her daughter at the castle. "I'm sure she is."

"You don't believe me?"

"I don't know you. Or your mom," he added. He might be predisposed to have certain ideas, but life had taught him that people had many facets to their personality. Some were little more than subtle shifts, while others could be as different as night and day.

"She's a good mom."

He opted not to respond, doubting anything he said would go over well. "How old are you?"

"Sixteen," she said, drawing back her shoulders.

He raised a brow and stared at her, hard. "Try again."

She glared back. A minute of silence passed, then her shoulders drooped. "Twelve."

"And where's your mom now? A question only, not a judgment," he added when the spark of defiance returned.

He almost regretted asking when her bravado slipped and she looked every one of her scant twelve years of age, lost and unsure.

"I don't know," she said. Then lifting her chin, all but daring him to judge, she added, "She left me here two weeks ago."

CHAPTER TWELVE

Monk held back the sigh threatening to escape. His fucking father. Bringing a *mother* and her child to the castle. Whether he knew about Kendall didn't matter—no single parent should be lured into the things that happened in the dungeon.

But none of that was anything Kendall needed to hear. "You cold?" he asked, lifting his chin toward her. Her clothes looked clean but thin, and the top, by design, left her midriff bare. Another judgment he wouldn't pass on her mom, although he wondered about the appropriateness of it for a twelve-year-old.

"A little," she admitted, wrapping her arms around her body. Another sign of vulnerability.

"Let's get you a sweatshirt. And some food," he said, turning and heading toward the staircase. He didn't wait for her—wanting her to understand she had choices—but he kept his ears tuned. He did allow a tiny bit of relief to ease his worry when her light footsteps fell in behind him.

"You grew up here?" she asked.

"Yep."

"Must have been wild. It's an actual fucking castle. I heard people say it was brought over from France."

"Italy," he corrected, opting not to police her language. If dropping an f-bomb every now and then gave her the illusion of some control, some maturity, who was he to argue?

"Did you like it?" she asked.

"The castle's all right. Didn't make me popular with the kids in town."

"Everyone assumed you were a rich asshole?"

He inclined his head as his feet hit the landing of the ground floor and he started toward the tasting room. Dulcie had picked up a few items of clothing for him from one of the chain stores in town. The sweats and sweatshirt would be huge on her, but better than the thin cotton she had on now. He'd give her a pair of socks, too.

"Pretty much. Didn't help having a father who liked to flash the money around. Made him popular with a certain set —and all the nonprofits he donated to—but kids are a different story. Here," he said, tearing the tags from the clothing and handing them over. "They'll be huge, but you can roll them. If you need a belt, Roger probably has one we can punch a hole in for you."

She took the clothing and cocked her head. "You call your dad by his first name."

He considered glossing over his relationship with his father, but if he wanted information from Kendall, he better be willing to offer the same. "My father was a shit human being. When I was not much older than you, he put me in situations that no one, especially not a child, should be in. I left the day after high school graduation. Didn't come back until after he died. This"—he lifted his arms, indicating the castle and every-thing in it—"is now all mine and as you can imagine, I'm conflicted about it. There's a lot of family history here going back several generations. And a shit ton of money. But there are also bad memories and things I'd rather not be reminded of."

Her dark eyes studied him with a wisdom she shouldn't have at her age. She might not know the exact things that had happened to him, but she got the gist.

"You gonna take the money and run, as they say?"

His lips twitched. "If only things were that simple."

"What's not simple about that?"

"Go get changed. I'll make some food since it looks like my arrival home might have interrupted your dinner. We'll talk more when you get back. I'd point you to the bathroom, but you probably already know the way."

The imp grinned at him, then darted out.

When he heard the bathroom door close, he pulled out his phone, texting Mantis as he headed to the kitchen.

Monk: *New development, there's fucking kid living here. She's been here two weeks. Her mom was one of my father's party "guests" and left her behind. Name's Kendall. Can you see if Leo can find out anything?*

Then he added a brief description of her. He wished he had a picture to send, but he didn't want to creep Kendall out by taking one.

Mantis: *Done and she okay?*

Monk: *TBD, tough, but weren't we all?*

Mantis: *A place we all know too well. Let us know if we can help*

Monk: *Getting Leo on it is all I need for now. Will update you when I know more*

Setting his phone on the counter, he opened the small fridge. He'd gone through most of the cured meats and cheeses, but he'd spotted another industrial fridge/freezer in the laundry room so decided to look there.

Hoping she wasn't vegan or vegetarian, he snagged a packet labeled "Asian Bites" and headed back to the kitchen.

"That's a good one," Kendall said, appearing in the door. She swam in the clothing but looked comfortable. "I grabbed one of those things that ties the curtains back and used that," she said, lifting the sweatshirt to show him the shiny gold rope edged with fringe circling her waist.

"Whatever you need."

"After what you said about your dad, I didn't want anything of his anywhere near me."

He chuckled at that. "Can't say I blame you." He started the small oven and set the twelve little spring rolls on a pan. He'd sauté the dumplings, then heat the chicken skewers over the gas flame.

"You found the food?" he asked.

She hesitated, then nodded. He sensed her apprehension more than saw it. "Good," he replied. "Where are you sleeping?"

Again, she hesitated. "Third floor, north room."

"The one close to the fire escape?" She nodded. "Smart girl," he said. It killed him that she needed to think about having an escape, but he was glad she was smart enough to do it.

He finished preparing her meal in silence. Once he plated everything, he gestured her to the tasting room. "I'll make a fire, and you can eat there."

She followed him out, taking the plate from him when he handed it to her.

"Do you want me to help find your mom?" he asked. Well aware that the question might raise a mix of emotions, including helplessness and vulnerability, he kept his back to her, giving her space to experience them without feeling under the microscope.

Setting a log in the fireplace, he waited. He set another before checking the kindling underneath. He was reaching for the matches when she answered.

"Can you do that?"

"I have friends who can."

"No." Her answer came so swiftly that he turned. "They'll get the police involved. That's a one-way ticket to foster care, and that's a ride I'm not going to take."

He studied her, then turned back to the fire. Once the flames grabbed hold, he rose and took a seat on the same sofa he'd slept on the past few nights.

"Are you in school? Don't you think they might have already reported you missing?" he asked.

"I do online school. My computer's upstairs and the internet security here is shit. The password is taped to the inside of a desk drawer in one of the offices. I found it years ago."

Ignoring the fact that she'd obviously been to the castle before, he frowned. "Online school. That's a thing?"

The look she shot him was pure tweenager. "You're not *that* old, dude. Yeah, kids can learn online."

He rolled his eyes. "I know there's online learning. I didn't know it extended to what, fifth graders? I don't exactly spend a lot of time with kids."

"Sixth grade," she corrected. "But I work at the eleventh-grade level. I'll be ready for my GED next year."

"You're a savant."

"I'm someone who spends a lot of time alone with my computer. May as well learn while I'm at it. Beats the shit out of reading about whatever scandal the newest pop star is getting into or who cheated on who in Hollywood."

"I agree. And I know a few geniuses, so no need to get defensive. My comment was an observation, not a challenge."

A glint of interest came into her eye. "What kind?"

"What kind of what?"

"Geniuses? There're all kinds. Painters, mathematicians, chemists..."

"They may be more than one thing, but I know them for their cybersecurity skills." Ah, that piqued her interest. He bit back a smile and lured her in. If he got her interested in Leo and Sabina, maybe she'd let them help find her mother. Leo was probably already working on it, but he'd rather Kendall agree to the help than feel as though he went behind her back.

"Sabina runs the cyber team at a private security company called HICC. Leo is on her team. Ava also works there, but she's on family leave now. Gave birth to twins recently. The last person on the team is another Collin, but he works mostly on developing new technology hardware rather than the hacking-type stuff Leo and Ava do."

"Hackers?" She straightened in her seat.

"White hat, of course. But between you and me, they might skirt a few laws to make sure the right things happen."

She watched him as she ate another spring roll. Then a dumpling. He knew the power of silence, of letting people have the time to think. Especially those who had so little control.

She finished a skewer, then asked, "Are those the people who might help find my mom?"

He rose from his seat and walked behind the tasting bar as he answered. "There's no 'might' about it. They will if I ask them. But yeah, it's them."

"How can you be so sure?" she asked.

Bending down, he examined the contents of the fridge. "Water, some sort of fancy fruit soda, or ginger beer?"

"Fruit soda."

He nodded and grabbed a can for her and a beer for him. "I

can be sure because they're practically family. Not blood family, but it's...a little complicated."

She raised a dark eyebrow. "You called me a savant. I can handle a little complicated."

"Touché," he said on a chuckle, before telling her about his fourteen brothers and Mantis and Charley and Joey and Leo. "Like I said, complicated. But it is what it is. Family isn't always what we're born into. Thank fuck," he muttered, then grimaced. He didn't need to encourage her language.

She snorted at his expression, then quickly covered her nose as the sip she'd taken hit her nostrils. He laughed as she wiped her face with a napkin, all while rolling her eyes.

"That stung," she said on a smile, tucking her napkin back under her plate.

"Yeah, it does."

"Will they really help?"

"I told you they will."

"And they won't call the cops?"

"I can't promise that." Her expression shut down, but he wasn't going to lie to her. "If they find out your mother's been hurt or needs help or is in danger, they might need to call in law enforcement. But if that's the case, they won't do it without talking to you first. I can also promise they won't report her for leaving you here. Especially not if they know you're in good hands."

"Yours?"

"If you're not comfortable with me, like I said, I have a huge family-by-choice, including several new sisters. The Warwick family—Charley and Joey's family—would step in, too, if you'd rather be with someone else."

"I can just leave."

"Why head out on your own when you have options?" he said, knowing he couldn't push her. "I get that trusting people isn't easy, that it probably goes against everything your survival instincts are telling you. I won't belittle that because those instincts have kept you alive. Sometimes, though, when presented with a novel situation, those instincts can be off. But I can't make you trust me. That's a decision you have to make."

"Can I sleep on it?"

"Yeah, but don't bail on me tonight. I've already got a lot of shit going on and you'll give me a heart attack if I have to worry about you, too."

"I can take care of myself. You don't have to worry about me."

"Too late." He didn't miss the brief flare of hope in her eyes.

She blinked and looked away, taking another sip of her drink. Several minutes passed before she turned back and nodded. "I'll stay."

"Thank you," he said, rising and holding his hand out to take her empty plate. She hesitated, confused by the offer, then handed it over. "Why don't you head up and get some sleep. I can turn the heat on in that part of the castle, too, if you like."

She blinked again, then nodded and started for the stairs. He followed but stepped into the kitchen as she continued down the hall.

"Collin?"

"Yeah," he replied, popping his head out the door.

She stood at the bottom of the stairs, her hand on the doorjamb. "You said you have a lot on your plate right now. Is one of those things your dad—Roger's—murder?"

CHAPTER THIRTEEN

Helia rolled over in bed, her big empty bed, and stared at the pillow beside her as memories of the night before flashed through her mind. Collin's friends hadn't been what she'd expected, and yet they had. Was that even possible? To be two opposite things?

They were both big and, though not scary, had an edge of supreme confidence and competence that made people think twice about approaching them. But they'd also been funny and caring. She wondered if the rest of the Falcons were the same. If so, walking into that clubhouse would pack a punch to a woman's ovaries, that was for damn sure. Although for her, Collin did more than that.

The smell of coffee wafted into her room—thank you, automatic maker—and she rolled onto her back. Tomorrow, they'd start preparing for the last three events of the year. Today, she had only paperwork and orders to address.

Which left her day mostly free to think about Collin. About his rare smiles that came more frequently now than a few days ago. About his kindness and willingness to help with the wedding the past weekend. About him living in that massive home—if one could call it that—alone. She didn't like that idea.

Sliding her feet over the edge of the bed, she rose, a plan forming. She'd respected his desire to be alone at the castle that first day back, but he didn't need to confront his past on his own anymore. He might think so, but what he thought he needed and what he actually needed were two different things. And he *needed* to know he wasn't alone.

Hoping a little caffeine in her system would help her figure out how best to approach the topic with him, she headed downstairs. Maybe if she spent the day with him at the castle, he'd suggest walking through the building? Or should she force it?

The options percolated in her mind as she flipped on the gas fireplace, then wandered into the kitchen. Pouring herself a cup of dark brew, she stared out the window over the sink as she took her first sip, the heat of the liquid warming and waking her.

A turkey vulture swooped across her view, the black form stark against the white winter clouds. It circled out of sight, then came back again, before moving on.

She frowned. Turkey vultures were common in the area, but they didn't tend to hover over the vineyards. Carrion wasn't common among the vines, at least not remains big enough to attract—she leaned forward to see better and counted—five.

What the hell had died out there?

Curiosity woke her faster than coffee, and she jogged upstairs to change. Ten minutes later, dressed in leggings, a flannel top, and her trusty puffer vest, she pulled on her boots and opened the door.

To find Collin on her doorstep, hand raised as if about to

knock. She startled and stepped back, her hand going to her chest like some Victorian maid. It was then she noticed he wasn't alone. A young girl wearing a pair of ripped jeans and a sweatshirt that could only be Collin's stood behind him.

"Well, I'm glad I didn't curse up a storm when you scared the hell out of me," she said, chuckling away the shot of nerves.

Collin grinned and hitched his thumb behind him, pointing at the girl. "She has a mouth like a sailor. I'm pretty sure she could teach you a thing or two."

She laughed but eyed Collin at the same time. She hadn't expected to see him on her doorstep, but when had he collected the child? She didn't see any worry or concern in his expression, so she dropped her gaze to the girl.

"Helia," she said, holding out her hand.

Dark, watchful eyes swept over her before shifting to Collin. He nodded. "Kendall," she said, her thin, delicate hand lifting cautiously. A short curtain of nearly black hair fell away from her face as she raised her chin to meet Helia's gaze head-on. Not so much in challenge—okay, maybe a little of that—but mostly as if to claim her place in the world. To be seen.

"We came to ask if you wanted to join us in town for breakfast," Collin said. As if it was completely normal for him to show up with a sprite of a girl when Helia'd left him in the company of two of his burly brothers the night before.

The look Kendall slid his way made it clear the "we" in that sentence was him. Helia chuckled. She had no idea what was going on, but she wanted to find out. And since Collin was on her doorstep, he wanted her to find out, too.

"Sounds good," she said. "Want me to drive? Then you don't have to walk back to the castle."

Collin looked at Kendall. A beat passed before she nodded.

"Great. You mind if we stop somewhere for Kendall to pick up a few clothes after we eat?" he asked. Kendall studied her feet, the gesture telling Helia two important things: she'd been on her own for a while, *and* she was smart enough to accept help.

"Happy to," she said. "I know a few places that might be good options. Before we go, though, I want to see what that's about." She pointed to the circling birds. There were now six.

Collin's gaze tracked them, a small frown tugging on his lips. He'd trimmed his beard again, leaving the hair silky and shiny. She'd never been a beard girl before, but she found herself wanting to touch it, to feel it under her fingertips, to know if it was as soft as it looked.

"Why don't you two stay warm inside and I'll have a look," he said.

Kendall narrowed her eyes at the suggestion before shifting them to meet Helia's. The girl talk was strong in this one. Helia nodded in agreement with her unspoken opinion.

"No dice, Collin," Kendall said. "We'll check it out together, then go to breakfast."

His gaze dropped to her. The gangly skin-and-bones girl looked even tinier beside him, but no one could miss the glint of stubborn in her eye.

"Fine," he huffed, before brushing past Kendall and heading toward the vineyard.

Helia winked at Kendall and might have caught a glimpse of a smile before she shut her door.

Falling into step behind Collin and beside Kendall, a thousand questions hovered on the tip of her tongue, but she couldn't decide where to start. She didn't want to interrogate the girl, but, well, she kind of did.

"Collin said he's known you a long time," Kendall said, surprising her by starting the conversation.

"We met when I was fourteen. He spent a lot of time here."

"Yeah, he said he came to hide from Roger's parties."

Helia swallowed but nodded. No girl should know about the parties Roger Wilde used to throw. Collin had only ever told her bits and pieces of what went on in the dungeon of the castle, and even after all these years, they still made her stomach turn.

"He came for other reasons, too. He's close to my parents and friendly with my brother." She paused, then added, "But yeah, he came to get away from home."

"Your parents were okay with that?"

"They never hesitated. They love him like one of their own."

"And you? Do you love him like a sister?"

Not even close, but Helia bit back the words that wanted to escape. She'd never named her feelings for Collin, not as an adult. She'd never had a reason to until he came back into her life a few days ago. But *sisterly* was not among them. In fact, the memory of his arms around her when she'd jumped into them, then clung to him like a monkey, had given her fantasy fodder. He'd held her so easily, smelled so good, felt so warm, that her mind refused to forget. Nor did it stop at the memory. No, it had created an entire fantasy around that moment, one involving her back to the wall, legs around his waist, and no clothes.

"It's a little complicated," she managed to answer. Kendall snorted and wiggled a dark eyebrow at her, drawing a laugh from Helia, too. "Fine," Helia said. "Not sisterly, but what it is, I don't know."

"What do you mean you don't know?"

"Nosy much?"

"I've been hiding out in the castle for two weeks on my own. I haven't talked to anyone else until last night when Collin found me. I'm making conversation."

Oh, that raised so many more questions. *Two weeks?* What

had she been doing for two weeks and how had she ended up there in the first place? But first things first.

"Nice try, sister. You're nosy."

They took ten steps before she answered. "Maybe," she said as Collin held up a fist.

"Are we supposed to know what that means?" Helia asked.

"It's a military or law enforcement thing. It means stop," Kendall said.

"Look at you, smarty-pants," Helia said, following Kendall's direction and stopping. She didn't really want to, but if Collin found something gross, she didn't want Kendall to see it, and she doubted the girl would be willing to stay behind on her own.

A breeze rustled through dry vines and rippled across Collin's flannel shirt, flaring the unbuttoned edges out. His broad body blocked their view, and alert, wary tension flowed off him in waves.

Kendall made to step forward, but Helia put her arm out. She opened her mouth to protest but shut it when Collin turned around.

"Back to Helia's," he said, holding his arms out and all but shooing them the way they'd come.

Kendall cocked her head. Collin's gaze shifted from her to Helia, and he gave a tiny shake of his head. "It's too cold to stand out here arguing over what to do," Helia said, tapping Kendall's arm lightly. "Let's head to my house and you can interrogate him in front of my fire."

Kendall's gaze darted between them, then she heaved a sigh big enough to lift the world—leaving no doubt what she thought—then muttered something probably unflattering, turned, and started walking.

Helia let Kendall get ten feet ahead before glancing over

her shoulder at Collin. He gestured for her to follow but stayed close.

"It's a body. A human one," he said quietly, catching her when she stumbled.

"A body?" A stupid thing to say. He'd hardly misidentify *that*. But finding a body in their vineyard had definitely not been on her bingo card for the year.

"Male. Definitely dead but turned away so I couldn't see his face."

"Someone from Sundaram?" she all but whispered. They paused when Kendall shot them a look over her shoulder. Her eyes narrowed, but a step later, she faced forward and trudged dramatically toward Helia's house.

"I don't think so. He was wearing a suit."

"Good. I mean, not good, but good," she said. No one who worked at Sundaram, or who lived on the property, ever wore a suit.

"Blondish hair. Under six feet tall, but hard to tell exactly. He was curled on his side," he added.

She didn't know many blond men, and at this point, it wasn't worth speculating. Ha, who was she kidding? In the five minutes before reaching her little abode, she ran through every memory she had trying to identify men who met Collin's description. By the time they reached her door, she had five possibilities.

"I need to call the police," Collin said when he shut the door behind them. Kendall didn't even try to hide her panic.

"If you want to stay here, we can keep them out of Helia's house," Collin said to her. "We can meet them at the main building." He paused. "Or you can go back to the castle. You know the way, and I can give you the code to get in."

Her eyes searched Collin's. "You're not going to tell them?"

"I told you I wouldn't. As far as you're concerned, my priority is reuniting you with your mother," Collin answered.

The girl stilled, then swallowed. "Can I stay here?" she asked, her tentative gaze flickering to Helia.

Helia nodded. "Of course. You may want to stay upstairs, though. And away from the windows," she added, hoping she wasn't harboring a felon.

Collin cocked his head. "You have your phone, right? You can watch something while we deal with the police."

Slowly, Kendall nodded.

"Why don't I show you where everything is and get you the Wi-Fi code," Helia said, setting her hand on Kendall's shoulder and turning her toward the bedroom. Five minutes later, she and Collin exited the house and headed toward the main building.

"What about CCTV?" Collin asked.

She waved him off. "It's all over the place by the gates and the main buildings, but not out by my house or the vineyards. If we have to turn over more footage, they won't see her." They crossed the courtyard side by side, the packed gravel crunching under their feet. "When we were upstairs, I told her what you saw," she said. "Who is she?" Helia asked. "No, scratch that. You can tell me later. What I really want to know is why did she say this has been the *third* murder in less than three weeks?"

CHAPTER FOURTEEN

Monk huffed out a breath as they walked to the main building. "Let me call the police, and I'll tell you while we wait."

Helia's hazel eyes searched his. For a moment, he got lost in them. He'd heard that saying a thousand times before but always thought it ridiculous. You got lost in the woods or when driving through a new city. Not in someone's eyes. He had no other way to describe it, though. No way to describe how time slowed, or how there seemed to be an invisible magnet between his eyes and hers, making it impossible to pull away. Or how the connection between them conjured images in his head, recalling the past but also hinting at a future. And he definitely had no way to describe the feelings roiling through him. Want and desire were the obvious ones. But something deeper lay at the foundation of it all, something binding him to her in a way he couldn't—wouldn't—deny even if he didn't understand it.

"Helia? Collin?"

He held Helia's gaze for one more beat before turning. "Vanessa, it's good to see you again."

"You, too," she said, walking over and giving him a hug. "What are you two doing out here?" she asked, hugging Helia, too.

He glanced at Helia, who nodded. She'd tell her mom while he called the police.

He stepped away and dialed 911. By the time he was done giving dispatch the details, Vanessa and Helia stood in mirrored poses, one arm crossed across their stomach, the other elbow resting on top, fingers covering their lips.

"The police are on their way," Monk said, rejoining the pair.

"I texted Harry. He'll be down in a second. He was getting out of the shower," Vanessa said. "You didn't recognize him?" she asked.

Monk shook his head. "I didn't see his face. Even if I did, I don't know a lot of people around here. I probably wouldn't have recognized him anyway."

The door opened and Harry strode out. "What the hell? Who is it? Where?"

"We don't know and over there," Helia answered, pointing to where the birds still circled.

Harry cursed under his breath and started forward, but Monk put a staying hand on his arm. "The police are on their way. It's best if we stay here."

Harry wanted to argue; Monk saw it in his posture. But in the end, he nodded and wrapped an arm around Vanessa.

Helia stepped in front of him, putting her back to her parents. Heat flooded his body, sudden and strong, when she set her hands on his chest. He covered hers with his, more to steady himself than to keep hers there. "Who's the third?" she asked. "The third murder?"

Her parents had moved off to sit on a bench in the filtered sun, leaving them space. Helia's fingers curled into his shirt. He tried ignoring her scent as her warmth wrapped around him.

"Kendall thinks Roger was murdered," he said, the ugly statement dousing the simmering heat between them. Her eyes widened. Lifting a hand, he set a finger across her lips to stop whatever she'd been about to say. "I don't doubt what she heard, but I don't know if it's the full story. And since Roger was cremated, we may never know."

"What did she hear?" Helia asked, her lips moving under his touch. Mesmerized by the softness against his work-roughened skin, he traced the cushion of her lower lip. Her pupils dilated and her tongue darted out, the tip grazing his finger. Lust exploded through him swift and consuming, sucking the breath from his lungs. Her fingers curled into his shirt, clinging to him. His body wanted nothing more than to carry her off somewhere private, somewhere they could do all the things they'd done as teenagers. All the things that would be so much better than he remembered.

And he remembered often. Helia had been and would always be the only woman he ever wanted. She'd cemented her place in his life years ago. Not by doing anything as cliché as "slipping through his defenses." No, she'd given him her love, her support, and the space to *choose* to let his defenses down. His choice. A freedom his father had taken from him that she'd given back.

Harry coughed, and Monk pulled his gaze from Helia. The primal beast inside him roared at the broken connection, but the scared, injured child also buried inside him breathed a sigh of relief. He wasn't ready to go there with her again, not yet. As much as his body craved her, his mind, and heart, carried too many questions. He needed to be sure that what he felt now— what they felt—wasn't just a remnant of who they'd been.

He took a tiny step back, not out of reach, but enough to let the cool morning air fill the space between them.

"She heard a man and a woman talking," he said, answering her question. "After they took Roger's body away, I guess some people stayed in the house to clean up, knowing it would be shut down for a while. She never saw them, but she heard a woman say that 'it finally worked,' and 'who knew it would take so damn long.' The man asked if she was sure 'it would be undetectable' in the autopsy. She assured him it would be."

"What the hell was Kendall doing there in the first place?" she demanded. He wouldn't lie, he liked that her first concern was for the young girl.

"Her mom liked Roger's parties. She left her there after the last one. I'm guessing it was a week or so before he died. Kendall swears she'll be back."

"Her mom's done this before."

Not a question, but Monk nodded.

"How old is she? The look in her eyes is far older than I'm guessing she is."

"Twelve."

Helia winced. "Jesus."

"Yeah," he agreed.

"Is there any way we can find her mom without alerting the police?"

"I'm trying, but I don't know her last name or her mom's name."

"You didn't want to push," Helia said.

Again, he nodded. "I told her I have friends who can help find her mom under the radar, but I didn't force the issue. I'm hoping she'll eventually trust me enough to share those names so I can pass them on."

Helia patted his chest, but her eyes were on the vineyard,

her mind somewhere else entirely.

The sound of tires on the drive had all four turning. Helia's hand dropped from his body—a contact he sorely missed—but she didn't move far.

Two police cars pulled into the courtyard, Harry directing them where to park. By the time the four officers were out of their vehicles, a third arrived with Jess behind the wheel and Carter beside her.

Helia shifted to his side, her fingers gently brushing his. Not letting himself think of the consequences, he wrapped his hand around hers.

"Harry, what can you tell us?" Carter asked, striding over as the officers collected gear from the trunks of their cars.

"Nothing," Harry said. "Helia and Collin found it," he added, regret heavy in his voice. As if he wished he could take this on himself rather than leave it to him and Helia.

Carter and Jess eyed them. Both detectives dropped their eyes to his hand closed around Helia's as they approached.

"What can you tell us?" Carter repeated.

"I came over this morning to see if Helia wanted to head to town for breakfast," he said, with a subtle squeeze of her hand. "She was on her way out to check the birds."

"Birds?" Jess interrupted.

Helia pointed with her free hand to the still-circling vultures. "We don't get a lot of vultures around the vineyards. Well, not around these vineyards. I saw them out my kitchen window and thought it was weird. I wanted to investigate. As Collin said, he was standing on the stoop getting ready to knock when I opened the door."

"We decided to check it out before breakfast. I wasn't really expecting much. Maybe a dead rabbit or other small animal," he said. "But well, that's not what we found."

The two detectives raised their gazes again to the circling birds. "It's there?" Jess asked.

"He is, yes," Monk answered.

"What's the best way out there?" Carter asked.

Helia pointed to the dirt alleyway between two vineyard blocks they'd walked down. "Down there, then turn right at maybe the thirtieth row or so. I wasn't counting so don't remember. But you can follow the birds."

Carter nodded to the four officers, who gathered their kits and headed out. Monk wished the detectives would go with them but hadn't expected them to. They'd wait until the scene was secure before adding extra footprints.

"How do you know it's a man?" Jess asked.

"I didn't see a face, the body was turned away on its side, but they were in a suit," Monk said. "It fit like a man's. Short blond hair, one hand flung over their hip, the hand looked male, too. Large. But I guess, to your point, I don't know for certain."

"Did you touch anything?" Carter asked.

Monk shook his head. "I stopped twenty feet away. Helia was behind me."

"I didn't even see it, him, whatever. Collin blocked my view."

"You didn't check to see if he was still alive?" Jess asked.

Monk gave Helia's hand another squeeze. "There was no point."

Carter and Jess stilled, like predators preparing to hunt. Information, for now, but they'd turn to him—or Helia—eventually.

"Meaning?"

He hated having to answer with Helia at his side, but her fingers curled around his, as if telling him it was okay.

"His side is split open. Like someone took an axe or

machete here." He pointed to his waist, right above the top of his jeans. "The cut ran all the way to his spine. His hips twisted away from his torso."

Both Carter and Jess blinked. He'd seen much worse in the military, but he doubted the Napa Valley detectives regularly encountered that kind of brutal violence. Vanessa paled and made a small sound of distress. Harry wrapped his arm around her as Carter and Jess shifted to form a circle.

"When was the last time you were out that way?" Jess asked.

Helia's parents looked at each other, then to her, before Harry answered. "We lease the vineyards to a winery so have no reason to be out there, as they do all the maintenance. I honestly can't remember the last time I was that far out." Vanessa nodded in agreement.

"A photographer from the wedding last weekend wanted a wide shot of the venue and we walked about fifty yards down the alley, but not as far as where we were today," Helia said.

Turning to him, Carter asked, "Where's your car? Did you walk here?"

Monk dipped his chin. "I did, but as you know, Bacco is that way," he said, pointing the opposite direction from where they'd found the body.

"Have any of you heard anything unusual in the past day or two?" Carter asked.

Again, Harry and Vanessa shared a look before shaking their heads. Helia did the same with a confused shrug.

"It's far enough away that if someone came in through one of the other alleyways, no one here would hear it," Monk said.

"Any cameras out there?" Jess asked.

Helia shook her head again. "We're more concerned about the grounds here and the venue buildings."

"Are there ways to access the vineyard that don't require passing through here?" Jess asked.

The Shaws all nodded, but Harry answered. "From Sundaram, you can only get there by foot. The landscaping and hardscaping make it impossible to drive there from here. But there's access from the connector," he said, referring to one of the many roads that ran east to west across the valley floor, connecting the Silverado Trail to Highway 128. "The winery that leases the vineyard uses a few spots along there for access."

"Which winery?" Carter asked. Harry gave the name of a company that owned several labels. They'd been around for years, which was the only reason Monk recognized it.

Carter pulled his phone from his pocket, then glanced at Jess. "They're ready for us."

Jess nodded. "If you all could stay available until we clear you?"

"We have three events this weekend. Can we move around the property?" Vanessa asked. "We won't leave this area, but we have employees coming for a planning meeting."

"That's fine," Jess replied. "Please keep them on the immediate grounds. And again, if you could stay available in case we have any follow-up questions."

They nodded, but Jess and Carter had already turned. By silent agreement, they watched the detectives leave. When they were far enough away not to hear, Harry asked, "Are you two okay? Do you want to come in for breakfast?"

Monk didn't want to leave Kendall longer than necessary and was about to make an excuse before Helia could agree, but she cut him off. "No, but thank you. We'll go back to my place and scrounge some food there."

Her parents studied them, Vanessa's eyes dropping to their interlinked hands. He made to let go, but Helia held tight.

"Let us know if you need anything," Vanessa said.

"Or hear anything," Harry added.

"You, too," Helia said, before leading him away.

He squeezed her hand. "You know what your parents are going to think," he said when they were too far away for them to hear.

Helia stared at him, blinked, then cringed. "Oh, I'm sorry. I hope I didn't make things awkward for you."

This time, he held tight. "I wasn't thinking of me. I'm good. More than," he added quietly.

He felt her eyes on him as they stepped out of the courtyard and onto the path leading to her house. He didn't quite hold his breath, but it was damn close. Had he said too much? Should he have kept his mouth closed?

Finally, Helia smiled and gave him a little shoulder bump. The tension in his neck eased. He still didn't know if what he'd said should have been said, but it was the truth.

"Stay upstairs," Helia called out when they stepped into her house. Then to him, she said, "I'll get the curtains in the kitchen. You get these." She waved to the ones in the living room. Her protectiveness of Kendall didn't surprise him, but still, his heart flip-flopped in his chest.

When they were properly closed in, she called for Kendall to join them. A beat later, the tweenager jogged down the steep steps, her long gangly limbs reminding him of a newborn foal.

"Are they gone?" she asked, pausing at the bottom.

Monk shook his head. "They have to deal with the crime scene, remove the body. It's going to be a while."

"Why don't I make us breakfast," Helia said. "Egg-and-bacon sandwiches?"

"Sounds good," he answered. Kendall nodded but didn't say anything. "I can put more coffee on," he added.

"Can I help?" Kendall asked. Judging by the slight falter in

Helia's step, the request surprised her as much as it did him. She didn't skip a beat, though.

"Of course," she said. "Do you want to take the eggs or the bacon?"

"Bacon," she said so emphatically both he and Helia looked at her.

She made a face. "I know everyone says pigs are supercute and so smart and all that. But we were in Texas once and I saw a wild one attack and kill newborn twin lambs. It like, went on a frenzy or something. I've hated them ever since."

Monk stared, then dragged his gaze to Helia. Her eyes met his, and they both barked out a laugh.

Kendall ducked her head, her ears pink. Helia wasn't having any of that, though. Wiping her eyes with one hand, she grabbed Kendall's hand with her other. "Come on, Killer. I have a pound of bacon that's awaiting your revenge. And remind me not to get on your bad side."

CHAPTER FIFTEEN

"How on earth do you know about Wham!? They were broken up probably before your *mother* was even born," Helia demanded. She and Kendall were in a heated game of Trivial Pursuit, but Collin was playing along purely for the entertainment value.

Kendall grinned as she slid the little pink plastic triangle into her game piece, completing the circle. "My mom hung out with a guy in a band for a while in Seattle. His dad was his manager and a pretty cool guy. Way into all kinds of music. We talked a lot."

Helia flickered her gaze to Collin, whose eyes dimmed briefly in concern. Kendall had talked about being in Texas and Seattle, and earlier she'd mentioned living both in LA and on a ranch in Idaho. Helia had moved around a lot as a kid, too. She'd been a military brat until moving to Napa, though, and despite living in six countries growing up, there'd been a stability to their lives.

"Bathroom break," Kendall said, hopping up.

When she closed the door of the powder room, Helia raised

her eyebrows at Collin. "There's not much I can do unless or until she trusts us with her mom's name," he said, keeping his voice quiet.

"Even when you find her, I'm not sure that being with her is the best thing," she responded. "She's exceptionally intelligent and seems to *love* learning. She deserves the chance to do that somewhere stable."

She could see the agreement in Collin's eyes, but a knock at the door cut off whatever he'd been about to say.

"Yeah?" Collin called, rising.

"It's Carter," came the answer.

Helia hesitated, then making a quick decision on how to buy them time to hide Kendall, called back, "We'll, um, we'll be there in a second."

Collin shot her a questioning look, and she mouthed "Trust me." His brows dipped but he remained still.

Helia darted to the powder room and knocked softly enough that neither Carter nor Jess would hear. When Kendall cracked the door open, Helia waved her farther inside. She took two steps back, bumping into the sink, her eyes wide with panic.

"We'll get them away from the house," Helia whispered, pushing aside the shard of pain lancing through her at Kendall's fear. "Wait ten minutes after we leave, then head upstairs. We'll be back as soon as we can."

"You're coming back, though?"

Another shard through her heart. "Can I hug you?" Helia asked. Kendall blinked, then nodded. Helia didn't hesitate in wrapping her arms around the slight girl. "We will be back as soon as we're done. Your memory is astounding, so I know you'll remember this when I tell you," she said before rattling off her phone number. "Call or text anytime." Kendall gave a jerky nod. Because she couldn't help herself, Helia gave her one more quick squeeze, then reached over and flushed the toilet. Kendall cocked her head in question, but Helia slipped out, not pausing to explain her plan.

When she returned to the living room, Collin stood where she'd left him, an almost identical look of confusion on his face. Without giving herself time to question the sanity of the plan, she stopped inches in front of him.

"Can I kiss you?"

Collin canted his head. They had chemistry, always had, probably always would. But with his history, she wasn't about to lay one on him without his consent.

She gripped the sides of his flannel and pulled him closer, her lips to his ears. "The window shades are pulled. As far as they know, we're in here together. Making it look as if we were in the middle of *something*—if you know what I mean—is the most obvious way to explain the extra time we needed to open the door."

This close to him, his subtle scent wrapped around her. She could lie to herself that the kiss was just to protect Kendall, but she wanted it, too. She wanted to know if the same hunger they'd felt all those years was still there. She suspected it was, but unlike her, Collin wasn't a man to dive in headfirst without consideration. They were probably well balanced in that way, but in this moment, she needed him to decide fast.

His dark eyes bored into hers. She saw questions and doubts but also more. To her utter shock, he slid his hands into her hair, cupped her cheek, then tipped her mouth up and covered her lips with his.

Heat, desire, need, and want detonated through her as his mouth moved over hers in a kiss that felt far more real than even she anticipated. Sliding her hands up, she ran a palm over his beard, its silky bristliness surprising her, before spearing her fingers through his thick dark hair.

His thumb moved under her jaw, his hand wrapping around her neck as his other left her hair and traveled south, landing on her ass, pulling her closer. He kissed her as if he needed her for his next breath, as if he'd devour her if she let him.

And she desperately wanted to let him.

Only another knock sounded, this time sharper, harsher, than the first.

Collin jerked back, his eyes searching hers. Withdrawing her hand from the short strands of his hair, she drew her thumb across his damp lips. "I'm not going to lie, the idea started as a distraction, but I wanted that." His eyes held steady on hers, and while she didn't see regret there, a shadow lurked. "And I think you did, too," she said before stepping away.

Opening the door, she intentionally made a production of running her hands through her mussed hair and pulling her sweatshirt around her body. "Sorry, we were in the middle of..." She shrugged. She wasn't the least bit embarrassed by what had happened, but she hoped she blushed a little for show.

Carter's and Jess's gazes darted to Collin. Hers followed. The hair on the right side of his head stood on end, his flannel was askew, and he wore the unmistakable look of a man who'd been kissed within an inch of his life.

Jess's lips tipped into a small smile, but Carter glared at them. "May we come in?" he asked.

Helia shook her head. "We can go to the main house. Anything you have to say or ask will need to involve my parents."

Carter started to argue, but Collin stepped forward, took her hand in his, and ushered her out. Carter and Jess stepped back on instinct, and he shut the door behind them. Not having any choice, the detectives followed as he led them to her parents' place.

Ten minutes later, they were seated at the large kitchen table. When everyone settled with their drink of choice—tea for her, coffee for everyone else—her dad set his elbows on the table and asked, "What can you share?"

Carter pulled out his phone and tapped the screen. "Do any of you know Kurt Fisher?"

Beside her, Collin shook his head. She didn't need to reach for the phone to see the picture. "Yes," she said. Carter and Jess turned sharp eyes on her. "He used to work for Yoshi Ito," she continued, then as an aside, she added for Collin's benefit, "Yoshi is the broker who imports fish from Japan for a lot of the restaurants in the area." Jess and Carter both took notes. "But he has dark hair, not blond, and Collin said the body had blond hair."

"Likely lightened. His driver's license shows him with dark hair," Jess answered. "Were you close?"

Under the table, Collin's large hand slid over her knee. She lowered hers and set it on top of his, the heat seeping through her leggings.

Helia shook her head. "No. We do some business with the company when Akin needs those goods. But Kurt moved away several years ago. Two, maybe three. Maybe longer than that." She paused. "Last I heard, he was working for some business in San Francisco."

Her mother nodded. "I remember Asuka, Yoshi's wife, telling me he had a restaurant job in the city. He was young and wanted to live somewhere a little more exciting than Napa Valley. I think he had family there, too."

"A brother," Carter confirmed.

"And you weren't close?" Jess asked, directing the question to her. Collin's hand twitched again.

"We weren't," was all she said. Collin's hand relaxed.

"You never dated?"

This time, she tightened her hand on Collin's. She'd learned from her first go-around with them to only give answers to the specific questions.

"Never," she answered.

"He ever ask you out?" Carter asked.

"No."

"If you don't mind, we'd like to search the premises," Carter said.

"Not without a warrant," Collin said, drawing everyone's attention. "This business and the vineyards are separate companies, right, Harry?"

Her dad nodded. "They are. We have an LLC that leases the vineyard, and then Sundaram is another."

"It's at least a half a mile between the property here and where the body was found. Asking to search Sundaram is like asking to search a boutique four blocks from the bank when there's been a robbery. The two businesses are unrelated, and Sundaram isn't even the closest structure to where the body was found. That would be the winery to the west and the one to the north. Not to mention, the victim was dumped in that vineyard, not killed there."

Her parents had always liked Collin, but a new sort of respect, layered over the affection, reflected in their eyes. As if realizing he was no longer the child they'd taken in, but a man with knowledge and experience.

Carter tipped his head. "How do you know he wasn't killed there?"

"It's not brain surgery," Collin replied. "Whoever killed him nearly severed his torso from the rest of his body. The blood spray would be massive, and I saw none of that. Not on the ground and not on the vines where it would clearly show up against the pale winter color of the trunks and branches."

Silence fell across the room before her dad spoke. "Is that true? He was dumped but not killed there?"

Carter and Jess shared a look. "It's an ongoing investigation. We can't comment on that."

"Then we'll take that as a yes. I trust Collin to know what he's talking about," her dad continued. "About the body and the search."

Another look passed between the detectives before they rose. "Thank you for your time," Jess said. "We'll be in touch."

"I'll walk you out," Harry said.

In silent agreement, she, her mom, and Collin moved to the window and watched as Harry escorted the detectives to their car. The three paused to talk, Harry gesturing to the two police cars, then to the field. Carter and Jess didn't look happy, but both shook his hand before climbing into their vehicle.

"Well, that was interesting," Harry said when he returned to the apartment. "I asked them to have the police move their cars to the other property. Was the man really dumped?" he asked, turning to Collin.

"He wasn't killed there, I can promise you that."

"Why were they so interested in whether or not you ever dated him?" her mom asked her.

Helia lifted a shoulder. "I don't know. Maybe because Justin and I dated and for some reason, they think the two murders might be related."

All four turned back to the window. Two officers trudged through the vineyard toward parked cars.

"Carter said they'd be another few hours before they clear the field. I called Jeff to let him know," Harry said.

"Jeff is the business manager for the winery that leases the land," Helia said to Collin. He nodded in thanks for the clarification.

"What now?" Vanessa asked.

"Now we go back to my house," Helia said. "Collin has some shopping to do, so we'll head out in a few minutes."

Her dad's gaze lingered on the window. "I don't like this."

"I don't much like it either," Helia admitted. The questions about her and Kurt had rattled her. Only Collin's hand on her leg kept her grounded.

"I have friends who can look into it," Collin said. She wasn't the only one to turn her attention to him. He flashed a rueful smile. "I know interesting people. I already have them poking around Justin's murder. They'll be happy to add this to it."

"The kind of people it would be better for us to not know about?" her mother asked. After twenty years in the military before starting Sundaram, her parents were no strangers to subterfuge.

Collin chuckled, a warm, familiar sound. "Nothing like that. They are a very legitimate company who happen to have a ton of connections, crazy smart people, and, in a roundabout way, see me and my brothers as family. And they'll do anything for family."

Her parents studied him a moment longer, then her mom stepped up and hugged him. "I'm glad you're back in our lives. Not because of this, not because of what you can do to help us, but because we get to know the man you are, the man you've become. And I very much like that man."

Collin blinked and hugged her mom back. When she stepped away, her dad took her place, echoing his wife's words.

Sensing the mood was heavier than Collin wanted to linger in, she looped her arm through his. "On that note, Collin and I will now go in search of socks and T-shirts and other necessary items. You guys need anything from town?"

Her parents shook their heads and after another round of hugs, she and Collin headed back to her house.

"We need to sneak Kendall out," he said, sounding happy to be talking about anything other than murder.

She nodded and smiled. "We do, and I have the perfect plan."

CHAPTER SIXTEEN

"What's your plan?" Monk asked, more curious about Helia's delight than the actual details.

"My car has tinted windows. I'll pull it up to my house, she can pop in the back, and we can drive away. So long as she leaves from the front door, the police in the vineyard won't see her. And if she stays down, the cameras won't pick her up in the back seat."

He chuckled. "Why do I feel like you've done this before?"

Looking over her shoulder at him, she grinned. "Down in San Diego, I had a friend in the military. I might have helped her take a little unauthorized leave for a few hours here and there."

That grin. It would kill him one of these days, he was certain. A little mischievous, a lot confident, and a whole bucketload of sexy, he'd always been a goner for that look on her.

And he'd kissed her.

Well, technically, she'd kissed him. But he sure as hell had kissed her back. A twist of doubt curled through his stomach into his chest. Maybe it would end with that, with that one searing kiss. Thinking about anything more brought up all sorts of thoughts and feelings he'd rather not confront.

He snorted to himself at that thought. Not a month ago, he'd been telling his brother Philly that shit festered, and it was better to get it out and deal with it. Apparently, what was good for the goose wasn't good for the gander.

They halted as a car pulled into the courtyard and parked by the side of the kitchen.

"Greg and Akin," she said.

"Who's Greg?" He'd met Akin the day he'd helped with the wedding and liked the easygoing but exacting chef.

"Our kitchen manager," Helia answered. "He takes care of the supplies, repairs, hiring, that sort of thing."

"What's going on?" Greg asked, his gaze darting to the activity in the field as he and Akin joined them. Tall with thinning brown hair and the ruddy skin of either an alcoholic or a Brit who's had too much sun in his life. The kind of man who tried to appear pulled together but never quite succeeded. Not that he needed to look a certain way to be good at his job.

Helia introduced him to the kitchen manager before giving them a brief lowdown on the events of the past few hours.

"Geez, that's the second murder in a week. It is murder, right?" Greg asked.

Helia nodded. "Based on what Collin saw, yes."

Both men turned their attention to him. "I'm guessing you weren't expecting to start your day with that," Akin said.

"Definitely not," he replied.

"Did you see anything else?" Greg asked.

Monk shook his head. He didn't need to repeat what he'd told the detectives about the blood spatter. He didn't have strong social skills, but even he knew certain information was best left unsaid.

"Did either of you know Kurt Fisher?" Helia asked.

"The fish broker?" Akin asked.

"Didn't he move to San Francisco?" Greg added.

"Yes and yes," Helia said.

"It was him?" Greg asked, his gaze back on the vineyard. They couldn't see much from where they stood, only the occasional bob of a head as it moved around the crime scene and the top of the coroner's van.

"We think so," Helia replied. "At least that's who the detectives asked us about."

"I saw him the other day," Greg said. "Maybe four days ago. He was having dinner with Kelly at that new place over on the river. Do you think I should mention it to the police?"

"I'm sure they'll track his movements and figure it out, but if they reach out to you, it might not hurt to mention. Maybe they talked about something that could help shed some light on what happened," Helia replied. "Kelly is the social media manager for a lot of wineries, including Bacco," she added for his benefit.

"You okay?" Akin asked. His gaze taking in both him and Helia.

Helia waggled her head. "It's been an interesting morning." Akin's gaze landed on him, and he nodded in agreement.

"On that note, what are you all up to this morning?" Helia asked. As the three chatted about work for a few minutes, he took the opportunity to study the two men. Akin, the more intense of the pair, held Helia's gaze as they spoke, never looking away. Although Monk didn't get any vibes other than professional ones from him. Greg, on the other hand, looked as if his mind was bouncing in a thousand directions—from the goings-on in the vineyard, to the upcoming events, to the scratch on his car he kept eyeing. Watching him was exhausting.

"We have some errands to run in town, so don't let us keep you," Helia said, bringing him back to the conversation. "If you need anything, text. We'll be out for a while."

Curiosity flared in both men's eyes, but Helia didn't give it a chance to go any further. Taking his hand, she led them back to her place, where they found a nervous but not panicked Kendall.

"Come on, kid, we're busting you out of this joint," Helia said. "Well, really, we're going to get you some more clothes, but that sounded better."

Kendall's shoulders eased and she rolled her eyes but smiled. Monk didn't know what the rest of the day would entail, but he enjoyed seeing Helia charm the abandoned child.

Four hours later, they'd visited two box stores, three thrift shops—which Kendall delighted in far more than Monk would have thought—and the grocery store. With a café stop for pastries and drinks in between.

"I'll drive you to Bacco and maybe we can make a late lunch before I head home?" Helia suggested as they traveled north out of the city of Napa.

"Works for me," Monk replied.

"There's a bunch of board games in the tasting room, maybe we can play?" Kendall suggested.

"Do you know how to play blackjack?" he asked, craning his head to look at her sitting in the back seat.

She rolled her eyes. He'd noticed she used the gesture to either convey a silent "duh" or hide her discomfort. This eye roll was definitely the former.

"Dulcie's the best of the Falcons. Maybe we can play a few rounds," he said.

Wariness entered her expression. "Who's Dulcie?"

Hell, in the chaos of finding her the night before, then the body that morning, he'd forgotten she hadn't met his two friends the way Helia had. He was sure she'd heard them, though.

"He was at the house yesterday. The softer spoken of the two. The other is my brother Lovell."

"Lovell is Black," she said, confirming his suspicion she'd seen them even if they hadn't seen her.

"That is true."

"You're not."

Ah, he got it. "Found family, remember," he said, reminding them of their earlier conversation.

"You can't pick your family," she insisted.

He sensed an argument brewing inside her. He didn't know the origin but suspected it had to do with both nerves and her own precarious position when it came to family. Her insecurity. He couldn't address that head-on; they didn't have that kind of trust, not yet, but he could make his opinion clear.

"I can and I did," he said, then continued before she could object again. "Dulcie has three younger sisters who all have him wrapped around their little fingers, but don't think he'll go easy on you when it comes to blackjack. That's his line in the sand."

"I suck at card games," Helia said, turning left onto the Silverado Trail. She'd sensed the tension, too, and was doing her part. He couldn't say he fell a little in love with her then, because he wasn't sure he'd ever been out of love with her, but he felt her solidarity far deeper in his soul than the words warranted.

"It's my face," Helia continued. "It's too expressive. Can't hide my feelings to save my life. It's also why I always work the back of the house for our events. You get a bridezilla in my view or an asshole CEO up in my grill and it's not pretty. I don't ever say or do anything, but everything I *want* to say or do is written on my face."

A mile ticked by in silence before Kendall spoke. "Can you play with us? I wanna see what that looks like."

He laughed. Helia gasped in mock outrage. "You want to make fun of me?"

Kendall's lips twitched, and she tipped her head shyly to the side. "Maybe. A little."

"The things I do for you, kiddo," Helia muttered, but loud enough for Kendall to hear. The tension eased in the car.

A few minutes later, they pulled through the gates to Bacco and up the drive. Dulcie was standing at the base of a ladder resting on the south corner of the castle. He waved, drill in hand, then followed their car on foot to the parking area. Monk had texted him about Kendall and the murder while Helia and Kendall shopped. He wasn't surprised to see the three of them arrive together.

Helia popped out first and darted over to give Dulcie a hug. She'd always been easy with her affection, but Monk was pretty sure at least a part of the greeting was for show. For Kendall's benefit.

"I got the cameras set up on the house," Dulcie said, as Monk strode over and gave his brother a one-armed hug.

"Thanks for that. We can tackle the wine caves tomorrow," he said. "Kendall, this is Dulcie."

"Weird name," she said.

"Kendall!" Helia said.

Dulcie shrugged. "Whatever, Kendall Jenner." Kendall narrowed her eyes at him and his taunt. "Or should I call you Savant? Isn't that what he calls you?" he said, tipping his head in Monk's direction.

"He calls me Kendall."

"Then Kendall it is. And for reference, my real name is Mateo, but my brothers call me Dulcie. We all have nicknames."

"It's a nickname?" she asked, a tiny prick of curiosity in her tone. Dulcie dipped his chin. "How'd you get it?"

Dulcie shrugged and smiled. "I'm Mexican by descent and, according to my asshole brothers—excuse my language—I'm sweet as sugar. They thought it would be hilarious considering what we did for a living."

"Dulcie means sweetie, though, not sugar," she said. "Dulce would mean sweet."

His brother's eyes lit. "You know Spanish?"

"Un poquito," she replied.

"You're right. But they decided Dulcie was easier to say than Dulce. I don't know why. Gringos," he added with a shrug. Monk rolled his eyes.

"What's your nickname?" she asked, turning to him.

"Monk," both Dulcie and Helia said at the same time.

"I don't think I want to know the origin of that name," Kendall said, making the rest of them laugh.

"You don't. Now let's get inside and make some lunch. It's getting colder, and I could do with a fire, too," he said.

"You get the fire, I'll get lunch," Helia said, leading the way inside. He followed behind her but didn't miss how Kendall tentatively came up alongside Dulcie, bringing up the rear.

"You're installing cameras?" she asked.

"Yeah. Monk's father didn't have any, and with the break-in the other day, we thought it was time. Probably past time. Roger had his reasons, none of which are valid anymore, so security, rather than privacy, is taking over."

"What kind?" she asked. "Of camera," she clarified.

And then they were off. He left the two talking brands, specs, bugs, and all sorts of tech things as he made his way to the fireplace. He got the fire going, checked in with Helia, then hauled the bags of clothes from the car to the laundry room. He considered starting a load but knew Kendall had purchased some personal items that she might not be comfortable with him seeing. And since she and Dulcie had slipped back outside so he could show her the setup, Monk left the clothes and wandered into the kitchen to find Helia bent over, peering into the oven.

He stared at her ass for longer than he should, remembering the feel of it in his hand when they'd kissed that morning. Forcing his mind back to Kendall, he cleared his throat.

Helia straightened and spun. "You startled me."

He made a face. "Sorry, moving quietly is habit. What did you decide?" he asked, nodding to the oven. They'd bought enough food for several meals.

"BLTs and french fries. The sandwiches are ready to be assembled, just waiting on the fries."

His stomach rumbled, making her smile. "I wanted to get some of those clothes washed for Kendall, so she has clean pajamas and…stuff. But she might not like me going through some of those things. Would you mind…?"

"Say no more. I'll start a load if you keep an eye on the fries?"

"Deal." He moved into the small kitchen.

Helia paused in front of him on her way out. Then reaching up, she patted his chest, went up on her toes, and kissed his cheek. "You're a good man, Collin," she said before disappearing out the door.

CHAPTER SEVENTEEN

Helia folded a shirt and set it on the growing pile on the shelf beside the dryer. Kendall had offered to do her own folding, but Helia thought she could use a little spoiling. She hadn't talked much about her life, but she'd dropped enough tidbits for them to know she'd been the adult in the relationship.

A burst of laughter filtered down the hall from the tasting room. Dulcie and Kendall had moved on from blackjack to Texas Hold'em, and she guessed one or the other had landed a sneak attack.

"You all good in here?" Collin asked, stepping through the door.

"You're good with her," she responded.

"I'm hoping she'll trust us enough to tell us her mom's name so we can help find her. You're helping with that. By spending time with us."

"You ever thought about having kids?" she asked, knowing the question had implications, even unintended ones. The kiss they'd shared that afternoon had been playing on repeat in her head all day.

She expected, maybe anticipated, either a general panicked "no" or an emphatic "yes." The steady, piercing study she received from his dark eyes had her setting a pair of jeans on the counter and turning to face him more fully.

"Actually no," he said, his voice quiet. "I like kids. Just assumed it would never happen for me."

She cocked her head. "Why not?"

Before he could answer, her phone rang. Pulling it from her pocket, she frowned at the ID, then flashed it to Collin: Napa Police Department.

"Hello," she answered. Collin gestured for her to put it on speaker. She tapped the button, then held the device out.

"Helia? It's Carter."

"Hey, Carter."

"We have a few more questions; can we stop by to talk?"

She glanced out the window into the darkness. Granted, night came earlier in the winter, but still, it was after six.

"I'm not home right now," she replied. "I can talk over the phone, or we can meet tomorrow."

Carter paused, then sighed. "Can you tell me what kind of car you drive?"

Her brows dropped so fast she wondered if they'd stay there permanently. "A Mini," she replied. Collin had barely fit into the passenger seat. Thankfully, Kendall, though tall, was flexible enough to sprawl across the back bench, allowing him to put his seat all the way back.

Beside her, Collin crossed his arms and glared at the phone. His facial expressions had always been subtle, and they'd grown even more so since his childhood. Still, she knew him well enough to catch his micro-expressions. And right now, the tension in his jaw and the tiny crease at the corner of his left eye told her he Was. Not. Pleased.

"Does Sundaram have any other vehicles?"

Collin nodded for her to answer. "Yes, we have a van and a truck."

"And do you drive those?"

Again, Collin nodded. "I do. Several of us do, when needed. But I don't think either has been taken out since last weekend. Why?"

"And you say you haven't seen Kurt Fisher for a few years?"

Collin pulled out his phone and started typing out a text.

"Since before he moved," she answered. "I told you, I don't remember exactly when he moved, but I hadn't seen him in a while when I heard about it. Again, why?"

"Because we have a witness that says they saw you with him last week," Carter replied.

She sucked in a breath. Impossible. She opened her mouth to say as much when Collin set a hand on her arm and held out his phone out. He'd written a note, not a text.

"Ask when," it said.

"When did this witness say they saw us?"

"A week ago, Monday."

"What time and where?" she asked, not needing Collin's notes to tell her what to ask next.

"Midmorning, near the Mount Saint Helena trail."

She shook her head. "Aside from wedding season during the spring and summer, November and December are our busiest months at Sundaram. Not only was I *not* hiking on a weekday morning, but it's a nearly ten-mile trail that takes five to six hours. It would never even cross my mind to try it during our second high season."

"And last night?"

"What about last night?"

"Where were you?"

Collin arched his brow and lifted his eyes upward, almost making her laugh. "Between what hours, Carter?"

"Ten and two in the morning?"

She snorted. "In bed like most people who live in the valley who aren't working hospitality that night."

"You didn't go out?"

"Not during those hours. I'd been out to dinner with Collin and two of his friends."

"Where'd you go?"

"Guichos Tacos. Saw a couple of other folks there, too."

"That unregistered food truck on the south side of town?"

"Yes," she confirmed. No way was she going to comment on the other thing. Food trucks like Guichos, ones that fed locals at reasonable prices, were a battleground between those who embraced economic diversity and those who wanted a dozen new Michelin-star restaurants.

"What time did you get home?"

"Nine. A little after. I went to bed straightaway."

"You didn't go out again?"

"It would be hard to go out again when I was in bed asleep."

"And you didn't hear or see anything in the vineyard? Don't you have a window that looks out that direction?"

"I do. But again, it would be hard to see anything in the field when my curtains were drawn and *I was asleep*."

Collin grinned and held up his phone again. She read the message but wasn't sure if she was supposed to volunteer the comment or if it was a heads-up as to what was coming.

"I understand there's no CCTV out by your house or the vineyard."

Ah, a heads-up.

With her eyes on the response Collin had prepped for her,

she answered. "There isn't. But as you saw, it's impossible to drive out to the vineyard from Sundaram. From my house, you'd have to go out the main gate, where there is CCTV, then circle back on the connector road. If you're thinking I killed Kurt somewhere, loaded his body into a vehicle, then dumped it in the vineyard between ten and two last night, you'll have to think again."

Carter paused. He must have put a hand over the receiver as all they heard were muffled voices before he returned twenty seconds later.

"Thank you. We'll be in touch."

She disconnected the call, then set her phone on the dryer. "Well, that was exciting."

"That was annoying. Any reason they'd focus on you?" Collin asked, irritation deepening his voice. The tone raised the hair on her arms, as if each little filament was seeking him out.

She made a face. "Even less reason than they had for Justin. I knew Kurt, but we weren't overly friendly. He dated someone on our waitstaff, so we'd occasionally see him around, but we didn't spend any time together." She paused. "I'm a little slow to this game, but is it weird that my name has cropped up in two murders in the past week? I don't think Napa has ever had *any* murders like these, and now there's two and I'm being questioned about both."

Any hope she had of Collin reassuring her died when his lips curled in and he frowned the tiniest bit.

"I don't like it either," he said. "I also don't like that people from your past keep cropping up."

She cocked her head. "People from my past?"

"Justin and Kurt, but also Trish and Derek. Not to mention Derek was giving you a hard time."

"I don't know what to tell you about Derek, but as for Trish, people come and go from Napa all the time. And given that I went to school here for five years, it's not unusual for me to know folks moving home. Usually, people who left because they hated it but now realize it's not a bad place to live."

He didn't look convinced, and she fought the urge to tell him he was overreacting. She didn't want to go down a weird rabbit hole of conspiracy and fear. On the other hand, she also didn't want to turn a blind eye if something weird *was* going on, even if she couldn't fathom what it was.

Collin lifted a hand, as if to touch her, then dropped it again. "What time do you need to be home?"

She reached over and tipped her phone up. Almost seven. "I should probably head out now." She'd never thought of the castle as remotely cozy, but with the four of them tucked into the tasting room, the card games, the food, the fire, and the Christmas tree lit, she could almost forget the rest of the world existed.

But it did. And she had three parties in the next few days. None were particularly difficult, but no one working for Sundaram took anything for granted.

"I'll drive you," Collin said.

"It's my car."

"I'll walk back. I could use the exercise."

She doubted that but didn't argue. "Let me finish this load of folding, and then I'll be ready. Won't be five minutes."

His eyes held hers, as if he had something to say, some world to share with her, then he nodded and stepped away.

Fifteen minutes later, following an extended round of goodbyes and making plans to see each other again, she and Collin climbed into her car. The ride was silent, though not uncomfortable. The hustle and bustle of the valley gave her energy, but she loved these quiet times when it felt as if the land breathed again.

They pulled through the gate as a car and van passed.

"Who's that?" Collin asked as she waved.

"Felipe and Greg."

"The kitchen manager?"

She nodded. "Felipe is the floral supplier. He was probably making a delivery for the upcoming events. We have a cooling room to keep flowers in, so if they aren't the sort to wilt or go off, he'll frequently deliver them a few days before they're needed."

"Kind of late," he said, as she pulled into the spot beside her house.

She tipped her head. "It feels that way because it's so dark."

The look Collin shot her was inscrutable. "I'll walk you to your door."

The door was all of twenty feet from where she parked, but who was she to argue? Maybe he'd even kiss her good-night. Although if the way his hand fell away from her in the laundry was any indication, she'd need to initiate it. Which seemed like a good idea to her. Surely a planned kiss couldn't be as good as the surprise kiss she'd laid on him earlier. And if it wasn't as incendiary, maybe she could stop obsessing about it.

Collin opened her door, startling her out of her thoughts. She hadn't even noticed he'd exited the car.

"Ready?" he said, holding out his hand. Not a kiss, but she'd take the offer, and she slid her palm into his. She'd always liked the subtle, almost innocent yet intimate, connection.

Hand in hand, they strolled toward her front door. She'd left the lights off in the house, but the motion-sensing one on her porch flickered on when they approached. She blinked at the sudden bright glow in the dark night, then stumbled as Collin hauled her behind him.

She hadn't seen anything, but his reaction triggered her

fear instincts, and she tucked herself against his back. Curling her hand into his flannel shirt, her heart running like a conga line in her chest, she asked, "Collin?"

"Did you close the door when we left?" he asked.

She tried to peek around his wide shoulders, but he nudged her back with his arm, his hand resting on her hip.

"Yes. And locked it. I always do. Force of habit when you regularly have strangers partying on the property." She hesitated. "Why?"

A cricket chirped somewhere out in the vineyard.

"Go back to your car, get in, and lock the door."

"Um, no."

He didn't shift from his protective stance, but his eyes met hers over his shoulder.

"No?"

"No. What's going on? And if it's dangerous, I'm insulted you think I'd leave you."

"You do realize that I spent ten years chasing and hunting terrorists and really, really bad guys. And gals."

"But you don't do that anymore. You've closed that chapter, started a new one, now you're a business owner, brother, friend, and so many other things that don't involve hunting terrorists and really, really bad guys and gals. You're also my friend and I'm not leaving you." She lifted her chin for good measure. She had no doubt that if he wanted, he could throw her over his shoulder and dump her in her car. But he couldn't make her stay.

She waggled an eyebrow in challenge.

"Now is not the time for that," he grumbled. "Your front door is open."

"What!" she gasped, moving to get a glimpse. Again, he forced her behind him.

"When I tell you a building is burning, you don't run to it, woman," he said.

"What were you saying about hunting terrorists?" She might have heard a snort.

"Fine, stay behind me," he conceded.

She had no problem with that. Gripping his shirt, she shuffled forward with him, inching toward her house. When they reached the door, he stood to the side, sandwiching her between his body and the wall, and set his hand on the wide planks.

She held her breath as the heavy wood swung slowly open. Collin paused, maybe to listen, although the rush in *her* ears muted most sounds. A million years seemed to pass before he stepped around the frame and into her living room. Pulling her in with him, he gestured for her to keep her back to the interior wall.

"Stay there. I'll check this floor."

Before she could answer, he was halfway across the room, silently moving through the space. She watched him check furniture, the hall closet, and the bathroom, before he disappeared into the kitchen.

Less than a minute later, he reappeared. "It's clear down here. Any chance you'll lock yourself in the bathroom while I check the rest of the house?"

She weighed her options. "Will it make this go faster?"

His head tipped an inch to the left. "If I find something, yes. Dealing with it will be easier if I know you're safe."

She made a face. "That's such a cliché."

His brows dipped. "What is?"

"That you can do your job better if you don't have to worry about me."

He frowned. "Not sure if it's a cliché, but it's true."

"I'm not a damsel in distress."

"No, you're a damsel who doesn't know the first thing about hand-to-hand combat. I'm a guy who doesn't know the first thing about planning a four-hundred-person event. We have different strengths."

Well, when put like that... "Fine, I'll stay down here."

She tried not to read too much into the look of relief on his face as she crossed the room. Letting herself into the small powder room, she locked the door, then leaned against the vanity. She didn't hear Collin's footsteps on the stairs, but the distinctive creak of her closet door traveled to her with the subtlety of a banshee's screech.

True to his word, not five minutes passed before he jogged down the stairs, this time not cloaking his steps. "You can come out," he called.

"Nothing?" she asked, opening the door a slice. A dumb question since he wouldn't have told her to come out if that hadn't been the case, still, she felt compelled to ask.

"Well, someone was here, but they aren't now," he answered, stopping in the middle of her living room and crossing his arms. She probably shouldn't be noticing his biceps, but it was hard not to. He was primed for a fight, and they were bulgier than usual.

"How do you know? Other than the door?" she asked, focusing on the more important, if far less interesting, topic.

"Unless you've grown sloppy in the past seventeen years, you never would have left the closet the way it looks now."

She sucked in a breath and stilled. Then like a rubber band snapping, she bolted upstairs to her room. Halting in the door, her gaze swept over the space. Her bed hadn't been touched; neither had her bedside tables, lamps, and dresser. But her closet...

Nausea churned and boiled in her stomach. Gentle and steady fingers landed on her back.

"That wasn't you, was it?" Collin asked, the words sounding pained.

She shook her head. In the grand scheme of things, it wasn't as bad as she expected. Several dresses hung halfway off hangers, three coats lay strewn across the floor, and several shoes were tipped over and no longer in matching sets. Taking a second, slower look, she also noticed three button-down blouses, still on their hangers, lying on top of the coats, and her robe crumpled and shoved against the back of the closet.

"No, this wasn't me," she said.

"Do you want to call the police?"

She stared at her things. She'd need to go through it all to see if anything was missing, but nothing obviously stuck out to her as being gone. The relief she should feel was tempered, though, by the knowledge that someone had rifled through her belongings.

She set a hand on her stomach in a futile attempt to still the drunken butterflies stumbling around inside. A warm palm settled on her neck, Collin's fingers gently rubbing some of the tension away.

She inhaled deeply, held it to the count of four, then let it out. "Do you think they left prints?"

Collin didn't answer right away. "Hard to know. Why?"

She turned to face him. He kept his hand on her neck, and she settled against him. "If nothing is missing and there aren't any prints, I don't want to get the police involved. Not after..." *Not after they questioned me about two murders* remained unsaid.

A look she couldn't describe crossed over Collin's face. "Why don't you look through everything then we can decide. What can I do?"

She leaned forward, resting her forehead on his chest. "Nothing, you're doing it," she murmured as his other hand swept soothingly up and down her back. "I just need a minute."

"Take all the time you want."

She breathed deeply, inhaling his scent and warmth as she pulled her shit together. Twenty breaths later, she stepped away. "Okay, I'll tackle the closet, but then what?"

"If anything is missing, we call the police." She nodded. "Either way, though, you shouldn't stay here tonight."

An entirely different type of butterfly swarm took flight in her stomach. "Where should I stay?"

"Helia."

"The castle," she said. "You want me to stay at the castle."

CHAPTER EIGHTEEN

An hour after leaving, they returned to the castle. Sure, he could have suggested Helia stay with her parents, but then she'd be out of his sight, and he'd be unable to protect her. Neither option worked for him.

"What are we going to tell Kendall? And Dulcie?" she asked, clutching her overnight bag. At least her intruder hadn't taken anything, not even the intricate diamond necklace given to her by her Indian grandmother.

"The truth, I guess?" He knew nothing about twelve-year-olds, but he was getting to know Kendall. Between her trust issues and being far too old for her age, hiding things from her would do more harm than good. He'd *like* to coddle her, maybe give her some of her childhood back, but now wasn't the right time.

Helia tipped her head, the security lights Dulcie installed earlier catching strands of gold and copper in her hair. "You're right. I hate it, but you're right."

He pulled into a spot beside Dulcie's truck, and they climbed out, their steps heavier than they'd been an hour ago.

He reached for Helia's bag but dropped his hand when his phone rang. Pulling the device from his pocket, he checked the name. Leo. He needed to take the call but didn't want Helia to hear. She didn't need to know the extent of his paranoia when it came to her safety. Not wanting her to stay alone after someone broke into her home was one thing; knowing he had someone looking into Derek, Trish, Justin, *and* Kurt was a whole different level.

"I need to get this," he said, slowing his steps.

Curiosity flickered across her expression, but she nodded and said nothing.

"Leo," he said, typing the code into the door.

"You've had an interesting day," came the younger man's reply.

"That's one way of putting it."

Helia slipped into the castle. He felt bad leaving her to explain her return to Dulcie and Kendall, but he closed the door behind her, then leaned against the cold stone of the entryway.

"Where do you want to start?" Leo asked.

"The pistol," he replied.

"Good choice. It was used in a drug bust gone south in Jacksonville seven years ago. A young cop was shot. He survived but is no longer a cop since the bullet went through his spine and left him a paraplegic."

Monk gave a fleeting thought to the young man whose life had irrevocably changed in that instant. But the question that occupied most of his thoughts was, "How the hell did my dad get hold of a gun from Florida?"

"And it's not the first time the state has cropped up in the weirdness that's going on," Leo pointed out. "Derek Weber and Trish are from Florida, too."

"Any news on Trish?" Monk asked.

"She's next on the list," Leo replied.

"What about Flannery? Or Kurt Fisher?" He felt bad dumping so much on Leo but knew the cyber expert would be offended if he didn't. He did decide, though, that he and Joey would be getting a case of Bacco wine for Christmas.

"No updates on Flannery as far as the police are concerned. They're still combing through the evidence. There's nothing being tested for DNA so it will be a slog. Old-school detective work."

"That may be what the police are doing, but what about you?" Monk asked as the door swung open.

"You should come in," Dulcie said, standing in the doorway. Monk raised an eyebrow. "The ladies are speculating like crazy what that call is about, and I think it would be best for everyone to be on the same page." He paused, then added, "Not that I think a twelve-year-old should be hearing the things you're probably hearing, but Kendall isn't your average twelve-year-old."

Monk sighed, not really surprised by the development. They knew about the murders. Kendall knew about his cyber expert friends. Between the two, who knew what stories they were concocting.

"Hold that thought, Leo. I'm going to join the group, which will include Helia and Kendall—who is twelve. Don't hide things from her, but if you could..."

"Not get graphic?"

"Please."

"Not a problem. Why don't you update them on what we covered, then I can pick it up."

He mumbled a thank-you as he entered the tasting room behind Dulcie. Helia and Kendall both blinked at him with wide eyes, not hiding their surprise at his willingness to bring them into the fold, so to speak.

"Leo Gallardo, a cyber expert from HICC, a security firm in Mystery Lake, is on the line. I've been asking him to look into a few of the things going on here," he started.

"Like the murders?" Kendall asked.

"That's Kendall," he said to Leo. "And yes, the murders. But also the fact that I found a pistol in my father's room along with—" He hesitated, wondering if it would be going too far to talk about the drugs in front of Kendall.

"Drugs," she said.

The fact that she knew—or guessed—didn't make the regret he felt at her having that kind of knowledge any lighter.

"Yeah, drugs. I don't know what kind. Lovell dropped them at HICC to get tested."

"Drugs?" Helia repeated.

"Roger has been into them for as long as I can remember," Monk said, holding her gaze. "I knew he was a user, but I found more than what a single habit could support. Or even a year's worth of his parties."

"So is my mom," Kendall said.

Monk swung his attention to her. Not once had she mentioned her mom since waking up that morning. She gave an awkward shrug. "She's been on and off them for as long as I can remember. She's fine for a while and then...well, then she isn't. That's how we ended up here a few weeks ago. The parties here give her everything she needs—food, drink, drugs, a place to crash. Sex." That last word, spoken so quietly, ricocheted across the room.

Conflicting emotions crashed through Monk at her admission. He desperately hoped they'd find her mother so Monk could drive some sense into her. Intellectually, he knew that wasn't possible—you couldn't help people who didn't want to be helped. But that didn't stop him from wanting to protect Kendall.

Another part of him hoped they never found her, though. Kendall might be better off without her. It wasn't his call to make, of course. But if it came to that, he and the Falcons would take her in if she didn't have any other family. She deserved a safe place, a place she could thrive. He wanted to see her laugh and go to school. And chase whatever dreams she had.

Leo cleared his throat. "If you want me to find her, I'm happy to look."

Kendall's eyes shot to Monk's. "It's up to you," he said.

She nodded but didn't answer. She didn't shut the option down, though, either.

"Okay," Helia said, drawing out the word. "So, what were you two talking about before Dulcie dragged you in?"

Monk wanted to brush the question—the whole topic—off; instead, he filled them in on the gun and the Florida connections.

"Trish?" Helia asked, her expression conveying the same doubt he'd seen earlier.

"I know you think it's a stretch, but she's from Florida and is someone from your past who's reemerged into your life," Monk said.

"Could she be the woman I heard?" Kendall asked.

"What woman?" Leo and Dulcie replied at the same time. Kurt's murder had taken precedence, and he hadn't updated either on what Kendall overheard. He nodded to her to fill them in.

She drew back in surprise, then, as if making up for the momentary lapse of confidence, she snapped her spine straight and repeated what she'd told him.

"It couldn't have been Trish," Leo said when she finished.

"Why not?" Kendall asked, curiosity rather than challenge in her tone.

"I did a quick look at her while you were talking, and she flew into San Francisco four days ago. Before that, she was in Miami, but the day Roger died, she was in Hong Kong. I'm not saying she wasn't involved in Roger's death, but she couldn't have been who you heard."

Kendall stared at the phone. "You got all that in the, like, ninety seconds it took me to tell you what I heard?"

Leo chuckled. "Yeah, we're good like that."

"So what have you found out about the other two dead guys?" Kendall asked.

Monk cast Helia a questioning look. Should he be worried about her interest? Not in the sense he thought she had anything to do with it, but was it healthy?

Helia's eyes widened and she shrugged, not having any idea either, apparently. Dulcie cleared his throat and gave a tiny shake of his head. Since he was the only one experienced with kids, Monk decided that, as weird as it felt, he'd trust his brother and let Kendall lead the discussion.

"Nothing new on Flannery," Leo answered.

"The guy who was found dead in his home a few days ago?" Kendall clarified.

"The same," Leo confirmed. "I was about to update Monk about Kurt Fisher when you all came into the conversation."

"And?" Kendall pressed.

Monk leaned back against the sofa. Beside him, Helia tucked her legs underneath her, her body listing into his. Pushing aside whatever Dulcie or Kendall might think, he laid his hand, palm up, on his thigh. Without hesitation, she slid hers over, twining her fingers with his, then rested her head on his shoulder. Dulcie's eyes bounced between them before settling on Kendall.

"Kurt Fisher did leave the valley to work with a restaurant in San Francisco. That was three years ago. He lasted there about a year and a half, and he's been bouncing from job to job ever since," Leo said.

"Addiction issues?" Monk asked.

"There's some evidence of that, but nothing conclusive. His most recent job is an interesting one, though," Leo replied. "He works for Wei Zhao. Or rather, he worked for Wei Zhao at one of his smaller enterprises."

"Which sounds not legit," Kendall said.

"Zhao operates several legit businesses but has just as many that aren't. The one in San Francisco that Fisher worked for was a fish import business."

"Interesting," Helia said. "Trish is in the import business, too."

"I imagine Flannery is as well unless all the accessories his mother's business sells are made in the US," Monk said.

Her fingers danced over his hand. "They aren't. Made here, that is," she said. "I know several come from a few different Asian countries. Not sure about all of them, though."

"Are we thinking drugs?" Kendall asked. "As in they're all associated with importing them into the country and something happened leading to Flannery, Fisher, and Roger being murdered?"

"*We* shouldn't be thinking about any of these things," Monk said. "*You* should be, I don't know, focusing on schoolwork or boys or girls or what nation you want to take over when you're an adult."

Kendall snorted. "I told you, I've already tested out of most of the eleventh-grade classes. I think I can take a break for a few days. Not into boys or girls, yet, but figure I'll get there eventually. And if I ever take over a country, I'll do it from the background, and no one will ever know who's really running the show."

Dulcie laughed; so did Leo. Monk shook his head, and Helia muttered, "Terrifying."

"Back to the question, are we thinking they might all be involved in some sort of drug trade?" she asked.

"It's not out of the realm of possibility," Leo said. "But we don't have enough info yet. Trish Peterson needs looking into, and I want to see what crops up with Kurt in the next few days. Flannery's death was violent, but Fisher's was brutal. It takes a certain kind of someone to do what was done to either, but especially Fisher."

Kendall bobbed her head in thought. "Okay, fair. What about the drugs? Has HICC tested them yet?"

Monk let his head fall back, and he huffed. "Can someone please tell me why we're letting a twelve-year-old run this conversation?"

A beat passed, then Dulcie spoke. "Because she's probably smarter than we are. I mean, we have her on life experience, but..."

"And you're trying to gain my trust so I'll let you help find my mom," Kendall said. He lifted his head. She grinned at him. "I know what you're doing and, well, I appreciate the effort. No one's ever really cared whether I trust them or not. It's a little awkward, but in the kind of way a new sweater is awkward—it's uncomfortable because it's new and I'm not sure how it's going to fit or if I like it or if I do like it, whether it will change over time and become my favorite or one I hate. But I appreciate you giving me the sweater."

He stared at her, then snorted a quiet laugh. "That is a weird analogy, but I can go with that. Carry on, then."

Her grin turned into a smile, something he'd seen more and more of as the day had gone on. He suspected her nature leaned toward being optimistic and easygoing, but life had never given her the chance, or reason, to be either.

"So, the drugs, Leo?" she asked again.

"A custom mix of cocaine, GBL, and amphetamines."

Dulcie let out a low whistle, and Kendall's eyes grew big as she muttered a "Holy shit."

"I'm not surprised," Monk growled.

"Call me naive or whatever, but what does that mean?" Helia asked.

"It means Roger, or someone he knows, created a drug cocktail that lowers pain thresholds, reduces inhibitions, and jacks up sexual need," he answered. Not quite what Roger had sneaked into his system all those years ago, but probably not far off. "How are you going to get rid of it?"

"HICC has contacts at the DEA. We're going to hand it over. It will be anonymous for now, but if it's linked to anything bigger, we can't guarantee it stays that way."

"I don't care about Roger's reputation, but I do care about Bacco's because a lot of people rely on the winery for work," he said. "If it comes to that, to needing to go public for whatever reason, we'll deal with it, though."

A contemplative pall fell over the room and phone. Finally, Helia spoke. "What now?"

"Now, you all stay safe and keep your eyes and ears open. We'll look into Trish—"

"It's not Trish," Helia interjected. Monk understood she didn't want to think that someone she'd been so close with could be involved in what they were thinking, but it had to be done.

"If nothing comes up then no harm, no foul," Leo said, easily. "We'll also keep an eye on the Flannery and Fisher investigations. I'm going to dig deeper into Fisher, too. Hey, Kendall?"

"Yeah?"

"Do you think you'd recognize the two voices from the day Roger died if you heard them again?"

"Yes," she answered without missing a beat.

"Good. Don't let that become public knowledge, but I'll see if I can get you some voice clips of a few players."

"Okay," she said, sounding way more excited than she should. "Can I get your number? Then I can text you mine."

Leo rattled off the digits and a few seconds later, they heard the whoosh of a sent text.

"Anything we can do?" Helia asked.

"Stay safe," Leo answered.

"Oh shit," Monk said. Three sets of eyes turned on him. "I didn't tell Leo about your house."

"What happened?" Leo demanded.

"Someone broke in. Nothing was taken, but they pawed through my closet," Helia replied, her hand tightening in his as she answered.

Leo let out a low whistle. "I'm sorry to hear that. Any idea what they might have been looking for?"

"No clue," she said.

"The door wasn't forced, but I didn't examine it closely. I'll do that tomorrow," Monk said.

"I…" Helia hesitated. "I don't mean to sound paranoid, but is this somehow all tied to me? I mean, I'm the one who's been questioned about the murders, people I know are cropping up from my past, and my home was broken into. I have no idea how it *could* be connected, but, I don't know, it feels as if I'm a part of this somehow."

He shifted his other hand, enclosing hers between his. "We don't know enough to make those kinds of connections now, but I agree, it feels closer than it should."

"Which is why you're here at the castle," Kendall said.

"I can't stay here forever. I have to be at Sundaram tomorrow to prep for this weekend's events," she said.

"I'll go with you," Monk said.

"And Dulcie will stay here with me," Kendall said. Dulcie's lips ticked up. She'd been alone for two weeks. Monk would have expected her to assert she was fine on her own. He liked that she hadn't.

"I will," Dulcie confirmed.

"Then that's the plan for now," Leo replied. "Touch base again tomorrow night? Or sooner if there are any changes?"

Everyone nodded and mumbled their agreement. Monk reached for his phone sitting on the table to end the call, but Kendall's voice stopped him.

"Leo?" she said, sounding far less confident than seconds earlier.

"Yeah?"

"Can you...can you look for my mother? Her name is Cindy Jacobs."

CHAPTER NINETEEN

Helia watched Dulcie and Kendall head upstairs to bed—Kendall to her third-floor nest and Dulcie to a room on the second floor Kendall told him he should pick. Apparently, it had a suit of armor and peekaboo windows that made it feel like a fairy tale and was sure to inspire interesting dreams.

Leaving her and Collin in the tasting room with the Christmas tree still lit up and the fire dwindling.

"Where do you want me?" she asked. The heated look Collin shot her told her she might have chosen her words better. But in a very Collin way, he didn't follow through.

"You can sleep in my old room. It's already made up," he said. "I don't know about the others."

"I can sleep somewhere else. I've made a bed or a thousand in my time."

His short strands of brown hair swayed as he shook his head. His beard hid his sharp cheekbones and full lips, though it highlighted his rich dark eyes—not a man who'd stop traffic, but one who'd garner a second look. Still, it had never been his looks she'd been attracted to. They didn't hurt, that was for sure. But despite his hardened body, his toned and inked arms, and the lethal way he moved earlier that night as he searched her house, he possessed a softness to him. Something gentle and...*childlike* wasn't the right word, not by a long shot, but something inherently *kind*. He'd been her best friend before she'd fallen in love with him. Now, standing here, watching him watch her, she wondered if she ever fell out.

Their lives had changed and gone in different directions. Hell, she'd married and divorced. But from the moment she'd seen him standing on the stoop of the castle, staring at the security keypad, he slid right back into her life as if he'd never been gone.

"You're thinking awfully hard over there," Collin said, his voice a low rumble in the quiet room.

"Is it normal that it feels like the past seventeen years never happened?" She paused. "No, that's not right. The past seventeen years definitely happened. And much of it has been good —for both of us. But it hit me that you've slipped back into my life, not as if you'd never been missing, but..." She inhaled, then let the breath out slowly. "I don't know what I'm trying to say. I guess, well, until a few days ago, we hadn't spoken in years, but it doesn't *feel* that way. It feels like you've always been there. That *we've* always been there. Even when we haven't."

Collin tipped his head and studied her.

"I guess it's one of those friendships that we pick up where we left off?" she continued. "Only that doesn't seem right either." And it didn't. They were both different people than they'd been as teenagers. And yet... She took a deep breath, remembering the kiss, the way he reached for her hand, the scorching looks he sent her. She didn't think too much about the words that came out next. "Now that you're back, I can't imagine you not being a part of my life again, but it's almost...

suspicious how *natural* it feels. And I can't tell if that's because of who we were to each other, or if it's because of who we *should be* to each other."

His nearly black gaze hadn't shifted so much as a millimeter.

"I freaked you out, didn't I?" she asked, forcing a tiny smile.

"You didn't freak me out."

Her eyes searched his.

"You're braver than I am," he said.

She scoffed quietly. "Says the man who hunted terrorists and really, really bad guys. And gals," she said, repeating his words from earlier.

The left side of his mouth ticked up into the ghost of a smile. "I don't know," he said. Now she cocked her head in question. "I don't know the answer to the question you asked. Is it what we were or what we should be that makes this"—he waved between them—"seem so easy? So right?" He hesitated. "I trusted you back then in a way I trusted no one else. And despite the years and lives we've led between then and now, that trust is still there. I don't understand it, I don't know why. I only know that it is."

"And that makes you suspicious, too," she said.

He nodded. "Of me, though. Not of you," he clarified. He opened his mouth, shut it, then opened it again. "Our past, the present, and any potential future is all twisted up inside me. And my need, my confusion, my...circumstances feel like a burden you shouldn't carry."

Her brows dropped. "Burden?"

He dipped his head and ran his fingers through his hair as he turned toward the fire. She couldn't tell if he was thinking or opting not to answer, so she waited. A few minutes passed before he jammed his hands on his hips and lowered his head.

His shoulders rose on an inhale and his head lifted, though he didn't turn toward her.

"You are the only woman, only person, I've ever trusted with every part of me. With the parts of me that my father and his fucked-up life stole." He paused. "That's a weight I don't want to put on you."

She understood the words, but it took a moment for the meaning to sink in. When it did, disbelief, pain, and anger tore through her. Anger at Roger and everything he'd done to his son, pain on Collin's behalf for what he'd experienced, for the betrayal of his parent. And disbelief that...

"I'm the only woman you've ever trusted enough to be intimate with," she said, still processing that reality as the words came out.

A log shifted in the fireplace; Collin inhaled. A beat later, he faced her, a sad smile playing on his lips. "The nickname Monk didn't come from nowhere."

Her heart shattered for him.

"While I was in the military, I moved around a lot, deployed, all those things. It didn't leave a lot of opportunity to build the kind of trust I apparently need. And by the time we settled in Mystery Lake, I'd sort of gotten used to it not being a part of my life, I guess. I mean, I've been with women before. It wasn't like I never hooked up. But..."

"But you didn't let them touch you, please you," she said. As teenagers, he'd always focused more on her pleasure than his. She'd appreciated it, of course, but she'd wanted him to experience the same. They'd been together months before he let her touch him, let her take him in her hand, in her mouth, then eventually into her body.

He didn't so much nod as sort of bob his head at her comment.

She needed time to let what he'd told her sink in, but she didn't hold back asking, "Why would that be a burden to me?"

"You don't think carrying the weight of my seventeen years of celibacy would be a burden?" he asked, crossing his arms. "Or the fact that you're the only woman in my life who seems to be able to fill that need?" He paused, his chest rising and falling in rapid, but smooth, breaths. "My insecurities, my past, my scars...they're mine to carry, Helia, not yours. And no, I don't think it's fair to ask you to hold them, too."

The decision not to argue with him came easily. His reasoning might be grounded in truth, but it was flawed in execution. He wouldn't hear that now, though, if she pointed it out. If she pointed out that her choices were her own, and what she should or shouldn't carry, her decision.

No, instead, she focused on the man in front of her. The man whose shoulders were so tense he probably had the beginnings of a headache. The man whose arms were crossed, not in defiance but in protection. The man who stood rigid and still, waiting for a battle.

Well, he wasn't going to get one from her.

She crossed the short distance between them, his eyes tracking her every step. Reaching up with both hands, she gently pulled his free from where they'd been tucked under his elbows. Closing that final distance between them, she pressed her body to his, resting her cheek on his chest and wrapping her arms around his waist.

She didn't have any answers as to whether they would or should become anything more than friends. But if anyone needed a hug, it was Collin. Collin and every facet he held inside him—the scarred boy, the fierce soldier, the friend, the brother, the man.

"Helia," he said, his voice a harsh, cracked whisper.

"Shut up and hug me back," she mumbled.

Because he was the person she knew him to be, he didn't disappoint. Slowly, his arms lifted from his sides and wrapped around her. A beat later, his cheek rested on the top of her hair.

"This is a mistake," he murmured as his arms tightened.

"Yeah, you really seem to regret it," she replied. The swat on her butt surprised a laugh from her.

"Smart-ass," he said before brushing a kiss on the crown of her head, his hand lingering on the curve of her behind.

"Collin?"

"Yeah."

"You don't need me."

He pulled her tight against his body, the bulge in his jeans pressing into her belly. "You sure about that?"

She was tempted to play along, but what she had to say was important. "I understand what you're saying, that when someone needs someone else, that can be a weight to carry, maybe even a burden. But you *don't* need me. In the same way that I don't need you. We've lived seventeen years of our lives apart. We've built businesses, have our families. We've *lived*." She pulled back enough to look him in the eye. When his gaze met hers, she continued. "We did all that without each other." She paused. "But I'm telling you now, and you need to respect what I'm saying, it's okay to *want* me."

He stared at her for a long moment. "Wanting you isn't the issue."

She rolled her eyes. "I didn't mean that in a physical way. Well, not entirely."

"Neither did I."

She held his gaze. "Then what is?"

"Keeping you."

"I don't understand." It seemed like she *should* understand, but she didn't. Maybe because he'd never really lost her in the first place, although granted, he may not know that.

"Aside from my obvious issues, your life is here. You and your parents have built an amazing business. Mine is in Mystery Lake."

"Where you and your family have built your own businesses," she finished. He'd never live in Napa Valley again, not only because his family was in Mystery Lake, but because of the memories.

Deep inside, she'd always known that. It was why she'd been able to let him go the first time, though it hadn't been easy. He'd changed in the seventeen years he'd been gone, but she'd still never ask him to live day in and day out with those reminders. And she'd never considered leaving. Not that she wouldn't, only that she never had.

All these thoughts were putting the cart before the horse, but she understood why Collin raised the issue. Parting as kids, with their whole lives ahead of them, was one thing. But as adults—adults who knew more about life, themselves, what they valued, and who they wanted—it was an entirely different thing. Put in that light, maybe starting something without having *some* idea of whether it could work wasn't the best idea.

Then again, the past week of surprises had reminded her that life was short and often unpredictable. She didn't discount his concerns, but did they really know what would happen in the next year, month, week, or even minute? She had no desire to set them up for heartbreak, but passing up what could be an amazing experience because of how a future might or might not unfold didn't seem like a great idea either.

Resigned to not having an answer tonight, she tucked her head against his chest again. Again, his hold tightened. "Come sleep with me," she said. His body jerked against hers. "Just sleep," she continued. "We've both said a lot of things tonight that bear some thought. But my house was broken into, a dead man left ten minutes from my door, an ex-boyfriend murdered, and I found out that some crazy concoction of drugs might be making its way through the valley and that Roger might have been poisoned. I'm not super upset about the latter, but it would be nice to fall asleep with your arms anchoring me to something good."

Under her ear, his heart rate increased. Not a rapid beat, but a steady, heavy thud. "We might regret it."

"We might not," she countered.

Another log shifted in the fire, and the ambient light dimmed as it rolled against the back of the hearth.

A heavy sigh ruffled the top of her hair. "Let's head to bed, then."

She knew better than to say any more. Stepping back, she took his hand and let him lead her wherever he intended to go, likely to his old room.

Grabbing her bag as they passed, he ushered her toward the back stairs. Two floors later, they entered the south tower —a rounded room dominated by a spiral staircase carved into the stone, a massive four-poster bed, and a gorgeous armoire. To her right, a door led to a bathroom. A duffel, presumably Collin's, sat on the bed.

She took her bag and headed into the bathroom. Ten minutes later, she emerged with her face washed and moisturized and her teeth clean, wearing her favorite pajamas—drawstring pants and a button-up long-sleeve top in the softest bamboo. She didn't make a point of looking good while she slept, but the sage-green of the material went well with her eyes.

Collin's gaze slid over her before he grabbed his stuff and disappeared into the bathroom.

Throwing back the comforter, Helia climbed into bed, literally. She wasn't short, but damn, that bed needed stairs. Loosening the blankets as she moved, she scooted over, making room for Collin closer to the door.

She had her head nestled in a comfy pillow when the bathroom door opened and he stepped out wearing boxer briefs and a T-shirt. She didn't hide her appreciation.

He paused, backlit by the bathroom light, his eyes flickering over her tucked into bed. His chest rose on a deep inhale, as if bracing himself, then he flicked the bathroom light off. His feet were silent on the stone floor, and she startled when the bed shifted as he joined her.

"It's me," he said.

"This place is very gothic."

He chuckled as he settled beside her. "You have no idea."

She'd ask him about that later, but for now, she wanted to curl up next to this blast furnace of a man. Once he settled, she scooted over and nudged her way under his arm, throwing one of hers over his belly and sliding a leg on top of his thigh.

Another sigh.

"Don't be alarmed if, well, certain parts of my body don't get the message that this is about sleeping."

She snorted. "I'm thirty-five, Collin. I'm well aware of how a man's body can react of its own accord. Now wrap your arm around me."

He hesitated, then shifted, his arm banding behind her back, holding her to him. She settled her head in the dip of his shoulder below the collarbone, then smiled when his lips brushed the top of her hair.

"Now relax," she said.

"Bossy," he muttered, but she heard the affection in his voice.

"Leadership qualities," she replied.

"Ahh, Helia, what are we going to do?" he whispered. The last words she heard before drifting off to sleep.

CHAPTER TWENTY

S hards of panic sliced through Monk, dragging him from sleep and into confusion. His heart raced; a thousand needles pricked his skin as his pores expanded. Sweat coated his body, and his chest jerked as he gulped for air.

"It's okay," he heard. Only it wasn't. It was anything but okay. Roger was back. He was going to drag him down to the dungeon and...and...

"Collin." A soft voice, a female voice, cut through the panic. A lighthouse he could make out but not see clearly.

"Collin." A small hand settled over his heart. "You're okay. You're okay."

The hand shifted, sliding up over his neck, his jaw, then into his hair. Gentle. Soothing.

"Open your eyes," she said.

Answering the siren's call, he did as asked, blinking against a sudden onslaught of light.

A curtain of honey-gold hair brushed against his shoulder. Hazel eyes hovered over him. "Helia?"

His heart tripped again as someone knocked on the door.

He jerked his attention to the solid wood, calculating how to get Helia safely away from Roger.

"It's Dulcie," she said, her voice soft but firm.

Dulcie.

Helia continued stroking her fingers through his hair as reality reasserted its place in his mind. He wasn't a thirteen-year-old boy. Roger was dead. Helia was beside him. His brother, his family, was knocking. Not Roger.

Another knock.

"Coming," Monk said, sitting up. The move dislodged Helia's hand, but he grabbed it and set a kiss on her palm before sliding off the stupidly tall bed.

"You okay?" Dulcie asked when he cracked the door open.

Monk ran a hand over his face and through his hair. "A bad memory. I'm good."

Dulcie's dark eyes studied him, then, either happy with what he saw or willing to let it go, he spoke. "There are two women who came through the gates of Bacco."

Fog still clouded his mind, and it took him a few seconds to remember that while he'd changed the house security code, he hadn't changed the one for the gate. Alessio and the field workers needed access, even during the month off, and leaving the gate as-is had seemed easier.

"Any idea who?" Another sign that his mind hadn't cleared. How the hell would Dulcie know anyone from Napa other than those currently in the castle?

Dulcie shook his head. "One is an older woman, big black-rimmed glasses. Reminds me a little of Edna from *The Incredibles* but with white-blond hair."

"That's Gretchen," Helia said, coming to stand behind him.

Dulcie's gaze darted over his shoulder, more curious than surprised at her appearance.

"The business manager?" Monk asked, recalling the name he'd seen in the papers the lawyer had forwarded him.

Helia nodded. "The CEO, really, in all but name."

Monk nodded. "What about the other?"

Dulcie tipped his head. "Younger woman, maybe early forties. Has hair like Helia's." Both men looked at her.

"Was she driving a Lexus SUV? Not the huge one, but the midsize one? Blue?" Dulcie nodded. "That's Kelly Carter. The social media manager Greg mentioned the other day."

The last thing he wanted to do after his little trip down PTSD alley was deal with Bacco business. Although maybe the wake-up call would do him good.

"Where's Kendall?" he asked.

"Staying out of sight. She's in her room with her headphones on. Said she had some schoolwork to finish. She'll probably be done with college by New Year's."

Monk smiled at that. "Can you hold them off for five minutes?" Dulcie nodded and headed toward the stairs as Monk shut the door.

"Need anything?" Helia asked as he took a deep breath.

"A quick shower, a cup of coffee, and a chance to let my brain catch up?"

Smiling, she brushed her fingers through his hair again. "Can't help with the first or the last, but I can make you a cup of coffee while you shower?"

An image of them showering together took hold, but he forced it away. "Thank you," he said, "I'd appreciate it." Her eyes held his, and he flexed his fingers to keep from reaching for her.

"Thank you," he said again. Then, giving up the ghost, he slid his hands into her hair and kissed her forehead. The pull to stay connected to her, touching her, sank deep into his body, but his phone dinged with a security alert from one of the cameras. Reluctantly, he let her go and strode toward the shower, keeping his steps steady so as not to be tempted to return to her.

Seven minutes later, he stepped onto the porch to find Dulcie chatting with the two women. Two sets of curious eyes landed on him. One, bright blue, rimmed by a pair of thick black glasses, assessed him. The other, a light brown pair, raked over his body with an interest he didn't welcome.

"You don't look like your father," the older woman, Gretchen, said.

"Thank god. I'd hate to wake up every morning and see that face in the mirror." The words might sound like a jest, but judging by the way Gretchen's eyes narrowed, she knew it wasn't. And she agreed. "Collin Wilde," he said, holding out his hand.

"Gretchen Roan," she replied, taking his. "Business manager at Bacco. I ran into Clyde at the memorial, and he said you were here. Thought I'd come introduce myself." Clyde was his father's lawyer, and Monk suspected she wanted more than to introduce herself.

"Why don't you head into your office, and I'll join you in a minute," he replied.

She gave a curt nod, then passed Dulcie on her way in. With a nod to Monk, he turned and followed her. Keeping both women outside, especially with the temperatures hovering in the high thirties, might seem rude, but he wasn't ready for people to start thinking they were welcome at the castle.

And he didn't like the way Kelly eyed him and Dulcie. Especially not during what he assumed was a professional visit.

When the door closed behind his brother and Gretchen, she shifted her attention to him. She didn't bother hiding her speculation or interest.

"Two of you here. I didn't know Helia had it in her. Can't hardly blame her, though," she said, waggling her eyebrows.

Monk straightened, crossing his arms and fixing Kelly with a hard look at her implication. Neither the content nor the timing even remotely appropriate.

"Can I help you, Ms....?"

"Call me Kelly," she said, flashing him a smile he'd seen on dozens of women looking to add a notch to their bedpost. Between that look and her comment about Helia, it cost her a client. The Falcons had plenty of experience with web design and social media; they didn't need her.

He stared, waiting to see what she'd say. "I'm the social media manager for Bacco," she started. "You've probably heard of me." When he didn't respond, she continued. "Anyway, Trish Peterson mentioned you were here. You met her a few nights ago with Helia at that taco place in town." Again, he didn't respond. Her brows dipped, but she carried on. "I thought I'd stop by and see if you were planning to reopen the tasting room for the holidays and discuss what updates we should publish."

He shook his head. "No updates. The tasting room will stay closed until mid-January as planned." He wanted to change the login and passwords to the backend of the site before firing her.

She frowned. "This is a big time of year. You're losing business."

It wasn't, not really. Sure, the valley saw a bump in tourism the few weeks around Christmas and New Year's when folks took vacations, but it was hardly booming. Clyde had sent him enough of the financials for him to figure that out.

"The winery can afford it," he replied. Besides, he wasn't about to call employees back in. By now, several probably had other temp jobs for the month, or had planned vacations, or were simply enjoying the downtime.

"Really, you're missing out. You could throw an impromptu New Year's party or celebrate your dad's life with some big event. He would have liked that. Would have liked people raising a glass or ten in his name."

If he hadn't already decided to fire her, the familiar way she spoke about Roger would have made the decision for him.

"Not interested. I'll let you know if anything comes up that needs your attention," he said, setting his hand on the door.

"How about a cup of coffee, and we can discuss some spring changes?" She inched closer.

He narrowed his eyes. She stepped back.

"Right," she said. "Do you mind if I peek into the other office? Not Gretchen's but the one beside it? I was here a few days before your dad died, and I think my earbuds fell out of my purse. Lipstick, or my compact, I wouldn't care, but they're the expensive ones. I wasn't expecting anyone to be here and had resigned myself to waiting a month, but then I heard about you."

"I'll look and let you know if I find them." No way in hell was he going to allow her inside.

"They're small. You might miss them."

"I'm thorough," he replied, opening the door. "I'll let you know." He stepped inside, shutting the door with a definitive click. Turning his back on her, he pulled out his phone as he walked toward Gretchen's office. A fish-eye view of Kelly lingering on the porch filled his screen through the security app, her narrowed eyes and tight jaw absent any sort of come-hither look.

He paused at the office door, wanting to make sure she left. Ten seconds passed before she stomped off the porch.

"I'll make sure she leaves," Dulcie said, stepping out of the business office. "You should go in and talk to Gretchen. I think you're going to need her."

With that cryptic statement, he entered the room to find her sitting behind the desk, computer booted up, her glasses perched on the top of her head, and her body leaning forward.

"What do you know about your father?" she asked, not looking up.

"Nothing in the past seventeen years. More than I ever wanted to in the eighteen prior to that."

She sat back, assessing him again. "I looked into you when I learned Roger had a son." He decided it was prudent to stay silent. "You and your friends run quite a few businesses."

"Seven." He was proud of what they'd built.

"What's your employee turnover?"

He blinked. Not a question he expected. "Next to none, considering the business models."

"And considering you help people escape abusive situations and, if they want, give them jobs until they feel comfortable moving on?"

He sat. "You've done your homework." The work he and his brothers did to help people who needed a hand wasn't common knowledge.

"Petra Green."

He cocked his head.

"She's my niece."

He sat back. "Lived in Bend, Oregon, and married to a man who used both her and their son as his punching bag." Gretchen nodded. "That was a bad one."

"It was. Could have been worse without your help, though," she said. "She told me the names of the men who helped her. I remembered yours because of the last name. But as you can imagine, thinking someone like you could come from someone like Roger? It was a stretch, so I let it go until Clyde mentioned you at the service."

"You seem to hold the same opinion of my father as I do. What's made you stay?" He didn't mean to sound suspicious, but hell, he was.

She chuckled and leaned forward again, eyes on her computer. "Bacco employees. Twenty-two full-time and forty-five part-timers, mostly the field workers. I didn't know what kind of man he was when I hired on. By the time I figured it out, those people were family to me. Your father and I came to an agreement. He'd leave me to run the business as I saw fit so long as his bank account stayed where he expected."

Monk doubted she knew the full scope of how depraved Roger Wilde was, but he wasn't going to ask. "I saw the financials. Even with whatever cash you transferred to my dad, the winery is doing exceptionally well."

She nodded. "Fair wages, good benefits—they inspire loyalty. In the long run, loyalty is a good investment."

"I'm surprised Alessio hasn't gone off and started something of his own. By this point, he must have a following. One unconnected to the Wilde name."

"With what land? He makes a good salary. One of the best in the valley, but it's not enough to buy here."

Monk conceded that point even as an idea started forming. He needed to sort out things with Helia and the murders first, though. "Did you come in today to take my measure?"

She inclined her head. "More to confirm my instinct. So far, you're not disappointing."

"But the day is young," he said with a smile.

She grinned back. She wasn't old, maybe her mid-sixties, but the smile made her look a decade younger.

"So," she said, sitting back. "Have you found your father's drug stash?"

CHAPTER TWENTY-ONE

Monk stilled. Had his gut been wrong? How else would Gretchen know about the drugs? He doubted Roger ever bandied it about. Was she part of that whole scene?

"Drugs?" he said.

She sat back again, a look of empathy washing through her eyes. "You and your father may not have been close, but I still hate to tell you this. Over the past year, it's become clearer and clearer that he was using something. What, I don't know, but it wasn't recreational marijuana. Based on his manic behavior, I'd guess an upper of some sort." She paused, her gaze drifting to the window. She sighed. "I have no idea what you plan to do with this place, but I'd hate for someone to find his stash, whatever it was, and end up in a bad situation. I hear that it only takes one use for a person to get addicted to some drugs."

He studied her, his eyes—and his scientific Spidey sense—searching for any signs of deception. But he only saw a vague expression of sorrow. As if saddened by the impact drugs could have on people.

"Coffee," Helia said, entering the room with Dulcie on her heels. She handed him a steaming cup with the perfect amount of milk while Dulcie passed one to Gretchen.

"Where's Kelly? Dulcie said she was here," Helia asked, parking herself on the arm of his chair.

"She needed to leave," Monk replied. Dulcie arched a brow but took a sip of coffee rather than comment.

Only Helia noticed. "What was that look for?"

"There was no look," Monk replied.

Keeping his eyes fixed on his coffee didn't keep him from feeling the weight of Helia's stare. He'd never had a mom, but he suspected this was what a "mom stare" felt like.

Dulcie cleared his throat. "Monk told her to leave. She was eye-fucking him, and he didn't like it."

Silence.

"Bitch," Gretchen muttered at the same time Helia said, "Well, can't say I blame her."

All three turned to Helia. Her eyes skittered around the room, then she blushed, a hint of pink beneath her honey skin tone. "Fine," she huffed. "I'm not going to go so far as to say what Gretchen said. It's not as if Kelly knows she's encroaching on my territory. But I will concede it's inappropriate as I'm guessing she came by for professional reasons."

Monk fought a smile at her possessive statement. From any other woman, he would have hated it, but an odd sense of pride rolled up in a warm hug wrapped around him at her words.

"She also implied that you were having a threesome with me and Monk," Dulcie added.

Helia choked on her coffee. "That bitch!"

Gretchen cackled, Monk chuckled. Dulcie always did have the ears of a bat. That fucker could hear a sand snake slithering across a dune from half a mile away.

"I hope you weren't friends," Monk said.

Helia narrowed her eyes. "We didn't get together and braid each other's hair, but we were friendly acquaintances. You know how small the valley is for us business owners. And it's not that I have anything against people who do that—so long as it's consensual—but implying that about me to someone she doesn't know? And during a professional visit? What if you'd been a conservative client? She could have cost me business."

"Well, you're better off without her as far as I'm concerned," Gretchen said. "Never did like her. She and Roger were friendly—not in *that* sense, but as if they had a secret club only the cool kids got invited to. I tried to change over to Neil Vonhersh for our marketing—you know him?" she asked, looking at Helia, who nodded. "Well, Roger wasn't having any of that."

"You have my permission to switch," Monk said. "But let's change the login and password to the site. I want her locked out before she learns her services are no longer required."

"Give me five minutes and it will be done," Gretchen said.

"In the meantime, I need to head home," Helia said. "We have an event tonight and two tomorrow." She paused, a flicker of a smile appearing. "And then we shut down for two weeks."

"You don't host New Year's events?" Monk asked, somewhat surprised.

She shook her head. "They can be profitable, but they are also a huge hassle. People drink too much, do stupid things. We decided a few years ago that they weren't worth it."

Visions of taking her to Mystery Lake danced in his head like the proverbial sugarplums, but he shut the thoughts down. She wouldn't want to leave her family for the holidays.

"I'll drive you home," he said, rising from his seat as Gretchen typed away.

"Why don't I do that, and you can stay and talk with Gretchen," Dulcie offered. "You probably have a few things to catch up on."

Monk caught and held Dulcie's eye. He hadn't missed Gretchen's comments about Kelly. Was she the woman Kendall heard talking the day Roger died? If she and Roger were as close as Gretchen suggested, she would have had plenty of time to poison him. Which meant Monk needed to take a closer look at her.

"My car is here, remember," Helia said. "My coat's upstairs, though."

"I'd rather Dulcie drive you. Then he can walk back," Monk replied. Her eyes held his, bounced to Dulcie, then landed back on him. Slowly, she nodded.

He let out a breath and set a hand on her hip. "I'll head up with you. I want to grab something warmer, too." He didn't, but he wanted time alone with her before she disappeared for the day.

Dulcie shook his head and grinned at his less-than-subtle subterfuge. Even Gretchen's lips tweaked into a tiny smile. He ignored them both and ushered Helia out. He didn't know what he wanted to say or why it felt important to have a few minutes with her, but none of that mattered when he closed the bedroom door and a beat later found his back against it and Helia's body pressed to his.

"I wish I didn't have to go to work today," she said, her hands on his chest.

He speared his fingers through her hair, resting the pads of his palms against her jaw. He wished she didn't have to go, too. "Will you come back tonight?" he asked.

"That depends," she said.

"On?" he asked, his eyes locked on her hazel ones, now more green than brown.

"Give me a good reason."

He didn't pretend not to know what she meant, and the conflict that roared to life inside him would have brought him to his knees had he not been pressed against the door.

Did he want to kiss her? Desperately. Did it terrify him? Completely. Not because he hadn't kissed other women, but because this was Helia. And because he wasn't sure he'd ever be able to let her go again if he did. Visions of a life with her, one filled with laughter and love and, most of all, trust, teased his heart and mind. In the deepest, darkest parts of him, he wanted it all. He wanted it all and more. But the boy he'd never been able to truly leave behind—the one who'd been used, abused, and betrayed—still whispered in his ear. Still told him there was much to be afraid of.

"Collin?"

His gaze had drifted to the floor, and he looked up.

"Kiss me," she said. He hesitated. A look of understanding flashed in her eyes. He thought she might step away, and panic had him tightening his hold on her. Her eyes softened. "Take the leap, Collin. It's just you and me, and you know I'm not going to let you fall. Not alone, anyway."

Slowly, like a wisp seeping into his psyche and taking shape, he realized this moment wasn't about the future. It wasn't about what he and Helia might become or what the next week or year might hold. It was about the past. About reassuring that young boy that people *could* be trusted. That *he* could be trusted to take back what had been stolen from him so long ago.

Helia must have seen the revelation in his eyes, because a flicker of anticipation lit hers, and her fingers curled in his chest. Lowering his head, he brushed his lips against hers. The touch wasn't tentative, but it was new. A connection he wanted to draw out, absorb, savor.

Again, his lips slid over hers as she lifted her face, inviting him to take and give. She held him close, slipping her hands around his waist, her delicate fingers gripping his sides.

When his tongue touched her lips, she opened. Desire rolled through him, but it didn't take control. Not at first. As the doubts and distrust and pain of his past slid away with each touch of their tongues, it grew stronger, though. Not washing away the past, but quieting it, giving it permission to let go.

Angling his head, he deepened their connection, drawing a sound of need from Helia, triggering a primal need in him. Sliding one hand down the curve of her shoulder, along the arch of her back, it settled on her behind. Shifting his leg between hers, he pulled her body closer, her heat searing his thigh.

"Collin," she said on a strangled whisper as he pulled away, kissing a line down her throat. He rocked her against him, drawing a gasp as her fingers dug into his sides.

The need to hear her come undone tore through him. To see her expression when she came. To have the scent of her arousal surround him.

Gripping her hip, he shifted his thigh, her short gasps telling him the angle and pressure was exactly what she craved.

She muttered his name again, but he covered her mouth with his. He was a man on a mission now. He knew exactly what he wanted and how to get it. Helia would have her reason to come back to the castle, to him, when her workday was done.

Kissing her hard, tasting her with every touch, he rocked against her, his movements quickening with her breath. With two layers of denim between them, he couldn't feel the first flutters of her orgasm, but he could hear them. In her staccato breathing, in the tiny, gasping sounds coming from her throat. And he could feel it in the way her back bowed under his hands, in the way she drew away from his kisses, wholly lost in the feeling taking over her body.

When her head fell back and her eyes fluttered closed, her body going taut under his touch, his own responded. For a split second, embarrassment threatened to douse the heat of the moment, but he let that thought flit away. He let it dissolve into nothing, instead choosing to focus on experiencing this pleasure with Helia.

Sensing his arousal through her own haze of desire, she pressed her core to his thigh, shifting her hip against the zipper of his jeans and the raging erection that fought for release—in every sense—on the other side.

"Fuck, Helia," he muttered, his other hand dropping to her hip to hold her tighter.

"Collin," she responded on a breathy huff that trailed off to a long, low moan as her body tumbled over the edge. The feel of her, the knowledge of the release he'd given her, brought him to his own on a rumbled groan that matched hers.

Holding each other as their bodies came down, he let his head fall against the door as hers came to rest on his chest. Without thought, he lifted a hand to cradle her there, holding her to his heart as their unsteady breathing slowly evened out.

"That was some kiss," she muttered, her lips brushing his shirt and drawing a sated chuckle from him.

"Will you come back tonight?" he asked. He wouldn't presume they'd take things any further than they had, but if she was willing, his mind had already conjured a hundred and one ways to worship her.

"Will you let me touch you? Taste you?"

An obvious answer for most men, but they both knew that in this, he wasn't most men. Still, the thought of her doing to him even a tiny percentage of the things he wanted to do to her had his body coming back to life.

"If that's what you want," he managed to say.

"I definitely want, but do you?"

He pressed his hips against her. "What do you think?"

She chuckled softly, the sound fading to a sated silence as they savored the quiet moment of connection.

Finally, dropping a kiss on her hair, he shifted away, reluctantly separating them. "You need to get to work," he said.

She ran her hands through her mussed locks. "And you need to change your pants."

Again, the thought struck him that he should be embarrassed, but the hot look in Helia's eyes, as if she'd enjoyed sending him over the edge, stopped him. "Thankfully, I have a second pair," he said with a grin. A load of laundry a small price to pay.

She stared at him for several seconds, then, with a shake of her head, she stepped forward and gave him a big smacking kiss. "I'm going to leave *now*. It's not a good idea for me to be in the room when you change your pants. I might get all sorts of ideas that will keep me here, and we both have things to do today." And with that, she nudged him away from the door and stepped out. "I'll tell Gretchen you'll be down in a few," she added over her shoulder as she walked away.

He watched her go until she disappeared down the staircase. Tempted as he was to replay the last fifteen minutes again and again in his head, he shut the door, changed quickly, then started down the stairs only to halt a few steps down, turn around, and head to Kendall's room.

Knowing she probably still wore her headphones, he knocked loudly on the heavy door. A beat passed before she called out for him to come in. He hadn't set foot in the room since he'd been back but wasn't surprised to see it neat as a pin. She'd had enough instability in her life that she was no doubt ready to flee at a moment's notice with everything she owned. He both admired and hated it for her.

"Gretchen Roan is downstairs; she manages Bacco. I didn't get any indications that she's involved with Roger and his life in any way, but I wanted to be sure she's not who you heard the day he died. Would you mind coming downstairs to meet her? Or if you don't want to meet her, you can listen in from the hallway while she and I talk, and you can text me if her voice is familiar?"

Kendall shook her head. "Don't need to. I know it's not her. I heard her here a few times, talking to other staff people before Roger died. I know who she is, and it wasn't her."

Relief lifted a weight from his chest. He was going to need Gretchen's skill and knowledge in the next several months.

He dipped his chin. "Thanks. If you want to come down, feel free. We can tell her you're my niece or sister."

A look flashed in her eyes, but she shook her head. "Thanks, I'm almost done with this module. I hate the subject so want to get it over with."

He grinned at her tone, one of the few times he'd heard her sound like the tweenager she was. "What module?"

"Coding," she replied, making a face. "It's stuff I could do when I was six! It's so boring," she said, drawing out the "so."

"And you can't whiz through it?"

"It's timed!" she said in outrage. "They give you a prompt, then give you ten minutes to do it, but you can't go any faster if you finish early. Can you believe that shit?"

He arched a brow. He'd told her he didn't care too much about the swearing, but the words should be well-timed and -placed rather than gratuitous.

She rolled her eyes and reached for her headphones. "I'll come down when I'm done. Maybe we can search the house. See if we can find any clue as to who poisoned Roger. Or if his murder is connected to Flannery's or Fisher's."

There was something dreadfully wrong with dragging a twelve-year-old into a murder investigation, but once again, he opted to let it slide. If it kept her mind off the fact that her mother hadn't yet returned, he'd call it a win. A dubious one, but a win.

Jogging down the stairs, he found Gretchen where he'd left her, Dulcie and Helia gone. "Any chance you have a copy of Kelly's contract?" he asked.

She gestured to a file on the desk, not lifting her eyes from her screen. "I'm checking inventory, shipments, supplies, that sort of thing. Alessio's been monitoring this season's wine both remotely and in person. The stuff that's already been set aside to age won't be an issue, but he's racking a few varietals. He'll be wrapping that up by the end of January and will need supplies and people."

"Helia pointed Miguel out to me the other day at Guichos," he said, opening the file. "I assume his crew can help?"

Gretchen nodded. "They can. I'll get the supplies ordered, though. I also reconciled the books to date and paid a few bills. You can terminate that contract for convenience at any time," she added, looking up and nodding to the papers in his hands. "I've changed the login and password. Password is ding-dongthewitchisdead." He snorted a laugh. She smiled, then rattled off the new login.

"Want me to call Kelly?" she offered.

"I get the feeling you'd like that," he replied, chuckling.

"Possibly," Gretchen said, holding her hand out for the file.

"Anything you need me to do?" he asked.

She shook her head. "Everything can wait until after the

holidays. You probably want some time to figure out what to do with it all anyway."

"I'll admit, I haven't given it much thought. There have been other things occupying my mind."

"Like the murders and how they seem to be circling around Helia?" He blinked. "Very little goes on in this stretch of the world that I don't know or can't find out about."

"Handy skill."

She bobbed her head. "Mostly. Sometimes it's annoying."

"Do you have any idea why it's circling around Helia?"

She sat back in her chair. "I'm not so sure it's Helia. She isn't the only thing they have in common."

Before he could ask, his phone rang. Glancing at the screen, he rose. "Go ahead and call Kelly. I need to get this, but I'll be back in a few and you can tell me your thoughts."

She nodded as he connected the call, then walked out of her office. "Leo? What'd you find?"

"It's not good, and I think you need to sit down."

CHAPTER TWENTY-TWO

Helia and Dulcie navigated down the Bacco drive in silence. Outward silence, anyway. In Helia's head, her thoughts bounced from what she and Collin had done in his bedroom, to Kelly's weird comments, to picturing Collin changing out of his pants, to the dead body—bodies—hovering on the periphery of her life, to sleeping beside Collin, to wondering why Dulcie hadn't mentioned anything about it. There might have been one or two more thoughts about Kendall, her mom, and what killed Roger Wilde, too.

But mostly she wondered why Dulcie hadn't said anything about finding her in Collin's room. It was possible he was being polite, but when had a group of brothers *ever* been so polite as to not want the deets on their sibling, if for no other reason than to torment them at some later time?

With each quarter mile that ticked by, the tension in her body ratcheted up, waiting for Dulcie to ask something. When the entrance to Sundaram came into view, she couldn't take it anymore.

"I don't think I ever fell out of love with him," she said. "I had to let him go, to move on, when we were kids, but he was always there. Like this foundational thing inside me, grounding me. Not like a cement block tied to my ankle or anything like that. Whatever it is between us hasn't ever held me back from living my life. More like it's been a security blanket. No, that's not right either. It was like he taught me what it meant to be good and what I should expect from myself and the people in my life. He gave me a confidence that burrowed its way into my soul and let me try new things, have adventures, get my heart broken and know that I'd be okay. I don't regret the seventeen years we both went off and lived our lives —he has you all and I have a life I love, too—but coming together now feels right. As if we couldn't have done it before. I don't know if you believe in fate or soulmates or any of those things—hell, I don't know if *I* believe in them, but it feels like this is when we were supposed to come back into each other's lives."

Adrenaline from her rushed explanation tripped through her body, and she forced a deep breath as she waited for Dulcie to respond. Or at least acknowledge what she'd said. They reached the entrance before he obliged her.

"Have you told him any of this?"

She passed through the gate, then stopped. She wasn't quite ready to have her work life intrude on this conversation. "In a way, yes, we've talked about it."

Dulcie's gaze stayed fixed on Sundaram. "Good."

She narrowed her eyes. "Good? That's all you're going to say?"

His lips twitched. "Is there something else I should say? I sure as hell don't want any details about what happened in your room last night."

She blinked. Fair, she wasn't about to give him any, either. "You don't have an opinion on this? He's your brother."

"My opinion doesn't matter. Not at the end of the day. But if you're asking whether I have reservations, there's only one, and it has nothing to do with you as a person."

"Do I want to know? Wait, yes, I do."

He chuckled, then nodded toward Sundaram. "Your life is here and his isn't. It's not good for him to be here, not in my opinion. But I know Monk, and I don't doubt his strength. If he decides to stay, he'll figure it out." He paused. "He's been through enough pain and trauma—we all have—but if that journey has taught us anything, it's that life changes. If we're lucky and work for it, it can change for the good. I think you're good for him."

She studied him, her eyes unexpectedly tearing up. She wouldn't cry; well, maybe she would. Dulcie's words were everything she'd always wanted for Collin. Safety, respect, love, loyalty. His brothers gave him that, and it was all she'd hoped for him.

Throwing her arms around Dulcie, she squeezed. He startled, then wrapped his around her.

"Thank you," she said.

He patted her back much as she supposed he did for his sisters. "For?"

"For being the family he deserved all along."

Dulcie's arms tightened before giving her another pat and shifting back in his seat. "Now that that's out of the way, what's on your agenda for the day? Are you coming back tonight?"

She flashed him a slightly watery smile before continuing toward Sundaram. "I'll be back. We have a dinner event tonight, then a brunch and dinner tomorrow. After that, we're done for the season." The tires crunched on the packed gravel as she crossed the courtyard toward her house. She was about to tell Dulcie what time she'd be back when two figures emerged from the kitchen. She slowed and frowned.

"What?" Dulcie demanded.

"Nothing bad," she assured him. "Just weird," she added, rolling down her window. "Trish," she called out.

The woman jerked her head around, then approached with a smile. "Helia, it's good to see you." Her attention shifted to Dulcie. "And you, too."

Helia's hackles rose at the purr in Trish's tone. She didn't begrudge Dulcie the admiration, but honestly, between Trish and Kelly, didn't these people know the difference between personal and professional?

"What are you doing here?" she asked, her gaze shifting between Trish and Greg, who'd followed.

Trish waved a hand. "You mentioned that Sundaram sometimes imports food for events. I'm considering a potential business model to serve smaller, independent places."

"New business model?" she asked.

Trish nodded. "We all know the major importers in the area, but I'm exploring whether there's a market for smaller shipments of more unusual foods or from smaller farmers who don't have the inventory to do business with the big dogs. Kind of building on the idea of farm to fork, but cross-border."

That idea actually sounded interesting. A lot of restaurants would get on board with that kind of model, if for no other reason than to expand their own reputation for supporting small businesses.

"And consolidating the smaller businesses like ours helps make the import part a little more feasible," she said. Both Trish and Greg nodded. "Well, you're in good hands." She gestured to Greg, who smiled back. "I'm going to check in with Akin before seeing what help is needed for tonight."

Greg and Trish moved off, toward Trish's car. By the time Helia parked and started walking to the kitchen, she'd gone. "You don't have to stay, you know," she said to Dulcie.

"I'll head back once you're settled in your office," he replied. Not feeling the need to argue, she continued to the kitchen.

"Akin!" she called with a smile. The chef's gaze flickered up from a glass pan that held ciabatta dough, his fingers pressed gently into the top.

"*Arabinrin kekere*," he called back with a slashing smile.

"Yoruba for 'little sister,'" she said to Dulcie. "How is it going? Need anything?"

Akin shook his head. "We're representing seven cultures tonight—each food from a different country. I think they will be pleased," he said, referring to their clients.

"Of course they will, because everything you make is delicious," she said, earning her another smile.

"You hear Trish's idea?" she asked, picking up a carrot and taking a bite.

Akin's focus fell back to the pan. There were eight more lined up waiting for his final magic. His head bobbed. "More than one restaurant has been 'made' by finding that one unique thing to add to their menu. It's not a bad idea if she can pull it off."

"Are you interested?" she asked, leaning her hip against the counter. Dulcie propped his shoulder against the wall opposite, his eyes scanning the space.

Akin lifted a shoulder. "We're not a restaurant. Our reputation is built on everything Sundaram does, not only the food. It could be useful to us if we have a need for a unique product, but on a day-to-day basis, well, we shall see."

She considered his answer. They didn't need to brainstorm at the moment, though, so she pushed off the counter. "I'll be in my office. Text if you need anything," she said.

"I always do, *adunni mi*," he replied, already working on the next two pans.

"What did those last words mean?" Dulcie asked when they exited the kitchen.

"Sweetness, or something like that," she replied as they made their way across the courtyard to the main building.

"How long has he worked here?"

"Eight years, and we adore him," she answered. "Thankfully, he likes us, too. Likes that his days are different and he doesn't have to prepare the same menu over and over again."

"What about Greg?"

"He came not long after Akin. He wanted to leave San Francisco, where he worked in one of the high-volume, but high-quality, tourist restaurants. We needed someone to take over kitchen management. He doesn't make nearly as much with us, but he has a sane lifestyle."

"I can understand the draw of that," Dulcie said as his phone dinged. He pulled it from his pocket as they walked, then came to an abrupt halt.

"What?" Helia asked, her heart rate spiking. Dulcie's expression had gone disturbingly blank as he read the message.

He hesitated, then shook his head. "Not sure. Monk asked me to head back as soon as you were settled."

Her stomach pitched. "Why?"

Dulcie shook his head again, adding in a shrug.

"Go," she said. "I'm fine. I have twenty more feet to walk. But promise you'll text if something's wrong. Or if Leo's found anything. I'll be busy much of the day, but I still want to know."

He didn't hesitate to reassure her before jogging toward the vineyard. She wondered what Collin needed him for as his figure disappeared between the vines. As tempting as it was, though, she decided not to let her thoughts travel down dark rabbit holes. If something life-threatening had happened, he would have called.

Thinking of Collin, she switched directions and headed toward the event space. She had paperwork to do, but the thought of sitting at a desk made her antsy. She needed to keep her body occupied as she finally gave herself permission to pick apart the conversation she'd had with him the night before.

She understood his concern; his past and the way it impacted him weren't trivial concerns. But she felt humbled by his trust, by the role she played in his life. Not weighed down by it. And being the recipient of, and participant in, his enthusiastic "catch-up" period, well, it made her body tingle with anticipation in a way it shouldn't during the middle of the workday.

On the other hand, it tore at her soul that because of Roger, Collin had never experienced true intimacy. Not with anyone other than her, and they'd been little more than kids at the time.

"Helia?"

Her mother stood in the doorway, vase of flowers in hand, staring at her.

"Sorry, woolgathering," she said.

Her mom raised an eyebrow. "Anything to do with the reemergence of Collin?"

Yes, but she wasn't about to go into details. She and her mom were close, but no way was Helia going to share anything about the intimacies, physical or otherwise, that she'd experienced in the past eighteen hours.

"More about the murders," she replied.

"And your house," Vanessa added, concern settling in her expression. She'd texted her parents after she'd returned to the castle last night to tell them what had happened. They'd wanted her to come home but let it go when Collin and Dulcie promised to install a security system at her place.

"And my house," she conceded.

Her mother stared at her, then lifted the vase. "Help me with the finishing touches?"

"Of course," she said.

They entered the medium-sized dining room, already filled with winter greens and flowers. The tablecloth sat in a roll on the dining table, along with runners, and she headed for these first. The china and glassware lay stacked on a sideboard; they'd get to that next.

"What are you thinking about the murders?" her mom asked, setting the tall vase on a pedestal in the corner before standing back and eyeing it.

"It feels like I'm involved in a way I shouldn't be. First, they question me about Justin's murder because they found some weird letter, then Carter called last night to ask me about Kurt because someone said they saw the two of us together. I didn't know anything about the letter until they showed me, and I definitely wasn't with Kurt, so why focus on me? Or do I feel targeted because I've never been in this situation, when really this is all normal? Maybe they're out there questioning lots of people and I'm just not seeing the bigger picture." As she spoke, she unrolled the linen tablecloth. The white material with an embroidered frame of red holly berries making the room instantly more festive.

"I'm sure they're questioning a lot of people," her mom replied, straightening the other side of the tablecloth. "I don't like that they've come to you more than once, but since the idea of you being even remotely involved in either murder is ludicrous—not to mention your house being broken into—it makes me ask why."

Helia made a face. "That's exactly what I'm doing, asking why me?"

Her mom leveled her with a mom look. "I don't mean why *you*, but *why* you."

Helia paused, the linen fresh and crisp between her fingers. "I have to admit, you've lost me, Mom."

Vanessa chuckled. "Your life isn't small, dear daughter. In addition to everything you do at Sundaram, you're involved in the chamber of commerce, the tourism board, the animal shelter, and a few other groups." Another mom look came her way. For years, her parents had voiced their concern about the number of things she committed her time to. Not because the commitments pulled her away from Sundaram, but because they worried she'd stretch herself too thin.

That conversation was one for another day, though—or not—and Helia focused on what her mom meant. As the table slowly morphed into a holiday canvas waiting to be adorned, it clicked.

"You think Justin and Kurt might have some connection we don't know about, but whatever it is, I'm connected to it, too? Like maybe one of the organizations I'm involved in?"

"It only makes sense, doesn't it? Not that any of this makes sense," she said, smoothing out the cloth.

"It does make sense, actually."

Her mom flashed a wry grin. "Don't sound so surprised."

Helia laughed. "You're a constant source of surprises, Mom." She paused, eyeing the runners. Her mom had pulled three out, one a deep gold, one an elegant red with white tallow berries on it, the opposite of the tablecloth, and the third a rich dark forest green.

"Which runner?" she asked her mom, who had a better eye for decor than she.

"Gold," her mom replied. "With the dishware Akin chose and the decorations, the gold will even out the colors better."

She set the other two aside and together, they rolled the runner open. "It doesn't explain the letter or false sighting, but if you're right about Kurt and Justin being connected to an organization I'm involved in, it would explain why my name keeps cropping up."

"Not that I want you putting your nose anywhere dangerous, but I wonder what Kurt and Justin have in common? They're in different, though admittedly adjacent, lines of business, and I wouldn't have thought they were friends. But I certainly don't—didn't—know either well enough to say."

"Maybe the place to start is with me and the organizations I'm a part of?"

"I don't think you should be *starting* anywhere, sweetie. I think you should leave it to the professionals."

She should leave it to the professionals, but she wouldn't. Not entirely. She didn't want to go poking around. Napa was remarkably small when it came to full-time residents. Carter and Jess would find out faster than she could pour a glass of wine if she started putting her nose where she shouldn't. And the last thing she needed was to draw more attention to herself.

But she had Leo.

Well, Collin and Dulcie had Leo. If she gave him a list of organizations, he seemed the sort who'd be happy to look into whether any had a connection to Justin and Kurt. If he found one, he could point Carter and Jess in the right direction and away from wasting time on her.

"What are you thinking?" her mom asked, standing on the other side of the table, arms crossed, head tilted. Waiting.

She had no intention of worrying her parents any more than they were. She'd keep her plan to herself. But once the Sundaram machine got running and her help was no longer needed, she'd make a list and send it to Collin, who could forward it to Leo. She'd catch up with them all later tonight when she returned.

"Woolgathering again. Shall we set the table?"

CHAPTER TWENTY-THREE

The door opened, and Dulcie's footsteps echoed down the hall. He paused, and the low rumble of his voice was followed by Gretchen's before the footsteps continued. Monk ran a hand through his hair, then over his face, his eyes never leaving the flames in the fireplace.

"Monk?"

He turned, dipped his head toward his phone that lay on the coffee table, then went back to staring at the fire. In his peripheral vision, he watched Dulcie pick the device up and read the message from Leo. He held the phone for longer than a single reading required, but Monk didn't blame him—he'd read it three times.

"Fuck," Dulcie said, sinking onto the couch.

"Yeah."

"I think it's time to call in the family."

Monk nodded. "Yeah. Gretchen also placed an earworm in my head about the possibility of more drugs in the house. Like hell do I want anyone to stumble across anything, so we need to do a full search. The...dungeon needs to be taken care of. I haven't set foot down there." He paused and let out a disgusted huff. "Hell, I haven't even brought myself to go through the rest of the house except this wing, my old room, and a few other spots very briefly when searching for Kendall." He paused again. "And then there's that." He nodded to the device still in Dulcie's hand.

"And then there's this," Dulcie said, setting it back on the table.

"And it's Christmas Eve in four days. Fuck me," he muttered, slouching in his chair. Life was spinning too fast on its axle, tipping and wobbling to stay balanced. When it did find its footing and stabilize again, it would never be the same.

Not for him. Not for so many.

"One thing at a time," Dulcie said. "I'll call Mantis. I assume you're going to take care of that?" he asked, gesturing to the phone.

"Yeah."

"Have you already started the process?"

"Leo's submitting the paperwork as we speak."

"Any chance it will be denied?"

"Not unless there's an objection."

They both stared at his phone, then Dulcie rose and pulled his from his pocket. "I'll call Mantis and take care of Gretchen. You go talk to Kendall."

"Any words of advice?" Monk asked, rising and swiping up his phone.

"Honesty," was all Dulcie said.

Monk nodded. He couldn't be any other way right now. Even if he wanted to. With another deep breath, he stepped away from the fire and toward the stairs. Two flights later, he knocked on Kendall's door.

"Come in," she called.

His stomach churned, twisting and sour. Not bothering to

brace himself, he swung the door open and stepped in, his eyes meeting Kendall's dark ones. In seconds, he studied her, as if seeing her for the first time. Thin and gangly, but healthy. Taller than average and with her dark hair severely cut, sharp cheekbones, and wide-set eyes, she reminded him a little bit of a child version of Uma Thurman in *Pulp Fiction*.

"She's dead, isn't she?" Kendall said.

Monk bought himself a few seconds as he took a seat. Her feet were crossed under her chair, her hands resting in her lap. The tip of her nose started to pinken, and her eyes, though not yet tearing, were headed there.

"I'm sorry, but yes, she is," he said.

Kendall blinked several times. He wanted to tell her it was okay to cry; hell, he'd probably cry right alongside her. He didn't know Cindy from Adam, but her daughter was fucking amazing, so she had to have been a somewhat decent person.

"How?"

He felt the weight of his phone in his pocket. "Do you want me to tell you, or do you want to see what Leo sent?" After they'd spoken, Leo had forwarded all the details he could find about the death of Cindy Jacobs to Monk's email.

Her gaze flickered to her computer, as if debating whether she wanted a permanent reminder of the details at her fingertips. "Tell me."

"She died in a car accident between Truckee and Sacramento. No drugs or other substances were involved. Just a reckless semi driver who overcorrected on a turn and caused a four-car pileup. Your mother and a man in another car both paid the price."

A single tear tracked down Kendall's cheek, and of all the things he'd seen in his life, nothing had ever, or likely would ever, break his heart more.

"When?" she said, her voice cracking on the question.

"Three days ago. She'd been in Vegas and was, we believe, on her way back for you."

Another tear. One of his own matched hers.

They sat in silence, Kendall only occasionally twisting her hands in her lap as she stared at some spot behind him. The clock ticked by, minute by minute, but he'd stay until she told him to go.

She cleared her throat, dropped her eyes, then twisted her hands again. "What about her body? She wanted to be cremated. She'd joke about that all the time. Said she wanted her ashes dumped in the ocean so she could travel around the world."

"Then we'll make that happen," he replied, already ready to text Leo. He'd have to liaise with the police and Department of Social Services eventually, but for now, Leo had offered to take the lead.

More tears fell. He wanted to gather her in his arms, hug her, and tell her it would all be okay, but this moment wasn't about what he wanted. Kendall hadn't moved from her chair, and he sensed she needed the stillness, the lack of other stimuli, to process the news.

"What about me?" She'd been all fire and challenge when they'd first met. Now he saw the little girl she still was.

"My family and I do some work helping people escape bad relationships. Mostly women, but not all. A few years ago, a woman we helped couldn't care for her two-year-old son while recovering in the hospital. We didn't want them separated or traumatized any more than they'd been, so a few of us went through the process of being preapproved as foster parents. Including me."

"Are you offering to be my foster home?" she said, her mind still as quick as always.

He inclined his head. "Leo has started the paperwork

already, but if you don't want that, we can find another option."

"Yes," she said. He cocked his head, unsure if she meant she wanted him to proceed with the application or wanted someone else. "I want to live with you." Relief flooded in with a strength he hadn't expected. In the few days he'd known her, Kendall had sneaked under his skin. He couldn't imagine life without her as part of it. Even if Cindy had lived, he would have kept in touch with her, always made sure she had a safe place to land.

"I'm glad," he said. Her shoulders eased, hopefully at the honesty she heard in his voice. "We'll have some details to work out, and we'll need to meet with Social Services, but we don't have to think about all that right now. Right now, is there anything you need? Dulcie is here, too, and my family is coming later today. It might be overwhelming, so I can keep them away from you, but I didn't want you to be surprised or caught off guard when they arrive."

"How many?"

"I don't know. Dulcie is talking to Mantis right now. Mantis is the president of the club. There are fifteen of us total, but some will have to stay in Mystery Lake to run the businesses."

She nodded, a slow, contemplative movement. "I'd like to meet them."

"They'll be glad. I know they'll want to meet you, too." He paused. Outside of the military, he'd never delivered a message of death, let alone one to a grieving girl of twelve who was now an orphan. She'd have a family—the Falcons would see to that —but for now, he could only imagine how alone she felt.

He let out a long, heavy exhale. "I'm not going to pretend to know how you may or may not feel, or what you may or may not need right now, but I will ask, is there anything I can do for you? I can make you an early lunch or some hot chocolate. I can bring it up here or, if you want to come down, I've found that staring into the fire has a way of settling me."

She didn't answer right away, and he didn't push. Another tear slid down her cheek. "If it's okay, I think I'd like to lie down for a little while."

"Of course that's okay. Whatever you need," he said, rising. He paused, taking in her hunched shoulders. With her big-sized personality and brains, she'd always seemed like a force to be reckoned with, even at her age. But now she looked young and so frail. He hated it. Hated she'd had the life she'd had, that her mother was who she was. That she hadn't had any stability in any way, nothing to ground herself to or feel she could rely on. Maybe it wasn't fair—he knew very little about Cindy Jacobs and maybe she really did do everything in her power to do right by her daughter. But looking at Kendall now, curling into herself, no doubt feeling so alone and scared, he couldn't muster any sympathy. It wasn't only that Cindy had died—she had no control over that, and for that, he was truly sorry. But for everything she'd put her daughter through *before* dying? Well, it might not be his place, but he wouldn't be forgiving her that for a good long while.

"I'm told I give good hugs," he said, his chest twisting at Kendall's red-rimmed eyes. "Something about being so tall and, well, big," he said, holding his arms out to the side.

She studied him. "I've never really been a hugging person. Not with anyone other than my mom." He could sense her wavering. She wanted a hug, wanted the basic comfort of one, but didn't trust it wouldn't be awkward. Like her new sweater analogy, she wasn't sure it would fit.

"We could try one. See how it goes."

A tiny light of amusement glistened in her eye. "My mom

always did like trying new things." She paused. "Sometimes they didn't turn out so well, but sometimes they did."

"Maybe in honor of your mom, you give it a try?" By sheer luck, that seemed to be the right thing to say. Kendall rose, then, unexpectedly, flew into his arms.

Even as tall as she was for her age, close to five foot six, she felt so tiny as her arms came around him and his wrapped around her back. She tucked her head against his chest, and it wasn't long before her tears seeped through his shirt.

He held her tight as she cried, rubbing soothing circles between her shoulder blades, making vows to himself to give her the life she deserved. One with stability, security, love, friendship. He'd fuck up occasionally, he was sure of that, but the Falcons would be there for them when that happened.

Minutes ticked by as they stood in her room, her silent pain filling the space. When her grip eased and her body sagged, he knew she'd reached the exhaustion phase of mourning—at least for the first time. Loss was a cycle that ebbed and flowed; for now, it had drained her.

"I want to lie down," she mumbled, her head still resting on his chest.

He eased away, and she turned, wiping her eyes and cheeks as she walked to the four-poster bed, her steps heavy as she crossed the thick wool rug.

He waited until she tucked herself under the covers before speaking again. "I'll text you an update on my brothers' ETA. Dulcie and I will be here all day, though, so don't hesitate to text if you need anything or come find us." The ruffle of the comforter was his only response. He waited another half a minute to make sure she didn't change her mind and ask for something, then turned to leave.

His body felt ten times heavier as he navigated back to the

ground floor, as if the weight of Kendall's grief pulled him down. When he stepped into the main room, Dulcie rose.

"How is she?" he asked.

Monk lifted a shoulder. "I don't think it was wholly unexpected, but still..."

Dulcie tipped his head in acknowledgment. "Mantis said they'll be here by early afternoon. Superman, Wesson, and Juan are staying back to cover the businesses, but everyone else will be here. I suspect the women will come, too."

Monk's phone dinged, and he pulled it out. "And Leo and Joey," he said, showing Dulcie the screen with Leo's message.

"A full house."

Monk snorted. "It's not like we don't have room."

The comment drew a smile that faded as quickly as it appeared. "Have you given any thought to what you're going to do with all this?" he asked with a gesture meant to encompass the castle and everything else he'd inherited.

Monk sank down onto a chair as he shook his head. "It's more than the castle. There's the wine business, the properties, and despite his many failings, Roger was good with money, so there are a shit ton of investments. More money than I could ever—or would ever want to—spend in my lifetime. I'll put some away for the network," he said, referring to the network of people the club worked with to extract people from abusive situations. "But other than that, I haven't given it much thought." He paused, then leaned back, emotional exhaustion rolling through him. "I've been too busy worrying about the murders and how or why they're circling around Helia."

Dulcie sat as well. "A more pressing matter than Bacco and your inheritance," he agreed. Gretchen would keep the business going in the short term, maybe the long term, too, if she was interested. And Alessio would manage the wine aspect. The truth was, with good people in place, the Bacco part of the estate could click along fine. He just wasn't sure he wanted anything to do with it. A question he could address once they sorted out the murders and how best to ensure Helia didn't get caught up in them anymore.

Of course, the best way to do that would be to solve them. Not for the first time did it feel as though an obvious piece of the puzzle was eluding him, something that explained why Helia seemed in the middle of the situation when she had nothing to do with it. Hell, she couldn't even kill a spider. She was one of those people who picked them up with a glass and gently set them outside. The idea that she was involved in not one, but two murders was laughable.

"Taking Helia out of the picture, which is hard to do given she's been questioned in both murders, why are all these people from her past—from *the* past—reemerging?" he asked.

"They may have reappeared in her life, but neither Weber nor Flannery left Napa," Dulcie said.

"Unlike Kurt Fisher and Trish Peterson," he said. "Both left and are now back."

"But Kurt and Justin are dead, while Weber and Peterson aren't."

"I think it's safe to assume Kurt's and Justin's deaths are connected. Maybe even my father's, too. It's too much of a coincidence to have three murders in the Napa Valley—men who worked in similar, though not the same, industries—and not have them connected."

"We just haven't figured out how yet," Dulcie said in agreement. "But are Peterson and Weber a part of it as well? Or is it coincidence that they reappeared in Helia's life now?"

"And if they are all part of something together, what would bring a wine merchandiser, a food importer, a restaurant manager, and a lighting fixture exec, or whatever Trish was, together?"

"I can see the first three having professional connections, but Trish?" Dulcie said. "Although we did see her this morning," he said. Monk pulled his gaze from the flames to his brother. "She was at Sundaram, talking to Greg, the kitchen manager. She's thinking about getting into the food import business, too," he said, before telling Monk what she'd told Helia that morning.

As he spoke, a picture wavered into focus before disintegrating. "If Trish goes that path, we now have three people involved in imports related to the food and wine industry—Trish, Kurt, and Justin—and one in the restaurant industry, Derek." He paused as the picture took shape again, this time, more like a puzzle. Not clear, but clear enough to see what might be revealed.

"Throw Roger in there and his drugs, and I have to wonder if there's a high-end drug distribution channel operating here in scenic Napa Valley."

CHAPTER TWENTY-FOUR

Helia glanced out the window as the first of the supplemental kitchen staff arrived, folks whose sole job was to ensure the food made it from the kitchen to the staging area. From there, the waitstaff would deliver it to the table and be the face of Sundaram for the partygoers, her and her parents lingering in the background in case anything needed troubleshooting.

Returning her focus to the inventory, paying bills, and placing orders, the familiar sounds of Sundaram coming to life for an event played like a comforting symphony in the background.

An hour later, a burst of laughter floated up the stairs as she shut the computer down, making her smile. They had great contract waitstaff, many of whom had worked for Sundaram for years. They might be joking and teasing now, but they'd be the epitome of professional when the guests arrived.

Rising from her seat, she leaned against the edge of the window. At three in the afternoon, the sun still hung in the blue sky, although this time of the year, the light felt soft and quiet, as if holding its breath for night to fall.

Her parents crossed the courtyard to the supply shed, the sight of her mom reminding her of their earlier conversation. She hadn't made a list of the organizations she worked with yet, and she pulled her device to open the notes app, only to find two missed messages. One from her mom reminding her to drop off a few items to the accountant in town that she'd promised to take care of before the holidays. The second from Collin asking her to call him when she had a chance. She frowned at the time stamp, three hours ago. She'd had her phone on silent and missed it.

Helia: *Sorry I missed your text, set my phone to silent then forgot*

Collin: *No problem, wanted to see when you might be back? I can come get you when you're done for the day*

She'd gone seventeen years without seeing him. Six hours wasn't even a blip.

Helia: *I have to head into town to drop off some paperwork. Come with me and maybe we can grab a quick bite before I have to be back at Sundaram?*

Just because she *could* go six hours without seeing him didn't mean she had to.

Collin: *I'm in town now, grocery shopping. Meet you after your errand at that coffee shop south of town by the grocery store. Don't remember the name*

At this time on a Friday, it would take her forever to get south of town.

Helia: *Can you venture back north? I need to wrap up a few things, then I'll head out. That will give you time to finish your shopping and then we'll both be closer to home*

She sent the message, then followed up with a link to a

small café far enough from the crowds that they'd be able to get a table.

Collin: *Deal, see you then*

She closed out the thread, then sent a quick note to her mom that she was going into town to drop the file and asking if they needed anything. When her mom replied in the negative, she grabbed the financial documents and exited her office, locking the door behind her.

She waved to the servers as she made her way through the building, stopping to talk with a few. By the time she made it to her little house, she'd almost forgotten what she'd come home to the night before. But seeing evidence of the new security cameras brought her to a halt. The cameras weren't installed yet, but a ladder lay against the house, and either Dulcie or Collin had started pulling the electrical lines.

Some of her anxiety eased knowing they'd been there. They would have searched the house when they arrived. Maybe when they left, too. Although it wasn't so much the prospect of someone jumping out of her closet that made her hesitate, it was the memory of the night before—that powerful, ugly beastie.

With a shake of her head, she forced herself to step forward, open the door, and walk in. Not giving herself any time to think about who else might have been in her space, she jogged up the stairs. Mechanically, she went through her drawers, gathering a few more items to take to the castle. Even once the security system was installed, she didn't plan to stay at home, not unless Collin stayed with her. She didn't know how much time they had together, and she had no intention of wasting any of it.

Well, that wasn't exactly true, she thought as she tossed her hair care products into her bathroom kit. They'd have the time they made together, but she didn't know what that time would look like. The distance between their respective homes and businesses was a real thing, not a hurdle that would simply fade away because it was inconvenient to their feelings for each other. Whatever happened between them would have to be a conscious, active decision on their part—one that involved compromise.

A heavy thought, but she'd rather mull *that* over than think about the break-in. And by the time she grew bored of ruminating on the possibilities for her future with Collin, she'd packed her bag and was headed to her car.

Twenty minutes later, she handed the documents over to the company's CPA and walked back out into the crisp late-afternoon air. Far enough away from the main part of town not to be filled with holiday tourist crowds, locals still browsed the shops and filled the cafés and restaurants.

Smiling at the festive atmosphere, she made her way toward the café to meet Collin. A family with two kids—twins—on push-trikes passed by, and she scooted closer to the building on her left, a high-end men's shaving goods shop. A few products for women dotted the window display, too, but the men's called to her. A familiar laugh pulled her focus in another direction, and Helia scanned the crowd. Standing at the door of a café, talking to a man Helia didn't recognize, was Kelly. Judging by the way she held her coat and a small to-go bag, they'd finished eating. Who knew which direction she'd head after saying goodbye, but Helia had no desire to run into her.

Double-checking the time, she ducked into the shop to have a look around, killing two birds with one stone. In the next few minutes, Kelly would pass by, or she'd head the other way. Either way, Helia would dodge her *and* have a chance to find a gift for Collin. Christmas was only a few days away, and while she and Collin hadn't talked about where they'd be or what they'd do for the holiday, she wanted to get him a present.

She wandered around the shop, half the size of its neighbors, reading labels, smelling products, and chatting with the guy behind the counter. Ten minutes later, she had a beard brush, some balm, and a conditioner in a small bag. She liked the scent, and the employee assured her it would soften Collin's beard. It didn't need softening, but since she planned to get up close and personal with that beard, she figured it was a present for them both.

With the sun behind the western mountains, the temperature had dropped, and she tugged her beanie down lower as she stepped back outside. She only wore her puffer vest, but at least her hair provided another layer of warmth across her back.

Dodging around a couple holding hands, she rounded the corner toward the café to see Collin striding down the street from the opposite direction. She paused and watched him, his long legs eating the ground, the purposeful way he moved, shoulders back, eyes alert. Hot as hell. She thought about the first day she'd seen him back, the way she'd jumped into his arms and how easily he'd held her.

He caught sight of her and lifted a hand, pulling her from the sexy thoughts forming in her head involving him holding her—against a wall, in the shower, really, the options were limitless. She smiled and waved. Forgetting the bag hanging from her wrist, it banged against her forearm just as a sting poked her in the side.

She jerked, more from the possibility of a bug crawling under her clothes than from the actual pain. Grabbing the hem of her shirt, she fluttered it, hoping whatever was inside took the opportunity to flee. She really didn't want to strip off her clothes in the middle of Napa, but the idea of a spider crawling all over her had her considering the option.

Her head started swimming, and confusion clouded her mind. It cleared for a moment as something fell to the ground. Only when she stared at the object she couldn't make it out. It seemed miles away, even as a small part of her brain insisted it was simply lying at her feet. The world started spinning again as her heart rate picked up. She could hear each thud in her head like a drumbeat and feel the rush of blood through her veins. Her skin chafed against the cotton of her shirt, the contact both the slash of a whip and the teasing brush of a lover's touch. Heat poured down her body as if she'd been submerged, headfirst, in boiling water. It was hot, too hot. Reaching for the zipper on her vest, her fingers fumbled to find the tab.

Frantically, she tried and tried.

A big hand came to rest on her back, and she jerked away. Only it held her steady.

"Helia!"

She knew that voice. Didn't she?

"Helia!"

She raised her eyes. A man, Collin, stared down at her, concern and...was that fear in his expression? She sagged against him. Everything would be okay. Collin was there.

As if through a tunnel filled with cotton wool, she heard voices. Some tense, some precise, some worried, but she took in none of the words. Something was happening, only she didn't know what. And whatever it was made it hard to care. The bombardment of sensations she'd initially felt had turned into an assault, one that lured her into welcoming it. And the more she welcomed it, the more euphoric she felt.

Something inside her insisted she needed to fight whatever

had taken over her body, but she didn't know if she had the strength. Or the will.

"Helia, we're two minutes from the hospital, hold on, sweetheart." A squeeze of her hand followed. "They'll make you better and then you can come home with me. My brothers are coming today, too. I want you to meet them," the voice continued. A warm breath of air washed over the back of her hand before two soft lips touched her skin.

Collin.

His brothers were coming? She wanted to meet them. She wanted to meet the men who'd given him the family he deserved.

She tried opening her eyes, her fingers twitching around his.

"There's my woman," he said, his palm brushing her hair back from her forehead. "Don't let go," he continued, his words clearer now, although they still held no context for her. She didn't know what had happened, what *was* happening, but she knew Collin was safe and so she squeezed his hand again.

"Hang on, Helia. We're at the hospital. The doctors are going to see you now. I have to let go, but I won't be far. I won't leave you. I'll be right here when you wake up."

She didn't understand what that meant, but she didn't want to let him go. A flurry of voices followed, none of which mattered to her. Only Collin mattered.

"Hold on, Helia," his voice came again, this time, close to her ear, his breath teasing her neck. "Hold on and come back to me." And then he was gone.

CHAPTER TWENTY-FIVE

Monk paced the waiting room, the two attendants keeping a sympathetic, if wary, eye on him.

A dart. A fucking poison dart.

He ran a hand through his hair, replaying those few seconds on the street in his head for the thousandth time. He'd spotted Helia coming around the corner and waved. She smiled, her brilliant, big smile that lit him up from the inside, and waved back.

And that's when everything had gone to shit.

She jerked, then started fluttering her top. He'd thought it weird, but they'd all been there before when some bug or insect ended up down their shirt. But in the few seconds it took him to reach her, confusion and panic took over her body, her eyes growing big, as if a war were happening inside her that she didn't understand. She'd been fumbling with her vest, mumbling words he couldn't understand, her heart racing like a Triple Crown winner when he'd set his hand on her back to steady her.

Then he'd seen the dart on the ground.

Drugs? Poison? He had no idea. He'd scooped it up and handed it to the EMTs when they arrived. He'd probably fucked up any fingerprints that might have been left on it, but he was hard-pressed to care. Helia came first, and if the doctors were going to counteract whatever she'd been dosed with, they needed to know what she'd been dosed with.

Vanessa and Harry came rushing into the room, stopping his path midstride. Behind them came Carter and Jess.

"How is she?" Vanessa demanded, hugging him.

"I don't..." Harry gave him a quick side squeeze. "I don't know," he continued, clearing his throat. "She was somewhat lucid when the doctors took her in. I think she knew I was with her."

The couple sank onto a pair of chairs, their hands gripping each other's.

"Can you tell us what happened?" Carter asked.

Between his anxiety and their past lines of questioning, Monk wasn't a big fan of the two detectives. For a split second, he considered blowing them off. But the memory of Helia's limp body in his arms spurred him to give voice to the memories playing on a loop in his head.

"A dart? Who uses a poison dart?" Vanessa asked when he finished, confusion heavy in her voice. He didn't blame her. So focused on Helia and getting the item to the doctors, he hadn't given it much thought. But what kind of person used a poison dart gun? In everything he'd seen during his time in the service, he could honestly say he'd never encountered one. And to have one used in downtown Napa?

"Someone with access to poison or drugs, who *doesn't* have easy access to Helia, but who didn't want to start a general panic by using a gun," he said, the picture growing clearer in his mind. With Helia tucked away at either Sundaram or the castle, she'd be a hard target to reach. But a shooting on a public street would cause mass confusion and call attention to the situation that the person responsible didn't want. A dart was nearly silent and practically unnoticeable. Had he not been there, and focused on Helia, it probably would have gone undiscovered altogether.

Problem solved, efficient and thorough. If it hadn't been for him.

His stomach lurched at the sheer coincidence, at the reality of how close they came to losing her. He didn't know what poison or drug the dart contained, but he doubted she was meant to live through it. The fact that he was there, found the dart, and had EMTs on-site in less than five minutes was probably the only thing standing between Helia's life and her...he wouldn't even think it.

He muttered a curse and sank onto a chair beside Vanessa. She reached over and grabbed his hand. "She'll make it. I know she will."

Nothing else was an option, so he nodded.

"Could you tell where the shot came from?" Carter asked.

Monk cast his mind back to the incident, then shook his head. "Her left side was to a building, so it must have hit her on the right. The dart was on the ground by the time I reached her, though, so I don't know specifically where. If I did, I could give you a good guess."

Carter and Jess exchanged a look. "We'll get that information from the doctors."

They peppered him with a few more questions, most of which he had no answers for, before falling silent. Both detectives were leaning against opposite walls in the waiting room when a doctor stepped in.

"Mr. and Mrs. Shaw?" he said, his gaze scanning the room before landing on Helia's parents. Monk rose with them, and Carter and Jess straightened from their positions. The doctor's gaze darted to the two detectives before settling back on Vanessa and Harry.

"She's going to be fine, but let's find a private room where we can talk," he said. Relief nearly took Monk out at the knees; the only thing holding him upright was focusing on Vanessa. She'd sagged against Harry at the pronouncement, and Monk wrapped an arm around her other side as they followed the doctor out, Carter and Jess trailing behind.

When the door closed behind them, the doctor, a fit-looking man in his mid-fifties, crossed his arms. "She's going to be fine," he repeated. "Thanks to your quick work," he added with a nod to Monk. Monk didn't respond.

"The dart contained a lethal dose of a drug cocktail. I won't speculate about intent, but I will say it would have killed her if she'd gone untreated for any length of time."

Vanessa whimpered, and Harry mumbled comforting words as he pulled his wife closer.

"Where did the dart hit her?" Jess asked.

"Here," the doctor said, raising his arm and pointing to a spot on his ribs.

"She lifted her hand to wave at me," Monk said.

The doctor nodded. "That sounds right. It's not an easy spot to hit otherwise."

"Do you have a sample of the drug?" Carter asked.

The doctor nodded. "We did a quick analysis that allowed us to treat her with the right counteragents, but there's enough left to do a more thorough workup. Several people handled it, though."

Carter inclined his head. "Can you give us a list of everyone who touched it? We'll take prints to rule them out, then see if we can find anything. It might be a needle in a haystack—"

"But you won't get any pushback from anyone here. No one's seen an attack like this, and everyone will do what they can to make sure the person behind it is caught," the doctor said.

"Can we see her?" Harry asked.

The doctor nodded. "She's sleeping now, but will be in and out of wakefulness for the next hour or so."

"After that?" Vanessa asked.

"She'll wake more fully. She'll probably be tired for the next twenty-four hours, but so long as her vitals stay stable and she stays on the track we expect, she can head home tonight."

Vanessa and Harry would want her home. He understood the need to keep their daughter close. But he had ten of his brothers coming, and two of their partners, Callie and Lina, were former FBI and CIA, respectively. Helia would be far safer at the castle than anywhere else. Vanessa and Harry wouldn't like it, but they'd agree in the end.

The Shaws asked the doctor a few more questions before thanking him. Carter and Jess followed him out, a nurse entering as they exited. A few minutes later, Harry and Vanessa sat on one side of Helia's bed and he on the other. He didn't like how limp her hand felt in his, but the warmth assured him that she was alive and healing.

The heart monitor and the background noise of the other machines in the room filled the silence. Twenty minutes passed before her eyes fluttered open.

They all stood. The motion must have startled her, and she drew in a sharp inhale as her alert, though sleepy, eyes tried focusing.

"Honey," Vanessa said, brushing a hand over her daughter's head. Helia's dazed gaze lingered on her parents, then flickered to him.

"What's going on?" she asked, then licked her lips. "Is there any water?"

He let go of her hand and poured a small glass, setting the

straw in it before holding it to her lips. She took a few long sips, then rested her head back against the pillow.

"Why am I so tired?" she slurred, as if moving her lips required more energy than she had.

Uncertainty shadowed Vanessa and Harry's expressions. "There was an incident," Monk said, taking the task of explaining from them. Her hazy eyes tried focusing on him. "You were drugged, but we got you to the hospital and they've done their best to flush it out of your system. The doctor told us you'll be tired for the next day or so."

Struggling to comprehend what he'd told her, her gaze held his. "Drugged? How? What?"

"As to what, we don't know the details, but the police are taking over and will do the analysis," he answered.

"How?" she asked again.

He hesitated. "A dart gun."

Two lines formed between her brows. "Like a tranquilizer gun vets use on animals?"

"I'm not an expert on that weapon, but yeah, I imagine it was like that," he said. Her gaze drifted to her parents, then back to him.

"Why?"

The sixty-four-thousand-dollar question. "We don't know."

"But Carter and Jess will find out," Harry said with more certainty than Monk felt. He wasn't *unimpressed* by them, but they hadn't exactly wowed him with their skill.

She fell silent, and the second hand on the wall clock clicked down, seeming much louder than before. "It's tied together, isn't it?" she said. "The murders, the break-in at my house..."

He cast a probing look at her parents. Harry and Vanessa weren't the sort to gloss over the truth or sugarcoat things, but this was their daughter's life. By the expression on their faces, though, they wanted answers, too. It was a little intimidating that they were looking to him, these two people who had taken him in, protected him as a child. On the other hand, it meant they saw him as an adult now. And a capable one at that. A heady feeling took root in his body.

He nodded. "Yes," he said, his tone grim. "I think they are all connected."

Her eyes slid to her mom, and a look crossed her face, as if trying to pull up a buried memory. She blinked and turned back to him. "Connected to me or connected to something I'm involved with?" she asked. Before she could tire herself out more, Vanessa jumped in, telling him a theory she'd proposed to Helia earlier.

"Not a bad idea," he said when Vanessa finished. "We can look into it." The possibility of Justin and Kurt being connected through an organization Helia also worked with didn't account for Roger, who donated money, not time, but it was worth exploring.

Satisfied, she nodded, then sat back. "What are we going to do with Helia now? If they are after her..." Sundaram had two events the next day before they could lock down. Lots of people on the grounds. Lots of opportunity to get to Helia.

"My brothers are coming today," he said. "Well, most of them. They were supposed to be here already but got held up dealing with a work thing, then hit traffic with an accident on the interstate. The delay gave me time to head to the grocery store and meet Helia before they get here." His stomach once again revolted at how close he'd come to losing her. If that series of events—the work delay, then traffic—hadn't happened, he would've been home greeting his family, and she would have been on that street by herself. Someone would have noticed her fall, but he doubted anyone would have called 911 as quickly as she'd needed. Or seen the dart.

Pulling him from that dark path, Helia's hand squeezed his. "I'm looking forward to meeting them, but why are they coming now?"

Sorrow weighed heavy on his chest. The reason he'd wanted to see Helia in person was to tell her about Kendall's mom. It wasn't a message that should be sent over text or given by phone.

"A few reasons, but the main one being because I need help. I need help searching the castle for more of Roger's drugs." He paused. "And I need help with Kendall. We found out this morning that her mom died in a car accident. Probably on her way back to get her. That's what I wanted to tell you."

Her eyes teared. "No." He gave a tiny nod. "That poor girl."

"Who's Kendall?" Harry asked.

A complicated question, but Monk boiled it down, telling them how she'd been left at the castle by her mom and how he'd found her. He couldn't help mentioning how sharp she was and how she'd contributed more than her fair share of ideas to the Kurt/Justin situation.

Harry rubbed a hand over his face, and Vanessa dabbed her eyes when he finished. "That poor child," Harry said. "What will happen to her now?"

Monk's gaze flickered to Helia. Their relationship was barely getting started, well, Act 2 of it, and he was changing the stakes dramatically. Still, he couldn't, wouldn't, do anything else.

"Me and a few of my brothers are preapproved foster parents. It's a long story, but it's come in handy a few times in the past when we've needed to watch kids for a few days while their parent, usually their mom, heals." He held Vanessa's gaze before switching it to Harry. Both nodded in understanding as to what he meant, even as they looked confused as to how he'd be involved. A situation he'd explain later.

"As soon as Leo—"

"He's a friend of Collin's who works for a prestigious security company and is a cyber genius," Helia interjected. Her parents nodded again, although he could see a thousand questions gathering in their eyes.

"As soon as Leo told me about her death, I asked him to start the process of having me appointed as Kendall's foster parent." His gaze flickered to Helia. Something akin to pride shone in her eyes, but he doubted the reality of what that meant had sunk in. "The provisional appointment came through a few hours ago. We'll have to talk to a social worker after the holidays, but it's what both Kendall and I want."

Harry stared at him. Vanessa frowned, not in disapproval, but concern. "I'm not questioning whether you've done the right thing, Collin, but are you ready to parent a twelve-year-old orphan? Becoming a parent changes everything."

"And I imagine being a parent to a girl like Kendall, who hasn't had the most stable life, is going to pose even more challenges, but is anyone really ready to be a parent?" he countered.

A ghost of a smile touched Harry's lips, but Vanessa still didn't look convinced. Monk sighed. "Look, I know it will change things, my life, in ways I can't even imagine. But I can't, I won't, leave her to the system. She deserves better than that. All kids do, but she's the one I can help, and she wants the same thing. We'll get therapy, we'll do what we need to to make it work."

"That you both want it is a good start," Vanessa conceded.

"And not that you won't have to parent, but my guess is that you'll be more like a big brother than a father to her," Helia added. He'd considered that as well, then decided not to put any labels or expectations on what their relationship may or may not be. His priority was to provide her with a safe home where she could thrive. Everything else, they'd figure out as they went along.

A nurse popped in, putting a pause to their conversation. Three minutes later, Helia's vitals checked, she left with a satisfied nod. Harry turned to him. "You mentioned your brothers. Are you suggesting Helia will be safer with you?"

Vanessa made a small noise of protest, but Monk held Harry's eyes. "We have twelve former spec-ops soldiers staying in the castle, plus their partners coming too, which means a former FBI and a former CIA agent also make up the party. Yes, I think she'll be safer recovering there." He wanted to haul her off and tuck her into the tower, but he forced himself to look at Helia. "But I won't force you. If you'd rather be home, we'll figure it out."

She tightened her hold on his hand again. "I was planning to stay with you anyway. Now I'll get to meet your family and be with Kendall."

His fingers twitched against her palm. "Leo and Joey will be there, too. Kendall will like that, I think."

"When will they arrive?" Vanessa asked.

"In about two hours."

Helia clicked the call button as she swept them all up with her gaze. "Which gives me enough time to blow this joint so we can be there when they arrive," she said, all but daring them to challenge her.

Harry's lips twitched. Vanessa sighed in resignation. Monk smiled. No one challenged her.

CHAPTER TWENTY-SIX

Helia managed to bully the hospital staff into letting her go earlier than they'd like. It helped when Collin mentioned that one of his brothers was a field-trained expert medic who would keep an eye on her. Still, they hadn't been happy. Not that she cared.

Other than the fatigue, she felt fine. She hadn't fallen and hit her head or bruised or banged any other part of her body. Collin had seen to that. But the exhaustion...she'd never felt anything like it. It was as if a hundred-pound weight pressed in on her from the top while every muscle fiber simultaneously grew roots into the ground, pulling her down. And breathing? Intellectually, she knew her body wouldn't stop, but every breath felt as if she had to force air into her lungs.

Leaning against Collin, her arm tucked into his, they made their way into the castle. While she waited to be discharged, her parents had picked up her car from downtown, and her bag hung over his other shoulder.

"You doing okay?" he asked, keying in the security code.

"I'm fine," she said. More or less true. "Don't step away too quickly, though," she added, with a smile.

The look he shot her told her the attempt at levity fell flat.

"How long until everyone arrives?" she asked, as the door swung open.

"They stopped for gas at Cordelia Junction, so about thirty minutes."

"How was Kendall when you left?" she asked, keeping her voice low.

"Still in shock, I think. She requested mac'n'cheese from the store, though. I think it's a comfort food for her."

"Helia!" The girl in question popped up from the couch as they entered the tasting room. A fire blazed in the hearth, and Dulcie sat in a chair, a game of Trivial Pursuit on the table between them.

"Kendall," she replied, taking a step away from Collin. His hand lingered at her back, but he let her go.

Kendall froze about ten feet in front of her. Helia wanted to go to the girl. Wanted to wrap her in a big, safe hug, but she didn't want to do anything to make her uncomfortable and to date, she hadn't been very touchy.

"Can I...Can I hug you?" Kendall asked.

Tears pricked Helia's eyes, and she opened her arms. "Yes, please?"

The girl flew toward her, wrapping her thin arms around Helia's waist. Collin's hand at her back kept her steady as she embraced Kendall.

"I'm so sorry, sweetie," Helia said, her voice quiet, her heart breaking for the young girl who'd experienced far too much in life already.

Kendall's arms squeezed her, and she sniffled. "I'm glad you're okay," she said, her voice muffled.

"Me, too," she murmured. They held on to each other, a moment that needed no words.

Finally, Kendall stepped back. Helia let her go, but hid her surprise when Kendall kept hold of her hand and pulled her toward the couch. "You should lie down," she said.

Helia didn't have much experience with grief or loss, but it wasn't hard to figure out that Kendall was dealing with hers by taking care of Helia. And so Helia let her. Taking a seat, she curled her legs underneath her, then accepted the blanket Kendall handed over. She had no intention of sleeping, but between the fire and the blanket and the comfortable couch, it might be harder to keep her eyes open than she anticipated.

"Do you want any water or anything?" Kendall asked.

Helia shook her head. "Sit with me. You can tell me about how badly you're beating Dulcie at the game," she said, waving to the board on the table.

"Pretty badly," she replied.

"How you know so much about movies that came out before even *I* was born or about countries that don't even exist anymore is beyond me," Dulcie grumbled, pulling a small smile from Kendall.

"While you two are catching up, Dulcie can help me with the groceries."

"I'm glad your truck stayed cold enough they didn't go off," Helia said.

He waved the comment off. "Makes things easier, but it wouldn't have been a big deal. I would have sent one of my brothers later," he said, before he and Dulcie left the room.

Kendall sank onto a cushion on the floor, her back to the fire. "Are you sure you're okay?"

She'd already lost one person today; Helia wasn't about to let her worry about losing another. "I'd lifted my arm to wave to Collin, and the dart hit me in the side, not my biceps, which probably saved me. Well, that and Collin's fast response."

Kendall nodded. "Your reflex reaction to lower your arm probably knocked it out before it could dose you fully."

"That's what the doctors think. And because Collin was smart enough to gather the dart, the doctors were able to analyze the contents and counteract everything. I'm tired. Like really, really tired. But there will be no lasting effects."

Kendall studied her, then slowly nodded again.

"It's a stupid question, but how are you?" she asked, keeping her voice quiet as the men traipsed in and out, shuttling the grocery bags to the larger kitchen at the back of the castle. Idly, she wondered if these trips were Collin's first time setting foot in that part of the building again.

Kendall's eyes dropped, and she futzed with one of the game pieces. "I don't really know," she said, a single tear dropping onto her hand as she answered. "Is that dumb?"

"No," Helia said without hesitation. The desperation in Kendall's expression broke her heart. "I'm not going to pretend to be some sort of guru on loss and grief, but you're dealing with a shit ton of emotional stuff right now. The death of your mom and, in many ways, the death of the life you've always known. Plus, there's the reality of a future that you probably never imagined and all the questions that come with what that's going to be like. Everything from new relationships to a new place to live to a new way of growing up." She paused, then huffed out a breath. "Now I'm stressing myself out, too."

A ghost of a smile touched Kendall's eyes. "Sometimes it's hard to know which direction you're going when you're in the middle of a storm?"

Helia blinked back tears. Out of the mouths of babes. "Yeah," she agreed. "And you're in one helluva storm right now, sweetie."

Grief dulled Kendall's expression, but she nodded. "Want to play?" she asked, gesturing to the board, apparently done talking about her mom.

"I don't think I can sit up for too long. Why don't you read out questions, and you can laugh at how many I get wrong."

Kendall's lips tipped up. "Done," she said. A few minutes later, Dulcie and Collin joined them. Dulcie took the seat he'd vacated earlier while Collin sat at the other end of the couch, tugging her feet onto his lap. He also handed her a pillow, and she stretched out, resting her head on the arm of the sofa, the pillow tucked underneath.

Kendall and Collin were in a dead heat when his phone dinged. Pulling it out, he glanced at the screen before tucking it away again. "That was the system at the gate letting me know it's been opened. Everyone is here."

Helia's stomach fluttered, although a gentler flutter than she'd expected. The attack on her life and Kendall's mom's death had a way of putting things in perspective. The exhaustion might have something to do with it, too. Stress required a lot of energy she didn't have right now.

The sound of cars filling the parking lot drifted down the hall, followed by car doors slamming shut. Helia swung her legs off Collin's lap and sat upright, but he stayed her when she tried to rise. "They'll understand if you don't get up to greet them," he said, rising.

By the time the first arrival walked into the tasting room, a man with dark blond hair and a pair of light green eyes, Dulcie and Collin flanked Kendall as they stood with their backs to the fire.

One by one, Collin's family trickled in. Ten brothers, five women, and Leo. The brothers were easily recognizable by their build and similarly watchful expressions. The group paused on the other side of the table, not a standoff, but a sort of assessment. The moment fractured when the one with the green eyes stepped forward.

"I'm Mantis, but I answer to Noah, too," he said, stepping forward and holding his hand out to Kendall. She looked to Collin, who reassured her with a nod and a gentle shoulder squeeze.

"I'm Kendall," she said, holding her hand out.

The tension broke, and everyone filed in after that. She appreciated how they started with Kendall. The girl needed to feel welcome, feel special. So did Helia, but she was an adult. And she liked that the club trusted her enough to understand what they were doing and not take it personally.

With sixteen of them, it took a while to meet everyone. Ten of Collin's brothers: Mantis, Philly, Stone, Viper, Marley, Lovell, Hawkeye, North, Scipio, and Einstein, who everyone mostly called Stein. And of course, Leo, who gave both Kendall and her a hug. Their five partners followed: the twins, Charley and Joey; Juliana, a lively blond librarian living with Stone; Lina, the ex-CIA agent Collin had mentioned, living with Viper; and Callie, the ex-FBI agent married to Philly.

Her head spun with all the new information, although Kendall seemed to take it all in, her gaze darting among everyone as they spoke. She might appear collected, but Helia wondered what she was thinking. If she and Collin chose to keep the foster relationship in place, this group would be her new family. And to go from having only one person in her life to so many? Well, to say it would be an adjustment was a gross understatement.

Eventually, the room settled down, though Helia wouldn't call it quiet, not with twenty people in it, and the group sprawled out between the chairs, the high tops, and the floor.

"If anyone needs anything to eat or drink, it's in the kitchen," Collin said.

"We stopped for a late lunch when we hit the traffic on the interstate," Mantis replied. "We're here to help—what do we need to do? At the very least, we have a shit ton of beds to make," he added with a smile that turned into a grimace when he glanced at Kendall. "Sorry, I'll watch my language."

Collin and Dulcie snorted. "We've come to an agreement about language," Collin said. "So long as the swearing is appropriate, in context *and* setting, we're not going to make a big deal out of it. And that applies to everyone in the room, right, Kendall?"

Kendall rolled her eyes. "Yes, Collin," she singsonged, earning a few chuckles.

Mantis didn't look so sure about that agreement but let it slide. "What do we need to do?"

Collin had taken the seat beside Helia, and she reached over, covering his hand with hers. He didn't look at her, but his grip told her he appreciated the support.

Inhaling, he started. "Other than this area, I've only been in my old room, Kendall's room, and Roger's. With a short dash through a few other parts when I was searching for Kendall."

Helia appreciated how his brothers didn't question his choices.

"I've thoroughly searched Roger's room, but nowhere else. Gretchen knew about Roger's drugs, and if it was common-ish knowledge, it made me worry there might be more than the one stash I found."

All eyes went to Kendall except hers, Collin's, and Dulcie's. "Kendall knows everything that's going on," Collin said to the group. She doubted they'd challenge him on that, but the firmness of his statement dissuaded any who might have entertained the thought.

"We need to search everywhere else. All the rooms, hallways, everything. Not to mention the secret passageways."

"There are secret passageways?" Marley asked, his eyes lighting up.

Collin winced. "More than a few. I know where they all are, but I think there's an architectural map in Roger's safe. I can look when we're ready."

"I claim the passageways," Marley said.

"I'm coming with you," Philly piped up.

Mantis waved a finger between them. "You two aren't going anywhere in this castle together. That's tempting more trouble than I want to deal with right now. Scipio, you're with Marley."

"C'mon, Mantis," Philly whined.

"There are swords on the third floor," Kendall interjected.

Philly blinked. Callie groaned. "Swords?" Philly repeated. Kendall nodded. "Like real swords?"

"Fifteenth-century, from what I could tell," Kendall said. "You'd think they'd be dull, but Roger kept them sharp."

"You are not playing with swords," Callie said.

Philly arched an eyebrow at his wife. "Don't even pretend you don't like playing with swords, woman."

"I like playing with one specific sword, which is why the possessor of that sword will not be playing with large, sharp, heavy fifteenth-century swords," she retorted.

Helia had expected Callie to shut down her husband's trip down double-entendre lane, and Callie's response so surprised her she barked out a laugh. Along with most of the others in the room. Even Philly chuckled, pulling his wife against his side and kissing her temple before whispering something in her ear that had her blushing.

"How many floors are there?" Mantis asked, bringing the room back to the task at hand.

"Three and the basement," Collin answered.

"And an extra floor on the towers," Kendall said.

"And an extra floor on the towers," Collin repeated.

Mantis nodded his head in thought, then rose. "Okay, here's how it's going to go. Marley and Scipio, you're on the passageways. Hawkeye and Philly, you're with Monk on the third floor and towers. Viper, Lovell, and Stein, you're on the second. Stone and North, you're on this floor. I'll take the basement with Dulcie."

"What about Leo?" Kendall asked.

"I'll grab an office and focus on continuing the background work," he said. "We passed a few on our way in, any preference for which I use?" he asked Collin, who shook his head.

A beat later, everyone, well, all the men, dissolved into their assigned tasks, leaving the women in the tasting room. A few cast worried looks as the brothers left, but most wandered over to the table and took seats, leaving the couch empty for Helia to stretch out again.

"Oh, my favorite," Juliana said, pointing to the board on the table as she took the seat Dulcie vacated. "Anyone up for a game?"

CHAPTER TWENTY-SEVEN

Kendall watched Collin, Dulcie, and the others disappear down hallways. She didn't want to give too much thought yet to the reality that they'd be her de facto family from now on. They seemed like good enough people—Collin was tight with them, and she liked Collin. And she liked how Mantis led the group; he didn't dictate or order anyone about. Sure, he'd divvied up the teams and proposed the strategy, but if someone objected, she got the feeling he would have listened.

Thinking of them as anything more than Collin's brothers made her mom's death more real, though. And while she knew it was real, it wasn't real-real. Not yet.

Not ready to let her mind travel any further down that path, she turned her attention to the women gathering around her. They were easier to think about than reality. Even if a little intimidating. They all looked so put together. Not high-maintenance, just grounded. Confident.

Juliana, the librarian at the presidential library. Not a job that interested Kendall, but it was pretty cool. The curvy blond also had a nice smile. The kind you'd expect from the girl next door, only Kendall got the sense there was more to Juliana than that. And she and Stone had brought their dog, Sherman, too. She'd never seen anything like the huge animal who'd come over to her as soon as he entered the castle, wrapped his wiggly body around hers, licked her hand, then darted off. She didn't know where he'd gone, but she hoped he'd come back. She'd never had a pet before and had always secretly wanted one. She'd never told her mother that, though. She hadn't wanted to make her feel guilty for not giving her one.

Then there was Lina. Dulcie had given her the lowdown on all the women while they'd waited for Collin and Helia to get back from the hospital. She was a CPA now, which Kendall didn't think was at all interesting, but she'd been a CIA agent early in her career. Her mom and grandfather, also both spies, had trained her from the cradle. Kendall didn't know what that meant, but it sounded kind of cool.

Callie had surprised her. Tall and elegant, all polished and put together with her perfect hair and smooth dark skin that held not a single flaw. Wearing fitted jeans, tall boots, and a deep green ribbed sweater, she could be in an ad for a ski resort. Dulcie told her that she was ex-FBI and now worked for HICC with Leo, but Kendall hadn't pictured someone so, well, sophisticated. Although she *had* made that remark about swords. And while eww, she had to admit, it was funny. And unexpected.

The twins were the youngest. Kendall didn't know by how much, but Dulcie had mentioned they were in their twenties. They were the granddaughters of a former US president—a real frickin' president. And they owned their own business. A successful one if Dulcie hadn't exaggerated. A shop that carried outdoor gear and a tour company that led guided hikes, camping trips, and other outdoor adventures. Kendall had never been hiking before, not intentionally, and thought she might like seeing Mystery Lake, her new home, through their eyes.

Her gaze traveled to Helia lying on the couch and lingered there. Dulcie, Collin, and even Hawkeye, who'd checked her vitals almost immediately after meeting her, all said she'd be fine, but she was pale. And barely keeping her eyes open. She knew Helia better than the others, but they'd still only met a few days ago. Even so, when Collin had called from the hospital, well, Kendall hadn't liked that. Hadn't liked the surge of emotion she'd felt. She didn't know if it had all been because of Helia or because of, well, everything. But it had made her feel twitchy and as though she was about to burst into tears. Dulcie had told her emotions were good and normal. He might be right, but that didn't mean she had to like them.

"Oh, my favorite," Juliana said, pointing to the board on the table as she took the seat Dulcie vacated. "Anyone up for a game?"

Helia shook her head and pulled her blanket up over her shoulder, but the other women took seats around the table.

"I love this game. Even when I lose, I win because I learn things," Juliana said. "Weird things, usually, but hey, what is life without a little weird. Can I start again?" she asked, tapping one of the round pie-shaped game pieces, nearly filled with colorful wedges. It took Kendall a second to realize she was asking her, and she nodded.

"Why did the guys leave you all behind?" Kendall blurted out. "I mean, I didn't mean, not that you shouldn't be here. Or that I don't want you here..." she stammered, blushing for the first time in her life. Wow, two minutes with this new family and already she'd fucked it up. They were going to think she was some bratty kid who didn't want their company.

Lina chuckled. "Nice, we have a budding feminist on our hands, ladies. Kendall, I'm going to like you."

Kendall's body sagged in relief, grateful Lina understood her poorly worded question. She offered a tentative smile. "It seems, I don't know, weird. They obviously respect you all, and it's not like they know the castle better than you since none of you have been here before."

"And it's weird that they left the little women behind?" Juliana finished. Kendall nodded.

"How much do you know about Roger Wilde?" Charley asked.

"More than I want to, but probably not even close to everything," she said. Even Helia's eyes opened and focused on her with that statement. "I mean, I heard things. I saw him around when, well, whenever my mom brought me here. And I know my mom's flaws." She paused, her gaze dropping. "I knew my mom's flaws," she corrected quietly. "She liked drugs and sex and to party. The castle was one of her favorite places. Gave me a pretty good idea of the kind of person Roger was."

Helia blinked, as if trying not to cry, although Kendall didn't know what she'd said that would cause that. "Do you need anything?" Kendall asked. "Water? Tea? Coffee?"

"If she does, I can grab it," Joey said. "Why don't you go share the couch with Helia."

The suggestion seemed weird, but she wanted to be closer to Helia anyway. The other women didn't *worry* her, but she felt more comfortable with Helia. Scooting by Lina and Callie, she sank onto a cushion on the floor beside her friend. Helia's hand touched her head, then stroked through her short hair.

"You know Collin and Roger have been estranged since Collin walked out at eighteen, right?" Helia asked. Kendall nodded. "There are reasons for that. Personal ones. I won't go into the details because those are his to share, should he choose to, but I will tell you that when Roger decided his son was old enough to enter his sick idea of manhood, this house was not a safe one for Collin. He has a lot of memories and a lot of demons in this castle."

"Those men, his brothers, they helped him heal. Find family," Charley said.

"There are no secrets among them," Callie said. The other women shot her looks that Kendall had no idea what they meant. Callie huffed. "Not anymore, and that was my fault," she said. Kendall wondered what kind of secret Philly had kept, but Juliana spoke, pulling her back into the conversation.

"They need to do this together," Juliana said. "As much for Monk as for themselves."

Kendall didn't understand.

"Those men would kill or die for one another—us, too, if it were to come to it," Lina said. "But what they've managed to do together that's even more remarkable is heal with one another. From their pasts, their scars, their histories."

Ah, she got it now. Sort of. "This is part of a process for them. Helping Collin fight this demon."

All the women nodded. Kendall didn't totally get it. She couldn't imagine having ties so deep to other people, but she understood. The guys hadn't so much left the women behind as the women had sent them off to undertake some sort of group therapy.

Helia's hand stroked through her hair again. Having someone other than her mom show her any affection felt weird. It wasn't pushy, though. And she sort of liked it.

"Before we start the game," Juliana said, "I have to say this, and I hope it doesn't make you uncomfortable, Kendall."

Kendall tensed.

"Don't start a sentence that way," Lina said with a shake of her head. "Now she's anxious regardless of what you were going to say."

Lina's teasing tone eased some of the tightness in Kendall's shoulders; the face Juliana made dissolved the rest.

"You're right, that was lame. I'll just say this," she said, turning to Kendall. "I'm so sorry about your mom. I lost both my parents in a car accident when I was seven. It sucks."

Kendall almost snorted at the understatement, but a nugget of appreciation stopped her. Cindy Jacobs was in no way an ideal parent, but the lack of judgment in Juliana's voice let her know it didn't matter. Let Kendall know that regardless of what kind of parent Cindy might have been, she was worthy of being grieved, of being missed, of being loved by her daughter.

Her eyes pricked. She turned away, blinking the moisture back. "Thank you," she said when she had it under control.

"Me, too," Lina said. "I lost my mom nearly four years ago. I miss her every day." She paused, then added, "And my father was murdered earlier this year. He and I weren't close. He wasn't an easy man. Not a bad one, just...different. I'm only now coming to realize that he parented me in the best way he knew how. I wish I'd figured it out sooner."

Someone else with a flawed parent. She didn't know if Lina meant to or not, but she'd laid out a thin connection between them, tying them together through a shared experience. Another wave of appreciation settled inside her. Lina understood what it was like to have a flawed parent and love them anyway. Understood that even flawed parents could love their children.

"I'm sorry, too," Callie said. When everyone looked at her, she huffed. "If we're talking about parents, I only have this to say: If you felt your mother's love, real love, in whatever form, then you're lucky. My parents are very much alive but are horrible people. They don't look it on the outside. On the outside, they are pillars of the community—my father is the district attorney, and my mother is a physician. But my childhood was filled with fear and anxiety and doing everything I could to stay out of their way. I haven't spoken to them since I moved out twenty years ago." She paused, then added, "I don't know why I shared that. It has nothing to do with you or your grief, Kendall."

Kendall stared at Callie, then blinked. Not to keep from crying this time, but she hadn't expected that sort of background from this beautiful, put-together woman. She didn't know what kind of abuse she'd experienced, but she'd seen enough to have a good idea of what it could have been like—even behind the walls of a fancy house.

"Thank you," Kendall said. Then taking a gamble, she added, "A lot of people judged my mom. She wasn't the best parent, I know that. But she loved me. In the best way she knew how," she said, repeating Lina's words. "A lot of people might think I'm better off without her, that I shouldn't love her because of everything she *didn't* provide. But I miss her, and I did—do—love her." She paused. "Maybe it's because you've all had the experiences you've had or, I don't know, maybe it's just you. But thank you for seeing my mom as someone who could still love me, even despite her flaws."

Someone sniffled, she wasn't quite sure who, but suspected it was Juliana.

"We're sorry you lost that," Charley said. She and Joey were identical, but there were a few tiny differences. Charley's right eyebrow winged up more than her sister's and had a small scar running through it. She also had slightly different earlobes than her sister.

"And you don't know us, not yet," Joey said. "But we will

always respect and share your grief. It's yours, and no one gets to tell you how to feel."

Helia, her eyes closed on the couch, nodded. "Always," she said.

Juliana sniffled again, then cleared her throat. Setting the game pieces on the board, she let out a dramatic exhale. "Okay, people, are we going to play?"

Kendall took in the group of women, a tendril of *something* taking root. She'd always miss her mother, always. But Cindy Jacobs was never coming back. If Kendall had to create a new life, maybe one with these women in it would be a good start.

CHAPTER TWENTY-EIGHT

By the time they finished searching the castle, it was well past dark. Being in the building, in the home that held so many bad memories for him, hadn't been as hard with his brothers at his side. No doubt their intention when they showed up en masse. They'd found a small bag of white powder in one of the third-floor rooms, but nothing else too incriminating. Although the stash of sex devices Philly found in one of the suits of armor raised a few eyebrows—both the content and the location.

Mantis and Dulcie wore matching grim expressions when they emerged from the dungeon, but all they'd said was that they hadn't found any drugs or weapons. Although they'd pulled Scipio aside shortly after, and Monk heard them strategizing about how best to clear out the space. He appreciated being insulated from the process. Too much depravity and pain had seeped into the walls for him to ever be comfortable down there.

Before meeting his brothers in the kitchen to start dinner,

he peeked into the tasting room. The world felt right when he saw Sherman curled in front of the fire, Helia dozing comfortably on the couch, Kendall perched beside Leo reading something on his laptop, and his sisters-in-law quietly playing a game. The world wasn't right. They had a murderer on the loose, Helia was in the crosshairs, Kendall's mom was dead, and he was taking on the raising of an orphaned girl. But in that moment, it felt that way.

"Amber would love this stove," Marley said when he walked into the kitchen, the scent of chili and corn bread filling the room. Amber was a woman they'd extracted from a shitty situation months ago. They'd brought her to their clubhouse to heal, and she'd stayed. All the people they helped were welcome to stay as long as they needed. Most only used it as a way station before heading to family or friends who helped them establish a new life. Others stayed, fell in love with Mystery Lake, and ended up finding their own lives in the mountain town. And a few, like Amber, took a little longer. Every day she came out of her shell a little more, though. But where she felt most free was in the kitchen. She loved to cook and was damn good at it. She'd been helping Dottie, their house mom/house manager, for months.

"She could do a lot in here," Stein added. The kitchen at the clubhouse was no slouch, but Stein wasn't wrong. In the years since he'd left, Roger had renovated this more private kitchen into a commercial space. Bacco had never hosted events, though, and it didn't make sense to Monk, but he'd stopped trying to understand his father a long time ago.

"This place would make a sic hotel or inn or whatever they call fancy spots people stay in down here," Philly said.

"Get Amber in here to cook for them and they'd come in droves," Hawkeye added.

"Guys." Callie's voice had all their heads turning. "Leo has something. Can you step away for a few minutes?"

The corn bread had four minutes left on the timer, so Monk simply turned the oven off and left it in there. Marley turned the burner down to low under the chili, leaving it to simmer.

They filed past Callie as she waited for Philly. When he came through the door, he slid his arm around his wife's waist and kissed her temple before taking her hand in his and trailing after everyone.

Monk's eyes went to Helia when he entered the room. Now sitting upright, with her chin resting in her palm and her attention focused on the end of the room, she'd tucked the blanket around her curled-up legs.

The group rustled up chairs and seats were taken—his right at Helia's feet. When everyone settled in, he turned to Leo. "Where's Kendall?"

"Here," she said, popping out from behind a whiteboard on wheels they'd dug up from somewhere, Sherman at her side. Shadows of grief flickered in her eyes, as they would for a while. But judging by the pen in her hand and the way she put her head together with Leo's, consulted his computer, then returned to behind the whiteboard, she'd found a distraction.

"Ready?" Leo asked.

A pause. "Ready," Kendall called back.

"Okay," Leo said as Kendall rotated the whiteboard. On it was a timeline with names and dates in different colors. "Kendall and I created this. We think it will help pull the picture together of what we believe is happening. The names and dates in black are the murders or potential murders. The names in red are those folks who have come back into Helia's life recently."

"And the blue are the weird events," Kendall stepped in, shooting a shy look at the large group.

He hid a smile as his brothers each responded with serious nods. Turning to the board, he scanned it, taking in the information. He reached the end, then bounced back to the beginning. "Hold up, why is Marcel Laurant on the board? In black?"

"Who's Marcel Laurant?" Stein asked.

"He was a sous-chef who worked at Sundaram two summers ago," Helia said. "He gifted a set of knives to Akin, our chef, when he left. It was one of those knives that was used to kill Justin Flannery."

Again, his brothers nodded.

"The thing is, Marcel never made it home," Leo said.

Helia startled at that. Truth be told, so did he.

"What?" Helia demanded.

"Kendall and I wanted to know more about the knife used on Flannery, so we started looking into him. He left here, traveled to Vegas where he worked for four months as a dishwasher, then disappeared."

"Why would he work as a dishwasher if he was a sous-chef?" Charley asked, leaning onto Mantis's thigh as he sat on the arm of the chair she'd claimed.

"Because he was hiding," Callie replied.

"From what?" Lina added.

"Let's walk through it all," Lovell said, a man of few words. "Once we have the lay of the land, then you can go down rabbit holes."

Kendall looked to Leo for direction. He nodded back. "Okay," she said, her voice strong but a little wobbly with nerves. "The timeline starts with Marcel's disappearance last fall. He left here in September, went to Vegas, then disappeared. There's no record of him being anywhere after the middle of January."

"He didn't leave the country," Leo added. "I checked."

"Then we leap ahead to Justin Flannery showing up in

Helia's life again, a little over five months ago. Next is Roger's death, here," Kendall said, pointing to the spot on the timeline. "We don't know when the poisoning started, though, only when he died. After Roger's death, we have Flannery's death, then Derek Weber showing up at Sundaram," she continued, moving down the line.

"Who's Weber?" Scipio asked.

"An ex of Helia's," Monk said darkly. Helia nudged him with her toe, and he slid his hand under the blanket, wrapping it around her foot.

"Not really an ex—that's why it was so strange," Helia said. "We went on two dates. There was only one kiss and a bad one at that."

He felt more than saw all his brothers' eyes travel to him at the mention of a kiss. To a one, the women snorted, chuckled, and even laughed. He didn't begrudge Helia a past; hell, she was a lot more normal and healthy than he was. But, yeah, he didn't like it.

"I'm not sure that helped, Helia," Mantis said, trying to keep a straight face.

Helia rolled her eyes. "Whatever. He's a nobody in the scheme of things."

"Who he is is a restaurant manager who lives far outside his means," Leo countered. "He's not as high on our priority list as some of the others so we don't know where the money comes from, but I'll figure it out tomorrow."

"Okay, what's next, K?" Lovell asked.

Kendall blinked at the big man, then ducked her head, hiding a pleased smile at the nickname. "The afternoon after Weber showed up, the police questioned Helia about Flannery's death," she continued, pointing to a blue marker on the timeline. "Then we have Collin finding the drugs in Roger's room, the two thieves, Trish Peterson moving back to town, the murder of Kurt Fisher, Helia's house getting broken into, Kelly and Gretchen showing up at Bacco, Trish showing up to talk to Greg at Sundaram, then the attempted murder of Helia," Kendall said, reaching the end of the line.

"Why are Gretchen and Kelly on the timeline?" Monk asked before giving the others a summary of who they were.

"It made sense for Gretchen to stop by," Leo said. "She all but runs this place. She'd want to meet you, make sure things were staying in order during the hiatus Roger stipulated in those weird-ass employment agreements. But Kelly seemed—"

"Weird," Kendall said. "She's a web designer and social media manager. They're good jobs—"

"Important ones for most businesses," Helia interjected.

"But of all the people involved in the business—the wine-maker, the vineyard crew, the accountant—why her? She's not exactly critical to the day-to-day operations," Kendall said.

"And it was a good thing she asked that question," Leo said with a huge grin that told Monk not only had they found something, but that he probably wasn't going to like it.

"We looked into her, did the usual searches, but then Kendall found her social media pages and clicked through a few of her posts."

"And videos," Kendall said, picking up the story. "She's who I heard here the day Roger died. The one talking about the poison."

Beside him, Helia gasped. His hand closed around her foot, steadying her, but the information shocked him, too. He hadn't liked Kelly from the get-go, but he hadn't expected *that* bomb. Neither had anyone else if the silence that followed meant anything.

A full minute ticked by before Helia spoke. "So Kelly and some unknown man murdered Roger? Are they tied to the other murders then?"

"How?" Lina asked. "How did they murder Roger? We know it was poison, but what kind and how did they administer it?"

"I'm a little more interested in the why," Callie said.

Monk nodded. "Given the ties to folks in the import/export business, we already considered the possibility of a drug ring in Napa Valley tied to this. But I agree, why kill Roger? The 'how' is interesting, but we may never know unless we get a confession. The standard blood work they do after a death showed nothing, and the body's been cremated."

Scipio walked to the board. He'd earned his handle as a nod to General Scipio of the Roman army, one of the greatest military strategists to ever live.

The room fell silent as he studied it, occasionally tracing an invisible line with his finger.

"Did Roger have any social media?" he asked.

"Very minimal, mostly about Bacco or charity events," Kendall replied

"Any way to tell if his schedule changed in the last year?" he asked. Leo started tapping at his keyboard, Kendall hovering over his shoulder.

A few minutes later, he looked up. "Based on his credit card bills, it did. A subtle shift, but it changed. Seven months ago, he went out for dinner or drinks at least four to five times a week. Four months ago, it was two times a week. In the month before he died, he went out only three times."

"But he was still hosting his parties," Monk said. "Or at least one," he added. He didn't like reminding Kendall of her mother and the situation that resulted in her landing at the castle. Darting a glance her way, he breathed a little easier seeing her glued to Leo's screen.

"He had a separate account he used to cover the cost of those—food, alcohol. Other things," Leo said. Monk was glad he forwent describing those other things. Neither he nor Kendall needed those details.

"Last year, he hosted an average of two parties a month, each lasting two nights. In the last four months, he hosted three total," Leo said.

"He slowed that down, too," Monk said. "What does that mean, Scipio?"

"K?" Scipio asked, turning away from the board.

"Yeah?"

"Did Justin have social media?"

She nodded. "The usual accounts."

"Any pictures with Kelly, Kurt, or Roger?"

"Kelly and Roger, yes. Derek, too. Not many, but a few from community events," she replied.

"Any chance he posted videos?" Scipio asked.

Kendall stilled, then lunged for her phone. "I didn't check that. I'll do it now."

"You think he was the second voice?" Lovell asked. "The one talking to Kelly?"

Scipio didn't answer. "What do we know about Trish?"

"In the middle of a divorce from her second husband, Mark Pena," Leo said. "Former resident of Miami. Worked for Pena's lighting import company while they were married."

"She seems like a woman who would have social media. K, can you check hers, too?"

"On it," Kendall said without looking up.

The room fell silent again. Helia shifted, leaning into him. Lifting an arm, he wrapped it around her shoulders. The tension in her body told him she was awake, but her eyes drifted closed.

The sudden blare of audio from Kendall's phone startled everyone, sending an uncomfortable ripple of laughter through the room.

"Sorry," Kendall winced, lowering the volume. The room quieted as the sound of a man's voice, presumably Flannery's, went on, humblebragging about his VIP access to BottleRock, the annual music festival held in the valley.

"It was him," Kendall said, ending the video. "He was the one talking to Kelly. I'll look up Trish now," she added, as if she hadn't just identified a killer.

"Helia?" Scipio said.

"Yeah?"

"Do you know who Sundaram orders its food from?"

"Yes, but not off the top of my head. We have a lot of vendors. Some we use regularly; those are mostly local. We also have a cadre of ones for the specialty items we need only when an event calls for them—things like spices from Thailand or India, fish from Japan, wine from Italy."

"Can Leo access that list?"

Her hazel eyes searched Scipio's face, then slowly, she nodded. "Our vendor management application is cloud-based. If you give me a laptop, I can log in to the system for you."

A device materialized from a bag beside the couch and less than a minute after booting it up, Helia passed it to Leo. Without needing direction from Scipio, he put his head down and started looking. He didn't bother explaining what for.

"Here's Trish's social media," Kendall said, handing her phone over to Scipio. He took a minute to flip through a few posts, Kendall directing him through the various apps. He squeezed her shoulder when he handed the device back and offered a quiet "thank you" before walking over to Leo and reading the laptop over his shoulder.

Leo pointed to a spot on his screen, and Scipio nodded. Looking up, his attention settled on Helia. Monk's body tensed. "Monk told us your mom's theory," Scipio said.

"What theory?" Callie asked.

"If this situation is like a Venn diagram, Helia's in a few of the overlapping circles," he said.

"But not at the center," Lina said.

Scipio shook his head. "She's not at the center." He paused, a shadow of worry reflecting in his eyes as they settled on Helia. "Sundaram is."

CHAPTER TWENTY-NINE

Helia's stomach lurched. "No," she whispered even as she saw the possibility. Collin's hand squeezed hers, and he pulled her tighter against him.

"How?" she managed to ask as she fought visions of her parents' business imploding. Everything they'd worked for since retiring from the military could go up in smoke. They'd have the land, sure, but that wasn't what they loved. Not to mention all the people who relied on the business for income.

"How is it at the center, or how did I come to that conclusion?" Scipio asked.

She'd meant the former, but the latter would let her postpone hearing the answer she didn't want to hear. "The latter."

"The timing," Scipio started. "Everything started a little over six months ago. You said you noticed Flannery coming around four to five months ago, which means he probably cropped up before that. It would have taken you a little while to see the pattern."

She nodded.

"Based on what K heard, whatever poison Kelly and Flannery were feeding Roger took some time to take effect," Scipio continued.

"You think those two things are connected. That Flannery was setting up a relationship with Helia that would be in place when Roger died," Lina said, nodding her head in understanding.

"But why?" Helia asked. "I saw Roger on occasion at events and things like that, but we never had dealings that weren't professional."

"We'll get to that," Scipio said. "First, I want to talk about Trish. Another person from your past, Helia." Helia nodded for him to continue. He walked over and handed her Kendall's phone. "Take a look at those pictures."

She scrolled through Trish's social media feeds, glancing at picture after picture. Some with girlfriends, most with a man Helia assumed was her husband given the way the two touched each other. In several, Trish sat perched on her husband's lap, his hand tucked between her thighs. In others, they were both caught laughing—genuine smiles of delight on their faces. And in a few, he was kissing her. Deeply.

"Trish and her husband," she said, handing the phone back. "And?"

"Do those pictures show a couple about to get divorced?" Scipio asked.

A rhetorical question, but she had to point out, "We don't know how old those posts are."

"We do," Scipio said. "The last one was posted seven days ago, but we can get Leo to run a time stamp analysis on them."

"Happy to, but not sure it's needed when we look deeper at Mark Pena," Leo said. "We didn't include him in our initial scope, and we should have. He's a well-known importer of high-end light fixtures. Handblown chandeliers from Murano, silver sconces from India, those sorts of things."

"But," Joey pressed.

"This is preliminary since I just started digging into him, but if the paper trail of his finances is right, he also appears to be part of the DKZ."

"No shit," Lovell—James—said.

Taking in the range of reactions to that information, everything from small frowns to raised eyebrows to disgust, several in the group knew something she didn't.

"What's the DKZ?" she asked.

"Stands for *da khukhi zai*. Pashto for 'the happy place,'" Marley answered.

"Started about twenty years ago by a group of US soldiers," Mantis jumped in. "Soldiers who lacked any moral compass and who decided that combat pay wasn't cutting it."

"They didn't so much go into business with the local producers of opium in Afghanistan as bully and terrorize them into it," Viper added.

"With the years of endless rotations into and out of that country, the group grew more powerful than they probably anticipated," Mantis continued.

"And the allure of that kind of money is impossible for some people to resist, so many kept at it when they discharged. Growing markets in the US and Europe," Collin said.

"The government knows they're doing it, knows the origin of the group, but because they're military..." James let the sentence hang.

Helia struggled to take everything in. Maybe it was the drugs she'd been given, or maybe it was because this situation was so far outside her reality that putting two and two together felt more like putting a round peg in a square hole.

"Was Mark Pena ever even in the military?" she asked. Not the most urgent question, but her mind wanted the baby steps.

"Served a single tour after college," Leo answered. "Deployed to Afghanistan."

"But Justin imported from South Asian countries, mostly Thailand and China," she said. "And you said Kurt worked for a company that had criminal ties, but also to South Asia."

"If you get a toehold in the drug world, expansion pays," James answered.

She blinked. "So this DKZ started with opium from Afghanistan, terrorizing a population of people who were already being terrorized by circumstances, and has expanded to other parts of Asia?"

"And South America. America's appetite for illicit drugs is unequaled. Europe's not far behind," Leo said.

"And Trish is involved in this, too?" she asked.

"Seems probable," Scipio said. "She was responsible for a large portfolio of imports for Mark's business. And with her showing up out here..."

Helia leaned forward, rubbing her fingers across her forehead before running them through her hair. Collin's hand splayed warm and steady across her back.

"Okay, so you think Roger, Kelly, and Justin were part of a distribution channel for drugs that Mark and Trish imported into the US," she said. Scipio nodded. "Two questions, no, three. First, how does that involve Sundaram? Second, how does Kurt come into this? And third, how can we keep Sundaram as clean as I know we are?"

"And fourth, why did someone try to kill you today?" Collin added.

"Yeah, that, too," she said.

"The second question ties to the first," Scipio said. "You said Kurt Fisher worked for a company owned by Wei Zhao?" he asked Leo, who nodded. "Wei Zhao competes for market with DKZ."

"Three months ago, Sundaram imported several food items from them for a large wedding," Leo said, looking at the computer she'd logged on to with the Sundaram vendor database. "That, in and of itself, isn't interesting. But what is, is the fact that for the past four years, you've used a different provider for the same goods."

"You think Kurt and Wei Zhao were trying to horn in on the DKZ market here in the valley and the DKZ killed Kurt because of it," Callie said.

"No absolute proof yet, but yeah," Scipio said. The former FBI agent held his gaze, then nodded, whether in agreement with the process or his deduction, Helia didn't know.

"So Sundaram is being used, as what, a sort of receiving center for the drugs that Kelly and Justin then distribute?" Helia asked, again feeling like a bottle of turpentine was swirling in her stomach.

Scipio nodded. "Food shipments, especially frozen ones like Sundaram receives, are rarely searched, and the dry ice it's packed with can impact scent detecting that the packages go through. It's a good place to hide drugs."

"Someone at Sundaram would have to be involved then," Helia said, wanting to cry. She wouldn't, but to say she hated the idea of her parents' business being used in that way would be like saying Mount Everest was a little more than a molehill.

"Someone in the kitchen, most likely," Scipio said.

Callie rose and started pacing the room in front of the whiteboard. "I agree," she said. "It's someone in the kitchen. Someone who can receive the packages and remove the drugs before anyone else notices. Which is also where Marcel, the former intern, comes in."

"What?" Helia asked. This kept getting worse and worse.

"I'm guessing he saw something in the kitchen that he shouldn't have. Then he disappeared to Vegas, hid in the shadows, maybe waiting to see if anyone came after him, before leaving the country."

"But he never made it," Helia said, a wave of loss rolling through her. She'd liked Marcel and didn't want to think about his body being somewhere in the desert, never to be found, because he'd stumbled upon something criminal at Sundaram.

"We should see if any of our players made a trip to Vegas around the time Marcel stopped working as a dishwasher," Callie said. "They probably sent someone to do their dirty work rather than get their own hands dirty, but it's worth a look."

"I'll show Kendall how to look for that while I keep pulling the other strings," Leo said, beckoning her over. Helia was hard-pressed to question Leo's decision as she watched the girl practically skip to his side. If he thought it was okay for her to be poking around whatever HICC systems had access to flight records, that was his call. She was an exceptionally bright child, and she'd need new things to keep her focused and challenged and out of trouble. Helping to catch a killer or killers might be well and good for now, but they shouldn't make a habit of it. A conversation she and Collin would need to have at some point.

"So the drugs come into Sundaram through food deliveries, then the inside man or woman collects them, and Flannery and Kelly feed them into the market?" Hawkeye said.

"Yes," Callie said, having picked up on whatever pattern Scipio saw. "Only six months ago, things changed. When both Roger's and Flannery's behavior changed." She paused, studying the board. "They were planning a coup."

"What?" Helia said again, feeling like a fish as her mouth formed the words.

"Prior to six months ago, the ring ran like a well-oiled machine. Drugs came in, the insider collected them, handed

MONK 277

them over, Flannery and Kelly put them into market." She paused. "But Flannery got greedy. He wanted to cut out the Sundaram insider. Or maybe the insider wanted out. For whatever reason, he was preparing to take that job over. Not by being hired by Sundaram—"

"But by being with me," Helia said. At least this piece of the puzzle clicked into place. "He wanted to get back together with me so that he'd have a reason to be around Sundaram and could be the one to collect the drugs when the shipments came in."

Behind her, Collin muttered a dark curse. She leaned back and set her head on his shoulder, draping an arm around his stomach. He dropped a kiss on her hair.

"But why kill Roger?" she asked. "He never came to Sundaram. And while I could see him being a distributor of the drugs, I can't see him really being a threat to the operation. He wasn't exactly a complex man. Give him a party, and that's all he wanted."

"I don't know the answer to that, not yet," Callie said. "Do you?" she asked Scipio and Leo. Both shook their heads. "What I can see, though, is Roger not so much involved in the distribution of the drugs, but in the marketing of them."

Beneath her arm, Collin's body tightened. "Meaning they gave him the drugs, he invited his cadre of rich friends up for a party, they experimented with them over a couple of days, then, when they walked away, Flannery and Kelly had a new set of customers."

"Or, if the attendees were already customers, he deepened their loyalty to the customized mixes," Callie said.

Another curse floated to her ears, fluttering her hair on his muttered exclamation.

"We need to know four things," Scipio said. "Who at Sundaram is the insider? Who killed Marcel, assuming he's dead? Why Roger was killed." His gaze settled on Helia. "And why someone tried to kill Helia."

"Which we can do after dinner," Mantis said, rising and pulling Charley up with him. "We've all had a long day. Some more eventful than others," he said, glancing at Helia. "Let's eat and then we can come back to it, tackling the question of who at Sundaram is involved first so that Helia can go to bed. You're holding up like a champ, but on many levels, this can't be easy for you."

She appreciated his concern and, truth be told, fatigue still weighed her down. She'd force some food into her body, but she didn't feel like doing much more than that. "Thank you," she mumbled as the others started rising. Kendall grumbled some sort of objection, but Leo leaned over and whispered something to her. She didn't look happy, but she clicked a few keys and closed the laptop.

Collin's family seemed to understand that between the medications given to her by the ER and the specter of her family's business being used to shuttle drugs, she hovered in a sort of foggy limbo, and they didn't force her into any sort of conversation. Just a quiet question here or comment there. Even Sherman gently checked in with her, setting his nose on her lap every now and then.

Collin brought out a few bottles of Bacco wine, but it sat unopened on the sideboard. A handful of his brothers looked curious but chose not to indulge. Those who did drink opted for beer. She'd seen Collin have a glass so knew he wasn't bothered by it, but it was kind of sweet how they stood by him.

She ate surrounded by the general din of conversation— not nearly as loud as she'd thought it would be, but lively enough to make it clear murder and drugs weren't the topics of the hour. Philly and Callie talked about their recent honeymoon; Dulcie and James chatted about a motorcycle they were restoring. Marley chimed in about a car scheduled to come in for custom detailing. And of course, the usual mountain talk about storms and the ski season. All gentle banter meant to soothe.

In the midst of this, Kendall sat between Stein and Dulcie, looking so tiny in her chair despite being tall for her age. She ate quietly, her eyes scanning the table, bouncing from person to person as they spoke, then bouncing around even more to gauge reactions to certain comments. Helia's heart went out to her. She couldn't imagine how it must feel to sit among this group of people she'd met for the first time a few hours earlier and realize they'd be a part of her life at least until she turned eighteen. And in the case of Collin, a big part of her life as her guardian. Sorrow and nervousness swam in her expression along with curiosity and maybe a tiny bit of hope. Kendall was smart; she wouldn't miss how tight the family was. And how settled they were in Mystery Lake. Her life would be very different than the one she'd had with her mother, but not all in a bad way.

When they'd finished the pot of chili, Charley, Joey, and several of the men peeled off to clean. Collin took her hand and led her back to the tasting room, the rest of the gang following. Only when they reached the room, Collin pulled her to the side, rather than toward the couch they'd been sitting on earlier.

"Scipio?" Collin called. He looked up as everyone retook their same seats and perches. "If Helia gives you access to the employee records, do you need her for this?"

Scipio's and Mantis's gazes landed on her. She didn't like being subject to that kind of scrutiny but found it hard to care because all she wanted was to trudge upstairs and fall into Collin's very comfortable bed.

"No," Scipio said after a tiny nod from Mantis. "We can

narrow down the pool from the broader list. We may have some questions in the morning, but those can wait."

"You can access those records in the same app as the vendor records, but I can stay up," she said. Both Lina and Callie snorted. Not unkindly, more in recognition of a kindred soul who knows a lie when they see one.

"Can and will are two different things," Collin said. "We'll see you tomorrow."

With that, he nudged her to the stairwell. And gentleman that he was, he waited until they were out of sight before sweeping her up and carrying her the rest of the way. She barely remembered her head hitting the pillow before dreams of clouds and warmth wrapped around her.

CHAPTER THIRTY

Despite having woken up to a woman in bed with him less than a dozen times in his life, he knew exactly whose hand traced the lines of his chest through his T-shirt. Maybe because it had always ever been only the same woman.

"Helia," he said, capturing her hand and pulling it to his lips. Her caresses were having a predictable effect. He'd never get back to sleep if he let her touches go any further.

She snuggled into his side, the smell of her hair surrounding him. He couldn't place the scent, too earthy to be vanilla yet too sweet to be herbal.

"Sorry," she said, her voice clearer than he expected in the pitch of night. "I slept so much today and now I'm wide-awake. I'll try not to bug you."

"You're not bugging me," he grumbled. He hadn't found pleasure with a woman in nearly two decades, but his body had no problem remembering, and every nerve rippled awake in anticipation.

He didn't have to wait long for Helia's restlessness to take over, and her hand slipped under his shirt, splaying across his hip.

"Can I touch you?" she whispered. As if he'd say no now. He'd laid all his cards on the table already. So had she. If she still wanted to play—metaphorically and literally—who was he to tell her no? Not when he wanted the same. Desperately.

"Yes, remember who you're with, though."

He'd meant to remind her of his past and his lack of experience. He'd meant it as a warning that he wasn't entirely sure how much he'd be able to take before his body did what aroused bodies do. But she chuckled and ran her hand up his chest, settling it over his heart. "I'm not likely to forget, Collin."

He sat up, and she rolled to her back, cocking her head in curiosity. The room was too dark to see her eyes, though, and he didn't like that. Rising from bed, he walked to the window and pulled the drapes open. Between the privacy of Bacco and being on the third floor, he wasn't concerned about anyone seeing him. In the moonlight, he pulled his shirt off, tossing it on a nearby chair.

Helia sat up, crossing one leg in front of her. She'd fallen fast asleep when he'd carried her to bed earlier, but he'd managed to divest her of her socks and jeans. At some point, she must have taken her bra off. Now she sat watching him wearing nothing but a T-shirt and underwear.

"Take the rest off," she said.

He complied, sliding his boxer briefs down and stepping out. In the filtered light of the room, her eyes took in every inch of his body. He swelled, a welcome pain, under her eager attention.

"Your tattoos, they mean something," she said.

"They do."

She studied him another minute, and he almost turned

around to give her the full 360 view but froze when she tore her own shirt off and tossed it on the chair beside his.

Shadows fell across her body, tracing the lines and curves of her skin. He ached to be touched, to feel her sliding over him, taking him inside her. His heart pounded, heavy and thick against his ribs, in anticipation of feeling her close around him. Of hearing the sounds she'd make. Of feeling her body bow, her muscles contract, and the vibration of her voice when she cried out.

He chose not to think about why he'd never been able to experience what he experienced with Helia with another woman. Or everything his father had done to him. None of that belonged in the room. None of it belonged between them.

"Take the rest off," he said, repeating her words.

She scrambled on the bed and soon her little black panties landed on the floor beside his boxers. Again, she crossed one leg in front of her, opening her thighs and exposing all of her to him.

Need, heat, desire slammed into him, and he all but growled as he stalked back to the bed, intent on only one thing. Touching Helia. Every part of her.

Sliding a hand into her hair, he tipped her head up, slamming his mouth down on hers in a demanding, feral kiss. Her hands gripped his biceps and although he had the height advantage, she gave as much as she took.

They kissed for hours, minutes. Who knew how long they spent feeling the heat, the history, and the longing that had always existed between them roar and soar back to life.

Then abruptly, it wasn't enough. He needed more. He needed more of her.

Taking a half step away, he sank to his knees, setting his hands on her knees as he lowered. Untangling her legs, he spread her thighs, tugged her to the edge of the bed, and set his mouth on her.

She jumped at the sudden contact, but a reverent moan followed as her nails dug into his hair. He took that as a green light to continue tasting her, devouring her. He wasn't sure how long he'd last once inside her, but he could stay here on his knees for her for hours.

Her first orgasm hit, and she arched her back into his eager lips, calling his name and chasing away any lingering doubts. Freedom replaced the shackles of his history, and trust flowed between them as strong and as unstoppable as the tide.

Reveling in the power of it, he slid a finger, then two inside her. She panted and moaned and whispered his name. His body wept when she came again, squeezing him, reminding him of what it felt like—what it would feel like—to be buried inside her.

He eased her down from her second peak, then kissed his way up her belly, pausing to take one nipple in his mouth, then the other. Her hands slid from his hair to his cheeks, and she tipped his head up and lowered her lips to his. She had the height advantage now, and she teased and tasted him before urging him over her.

He rose slowly, unwilling to release contact with her, and kissed her as she scooted back on the bed, making room for him. No words were spoken when he settled between her thighs, when he ran his hands down her sides, tracing the dip of her waist and the curve of her breast. When her hands stroked the line of his back and curled over his behind. No words were spoken when she lifted her hips and pulled him into her body.

He closed his eyes as he moved, her heat and her body so familiar yet all so new.

"Collin." Her fingers dug into the small of his back, her heels against his thighs.

He speared a hand through her hair and tipped her head up to his. Setting his lips to hers, he kissed her with a hunger that was all about her. No one and nothing but her.

"More," she managed to say between pants as his lips trailed a hot path down her neck.

He'd never not give her what she wanted, not in this. Sliding a hand down, he wrapped it around her hip, holding her still. She whimpered at not being able to move with him, but it turned into a moan when he withdrew, teased her entrance with a series of short thrusts before sinking all the way in again.

A throaty, needy sound escaped her body, and she stiffened as he held her firm against the bed, thrusting into her. When her nails dug into his flesh and her back arched, nothing had ever felt so good. Liquid heat poured from her body, lighting him on fire. Her muscles fluttered, then gripped him as if they never wanted to let him go.

In a haze, he heard Helia call his name one more time as he rode them through her orgasm, before finding his own with a blinding roar.

Temple to temple, they caught their breath as their bodies hummed and slowed with the memories. Slowly, she lifted a hand, the tips of her fingers tracing a line up his spine, over his neck, and to his jaw. On a gentle nudge, he raised his head and met her sated eyes.

There were no jokes, no words even. Just a rare certainty, both soft and strong, stretching between them. Binding them to each other.

She smiled quietly, her hazel eyes tender and wise. He leaned down and brushed his lips across hers before withdrawing and shifting to her side. Gathering her in his arms, he drifted off to sleep with a peace he hadn't felt in nearly two decades.

Sunlight touched the edges of their window when they woke again. Through two floors of ancient stone and wood, he heard movement on the ground floor. Dim but unmistakable. At least one person was up.

"How'd you sleep?" Muffled through the thick comforter, he could barely make out Helia's words.

"Better than I have in a long time," he answered honestly. The sex was a part of that, but not the whole reason. Or even the main one.

The blankets shifted and Helia's face emerged, her hair scattered across her cheek and forehead. He chuckled, rolled to face her, then gently swept the strands aside. He tipped his head to kiss her, but she set her fingers to his lips and held him in place.

"I have morning breath."

He raised a brow. "I don't care," he replied, his lips dancing over the pads of her fingers.

"I do," she replied, then wrinkled her nose. "I know. Not romantic, is it? But I don't want to kill you with my dragon breath."

"Want me to get a glass of water? Mouthwash? I think I saw some in the bathroom," he offered, making a mental note to leave a bottle of water beside their bed. He could make mint iced tea and leave it in a water bottle. That would do the job.

"I have a different idea," she said, rolling him onto his back and straddling him. He had no idea what her idea was, but he was on board with it. She ran a fingertip across his jaw, down his neck, then traced the line of pecs. "Tell me about this tattoo?" she asked, running her fingers over a series of white lilies about the size of her palm.

"Saint Maria Goretti is always depicted with lilies," he answered.

Her eyes lifted to his. "I didn't know you're religious."

"I'm not. But she's the patron saint of abused children—one of them, anyway. There's Mater Matuta and Bastet on there, too. I'm good with anyone, or anything, that wants to protect children."

"I know Bastet," she said, bending her head as she found the Egyptian cat. "But who's Mater Matuta?"

"Roman goddess. She had a focus on mothers, but children, too."

"And this?" she asked, touching a swirling pattern of colors that covered a shoulder and ran down his arm.

"It's a depiction of the Kurukshetra War from the *Mahabharata*. It's more nuanced, but it was a mythical battle where justice and righteousness prevailed over ego, greed, and envy."

She tipped her head as she followed one of the images with her eyes. "I remember my dad telling me that story."

"So do I."

Her hand stilled, and her gaze snapped to his. "When did you get this?"

He didn't even think about evading the question. "When I made it through basic training." Weeks after he'd left. He'd carried a part of her family—of her—with him all these years.

"Screw morning breath," she said, folding over him and slamming her mouth onto his. Fifteen seconds later, he'd rolled them over and pushed inside her. She came almost immediately, and he reveled in the feel of her even as he gripped her thigh, pulled it to his hip, and continued thrusting into her with a relentless pace. With a frenzied, almost frantic, need, they rocked the heavy bed. And when her breath caught in those tiny gasps of anticipation, he covered her mouth with his, swallowing her cry as her body locked around his. When the sensations grew too powerful to ignore, he ripped his lips from hers and threw his head back. Heated pleasure exploded through his body, and they came together.

The world came back to him—to them—in bits and pieces. When their breaths slowed, he released his hold on her thigh and rolled gently to the side. This time, rather than curl into him, Helia remained on her back. As if unable to move. He sympathized.

Twining his fingers with hers, they lay together in silence, the cool air swirling over their heated bodies, until one thought coalesced in his brain. "I never asked you about birth control. Obviously, I'm clean..." They hadn't talked about what would happen between them once the murders were resolved, let alone things like whether they wanted kids. Although he didn't hate the idea of her pregnant with their baby. It wasn't so much a caveman thing, but more a chance to build what he'd never had, a healthy family. He'd given up wanting it, but now...well, he wouldn't put the cart before the horse. He didn't know if she even wanted kids. Or if she did, whether she'd want to try to carry them herself or adopt.

"I have an IUD," she said. "I got one years ago, and while there hasn't been anyone in my life for a while, I like it because it keeps my periods lighter."

The muffled sound of the door closing followed by a truck, no make that trucks, starting, drew his attention. Sliding out of bed, he padded to the window.

"What's going on?" Helia asked.

He frowned. "I'm not sure, but five of my brothers just left."

"Maybe they went to get pastries?"

Philly's and North's trucks were in the lineup so that was entirely possible. But given the way all of the pickup beds had tarps tied over bulky loads, he had a suspicion about what they'd been up to that morning.

"How about we shower, then find out?" he suggested. She yawned. He frowned again. "I didn't even ask how you are this morning."

"If I'm experiencing a wee bit of fatigue, it's not from yesterday. It's the good kind. The *very* good kind. Now let's hop in the shower, then head downstairs and see what your family is up to."

The shower took longer with the two of them, but he couldn't have resisted Helia's soap-slick hands sliding over his body if his life depended on it. Besides, no one would expect them up early—not after Helia's day yesterday.

Thirty minutes later, they made their way to the kitchen. Callie, Scipio, Lovell, and Lina sat at the table, coffee mugs in hand, talking in low voices. Charley, Kendall, Mantis, and Stein were cooking breakfast and cutting up fruit.

Eight sets of eyes—nine including Sherman—noticed their entrance, but no one said a thing about what they must see. What happened between him and Helia felt written on every cell in his body. And to a one, his brothers had observational skills far above average. A necessary skill to survive first their childhoods, then the military. Still, they only received a few "good mornings," a few offers of coffee, and a couple asked how Helia was feeling.

He poured coffee and handed a mug to Helia, who joined Charley and Kendall at the fruit. Mantis passed his spatula over to Stein and nodded for Monk to follow him out. Helia glanced at them as they left but remained with Charley and Kendall.

"Scipio and Leo can give us an update when everyone is back," Mantis said as they entered a room along the back side of the castle. At one time, it might have been a dining room or morning room, but he didn't know and had never bothered to find out.

Neither took a seat in the masculine space with its dark paneled walls, heavy rich drapes, and a carpet that probably cost more than many people's cars. Oh, and a pool table. Monk didn't think they had any form of billiards in Italy when the castle was originally built, but at some point, Roger had turned the room into a game room.

"It's cleared out," Mantis said.

He didn't need to say more than that. Monk had had his suspicions when he'd seen the trucks leaving. The basement, the location of all his father's parties. The place he'd drugged his son and encouraged women to use his teenage body for their pleasure. The place he'd told his son that if he didn't like it, he wasn't much of a man.

Gone. He didn't have to ask to know that every stitch of furniture, every device, every instrument, every sheet, rope, and floor covering was gone. If he went down now, all he'd see were the bare stone walls and floor.

He might never make the trip down that flight of stairs, but it surprised him how much better it felt knowing it was empty.

"Know anyone who can smudge the place?" he asked with a wry grin.

Mantis chuckled. "From what I hear, I'm guessing Gretchen would be happy to."

CHAPTER THIRTY-ONE

An hour later, Collin's brothers were back from their chore, breakfast was eaten, the kitchen cleaned, and they'd all resumed their seats in the tasting room. Scipio paced the front of the room, the fire burning gently in the hearth an odd juxtaposition to the murder board that stood beside it.

"We still have open questions, but we came to a solid working theory last night," Scipio started. Perched at one of the high tops, Leo and Kendall nodded, each with an open laptop in front of them.

Nearly everyone in the room looked at her. Helia wasn't sure why. They'd all invested time and a lot of brainpower. This seemed like all of their fight now, not just hers, but she nodded for Scipio to continue.

"Here," he said, turning the murder board around to display a drawing more akin to an organizational chart rather than the notes and timeline on the other side. At the top was a name Helia didn't recognize, but connected by a line, beneath that box was Mark Pena's name. Beneath his was his wife's name, and under Trish's was Roger Wilde. Branching out under Roger were three names: Justin Flannery, Kelly Carter, and Akin Miller. Off to the side were two unconnected boxes, one with Derek Weber's name and the other listing Kurt Fisher.

"What are we looking at?" Helia asked.

"A drug ring," North said.

Scipio nodded. "Run by Johnny Haines out of Hong Kong," he said, pointing to the top box.

"How'd you get to that?" Mantis asked.

"Before you answer, why is Akin's name on there?" she interjected, setting a hand on her stomach, hoping the pressure would ease the acid burning there.

"Drugs are coming in from South Asia through Sundaram," Scipio said. "We don't believe they are distributed from there, but that is the point of delivery. Akin, as your chef, is in charge of ordering the food. It's possible it's not him. It could be your kitchen manager, Greg, but there are reasons we've settled on Akin. I can get into those now or as we walk through this," he said, gesturing to the whiteboard.

She wasn't ready to contemplate Akin's potential betrayal of Sundaram. Maybe that made her a coward, but she didn't care. "Start at the top, please."

Scipio nodded. "Johnny Haines is an American-born man of Chinese descent. Like Pena, he served in the military but then moved to Hong Kong after he discharged to run his uncle's export business. In addition to English, Cantonese, and Mandarin, he also speaks Thai, Vietnamese, Pashto, and Urdu."

"He speaks more languages than you do, babe," Viper commented.

"He sounds like a spook," Lina agreed with a nod.

"The CIA did try to recruit him, as did the Chinese government, but Johnny had other plans," Scipio continued. "Why get a shitty paycheck risking your life for a government who'd leave you high and dry at the blink of an eye when you can make millions trafficking drugs?"

"Well, when put like that," Callie said.

"Did Pena and Haines meet while serving?" Helia asked, her head spinning.

Scipio nodded. "Same unit. Deployed together. They've kept in touch."

"We have records of phone calls," Leo said, looking up.

"And a couple of social media posts of them together," Kendall added. Helia's gaze lingered on the preteen, but she chose not to revisit the question as to whether it was a good idea to keep her so involved. That horse had left the barn.

"Okay, so that's the link between Haines and Pena and presumably Trish. Where do we go from there?" she asked.

"We suspect Pena's the boss of the US operations of the DKZ, but the DEA would need to confirm that," Scipio continued. "Trish is, for lack of a better term, his lieutenant, in addition to being his wife."

"Which means?" Joey asked.

"She manages the people. She keeps everyone in line, organizes the logistics, that sort of thing," Leo answered.

"Basically, runs the show but doesn't get to claim the title of 'boss,'" Kendall said. Helia chuckled at the round of comments from the women in the room. Apparently, no matter the profession, women were still getting shafted in the workplace.

"Pena manages up while Trish manages down," Leo said. "Not that I disagree with Kendall's take, just telling you the organizational structure."

Stone crossed his arms, his gaze fixed on the whiteboard, Sherman lying on his feet. "Pena handles the relationship with Haines—"

"And Haines's inner circle," Leo interjected.

Stone nodded. "And Trish manages the downstream distributors. Based on your chart, that means she worked with Roger, who then worked with Akin, Kelly, and Flannery."

Scipio nodded.

"But the shipments come into Sundaram," Helia said. "Oh god, I think I'm going to be sick." Collin's big, warm hand settled on her back. Everyone else in the room sent her supportive but commiserating looks.

Scipio hesitated.

She took a deep breath and waved for him to continue.

A beat passed, then Scipio did as asked. "Last night, we realized that the police reports included no mention of Roger's cell phone. He had to have had one. No way was he making deals and running a business—even tangentially—without a phone. And there's only one landline in the building, and that goes to Gretchen's office and the tasting room."

"So we went on a treasure hunt," Leo jumped in. "Turns out, you all missed a place yesterday. The toilet tanks."

"The hell?" Collin said, his hand pausing in its strokes.

"Another great idea from the youngest member of our crew," Leo said. Kendall didn't look up but she smiled.

Scipio nodded. "Roger Wilde was a paranoid bastard. Had reasons to be even without being targeted for murder. We found his cell phone in a plastic bag in the tank of his toilet, and in two others, we found drugs. We've left the drugs where they are, but Leo and Kendall went through his phone last night."

"His text messages indicate he was the primary contact with Trish," Leo said.

"And I found a couple of pictures of the two. Not at events here in the valley, but in Florida," Kendall said. "One was from a party in LA, though. It was taken seven years ago. That's when we think they met."

Helia stifled a moan. Collin restarted his soothing rubs as he spoke. "Roger and Trish decide to start trafficking drugs into the Napa Valley. Pena and Trish broker the deal with him, but he doesn't have any way to get them into the valley without raising flags since Bacco doesn't import much."

"Which is when he brings in Akin. Or Greg," Helia said. "What better partner than a business that imports food frequently enough not to raise any red flags when shipments come through, but not so regularly as to raise red flags with customs agents."

Scipio nodded. "Once they arrive, Akin—or Greg—gets them to Kelly and Justin, who then distribute them." He paused, then he added, "With some coming to Roger both for his personal use and to use during the parties he hosted."

"Marketing the drug," Collin said, repeating Callie's suggestion from the night before. "He had access to drugs well before that, though," he added.

"He did." Scipio nodded.

"But not the high-end designer stuff you found in his room," Leo said. "When we tested it, our lab folks had never seen anything like it. The base drugs are the standard ones we talked about, but they've been customized and engineered in such a way that could only happen with the most modern equipment and knowledge."

"Why would Kelly and Justin kill him, then?" Philly asked.

Several people in the room nodded.

"They either found another broker or he became a liability," Callie opined. "And since the drug is hyper-engineered, I'm guessing it's the latter."

"It was," Scipio answered. "Leo ran Roger's text messages through some sort of program that I'm not going to explain because only about five people in the room will understand it, and I'm not one of them. The gist of it is, though, Roger was getting both reckless and careless."

"And forgetful," Kendall added.

"And forgetful," Scipio agreed. "Not anything major, nothing to expose them completely, but he slipped up enough publicly—saying things he shouldn't—that Kelly even mentioned it in a text to him. We think all three were getting nervous."

"Nervous enough to kill him before he said anything to implicate them," Charley said, her tone both curious and reflective.

Scipio nodded. "But once they killed him—and we may never know how—it created a leadership vacuum."

"A space all three—Kelly, Justin, and either Akin or Greg— wanted to step into," Collin said, leaning back against the couch. Sliding his hand forward, he wrapped his fingers around hers.

"And that's when things started getting ugly," Leo jumped in. "Flannery made an early move when he tried getting close to Helia. If he succeeded, he'd be spending more time at Sundaram, making Akin obsolete. Fulfilling two roles in the chain, receiver *and* distributor, potentially makes him more valuable to leadership."

"Also making him the first target," Dulcie said.

"Based on the shoe print in the carpet at Flannery's house, Akin was the likely killer. Knocking out his competition."

"I don't see it," Helia said. Everyone looked at her. "I mean, I see the scenario and don't disagree. But I can't see Akin being involved."

"He spends the most time in the kitchen," Scipio pointed out.

Helia inclined her head. "I'll grant you that, but he's not the one who places the orders. Greg does that."

"At Akin's direction, though?" Mantis asked.

She didn't want to concede that point, but she couldn't turn a blind eye. "Yes, at his direction," she said. "But Greg has final say on the vendors."

"You think Greg is the one we should be looking at?" Leo asked.

She sighed. "I don't know." Her gut said Akin wasn't involved, but what did her gut know about drug dealing and murder? It wasn't as if she had any experience to draw on. "I don't want to think it's Greg, either. But if it *is* one of them, I guess I could see it being Greg more than Akin. Akin loves his job. I mean, really loves it. Greg likes his, he likes the lifestyle it gives him in terms of it being a lot less stress than his prior job, but he doesn't love it like Akin." She paused. "Is there anything showing up in their finances? If they're selling drugs, I assume they're making money from it."

"Neither have shown any unusual financial transactions," Leo said.

"Where's the money?" Callie asked.

"Likely in an offshore account we haven't found yet," Leo answered.

"Will you find it?" Helia asked. What she knew about offshore accounts she'd learned reading thrillers.

"They will," Joey said. Leo flashed her a warm smile.

"If you haven't found it yet, why'd you settle on Akin?" Dulcie asked.

Scipio tipped his head to the side. "Proximity. Not a determinative factor, but a real one. He has the easiest access, the most natural access, to the shipments of food when they come in."

"And would be best positioned to remove the drugs when delivered to Sundaram," James said.

"To Helia's point, we shouldn't exclude Greg from the suspect pool," Scipio conceded. "When we dug into Akin, it made sense, but we didn't know that Greg selected the vendors. In my mind, that moves the needle back fairly between the two." His gaze scanned the room, looking for validation on the slight shift of focus. Everyone nodded. Helia agreed but couldn't bring herself to join the group. She was too close to both men to feel comfortable considering either a killer.

Pushing her opinions and personal wishes aside, she returned to the story Scipio was painting. "Okay, so chaos ensues after Roger dies, with the three parties fighting to take over the lead role. Justin is killed in the process, leaving Kelly and either Greg or Akin."

"Which is when Trish steps in," Leo said.

"To clean up the mess," Lina said with a contemplative nod.

"Exactly," Scipio replied. "Pena and his wife have a lot on the line if Kelly or Akin or Greg call too much attention to the situation—two people have already died, which is more than unusual for this area. If they start infighting even more, the higher the risk the whole operation will get exposed."

"Which is where we have some good news," Kendall said, jumping into the conversation as she flipped her computer around. "What do you think of this?" she asked. Sitting across the room, Helia couldn't make out the image, but those closest leaned in.

"A picture of Helia talking to someone at Sundaram?" Mantis said.

"That's not Helia," Callie said.

Kendall grinned. "It's not. It's Kelly. From behind, or even from the side depending on how they are wearing their hair, they look a lot alike."

Beside her, Collin sucked in a breath. "Helia wasn't the target of the dart yesterday, was she? It was Kelly."

"That is what we think," Leo replied.

"Trish and her husband have either decided that Greg/Akin will run the show and intended to take Kelly out of the picture. Or they've decided that neither will and they're cleaning house," Scipio said.

"I saw Kelly there, in town," Helia said, that snippet of memory coming back. "About ten minutes before I was hit, she was at a restaurant down the block."

"Another piece of circumstantial evidence to support our theory," Leo said. "If Trish knew Kelly was in the area, but not what she was wearing, she could have easily mistaken you two."

"Does that mean they'll kill Greg or Akin next? And try for Kelly again?" Helia asked, horrified at the thought. She had no respect for the dealers, but she didn't like the idea of them being murdered.

"We don't know which strategy Pena and Trish will take, killing one or both, but yeah, we think one of those two things will happen," Scipio said. Then added, "But as K said, the good news is, we don't think you're the target."

She wouldn't lie, relief trickled through her, but only a little. She'd not feel truly at ease until this was all over.

"What about Derek?" she asked, nodding to his solitary box. "And Kurt?"

Scipio studied the board. "Derek we're not sure about. We're still looking into him. We've only found a handful of social media pictures connecting him and Roger, but his spending habits are giving us pause."

"And Kurt?"

"We're sticking with the theory from last night," Scipio said.

"He wanted to see if Wei Zhao's organization should move in," Lina said.

"And encountered a strong 'no' from Pena's organization. Likely at Trish's hand. Maybe with the help of one of the others," Scipio agreed.

Helia hesitated to ask the question on her mind but swallowed her reluctance. "Collin said the killing was brutal and happened somewhere other than where we found him. Could Trish have done that on her own?"

"The killing, yes," Collin answered. "Assuming she had a sharp machete."

"But unless she killed him in the back of whatever vehicle was used to transport him to the vineyard, she had help," Callie said. "Kurt wasn't huge. A hundred and eighty pounds?"

"One ninety-three," Leo said.

"That's a lot of dead weight," Callie finished.

Helia's brain swam with all the information they'd gone over in the past hour. The picture Scipio, Leo, and Kendall painted was missing a few pieces, but still clear enough. At the heart of it all, Roger, Kelly, Justin, and either Akin or Greg were very likely involved in a drug ring. A business that left two dead and the others in the crosshairs.

"Okay," she said. "The drugs are at the center of it all. What can we do about that?"

Scipio shared a look with his brothers. Collin nodded at some unasked question, then Mantis did the same.

His gaze settled on her. "We need to bring in the DEA."

CHAPTER THIRTY-TWO

"The DEA?" Helia asked him. "Not the police? Not Carter and Jess?"

No doubt calling in the Feds sounded big and scary, but for those in the room who'd worked with them, it was less unpredictable than working with local police.

"There are two reasons," Monk said. Helia nodded, her hazel eyes filled with questions. "The first is that this is too big for the locals. Players like Pena and DKZ are not only out of their jurisdiction, but out of their realm of experience. The second reason is Sundaram."

"What about it?" she asked, her body tense in anxious anticipation.

"The Feds will see Sundaram as little more than a small piece of a much larger puzzle. They will have no reason to focus on it other than for the slice of information they can glean from it."

Her eyes slowly narrowed as the import of what he said sank in. "Whereas with local law enforcement, Sundaram will *be* the story."

He nodded. "Jess and Carter don't strike me as the most experienced detectives, but they don't strike me as gossips, either. I can't say that about the rest of the force they'd need to bring into this."

"And they'd end up handing it over anyway," Callie added. "Like Monk said, it's too big for them. They might salivate over the opportunity, but in the end, if they are *any* good at their job, they'll know it's too big."

She hesitated. "Okay then, the DEA it is. Do they have a hotline or something?"

Callie and Lina smiled. "They do," Callie said. "But I'm thinking Scipio has someone in mind to reach out to directly."

"I do," Scipio said. Monk already knew what he'd say, so he kept his focus on Helia. His father had brought this on all of them. A week ago, he didn't think he could loathe Roger Wilde any more. His revulsion had doubled for what the aftermath of his decisions was doing to Helia.

"A former teammate of ours is DEA now. He runs a team out of the LA office. We didn't want to put a call in to Reaper until we ran it by you," he said.

"Reaper? As in grim?" she asked. Monk bit back a smile. Helia had a habit of focusing on the small things when the big things got too big. Not that she avoided the big things, but she needed a little time to work her way around to them.

"From the pepper," Lovell replied.

Helia swung her head around to where he sat with Marley and Hawkeye. "His mom's from Trinidad. He pops peppers like candy," Hawkeye said.

Marley nodded. "We're talking food so spicy you can't even taste it."

"Why would you eat food you can't taste?" Helia asked.

The guys all chuckled. "Sometimes it's better not to taste the food they gave us," Mantis said.

"But he did it for the high, no question," Stone said.

"And the bragging rights," Philly added. "Remember the night he ate that ghost pepper raw?"

Hawkeye ran a hand over his face. "I thought I was going to have to perform some not-so-minor surgery."

"That bad?" Joey asked.

Hawkeye chuckled and shook his head. "Fucker ended up barely even breaking a sweat."

For the first time in too long, Helia smiled. "Okay, Reaper it is, then. Go ahead and make the call." She paused, then added, "But I don't want James to get in trouble for taking Roger's stash from Bacco to HICC. Will you make sure of that?"

Lovell's expression softened, a sight so rare Monk could count on one hand the times he'd seen it.

"Reaper won't let that happen," Lovell said.

"HICC won't either," Leo added.

Helia took a deep breath. "Okay," she said. "Let's get this thing started. Christmas is coming in hot, and while I doubt it will be wrapped up by then, I'd like it underway enough that we can all celebrate."

The room started moving, people rose from their seats, some went to the kitchen to make more coffee, a few asked if they could tour the wine caves, Mantis and Stone joined Scipio in a quiet corner to make the call.

Monk turned to Kendall, who was watching the goings-on with an anxious expression, as if unsure where she fit in to it all. "K?" he called. "Go for a walk with me?"

Her eyes darted to Helia, who seemed to know what he needed. Leaning over, she kissed his cheek before rising. "I'm going to give my parents a call." He gave her hand a squeeze, then turned back to Kendall, who nodded.

A few minutes later, dressed in jackets, hats, and sneakers, they closed the door behind them and headed toward the south vineyard, away from Sundaram. They walked in silence for a while as their bodies shed the intensity of the past hour. When they reached a trail that led up the steep hill, she asked, "What was it like growing up here?"

"Complicated," he replied. He paused, and they both turned to look out over the vineyard. They hadn't made it far up the hill, but they were high enough to see the vines stretching for miles, a patchwork of different wineries. "It's beautiful, of course," he started. "And I grew up with a silver spoon in my mouth, so to speak. Never wanted for anything."

"But Roger was your dad."

He nodded. "On the outside, it looked like a fucking fairy tale."

"But was really a nightmare?"

He paused before answering. "Parts of it, yes," he replied. "Parts of it left wounds so deep I don't know if they'll ever even form a scar. Some days it seems like maybe I can heal. Not completely, but enough that it becomes more of a twinge than pain."

"And the other parts?"

He thought of Helia and the Shaws. "Other parts are good. I met the Shaws when I was fourteen. They showed me what a real family could be. *How* a family could be. Because of them, I wasn't completely fucked up when I enlisted. Those years gave me the foundation to build and be a part of the family I have today."

He left it at that, and they started back on the trail, climbing toward the top. "We have a meeting with the social worker on January 4," he said. "I know it's a lot, but I need to ask you a few questions."

He waited for her to agree, a small "okay" came after a dozen steps.

"I live at the clubhouse now. I never had a reason to move

out. We'll have to stay there while we sort out next steps, but that's what I wanted to ask you."

"If I'm okay about staying at the club?" she asked. "I am. I like your family."

"They're yours too when you're ready for them," he said. "But that was only part of the question. We'll need a house," he continued. "I have enough savings to buy one, and the estate, well, if I wanted, I wouldn't ever have to worry about money."

"You don't want Roger's money," she said.

He inclined his head. "I don't. But I'd make exceptions. And it's not all Roger's. Well, legally it is, but it wasn't what he made or built. There's a huge chunk of the estate that's more or less intact from my grandfather. I can use some of that to buy us a house and start an account for your college."

She stumbled behind him, and he stopped to check on her. "College?" she asked.

He considered pausing but decided this conversation was better had on the move. "You're one of the brightest kids I've ever met. Granted, I haven't met a lot of kids, but even Leo is impressed, and he's a certified genius. If college is what you want, we'll make it happen." He let that sink in for a few minutes as they reached the top of the hill. The stone bench his grandfather had built decades ago still stood. He'd only been five when his grandfather died, but he remembered coming up to this spot with him. After brushing the seat free of debris, he sat. Kendall hesitated, then sat beside him.

"What I really wanted to talk about is the house, though. There's not a lot on the market right now because it's the middle of the ski season, but once the snow melts, we'll see more. If we know what we want, Stone worked with an agent we can ask to keep an eye on things for us." He paused again. "What kind of house do you want?"

"One with a roof and walls and running water and working electricity," she responded. "Other than that, I don't care."

He chuckled. It was that or cry. "You can do better than that, K. Do you want to be in town or have some land? There's not much lakefront property left, but there's some in the hills or on the rivers that feed the lake."

She took a moment to answer. "I don't know. Maybe after we visit, I'll know. I've always been around people, except when my mom took me to other people's property. I didn't like those trips, but maybe that was because she left me to figure it out on my own, and it was so different than the apartments I was used to. Maybe I'd like it." She paused. "But I like the idea of being in town. Close to people, but with our own space. It's a safe town, right?"

He nodded. "It gets a lot of tourists so has some of the usual issues, but overall, it's safe. Safe enough to walk around on your own once you're familiar with it. And Joey and Charley's store is downtown, as is their cousin's gallery, so you'll always have a place to go if something doesn't feel right to you."

"What about school?"

"Another question. There's a middle school that includes sixth, seventh, and eighth grade. That's where you'd fit age-wise, but you're beyond that intellectually. That said, I'm not sure I'm comfortable with you testing into the high school. For that matter, I don't even know if you want to go to school or if you want to keep studying online."

Birds swooped in the valley below; a gentle breeze rustled the trees. On a cool, dry day like this, Monk could barely make out the scent of the place, but after rain, or a hot summer day? Those memories were burned into his brain: damp earth mixed with the musky decay of the vineyards or dry oak that's been baked in the sun. To this day, if he caught a whiff of a similar smell, no matter where he was, his mind instantly flew back to this valley.

"What about Helia?" Kendall asked. "I mean, it's obvious you two are fu—"

He swiveled his head and raised an eyebrow at her. She snapped her mouth shut. She hadn't had the best role models for relationships in her life, but no way was he going to let her paint his and Helia's relationship with the same brush as whatever she'd seen with her mom.

"That you like each other. A lot," she finished.

He nodded, both acknowledging her effort and the comment itself. "We do. We haven't talked about the details yet, though." They'd have to at some point, but he had no idea how it would all work out.

"But you want to be together?"

He caught a tendril of hope, or maybe even wistfulness, in her voice that he hadn't expected. His heart tumbled a little more for her. She had every right to be jaded and hard. She *was* jaded. She knew more about the seedy part of the world than most adults—his brothers excluded. And yet she wanted to see, to be a part of, a happy ever after. That she even knew those existed in real life surprised him. That she believed in them made him want to wrap her up and make sure the tender parts of her heart had the same opportunity to grow as strong as her curiosity, intelligence, and wariness.

"We do and we will be. We just don't know what that will look like yet."

"If I stay in online school, it'd be easier for us to come down here to visit."

"First of all, you're done having to make your decisions and live your life to make someone else's easier," he said. "I'm not saying you turn into a selfish beast, but despite the life experience you've had, K, you're *twelve*. You need a chance to be a kid.

I know that's hard to imagine. You've probably never been a kid, not really. And losing your mom is yet one more shitty card you've been dealt." He wasn't sure he was being totally honest about that part. If Cindy had cleaned up her act, based on what he knew about Kendall, she probably would have been a great mom. But as it was, Kendall had a better chance at building a good life with him than she had being toted around the country to random people's houses. He knew the kind of people Cindy spent her time with—hell, Roger was the same. He refused to imagine what Kendall's life would have been like if Cindy had kept dragging her to one party after another once she started maturing.

"But Helia and I are the adults," he continued. "We will make the best decision we can given both our circumstances. You aren't an afterthought, though, K. Your life, whether that's school or if you want to play sports or pick up some hobbies, is as important as Helia's and mine."

She slipped her hands under her thighs and rocked back and forth, a subtle but telling motion. "Can we focus on the drug ring and murders for now?"

He couldn't help it—he barked out a laugh. A wry smile touched her lips.

"You know how many things are wrong about that statement, K?"

Her grin grew into a smile. "Yeah, but I'll be able to write one hell of a college essay when the time comes."

CHAPTER THIRTY-THREE

"Where's Helia?" Monk and Kendall asked at the same time when they returned to the tasting room.

"She wanted to check in on the two events at Sundaram. Lovell, Dulcie, and Einstein are with her," Mantis replied.

He trusted his brothers to keep her safe, but he didn't like her being out in the open. Sure, Kendall was probably right that Kelly had been the target of the lethal dart, but his head and his heart didn't seem to want to agree. And by the look on Kendall's face, she felt the same.

Not wanting to give her anything more to worry about, he squeezed her shoulder and moved on to the topic he and Kendall had discussed the whole walk back. "Did you get a hold of Reaper?"

Mantis flashed a smile Monk had seen a time or two. Some unholy hell was about to break loose.

"Turns out Reaper and his team, along with teams from Miami and New York, already have a case against Haines, Pena, and Trish Peterson. They've got eyes on all three but need to coordinate with international authorities before they pick them up, since Haines is out of the country."

"They've got someone up here?" Monk asked.

Mantis nodded. "Agent Perry. She'll be here in about twenty minutes for a briefing on what we have. Leo has already started the transfer of evidence, including the drugs you found, to the agency."

"It could be over soon?" Kendall asked. Monk wasn't sure if that was excitement or disappointment in her voice. Judging by Mantis's head tilt, he couldn't tell either. Which was concerning, as their MC president usually knew how people felt before they did.

"If all goes to plan, yes," Mantis said. "We might even be home for Christmas."

Kendall seemed confused by the idea of Christmas, and Monk made a mental note to drag Helia somewhere private so they could go online and buy her gifts. If they ordered today and he had them rushed, they'd make it to Mystery Lake by Christmas Eve. He could have them under the tree by Christmas morning.

"Do you have a tree?" she asked.

Charley laughed as she entered the room, carrying a couple of coffee mugs. "Do they have a tree. The main room in the club —it's called the lodge room because it looks like one with tall ceilings, big beams, a huge fireplace—has an eighteen-foot tree. It's over the top, but beautiful."

Mantis took one of the mugs from Charley, then pulled her to his side. "We do. None of us are religious, but we like Christmas. A lot of us never had much of one growing up." His gaze flitted to Monk. "Or if we did, it didn't hold any real meaning since our lives were generally a violent chaos. So now we put up a big tree, draw names for gifts, and spend the day eating too much and playing games." He paused, then chuckled. "It all sounds very Norman Rockwell, but we like it."

"But doesn't your family want you with them?" Kendall asked Charley.

"This is our first Christmas together, so we'll have to figure that out. As of now, the plan is Christmas Eve dinner with my extended family—which is *huge*—then Christmas Day and dinner with the club, followed by dessert with my immediate family."

"Ah, Kendall, good, you're back," Leo said, walking into the room. Then turning to Mantis, he said, "Joey's still in the caves with whoever else went out there, but she texted to ask if we need her to run to the store."

"We'll do an inventory and let her know," Mantis said, motioning for Monk to follow him into the kitchen.

"Joey loves music, and I want to get a full sound system for the shop she and Charley own and could use your help. I'm betting you know more about that kind of thing than I do," Leo said to Kendall, his voice fading as Monk and Mantis made their way to the kitchen.

Leaving tales of murder and drugs behind, they spent twenty minutes inventorying the kitchen then sending Joey the text. Feeding twenty people wasn't a stretch for them, but it did take planning. With a massive grill at their disposal, they decided on fajitas for lunch since they had the meat and vegetables for that, but they'd throw a couple of roasts in the oven to slow-cook for dinner.

By the time they finished plotting meals and making more coffee, his phone dinged with an alert. Agent Perry waited at the gate in a government-issued SUV.

Monk's first thought when he opened the door to her was *pocket Venus*. Books were thin on the ground while deployed, and he'd picked up a few romances in his time. The phrase seemed to apply only to stories set over two hundred years ago, so why the phrase popped into his mind as she stood on the stoop, he didn't know. No, scratch that, he knew. At no more than five foot two, her long dark hair, with a tiny hint of red, curled over her shoulders, resting on her more than ample cleavage. Her waist dipped in before flaring out to a full set of hips. Hips as full as her lips, relatively speaking, of course. A button nose, smooth, even skin, and bow lips gave her the look of a doll, but her big brown eyes, slightly tilted up at the edges, looked anything but innocent. They were eyes, what they looked like was a toss of the genetic dice, same with the rest of her physical attributes, so he didn't read too much into what he saw on the surface. Even so, if he'd ever been asked to cast the role of temptress in a 1950s film, he would have picked her.

"Collin Wilde?" she asked, her eyes darting between him and Mantis.

"That's me," he said, holding his hand out. She shook it with a brisk nod.

"Noah Streak," Mantis said, taking her hand next. "But you'll hear people call me Mantis."

Her gaze lingered, then turned to him in question. "Monk," he said. "After everyone gets here, we'll clarify as we talk."

Agent Perry's sharp eyes took everything in as they walked down the hall and entered the tasting room. Leo, Kendall, and Charley looked up from the laptop, the tree twinkling behind them, a fire burning in the hearth.

"I can honestly say I never expected a winery tasting room, in a castle no less, to be the center of an operation," Agent Perry said, her eyes flickering from the bar to the view of the courtyard, to the tall ceilings, huge oak beams, tapestries, and ornate windows.

Mantis chuckled. "When needs must."

For the first time since he stepped inside Bacco after

Roger's death, he saw the room as others might. Without the weight of his history, of his trauma, twisting inside him like something rotten. It would never be home, but Marley's and Hawkeye's comments about Amber cooking in the kitchen teased his mind. Unlike many of the other wineries of its size, Bacco had never been a restaurant or inn—thanks to the family's financial prowess, they'd never needed to open it up that way. But what if it could be? What if it *should* be?

A door opened at the back of the castle, followed by the sounds of feet treading on the thick floors and voices talking and laughing. His family's return from the wine caves halted his thoughts about the future of Bacco, then they zeroed in completely on Helia as she, Dulcie, Lovell, and Einstein entered the building through the same entrance he'd used.

Helia came straight to his side, and wrapping an arm around her, he welcomed the feel of her body tucked against his. He hadn't really been worried about her being gone, not with his brothers surrounding her, but he was glad to have her back.

It took a few minutes for Agent Perry to meet everyone, minus Joey, Juliana, and North, who'd headed to the grocery store. Another few minutes passed as Hawkeye insisted on making a pot of coffee. While everyone was getting settled, Monk pulled Agent Perry aside to explain Kendall's presence. Having a twelve-year-old girl part of the debrief they were about to have wasn't standard operating procedures, but he'd put a kibosh on the whole thing if Perry refused to include her.

After a few questions and more than a few dubious looks, she agreed. He didn't blame her for doubting his decision. Hell, he'd questioned it many times in the past few days. But he knew it was the right thing.

Dulcie gestured Agent Perry to a high top. She nodded to him, then took a seat and pulled out her laptop. Once the room quieted, Scipio walked through everything they'd put together in the past few days. As he talked, Agent Perry watched him progress through the timeline, then the murder board, occasionally dropping her attention to her computer. She asked a few questions along the way, her head bobbed a few times, and more than once her eyes narrowed.

When Scipio wrapped up, he, too, grabbed a chair and took a seat. "What do you think, Agent Perry?"

Perry remained focused on her laptop for a few seconds, then her gaze swept the room. "We didn't have Marcel Laurant in the picture," she replied, obviously not happy about the miss. "And call me Grace."

"No reason for you to," Dulcie said. Grace's attention swung to him. "You were focused on Pena, Haines, and Trish Peterson. Did you even know about Roger, Kelly, Flannery, and either Greg or Akin before you followed Peterson here?"

Her gaze lingered before pulling it back to the room. "We didn't. Haines's signature drug has shown up a few times in LA, which is how our team got pulled in. But compared to what's cropping up in other spots, the amounts are minimal, so our involvement hasn't been central to the case." She studied the murder board. "Derek Weber isn't involved," she said, nodding to the other solo box floating on the edge of the board.

"He lives far outside his means," Leo said.

"He won the lottery, literally, not figuratively, six months ago," Grace replied. "He bought a ticket in a small convenience store in southern Jersey when he was visiting a sick uncle. Walked away with ten million. He had it transferred to an offshore account in a business name to keep his own name out of the press."

Helia snorted. "Ten million in this valley isn't going to raise an eyebrow, let alone be worthy of press attention."

"Weird, but true," Grace agreed. "But in his head..."

"He's a much bigger deal than he is," Helia said. "Believe me, I found that out. He's not a bad acquaintance, which is why I agreed to a date. And stop that growling, Collin," she said, elbowing him and eliciting a laugh from the others. "Two dates, that was it. He's just not that interesting."

"He was seen with my father, though," Monk felt the need to point out, recalling the social media pictures he'd found.

"And he ended up on the DEA's radar," Einstein pointed out. "Not Marcel, but Weber. Why?"

Grace inclined her head. "Since Trish arrived in the area, she's met up with a bunch of people, including Kelly, Greg, *and* Akin. She's also dined at the restaurant Weber works at three times."

"An expensive place for a soon-to-be-divorcée who was basically begging me for work contacts a few days ago," Helia said.

"Which is exactly why we started looking into the restaurant. It was out of character for the story she was spreading around about her reason for coming back," Grace replied.

"Is there anyone else on your radar other than these players?" Hawkeye asked, nodding to the board.

"A few. People you'd know," she said, looking at Helia. "But no one we think is a threat, as they are further down the food chain and don't have any connections to Sundaram."

If Grace didn't report to Reaper, Monk would have asked more questions. But he trusted his old teammate. If he thought the Falcons should know something, he would have made sure Grace told them.

"What now?" Charley asked.

Grace exhaled. "Now I go over the evidence HICC sent over, and you all get on with your holiday plans."

"Any idea when it will be all over?" Helia asked. "I haven't told my parents anything about this and I won't. But it's going to impact our business and, well, I guess the sooner we get it over with, the sooner we can start damage control."

"Speaking of Sundaram, do you have any insight into whether it's Akin or Greg involved?" Monk asked. He'd been so focused on the same thing as Helia that he'd not bothered to ask the question they'd all lingered on for so long the day before.

"And do you think we're right about Kurt Fisher and Wei Zhao wanting into the market?" Dulcie asked.

Grace's gaze once again swept the room, evaluating them before answering. She let out a small breath. "Before moving to San Francisco, Greg Watson managed a high-end restaurant owned indirectly by Mark Pena. We've found no ties between Akin and either Haines or Pena," she answered.

Helia closed her eyes for a second, a brief moment to be thankful that one of her favorite employees wasn't involved. When she opened them, she squeezed his hand, then asked, "And Kurt?"

"There's no question DKZ and Wei's organization are at war. We have no evidence that Peterson was involved in Fisher's death herself, but we're investigating the possibility that she ordered it."

"Do you need us here, or can we head home for Christmas?" Leo asked.

Kendall's gaze shot to Monk, bounced to Helia, then landed back on him, the conflict clear on her face. She wanted to see Mystery Lake, but she didn't want to leave Helia. He didn't have an answer for her; maybe it was better that way and they could figure it out together. Or maybe this was one of those decisions he should make on his own to take the weight of it off her shoulders. Hell, he had a lot to learn about raising a kid.

"I'd prefer it if you did," Grace said, earning her a few

chuckles. "You've done a lot in the background to help our case. The prosecutors will be delighted. But no offense, we don't need any of you being tempted to step in when we make our move."

"Those days are over for us," Mantis said before his gaze slid over the room, touching on Lina and Viper, Philly and Callie, and Stone, who sat alone as Juliana hadn't returned from the store yet. "Well, mostly over," he amended.

An expectant silence fell over the room, then Grace hopped off her chair and started gathering her things. "I don't condone vigilante activity, but like I said, the prosecutors will be thrilled with the additional evidence you've collected. We'll also look into Marcel Laurant and see if we can find his family some answers," she added, directing the comment to Helia, who nodded in response.

"In the meantime, here's my card." She handed it to Monk, who'd stepped forward. "I'll send the evidence team over later today to collect the additional drugs you found, but let me know when you head out. The other players won't know the drugs have been confiscated, and we'll do our best to keep anyone from poking around."

"Some of the employees may come around over the holiday," Monk said, rising to walk her out. He only anticipated Gretchen and Alessio, and he promised to send their information to her so that the DEA had it on hand.

When he returned to the tasting room, he found it empty except for Helia. "Where'd everyone go?" He had a good idea, based on the sounds he heard, but the question had popped out. Maybe as an avoidance of what they really needed to talk about.

Helia held out her hand. "They're making a late lunch. Hard to believe it's only two in the afternoon."

"It's been a long day," he agreed, wrapping his arms

around her before lowering his lips to hers. He only allowed himself a small taste. He didn't trust himself to stop if it went any further than that.

"We need to talk," Helia said.

A vise closed around his body. "Do we have to?"

She smiled, her hazel eyes dancing. "And not about drugs and murder and things like that."

He started pulling away, thinking they should probably sit for the coming conversation. To his surprise, she held on tight. Catching his feet before they toppled over, he looked down at her in question.

A shyness he didn't usually see crept into her expression. "I've talked to my parents about Christmas, and we've come up with a plan. That is, if you and Kendall agree."

CHAPTER THIRTY-FOUR

Wariness crept into Collin's eyes, and her stomach threatened to revolt, but she took a deep breath and powered on. She was about to take them over a relationship cliff, and while she *thought* he'd be okay with it, the fact that they'd only been back in each other's lives for less than two weeks played in her head. Like her grandfather's records when they used to skip, playing the same five notes over and over again.

"Talk here or somewhere else?" she asked.

His head swiveled a little wildly, then he stepped away. Twining his fingers with hers, he led her down a series of halls to a smallish library in the back corner of the castle.

"I don't know what this room was originally," Collin said, flicking on a gas fireplace. "Roger made this upgrade when he did the others. Sometime when I was a kid." He paused and studied the flames. She remained silent as he prodded at some memory or thought. He came back to the room abruptly and gestured to the leather couch. "Shall we?"

She held out her hand, her body warming as his big one

closed over hers. When they were seated, he pulled the throw blanket off the back of the couch and draped it over her legs. "What's this plan?" he asked, the expression on his face reminding her of someone winding the handle of a jack-in-the-box waiting for it to pop out.

"I'm guessing you and Kendall both want to get settled in Mystery Lake." He opened his mouth, but she held up a hand to stop him. "I have no idea what the next few weeks or months are going to look like with Sundaram, so I'm only focusing on the next few days." He gave a hesitant nod. Her heart started fluttering, and she turned his hand over to trace the lines of his palm, more to give her own hands something to do as she jumped off this cliff.

"My parents want to meet Kendall. They've accepted she's going to be a part of their lives, and they want to welcome her to the family." She felt his head jerk toward her. Not that she saw it, since her eyes were fixed on his palm. "My brother and Patrick will be in tomorrow. I propose that we stay here and have Christmas Eve with my parents and brother's family, then after dinner we drive up to Mystery Lake so Kendall can wake up Christmas morning in her new home. I have a few weeks off, and she and I can spend the time getting to know the town and maybe learning more about the schools and that sort of thing. I say 'Kendall and I' because I know you have to work. Hopefully, we can troop around as a threesome when you have the time, though. What do you think?"

Several seconds passed and he said nothing. Nausea started crawling into her throat, sharp and bitter. But then he blinked, drawing her attention to his eyes. His glassy eyes.

"Collin?" she said, tentatively lifting a hand to touch his cheek. Only she didn't get the chance. Before she could even gasp in surprise, he had her across his lap, his lips on hers.

In a whirlwind of clothes, indiscriminate sounds, and

squeaks from the couch, what felt like a heartbeat later, an orgasm rocketed through her thanks to his nimble tongue and talented lips. Before she even finished, he pushed inside her, saying something. Lots of things. But consumed by the feel of him, by his unleashed need and trust, she couldn't make any out. Not that she needed to. His body, the way he touched her, told her everything. She shouldn't have questioned leading them over this cliff. They were already falling. And holding on to each other the whole way.

That heady realization, that certainty that he was *with* her through whatever the future might bring, brought her to the edge again, and together, pleasure erupted through their bodies in pulsing waves so strong they stole her breath.

They hung, suspended there in that moment, a moment much bigger than the physical, for the space of several breaths. Then, as it was wont to do, life inched its way back into their world.

Her spine released its tension and relaxed onto the couch. Collin didn't lower himself fully on top of her, but the tautness of his back eased under her fingers. Languorously, she traced the muscles, his skin damp beneath her touch, as they caught their breath.

She wanted the moment to stretch and imprint itself in her memory, but her hip digging into the back of the couch had her shifting. Collin lifted away but didn't rise. Instead, he stilled and gazed down at her, an impossibly tender look in his eyes, maybe even a hint of awe.

She ran her fingers along his jaw, then cupped his cheek. "I take it my plan works for you?"

"It's more than I ever thought to even hope for," he answered, his voice gruff with emotion. Her heart threatened to break for him—for all the holidays he hadn't had as a kid, for those he spent deployed in far-flung parts of the world, for the family he never thought he'd have. Yes, he had his brothers, but Collin's yearning for a family of his own, for a partner in life, had never been a secret to her. He'd never said anything, not at fourteen or even eighteen, but she'd seen it in the way he watched her parents, in the way he became a part of *her* family.

She tipped her head back, lifting her lips toward his. He obliged her invitation with a lingering kiss before withdrawing from her body and crossing the room to the massive dark oak desk. For someone who didn't have a lot of sexual experience, he was remarkably comfortable with his own nudity. Maybe the military made any sort of modesty difficult, but whatever the reason, she definitely didn't mind. In fact, she rather enjoyed the sight of him prowling around without a stitch on.

Finding what he went looking for, he returned with several tissues. "Sorry, there's no bathroom attached to this room," he said, handing them to her.

It took her a second to figure out what he meant; when she did, she shook her head. "There's one two doors down. I'll go use that to clean up."

He frowned. "Then you have to get dressed."

She rose and reached for her shirt. "As appealing as a day lounging around in the nude with you is, we have a house full of your family, a lunch that will be ready in a few minutes, and the rest of the holiday to plan."

He stared, then grunted an unintelligible word but reached for his own boxer briefs. After dressing quickly, she slipped down to the bathroom. When she returned, he was sitting on the couch, fully clothed, phone in hand, with no sign of what had happened moments before.

"What are you looking at?" she asked, joining him.

"We need to order Kendall's presents," he said. "I don't want to go too crazy, that will kind of feel like I'm trying to buy her affection—"

"I don't think you have to worry about that, but I see your point. It might be overwhelming."

"But I want to get her a few meaningful things."

"I have a few ideas," she said, pulling out her own phone.

His chuckle rolled over her like a warm blanket. "I knew you would."

Twenty minutes later, six gifts were on their way to the Falcons' clubhouse. Helia'd stopped him from texting Dottie to ask if she could wrap them, insisting they do it themselves. Midnight wrapping parties were part of the fun of the holidays. They were practically a requirement. His eyes had narrowed, and he'd cocked his head in doubt at that statement, but in the end, agreed. At her suggestion, he had, however, asked Dottie to make sure Kendall's room was ready when they arrived. She'd heard from Callie that Philly had happily agreed to give her his old one—right next to Collin's.

Helia veered off to the tasting room when they exited the back room, but a text from Kendall had her changing direction and heading to the third floor.

After knocking on the girl's door, she poked her head in. "You rang?" Helia asked.

Kendall paced the room, her baggy black jeans swishing with every step. A contrast to the silence of her sock-clad feet hitting the wool carpet.

Helia stepped inside, shutting the door behind her. Kendall paced to the other side of the room, then spun, the sides of her unzipped sweatshirt flying open to reveal the vintage Hello Kitty shirt they'd found in the thrift store.

"Christmas," Kendall said, coming to an abrupt stop, her already big eyes even wider. "I don't know anything about Christmas."

Ah.

"Well, not nothing," she continued, resuming her pacing.

"My mom and I celebrated every now and then. We even had a tiny tree a couple of times." She held her hand out to about four feet high. "She gave me a pair of socks and a new backpack one year. I got my computer three years ago. I gave her a silk scarf I found at a Goodwill and a wallet." She paused and cast Helia such a look of terror that Helia nearly reached for her. "I don't know what to do about Christmas. And...and my mom just died, and I don't know whether I should be excited or sad. And...and I'm worried that I'm going to do something wrong, that maybe I'll disappoint everyone by, like, being sad about my mom, and then they won't want me around because I'll be spoiling their day. And what about presents? How am I supposed to know what to get everyone, let alone have the money to pay for it?"

Helia couldn't take any more, and she stepped forward and gathered the girl in her arms. Kendall remained stiff as a board for about ten seconds, then melted. "What am I gonna do?" she said, her voice mumbled against Helia's shoulder.

"First things first," she said, glad she and Collin hadn't gone overboard on the presents. "Feeling all these things is fine. Don't ever think you have to feel, or not feel, something because of other people. You shouldn't do that ever, but in particular, you don't need to do that around anyone in this house. Or the Falcons clubhouse," she added, thinking of the few brothers who weren't in the castle.

"You know a little of Collin's background, and unfortunately, his story isn't unique among that group. And you heard Juliana, Callie, and Lina tell you a little about their lives. If anyone is going to understand how complicated grief and childhood can be, it's this group of people." She paused to let that sink in. Three breaths, then four, and Kendall's body relaxed.

"What about presents? I don't have any money for presents."

Helia smiled and led her over to the bed. Climbing up onto the big hulk of furniture, she scooted over, then patted the empty space beside her. "The good news is, one of the rules about Christmas is that kids aren't expected to give gifts. Not to everyone anyway. I picked up a few small things for Collin the other day but wanted to find one more present to put under the tree. Maybe we could find it together and it could be from both of us. And before you mention money again, your input is contribution enough. You hear things and see things that I don't. I'm going to take a wild guess that you're going to have a better idea what he might like than I will."

"I think he already got what he wanted for Christmas," Kendall said, nudging her with a grin as she snuggled against the stack of pillows.

"Rude," Helia muttered affectionately, making Kendall giggle. Smiling to herself, she tilted the phone for Kendall to see. "Now what do you think of this?"

CHAPTER THIRTY-FIVE

Helia hugged each and every one of the Falcons guys and gals as Collin tossed their bags in the back of his truck. After breakfast, he'd summoned Gretchen, Alessio, and Miguel to the castle for a meeting, then Alessio had offered to do a wine tasting for the adults before they headed out. Most of the group took him up on the offer, but Collin had declined on behalf of the three of them, stating he wanted to get to Sundaram. She couldn't tell if *he* wanted to be with her family or if he wanted to be sure *she* had time with them before they headed up to Mystery Lake. Or maybe he wanted time for her parents to get to know Kendall. Each option made her heart patter a little stronger for the man.

Kendall smiled and received hugs from everyone, too, but Helia thought a few quiet days at her parents' would be good for her before moving into the clubhouse. Sure, there'd be the awkwardness of meeting new people. But Kendall would watch Collin for cues, and Collin's relationship with them was solid, even after all these years.

"Ready?" Collin asked, his eyes jumping between her and

Kendall. Both nodded and climbed into his truck. After a few last-minute words with Mantis, they headed down the long driveway and toward Sundaram.

"Excellent timing," her dad said with a huge grin when they pulled up, her mother standing at his side. "Don't bother getting out. You can take us to get our tree." And with that, they climbed in the back seat of the cab, introducing themselves to Kendall as they did. Without a word, Collin turned around and headed to the only place they'd ever gotten their tree from.

As they had for years, the lot attendants—high school FFA kids—led them to a few trees set aside for local families. The pickings weren't vast, but they found a nice twelve-foot Douglas fir with a few gaps in its branches that her mom declared would be perfect for some of the larger ornaments to hang in.

An hour later, the tree sat proudly in the living room, lit up but not decorated, and Kendall perched on a stool at the kitchen island, cup of cocoa in hand, talking to her mom about cookies. Helia had worried that the flurry of activity would overwhelm her, but, probably exactly as her mom anticipated, it forced communication and conversations that helped break through any initial awkwardness.

"Is everyone on their way to Mystery Lake yet?" she asked Collin, who was helping her dad unpack all the ornaments from their storage boxes.

Monk chuckled. "Not even close. With Juliana and Lina there, Alessio is in hog heaven answering all sorts of questions."

"They don't mind the delay?"

Collin shot her a confused look before catching a glass ball that tumbled unexpectedly from its wrapping. "Course not," he replied. "They wouldn't have agreed to the tasting in the first place if they had a schedule to stick to. As it is, it's a unique holiday experience they're sharing together."

A practical answer that surprised her but shouldn't. She was 100 percent certain the Falcons crew wasn't always so laid-back. She'd heard the stories from all the women. But what mattered, and what didn't, seemed clearer to them than most people she met.

"We weren't sure what to get Kendall, but wanted to get her a little something," her dad said, keeping his voice low. "While we were looking for the tree, she mentioned that she's an Aries and her mother was a Cancer. While we were loading the tree, your mom called Jayne at the jewelry store she likes and had a simple necklace made up with a bloodstone and a moonstone charm—the zodiac birthstones—that we'll pick up later today." He paused, then added with a smile, "And then of course she couldn't resist and ordered her some clothes, too."

Helia smiled while Collin responded that she'd like those. The mention of the gift, though, reminded her of the beard products she'd bought downtown before the dart incident. They'd taken the bag with her in the ambulance, and she'd asked her parents to bring it home. She'd somehow had the presence of mind to keep it a secret from Collin, and her mom had tucked it safely in the closet in her room.

"I need to head over to my house for a few minutes," she said, rising from the couch and setting her hot chocolate on the side table.

Collin's gaze shot up. "I'll go with you."

She frowned. She definitely didn't want that. "It's across the courtyard and a little beyond. I'll be fine."

"Still, I'll go," he insisted, placing a box of glass ornaments on the coffee table.

"It's a few minutes and—" As if another reason might pop out of thin air, she looked frantically around.

"I'll go with her," Kendall said, walking into the room carrying a plate of cookies fresh from the oven. "And besides, you can see us the entire time, if you're that worried," she added, pointing to a window that would indeed give him a view of their journey.

"Is there something we should know?" her mom asked, joining the group.

Helia didn't like putting Collin in the awkward position, but it served her purpose. He wouldn't tell her parents anything about the upcoming DEA operation, but he also knew that he'd worry them if he insisted on going.

He rolled his lips and shot her a stern, mildly irritated but resigned look. "Fine. I'll keep an eye on you from the window."

"Really, should we be worried?" her dad asked.

Helia cast Collin a look, feeling a little bad leaving him to answer. She didn't want to risk a bigger conversation, though, so she gestured to Kendall, and they slipped out the door as Collin placated her parents.

"He's a little protective," Kendall said as they jogged down the steps.

"Not a bad thing, considering. But when I need to sneak his Christmas present back to my parents' so I can wrap and pack it, it's not ideal," she conceded.

They chatted quietly as they made their way to her water tower house, stopping to wave at the window before stepping in.

"Two minutes is all I need," Helia said to Kendall as she headed to the stairs. The girl nodded and wandered over to the fireplace to examine the pictures on the mantel.

Stepping into her room, she stilled. The air was off, and her skin rippled with awareness. Scanning the space, she saw nothing amiss. Except maybe the bed. She always left her comforter smooth, but now a large wrinkle ran down the middle. And the pillows lay askew. Slowly, she turned in a circle, cataloging the space. When nothing else jumped out at her, she decided Collin's unease, and the earlier break-in, were making her jumpy.

Walking to the closet, her eyes caught on the curtains. She stopped again and stared. She closed her curtains when she slept, but other than those nighttime hours, she kept them open.

With her mind focused on whether it meant anything that they were closed—as she couldn't remember definitively if she'd left them open—the familiar squeak of her bedroom door closing startled her. She spun, ready to laugh at herself for overreacting, but froze as the door swung nearly all the way closed. And Kelly stood on the other side, back to the wall, gun in hand.

Helia stumbled, her butt colliding with the dresser, knocking over two picture frames. One bounced against the wall before landing face down; the other clattered over the side, shattering as it hit the floor.

Her attention fixed on the gun. She'd never actually seen one up close before, but thoughts of Kendall squeezed in there, too. She hoped the noise alerted her that something was very wrong and that she managed to slip out of the house.

"Who were you talking to?" Kelly asked.

Helia could think fast on her feet when faced with a calamity at any one of the events she organized, but in this? With a gun in her face? She stumbled. "Huh?"

"You were talking when you walked in. Is there someone downstairs I need to take care of?" Kelly hissed.

Terror for Kendall had her answering with the first thing that came to mind. "I was talking to myself." Lame, but she had to go with it. "Grumbling. Collin didn't want me to come alone. He was being overbearing. I was grumbling about that to myself." She paused, fixated on the weapon pointed her way. "I guess I should have listened to him."

Kelly eyed her but didn't say anything. Three seconds passed, then she started forward. Helia took a tiny step back, all that the dresser would allow, frantically searching for a way to defend herself. The crocheted bowl she kept odds and ends in and the puffy cloth frame of the remaining picture offered little help, though. Kelly stopped a few feet away, grabbed one of the ties that held the curtains back, then resumed her path forward.

Adrenaline punched through Helia at what she knew was coming. She wouldn't go down without a fight, though, and she hoped Kendall was smart enough to slip out and book it back to the house. If Helia could hold Kelly off for even ten minutes, Kendall would bring Collin and the cops. She gave a moment's thought to placing her trust in a twelve-year-old, but Kendall wasn't your average preteen, and she'd rather place her faith in the girl than give it up altogether.

She'd never been in a fight before, but as soon as Kelly was close, she swung out at the arm holding the gun, then kicked out at her knee. Her former friendly acquaintance dodged both so easily, Helia realized how little she knew the social media manager. It seemed she'd barely taken a breath before Kelly's arm was around her neck, Helia's back to her front, and the gun pointed at her temple. She was too close for Helia to have any leverage to move, but still she struggled, clawing at Kelly's arm and kicking back with her heel.

"You're lucky I need you alive," Kelly said before a searing pain ricocheted through her head, dimming her vision and swirling up a cyclone of nausea. "That's better," Kelly spoke again. Before Helia could clear her vision and will the nausea into submission, Kelly had her hands and feet trussed.

Unceremoniously, Kelly dumped her on the floor. The

second thump to her head brought back the swimming feeling, and she closed her eyes, breathing deeply through her nose. She desperately wanted to call out, to make sure Kendall was safe, but she held her tongue. If Kendall hadn't escaped, she didn't want to alert Kelly to her presence. If she had, she didn't want Kelly to know help was likely on the way.

"Think about your choices, Helia. I'll be right back."

She opened her eyes wide enough to see Kelly's Chuck Taylors disappear out her door. "You didn't need to tie me up!" she called, wanting to alert Kendall in case she stayed in the house.

No reply came, and her stomach revolted again as the echo of Kelly's steps treading down the stairs brought her closer to Kendall. Potentially. Helia closed her eyes again and forced herself to picture Kendall running back to the main building, safe and able to tell Collin he was needed at the water tower.

She listened as Kelly paced the rooms below, opening cabinet doors and the half bath, her heart skipping several beats with each sound.

She didn't exactly feel a wave of relief when Kelly's footsteps climbed back to the second floor, but she did breathe easier knowing Kendall was safe.

"I'm sorry your boyfriend's overbearing," she said, walking back into the room. Helia eyed her as she grabbed a chair, spun it around, and straddled it, the gun hanging loosely in her hand now. "That's a red flag, don't you think?"

Helia blinked at the absurdity of the comment. "I think it's safe to say I suck at spotting red flags. After all, I didn't realize you were a murderous bitch. Sure, I thought you were cringingly crass when it came to men, but that's a far cry from a drug-dealing murderer."

To her surprise, Kelly smiled. "You figured it out? I thought so. That's why we're here. Or rather, why I'm here. When you got mistaken for me and that bitch Trish shot you with the dart, I knew your man wouldn't let it go. Same as I knew that dart was meant for me and that it was time I hightailed it out of town."

"Doesn't explain why you're here," Helia muttered.

"Sure it does. Trish wasn't the first person to mistake you for me. When Kurt was killed, I knew the shit was hitting the fan, and I came looking for your passport. I decided to hide out here after Trish tagged you with the dart, thinking it was me. Haven't found your passport yet."

Helia took a deep breath, then inched her way into a sitting position. A lopsided one with her back against the foot of her bed, but a sitting position, nonetheless.

"You're going to pretend to be me and what? You won't get away with it for long. People will notice I'm gone."

"Not if you're dead. And I don't need it to last long. Just long enough to make it to Mexico."

"Dead?" The thought of being one of Kelly's victims had a way of holding all her attention and the word came out little more than a croak.

Kelly shrugged. "You'll die in a fire here. No one will think to cancel your Social Security or passport or any of those other things, and I'll have plenty of time to drive south and cross the border."

Helia drew in a deep breath. It seemed the only thing she was capable of at the moment. At least she knew Kelly's plan. What the hell she'd do with that information, she didn't know.

"Why Roger?" she asked, mostly to kill time. She needed to calm her brain and give Kendall a chance to reach Collin, assuming she managed to slip out. Helia refused to think otherwise.

Kelly shrugged. "Tell me where your passport is."

"I'll tell you when you tell me." Even to her own ears, she

sounded like a petulant eight-year-old, but she didn't have much to lose. She tested her restraints, too. She didn't hold out much hope of slipping free, and if she did, she didn't stand much of a chance against a gun, but she had to try. If only for her own dignity. Unfortunately, knot tying was one more skill Kelly had, and her hands barely moved.

"Or you could tell me," Kelly replied, pointing the gun at her.

Helia swallowed, her vision focused on the tiny black hole staring at her. "If I'm dead, you'll never find my passport."

Helia counted to six, then Kelly sighed and lowered the gun. "He was getting reckless. Saying things to people he shouldn't say. Putting the whole operation at risk. He had early-stage dementia, did you know that?" Helia shook her head. "We just hurried it along."

Helia had never heard of hurrying dementia along. "How the hell did you do that?"

Kelly smiled, not hiding her vicious glee. "Bovine spongiform encephalopathy."

"Huh?" She couldn't muster more than that. Then her memory clicked in. "Mad cow disease?"

Kelly nodded. "Nasty thing that. Humans don't actually get it, but if they ingest infected meat, it causes another disorder. One with a long name that isn't relevant. It's a protein, prion, disorder, so doesn't show up in a standard tox screen."

"You infected him with mad cow disease?"

"Seemed fitting. It causes a lot of the same symptoms as dementia before the body finally succumbs to it. To the world, he was just an older man experiencing a very common older-person disease."

Helia would never admit it, but it was clever. It likely wouldn't work on a younger person, but someone like Roger?

No one would question a dementia diagnosis or a rapid progression of the disease. "How?" she asked.

"Like I said, it's protein-related. At my suggestion and on Trish's order, the drug lab created a similar prion, and we added it to his food—sushi I brought over to him, steak tartare Justin brought, the braised ribs Greg dropped off. It took a while, about seven months, to do the job, but he grew increasingly out of it, so no one paid him any mind. And when he finally died, it came as no surprise."

"And now you're going to kill me and abscond to Mexico to live a life of luxury on your drug money."

Kelly rolled her eyes as she rose. "Don't sound so holier-than-thou, Helia. Some of us don't have a family support net to keep us from hitting rock bottom. Now, where's your passport?"

CHAPTER THIRTY-SIX

Collin untangled a string of beads as he watched the window. Helia and Kendall had stepped inside five minutes earlier, and they couldn't come back into view soon enough.

"I get the sense there's more going on than we know," Harry said.

He was tempted to look away and meet the man's eyes, but he couldn't tear his attention from the water tower.

"There is," he replied. "We can't say anything about it, but we don't think Helia's in danger anymore."

"Which is why you're as nervous as a chicken with a fox circling the coop."

He started to smile, but the buzz of his phone stopped him. He anticipated a text from Mantis telling him they were leaving. His blood pressure leaped when Kendall's name displayed on the screen.

Kendall: *Hiding under the couch. Kelly is here*

"Fuck." The word burst from his mouth like a beast breaking its chains.

Monk: *Can you get out?*

Kendall: *Not leaving her*

Monk: *Are you safe?*

Kendall: *As can be, but wouldn't mind a little rescuing*

If he were in another state of mind, he might have smiled at that, but he didn't.

Monk: *Calling the guys, we'll be there in ten*

His hands shook as he sent out a group text to his brothers. He'd barely hit Send before a reply came in.

Mantis: *On our way. Dulcie knows the land best, he'll get us there unseen. Will text a meeting spot*

Monk didn't reply but headed to the room he and Helia had claimed and found his gun safe. Unlocking it, he pulled out his weapon of choice, gave it a quick once-over, then shoved it into the back of his jeans.

"Collin, what's going on?" Vanessa asked. She and Harry stood in the hall wearing identical looks of concern.

"I shouldn't have let her go on her own. There's...a situation. Call the police. No," he said, pulling out Agent Perry's card. "Call her and tell her we need her stat."

Harry took the card, eyeing it with confusion. He didn't have time to stop and explain why the DEA needed to be involved, though, and he pushed by the couple. To his chagrin, but not surprise, they followed him out. The echo of the gate bell rang as he made his way down the stairs. If that was Patrick and Kaden, maybe the couple would distract Harry and Vanessa enough for him to slip into the vineyard.

His phone vibrated with another text.

Kendall: *She tied Helia up, searched the first floor. She doesn't know I'm here. I should be safe*

Monk's jaw tightened. She'd be safer if she got out, but at least she'd given him an update.

He paused at the bottom of the steps.

Monk: *Stay quiet*

Kendall: *Duh*

Monk: *We're eight minutes out*

Kendall: *Helia's got her talking*

He didn't need to know what they were talking about, not now. And he was running too hot to be grateful that she was buying them time.

A familiar car skidded to a stop as he stepped into the courtyard. "Oh, fuck me," he said as the driver's door of the yellow Maserati opened. Monk glanced at his watch. Seven minutes until his brothers arrived. He had to deal with Weber.

"I'm here to see Helia," Weber said. "Mr. Shaw, Mrs. Shaw," he added, nodding to the couple, who'd followed Monk out. In his right hand, he carried a gift, but his left arm swung free. Monk paused, zeroing in on the appendage as Weber walked toward them.

"Oh hell, it was you," he said.

Weber paused and blinked. "Me?" he said, the squeak in his voice giving him away.

"You broke into Bacco looking for Roger's stash."

Weber backed up a step. In his peripheral vision, Monk saw another car approach, Kaden and Patrick. He hadn't seen either man for a good few years, but he hoped they kept up with the jujitsu they'd always loved.

"I...I did no such thing," Weber protested, sounding about as sure of himself as a newbie making their first high-altitude jump.

"Don't," Monk barked when he took another step back.

"Everything all right here?" Kaden asked, joining the gathering with Patrick at his shoulder.

Monk didn't have time for this. Agent Perry could deal with the fallout. "This man broke into Bacco the day of Roger's memorial looking to steal the stash of drugs Roger hid before he died. The drug ring is the subject of a DEA investigation, and I'd appreciate it if you two could deal with him, because at the moment, another player in that ring has Helia captive in her home. My brothers are here. We'll get her out, but again, if you could handle this"—he gestured to Weber—"I'd appreciate it."

The target of his comment dropped the gift and bolted toward his car, but Patrick and Kaden were already there. Monk didn't hesitate to turn back to his mission.

"When you bring her back, you and my daughter have some explaining to do, son," Harry called.

"Be safe," Vanessa added.

Their faith in him warmed him, but he didn't linger on it or the terror they no doubt felt at what their daughter might be going through. Pushing it all aside, he slipped into the vineyard and started making his way toward the water tower.

With the vines barren, leaving little cover for any of their movements, he crouched and did his best to stay out of sight, grateful for the earthy colors he wore. And the closed curtains. Those could work against them—it would be easier if they could see inside, but it also meant Kelly couldn't easily see them either.

Pausing behind an oak tree, he pulled out his phone and texted Kendall.

Monk: *Update?*

Kendall: *She's going to kill Helia, take her passport, and head to Mexico. Also, she confessed to killing Roger*

Monk: *Any weapons?*

Kendall: *Don't know, but I think she knocked Helia around. She's going to start a fire*

His vision went red, and he took a few breaths to force it back under control.

Kendall: *Helia told her where her passport is. Now she's insisting Kelly take her car*

Monk scanned the area. In his rush to get to Helia, he hadn't considered that Kelly *didn't* have a method of transport nearby. Had she expected to run through the vineyard?

Kendall: *Like weirdly insistent on the car*

Monk stilled, rolling that piece of information around, looking for how it fit into the puzzle. His gaze landed on her Mini parked beside the house. Time slowed as a picture formed, then in a flash it fell into place.

Monk: *Can you get out?*

Kendall: *I told you, I'm not leaving her*

Monk: *Kelly will start the fire on the ground floor to keep Helia from getting out if she breaks free of her ties. You need to not be there*

A beat passed before her response.

Kendall: *You're going to get her?*

Monk: *Wouldn't leave either of you for the world. Once Kelly's out, I'll slip in. I can lower Helia down from the top deck. My brothers will take care of Kelly. I promise*

He added that last bit with a silent prayer to whomever might be listening. Kelly was amateur hour compared to many of the ops he and his brothers had executed, but he knew how sideways they could go, too. Even with the best planning.

Kendall: *Okay, heading out the back door. I think she'll go out the front, closer to the car*

Monk: *Head to Vanessa and Harry. They've called Agent Perry*

He held his breath but true to her word, less than thirty seconds later, Kendall's slim form slid through the tiniest of cracks in the back door. Closing it softly behind her, she then darted into the vineyard and headed straight for the cover of the kitchen building.

A text from Mantis popped up on his screen: His brothers were in position. Monk responded with a summary of what

Kendall had told him and his plan. A beat later, he received a confirmation.

As they waited, a stillness stole through his body. He and his team had done this hundreds of times before. Failure wasn't an option, and success would come through executing the plan.

The curtains on the ground floor ruffled, as if someone moved rapidly around the room. From his location on the northwest side, he couldn't see the front door, but Mantis's text giving him the go-ahead came at the exact moment he spotted the first wisps of smoke filtering under the back door.

Trusting his brothers to deal with Kelly, he bolted toward the back door, well aware that throwing it open would add fuel to the flames that likely already licked the floors and walls. Still, it didn't stop him. Not pausing to assess the situation, he burst into the kitchen and dashed to the stairs, taking them three at a time. The first cough hit him on his second step, and by the time he reached the second floor, heat singed and stung his skin. Pushing through the thickening smoke, he ran into Helia's bedroom, flames claiming her first floor in a series of crackles and crashes.

He scanned the room but saw no evidence of Helia. Not willing to risk missing anything, though, he threw open her closet doors, then got down on his hands and knees and searched under the bed, too, the floor hot beneath his hands and bowing far too easily for his liking. Tucking away the knowledge that Kelly had likely used an accelerant—no way would a fire burn this hot and fast in December—he pulled his shirt over his nose and throat and left Helia's room. As he reached the door to the top deck, the first-floor staircase collapsed with a reverberating groan, taking some of the second floor with it.

The sound of sirens drifted into his consciousness, but only on the fringes of his focus. There, in front of him, propped up against the half wall, was Helia, her mouth gagged and her hands and feet bound to each other.

Breathing in the fresh air mingled with smoke, he knelt beside her, pulling the gag down first. He'd deal with the ties next, but he needed to know if she was conscious.

"Helia?" he called, the roar of the fire growing louder and louder.

Her eyes flickered open, but only a vague sense of recognition lit them. Judging by the spot of matted blood in her hair, she'd been hit and had a concussion, but she was alive. He chose to focus on that.

"We're going to get out of here," he said, hoping the flames weren't leaping out the windows. That would make it hard to lower her to the ground. So would her concussion; he wouldn't count on her being able to land on her feet. But first things first.

Pulling a knife from its ankle holster, he cut her free, then sliding his arms around her, he rose.

"Collin!" He heard a familiar voice and spun, hoping to god Kendall hadn't followed him in.

"Down here, Collin!" she shouted.

He inched over to the opposite half wall, testing the floor as he moved, then looked over the edge.

Kendall, Philly, Lovell, and Dulcie stood in the bed of his pickup that they'd backed up to within feet of what was left of the water tower. Kaden waved to him from the driver's seat.

He didn't stop his grin and nodded in acknowledgment of Kendall's plan. Brushing a kiss over Helia's brow, he whispered, "We're getting out of this. It's going to feel scary, but trust me."

She blinked in confusion, but her words were clear. "Of course I trust you."

He kissed her again before easing her body away from his. She panicked, gripping his shirt until he stopped. He didn't pull her back, though, just waited for her to look at him.

"Trust," he said.

She stared, then nodded and let go.

Gently, he eased her over the edge, then released her legs to dangle in the air. Holding her hands, he lowered her down into the waiting arms of his brothers. They caught her feet, and when Lovell gripped her hips and nodded to him, he let go. She dropped the last few inches into his brother's protective hold. As soon as they cleared her safely away, he swung over the wall, hung from the ledge, then pushed his body away from the building and dropped into the truck. His feet barely hit the bed before Kaden pulled away.

And it was none too soon as the front half of the tower collapsed, sending sparks and debris into the cold December air.

He gathered Helia and Kendall in his arms as the truck bounced along the dirt path back to the courtyard, slowing only to let the arriving fire trucks pass. Harry, Vanessa, and Patrick rushed over as soon as Kaden pulled to a stop.

"The ambulance is on the way," Patrick said as Vanessa and Harry climbed into the bed of the truck.

Monk adjusted his seat, pulling Helia across his lap and Kendall against his side. Lying his head against the back of the cab, he inhaled a small breath of fresh air, the cool, clean scents filling his body. He fought not to cough, but even if he ended up in a coughing fit to end all coughing fits, it was a price he'd happily pay for this moment. This moment with Helia alive, her chest moving in and out against his, and Kendall tucked into his side.

"Collin."

Helia's voice pulled him away from his moment of grati-
tude. Dragging his eyelids open, he looked at her.

"Kelly?"

His gaze flickered to Philly, Lovell, and Dulcie. He'd been
focused on her and had no idea if the rest of the plan had fallen
into place.

Philly grinned. "You were right, woman. Kelly didn't know
how to drive a manual."

CHAPTER THIRTY-SEVEN

Monk sat on his bed, fingering the piece of paper he'd pulled from an envelope Leo had given him that morning. Kendall and Helia were in the lodge room playing darts with Viper and Lina while the others lounged around the fire, picked at what little was left of Dottie's coffee cake, or tidied up after the spree of present opening that morning.

As he hoped, his family hadn't gone overboard with Kendall. Instead of each giving her a gift, they'd pooled resources and had Leo pick out a new laptop. In truth, they each could have bought her one, but she seemed to like the idea that it came from all of them. There were, of course, other gifts—the six from him and Helia, as well as a few bits and bobs in a stocking Dottie had made and that hung beside the others by the time they arrived after Christmas Eve dinner.

A text dinged on his phone, and he set the paper aside and pulled the device out. A short message from Reaper letting him know Pena, Haines, and Peterson had been charged and were being held without bail. As was Greg and a few other folks from the valley he didn't know, along with two dozen from Miami he'd have no reason to know.

Kelly's little stunt had sped up the DEA's timeline by several days, but thankfully, it hadn't impacted the case overall. His team had scrambled more than Reaper liked, but not more than they were capable of.

As for Derek, he folded before they'd taken him into custody. As Agent Perry had said, he wasn't involved in the drug ring, just stupid enough to give Kelly ammunition to blackmail him. Apparently, during some postcoital pillow talk between the two that Monk had no wish to picture, Derek had told Kelly that the winning lottery ticket he'd purchased wasn't actually his. His bedridden uncle had given him the cash and asked him to buy one last ticket, knowing he wasn't long for this world. Derek had thought the old man a bit on the crazy side but had agreed to make the run to the local convenience store because it got him out of the house, which smelled, according to Derek, like a cross between a hospital and a porta-potty. His uncle had died before the numbers were drawn, and Derek, stand-up guy that he was, hadn't mentioned the ticket to anyone, let alone anyone named in the man's estate.

Armed with this information, Kelly had blackmailed him to get close to Helia *and* break into Bacco to find Roger's hidden stash. After all, once she got rid of Greg and took over the ring, she'd need easy access to the Sundaram kitchen. Or she'd need someone else—Weber—with easy access to the kitchen.

They'd charged Derek with fraud and theft and a few other things, along with his cousin, who'd been with him at Bacco that day. Monk hadn't bothered to read through the laundry list attached to the arrests. As far as he was concerned, their role was over, and now they could focus on moving on with their lives and damage control for Sundaram.

Thankfully, Reaper and team had done what he'd hoped and been very clear in their public statements that Sundaram had willingly and proactively and at great risk to themselves reached out to the DEA once they'd realized what was going on. They didn't paint the Shaws as heroes; that wouldn't have stood up to scrutiny given that the case had started long before Helia was dragged into it, but they did emphasize their integrity and courage. It might not stop all the backlash, but it would help.

A soft knock came at his door, and he called for whoever it was to come in. The knob turned, and Kendall poked her head in. "You okay? Wanna come play a game of pool? I'll suck, because I've never played, but it might be a laugh."

He stared at her, tracing the lines of her face. She frowned at the scrutiny and stepped inside. "You're being weird."

He huffed a laugh. "C'mere," he said, gesturing to a spot beside him on the bed.

She eyed him, then crossed the room and sat.

He picked up the paper and once again fingered it. "I have one more..." What did he say? He saw it as a gift, but he wasn't sure she would. "Thing to give you."

"You've already given me enough stuff," she protested.

His eyes dropped to the top sheet. "This isn't a thing; well, it's not a tangible thing. Not in the way I can wrap it up and gift to you."

Tweenage exasperation crept into her eyes, but before it traveled from her expression to out her mouth, he handed the document over. She took it without shifting her gaze from his, annoyance morphing into concern.

"Read it," he said.

She held his gaze another four seconds, then dropped it to the paper. His blood grew thick as it thumped through his body, his heart thudding in a slow, heavy rhythm.

He counted his heartbeats as she studied the information. Twenty-six passed before her eyes met his again.

"Is this real?"

He nodded. "Leo found your birth certificate after he told us about your mom. He wanted to be very sure that the information it contained was truthful, so he managed to get samples while we were in Napa and ran a rushed DNA test. These results came back this morning."

He held his breath as he waited for her response.

"You're my half-brother?" she managed to say, the cracking of her voice an echo of his heart.

He nodded.

She blinked, her chest rising and falling with her rapid breaths. "Are you..." Worry crept into her eyes. "Are you okay with this?" she all but whispered.

He didn't bother to blink away the moisture gathering in his own eyes. "Yeah," he said, his voice hoarse. "I'm okay with it. I'm fucking thrilled," he said emphatically. He hesitated. "But what about you?"

She stared at him again, then a heartbeat later, her gangly arms wrapped around his waist, and she buried her face against his chest. Wrapping his big ones around her, he rested his cheek on her head. And held on to his sister.

EPILOGUE

"K back in school?" Philly asked, joining Monk in front of the fire in the lodge room. He nodded. The February ski-week break had passed and, along with Helia, the three of them had spent five days in the Caribbean soaking up the sun, swimming, and eating too much. They'd also spread Cindy's ashes in a current that would take her around the world.

"How's it going?" North asked, trailing Philly into the room.

"It's an adjustment," he replied. "She's smarter than most of the teachers, but she's not really there for the academics, so she does her work, aces all of her assignments and tests, and tries to catch up on the social stuff. Some days are easier than others."

"Juliana said she has her first sleepover this weekend, though," Stone said, lifting his head from the laptop he was working on nearby. Juliana and Kendall had grown close over the past several weeks, the contents of the presidential library bonding the two in a way that didn't make sense to the rest of them but didn't need to.

Monk smiled. "She does. Eloise is new to Mystery Lake, too, though her mom grew up here. They're going to start ski lessons Saturday morning." Charley and Joey had tried getting Kendall out on the slopes, but she'd been putting them off. She surprised him a few days ago when she said she and Eloise wanted to take lessons together. He'd readily agreed. Whether she ended up liking it or not was yet to be seen, but he thought sharing the learning experience with a friend her age was a good thing.

"Is Helia coming up this weekend?" Philly asked.

Monk nodded. "She's signing on the dotted line with the lodge on Friday," he said. The whoops of celebration made him smile. In a stroke of luck, the event planner at the big resort in town, owned by the Warwick family, had tendered her resignation after the New Year. A surprise event since she'd only been on the job for less than a year. But being away from her elderly parents was more of a strain than she'd anticipated, and she wanted to get back to the East Coast where she could help them out. Joey and Charley had quickly proposed Helia to their cousin, Brad, who ran the place, then put the two in touch. By the time they shook hands they'd clicked, but Helia hadn't been ready to leave Sundaram so soon after Greg's arrest and the DEA's operation.

In a complicated series of negotiations, the pieces slowly fell into place. The current event director agreed to stay through June, which would give her time to onboard Helia while also giving Helia time to manage the transition at Sundaram and turn her responsibilities over to her brother. Kaden and Patrick had always planned on moving back north in a few years. When the opportunity arose, they simply sped up their timeline. Patrick worked remotely and would keep his job. Kaden, who managed a successful art gallery, was happy to step away after nearly twenty years and fill Helia's role.

"She'll be up here a few days a week starting March, then full-time in June," he said. Smiling, he added, "I guess that means we need to find a house."

"I heard a rumor that the Italianate Victorian across the street and four doors up from Mantis and Charley is going on the market soon," North said.

"The one that looks haunted?" Philly asked.

North inclined his head. "It needs some work."

"That close to town, it will still go for a pretty penny," Stone said.

"He can afford it," Philly pointed out. He could. Kendall could, too. As soon as the holidays were over, he'd taken his sister to the lawyer who managed Roger's estate and made sure she was granted her fair share. He also asked HICC to see if Roger was listed as a father to any other children, but so far, they'd found nothing.

Once the ink dried on the paperwork, he'd proposed his idea for Bacco to her—turn it into a restaurant and inn that could be a training ground for the people the Falcons helped. Alessio, Miguel, and Gretchen had all been on board with the plan before he'd known about his relationship with Kendall. He'd been nervous bringing it up to her, but she hadn't hesitated to agree, and they'd both set aside a chunk of their estate to support the program. It would eventually become self-sustaining, but it needed start-up capital.

Other than the training program and Kendall's college, neither really had any wish to touch the money left to them, but when North mentioned the house, a glimpse of the future flashed through his mind. Kendall would love the gothic structure, and together, the three of them could make it a home. They'd have a table to share meals at, a porch to retire to on warm summer evenings, their own Christmas tree in the big front window. He could almost hear the pounding of feet running up and down the stairs.

He made a mental note to ask Charley who the listing agent would be. Very little happened in Mystery Lake that the Warwicks didn't know or couldn't find out. If Helia and Kendall were on board, they could have it fixed up and ready by the time Helia moved in June.

Lovell entered the room, scanned the area, then rested his attention on Monk. "You ready?" he asked. They had a vintage motorcycle in need of restoration in Sacramento that they'd agreed to pick up for a new client that afternoon.

Monk nodded and rose as Lovell's phone dinged with a text. He held up a finger asking for a minute, an unsettling stillness cloaking his body as he read the message.

"Lovell?" he prompted.

His brother slipped his phone back into his pocket, crossed his arms, and stared at the far end of the room. Knowing he'd speak when he was ready, no one said a word.

Whatever mental puzzle Lovell was working out must have resolved, and his gaze grew sharp as he turned back to the group.

"Houston, do we have a problem?" Philly asked, riffing on the astronaut who said the famous words, Jim Lovell. He was paraphrasing Jack Swigert at the time, but *their* Lovell was as apt to understate a problem as the original Lovell, so the name stuck.

"They let her out yesterday," he said. No need to tell them who.

"Fuck," Philly said.

"How?" Stone said in shock.

"Why are they only telling you now?" Monk asked. Only North remained silent.

Lovell inhaled, then exhaled with a shake of his head. "I agree," he said to Philly. "Probably her bevy of high-powered lawyers," he said to Stone. "And same answer as the last," he said to him.

Then running a hand over his bald head, he sighed and looked at Monk. "Can you grab the bike on your own? I need to let Mantis know someone might be heading our way to kill me."

ABOUT THE AUTHOR

Tamsen Schultz is an award winning author of the romantic suspense Windsor Series and an RWA Daphne Du Maurier Excellence in Mystery finalist.

In addition to being a writer, she has a background in the field of international conflict resolution, has co-founded a non-profit, and currently works in corporate America. Like most lawyers, she spends a disproportionate amount of time (and writing) about what it might be like to do something else.

She lives in Northern California in a house full of males including her husband, two sons, four cats, a dog, and a gender-neutral, but well-stocked, wine rack.

ALSO BY TAMSEN SCHULTZ

THE WINDSOR SERIES

1) A Tainted Mind (Vivienne & Ian)

2) These Sorrows We See (Matty & Dash)

3) What Echoes Render (Jesse & David)

4) The Frailty of Things (Kit & Garret)

5) An Inarticulate Sea (Carly & Drew)

6) A Darkness Black (Caleb & Cate)

7) Through The Night (Naomi & Jay)

8) Into The Dawn (Brian & Lucy)

9) The Puppeteer (The Prequel)

Also available in Box Sets!

WINDSOR SHORT STORIES

Bacchara

Chimera

The Thing About London

THE TILDAS ISLAND SERIES

1) A Fiery Whisper (Charlotte & Damian)

2) Night Deception (Alexis & Isiah)

3) A Touch of Light and Dark (Nia & Jake)

4) This Side of Midnight (Anika & Dominic)

5) Eight Minutes to Sunrise (Beni & Cal)

THE DOCTORS CLUB SERIES

1) Cyn

2) Six

3) Devil

4) Nora

www.ingramcontent.com/pod-product-compliance
Lightning Source LLC
Chambersburg PA
CBHW070839260626
47170CB00007B/2438